Love, Lies, And Ley Lines

by

Jeffe Kennedy

It's been years since the infamous smuggling team of Bandit and Goldilocks thumbed their noses at the fae authorities, running the priceless magical pixie dust desired by everyone from hedge witches to the storied magic academies. No one in the human principalities controlled by the fae can work even the simplest spells without the stuff. And without fae magic, humans will find themselves back in the dark ages of disease and fast mortality. But the enigmatic fae keep a tight grip on their monopoly of pixie dust, charging extortionate prices at their whim.

Bandit has been doing her best to get by on her racing wins and the quick thrill of one-night stands while her former partner and best friend, the powerful sorceress known as Goldilocks, is off playing house and having babies. But when Bandit gets the offer of a lifetime, she convinces Goldilocks to come out of retirement for one last, hugely profitable gig.

And if the Bandit picks up a mysterious and seductive hitchhiker fleeing his wedding, well that just adds a bit of spice to the job. When he refuses to tell her his name, she dubs him Prince Charming and only regrets that she won't have time to find out more about her enticing companion—and what he looks like under those fancy clothes.

As the Bandit and Prince Charming run distraction for Goldilocks and her precious haul, they face untold dangers penetrating the arcane fae realms.

All for gold, glory, and maybe even true love.

Or lust. It can be hard to tell the difference.

Dedication

To Kelly Robson

The fairy godmother of this book and the Dy to my Cha,

Besties and partners in crime forever!

Acknowledgments

Many thanks to Kelly Robson, of course, who helped with this book in so many ways and never lost faith in it.

Likewise to Agent Sarah Younger who worked with me on this concept and eventual book for years and never stopped loving it. Thank you for your unwavering support of my weird stories!

Deepest gratitude and appreciation to Laura Ann Gilman, whose mentorship—via the program at the Science Fiction and Fantasy Writers Association (SFWA) Nebula Conference—helped me focus on the elements to create this story.

Thanks to Tina Connolly, who almost certainly won't remember, but who asked me at the World Fantasy Convention in New Orleans what I was working on and was one of the first to hear the pitch for this book. Your excited reaction kept me going during a long journey with this one. We never know when the right word at the perfect time makes all the difference, and you did that for me.

Jennifer Estep, Alex Gurevich, Darynda Jones, Kelly Robson, Jim Sorenson, and Sarah Younger provided critical reads, for which I am grateful. Also myriad interns at the Nancy Yost Literary Agency offered feedback and proofing—and a fantastic mood board!—all of which I so appreciate.

Special salute to Jennifer Estep for suggesting the Amethyst rum scene.

Thanks to Jim Sorenson, for calling me out on the weight of coins, and to Alex Gurevich for being adamant on the metrics for my monetary system.

All the love to my cover artist, Ravven, who's been working with me for almost ten (!) years now, and who made herself a little crazy getting this cover just right. I adore the fan art. Thank you.

Many thanks to S.L. Prater and Gabrielle Landi for input on the back cover copy. And a grateful shout-out to the Tea Room for genre and cover advice. Adore you all.

Thanks to Alex Gurevich for providing a miraculous writing retreat in paradise.

Many thanks to able assistants Sydney Blevins and Carien Ubink. You two are the very best!

I'm grateful to wonderful friends Susan Lee, Megan Mulry and Minerva Spencer for general conversation and support. This book is in part about besties and you are in this story, too.

Love always to my other friends and family for the every day. I hesitate to name you because I'll inevitably forget someone, but I think you know who you are. Especially the ones who know all about the pussy sparkle.

Love, Lies, And Ley Lines

by

Jeffe Kennedy

~ Prologue ~

Nothing Like Fae Jail for Exploring Regrets

L IFE CAN GO to the seven hells faster than you can blink.

You can write that down. Maybe draw some kind of wisdom from it.

Cha wished she could claim to have learned a lesson from how quickly things had gone from excellent to sub-shitty in just a couple of days, but—let's face it—she'd never been a quick study. Besides which, her life had been far from that great to start. The past just looked that way, all shiny in the rear-view mirror, in comparison to her current situation: stuck in an egg-shaped, bastard-daddy-of-pearl Moonstone fae jail, a short future of torture, inquisition, and execution ahead of her.

It should've been a simple job. She sighed, adjusting her battered body into an equally uncomfortable curve of the cell wall, wishing she had a silver coin for every smuggler who'd said the same—right before telling how it had all gone bad. These were the criminal versions of fishing stories. The job that got away. The easy coin that had been anything but. Cha had listened to those tales, even paid for the ale of the sorry teller of them, and pretended to sympathize, all the while feeling smug that she'd never be so stupid, or careless, or shortsighted.

Or fall for the pretty, sweet-voiced bit of man-candy every-one could tell spelled trouble.

Right on schedule, as had happened every three minutes since she'd awakened in this opalescent prison, she thought of him. Azul. Those indigo-blue eyes and hair, those lips, his scent like sun-ripened blueberries, that devastating kiss that had rocked her world and tossed her into an abyss of unrequited lust.

And they'd said it couldn't happen to her. Not the infa-mous Bandit, with a stud in every town, and more lined up to volunteer for the opportunity. Falling hard for a guy, especially an unattainable one like the prince he claimed to be, just wasn't Cha's style. She'd barely stubbed a toe over a pretty bit of candy in the past. Now she'd broken something deeper than the ribs that hurt with every breath.

Azul was gone, never to be seen again. Her partner, Dy, was hopefully gone, too, and safe. And Cha was alone in fae jail, just as her mother had often predicted during Cha's admittedly troubled youth.

She should never have listened to Otto's proposition…

The Bandit

THE JAGUAR SNARLED as it tore up the ley line, sparkling white pixie dust billowing in its wake, making a glittering vortex like a phoenix's blazing tail. Cha mentally tapped into the enchantment stabilizing the line in the current race configuration and used her ley-rider senses to guide the jag as he traveled the floating boundary between the sleek carriage and the track. Looking ahead to the next obstacle in the course, she narrowed her keen eyes at what loomed in the near distance.

That was the key to winning: stay alert and present in the moment, ready to respond to changes fast, but keep an eye on the immediate future.

If she didn't miss her guess, the final challenge would be… Yep, there it was. The shine of sunlight and magic on a sizeable body of water. Cha was leading the pack for the moment— very few ley riders could compete with her, or her powerful jaguar carriage, Katu—but she didn't take that lead for granted. Another of her principles for winning: never assume you've got it made. Cha liked to win and did her best to ensure it happened as often as possible.

Speaking of not taking the lead for granted, look there: a ley rider she recognized surged up beside her and leapt to the fore. He was driving a sleek cheetah carriage, great for bursts of speed, but not the endurance of a full steeplechase. That bit of inexperienced bravado would cost him. Cha restrained Katu's territorial instinct to pour on more speed. The water obstacle she'd spied in the distance would require deft navigation. They might be on a smooth straightway for the moment, but this race was a marathon, not a sprint. Something a young, brash ley rider like the cheetah-driver, Garaile, didn't yet understand, even if he did have an expensive sponsor, probably one of the wealthy fae lords or ladies. Let him give full rein to his new cheetah carriage. Cha could be patient.

The crowd in the stadium roared, urging her on, shouting the handle she'd had since her smuggling days. *Bandit! Bandit! Bandit!* Everyone loves a champion and Cha had obliged them by being their favorite during her few years on the quasi-legal race circuit. Winning was always a thrill. Not quite as much as smuggling contraband, but it came close. Sex and winning races was all Cha got these days in the way of thrills, ever since her partner had bailed on her for a legit job.

The water hazard loomed into view and Cha studied it, trusting the jag to stay the course on the straightaway. That was another edge they had on the competition: Cha and Katu had been together since he was a kitten, newly enchanted, which was why he would always be her Katu, which meant kitten. They were a seamless team, Katu often anticipating

Cha's intentions, able to follow without explicit instructions, a distinct advantage in situations like this, allowing her to concentrate on sussing out the potential traps ahead.

This one was a doozy. The arena owner had gone all out for this tournament, as Cha had figured he would—gotta keep the crowds entertained—and hired a hydromancer to create a floating lake.

She had only seconds to assess it as they hurtled toward the apparently placid lake. The cheetah put on even more speed, Garaile clearly planning to take the big ramp straight ahead, conveniently positioned for a ley rider to jump the body of water entirely. *Too* convenient. Besides, that was no ordinary lake. The water shimmered with pale yellow magic, promising something else lay beneath.

Cha shook her head to herself, easing Katu back a hair more. No way that ramp would lead to a simple jump. As she slowed, a thoroughbred racehorse carriage shot past her, looking to overtake the cheetah, and the crowds roared their disappointment, shouting her name to urge her on. *Bandit! Bandit! Bandit!*

They should know to trust her by now.

The racetrack ley line branched just ahead. To most people, the racetrack looked as mundane as the roads they traveled. Anyone could get in an enchanted carriage and use the ley-line roads to get from here to there. But ley riders weren't most people. If you had a touch of the right magic— which meant one of your human ancestors went and got seduced by a fae, somewhere back in the bloodline—you could be a ley rider. Cha was fully human, humbly so, but she'd come into the world with a good dollop of the right magic. The ley lines lit up for her in brilliant clarity, like rivers of color, allowing her to sense their potency and stability.

At the looming fork, the most robust ley line led to that deceptively promising ramp. Several smaller tracks branched in other directions, offering less-enticing options. Two lines on either side of the ramp would shoot any carriage that missed the ramp straight into the water, a bog-standard penalty for any obstacle on a course like this. One more line, this one decently stabilized, led off to go the long way around the lake, an option for those ley riders whose vehicles couldn't make the jump. You wouldn't win taking that route, but you upped your odds of at least finishing, since you also wouldn't risk a devastating crash.

A fourth, spindly ley line, barely stabilized, coursed directly over the surface of the lake, barely discernible to any but the most experienced eye. But Cha had been ferreting out and riding barely-there ley lines since she hopped into her first kid's carriage, one enchanted from the faithful family hound, a plodding and gentle creature.

Yep, that ley line sitting on the water surface looked un-promising at best and treacherous at worst, but the racecourse mages who built the ever-changing tracks didn't leave loose ends. Sure, vanishing or dead-end roads were a regular feature—or a bug—of the rural countryside, where ley lines stabilized by ancient sorcerers rotted away in genteel splendor, used only by the impoverished or desperate. (Cha had been both.) But to deliberately create one on this course that would be soon disassembled was expensive in both time and magic.

Flyboys like Garaile—or that newbie riding the racehorse carriage—wouldn't know that, but Cha did. She processed all of that information in the time it took her to wink at the crowd as Katu hurtled toward the ramp. After a token battle, Cha allowed the racehorse carriage to jostle past her, the crowds howling disappointment as she dropped into third place. Katu didn't like it either. He loved to win as much as Cha did. But he went with her direction—and she made sure it looked like she was shooting for the main ramp, like everyone else.

Garaile's cheetah hit the ramp at full speed. Cha watched him, wincing in anticipation of the surely shocking outcome of that clueless choice. The cheetah carriage hurtled off the end of the ramp, catching air, with plenty of velocity to soar over the small lake to the finish line. Garaile's premature victory yodel echoed out—then cut off as a virulent yellow tentacle erupted from the lake, snatched them in midair, and yanked them into the water.

On their heels, the racehorse carriage balked at the sight and shied—failing to take the ramp and instead barreling down the boggy ley line to the right. A surprise twist of magic whipped them in a circle, bringing them under the ramp and sending them on a collision course toward the rest of the pack. A greyhound carriage nosing up beside Cha lost control as its rider tried to avoid the crash, unfortunately losing its purchase on the ley line and flipping. Cha grimaced for the rider who, catapulted from the carriage, went spinning across the active line. The protective suits and goggles could do only so much against the potency of direct contact with the high-test Moonstone pixie dust, and the unfortunate rider convulsed in a spastic fit as the mainlined magic scrambled their brains.

The crowd screamed in excited horror, as titillated by the carnage of such an accident as by the thrill of victory. Everyone knew not to touch ley lines without a carriage between them and the dust, but—outside of the races—few people ever witnessed what it did to a person. Even the ubiquitous and less harmful Obsidian black dust used by most of the human realms for basic transportation was dangerous and humans learned in early childhood to never, ever touch the stuff.

Pixie dust came from the fae realms. Even though everyone agreed it (most likely) had nothing to do with actual pixies, given their nasty and decidedly non-sparkly nature, the term persisted. Live pixie dust corrupted human nervous systems, mortal flesh unable to handle magic in such a distilled form. The Moonstone white race line was a full energetic level above the standard black, so it fried humans all that much faster.

Cha couldn't spare more than momentary sympathy for the unfortunate ley rider. She was too busy jockeying amidst the pack of carriages and navigating the line that raced Katu toward the ramp and a tentacle disaster of their own. No way would they be taking that ramp.

At the last moment, she wrenched their direction, sending Katu leaping at an acute angle, grazing the side ley and shooting straight for the apparently fragile line coursing across the lake's surface. A major risk, given that whatever that tentacle belonged to obviously lurked below, but she was gambling that the tentacle-beast had been enchanted to snag only airborne carriages taking the jump. Besides, she'd be cursed if she'd take the plodding amateur trail going all the way around.

The crowd gasped, a few people screaming as the jag hit the uneven ley line and shimmied, wobbling dangerously toward a dunking. Not far away, Garaile and his cheetah—the carriage back in animal form now that they were off the ley line, the enchantment broken, the cat none too happy for being soaked—paddled toward shore. Cha couldn't risk a glance at the snarl-up at the base of the ramp behind her, though by the sound of the shrieking, it was an unholy mess. She focused on Katu and his connection to the ley line, using her considerable skill and talent to hold them to the unstable magic.

Then she poured on the speed.

Katu's immaterial claws dug into the magic of the ley line, catching and gaining purchase, Cha guiding them toward the richest streaks of Moonstone magic in the cocked-up composite. As she'd hoped, the line wasn't a red herring. The wily mages had built just enough stability into the base of the ley line to get a carriage across. It reminded Cha of the bog tracks she'd once ridden over the drowned fae cities in her backwater home.

A tentacle shot overhead, and Cha ducked instinctively, showered with lake water in the open two-seater carriage. Pulling her sword, mostly because it would make the crowd happy, she swung it in a silver arc, nicking the tentacle and adding a bit of yellow ichor to the spatter. Sure enough, the crowd went wild. *Bandit! Bandit! Bandit!*

Time to go all out. Urging Katu into a final sprint, Cha

guided them over the bumps and pits of the uneven ley line, taking advantage of the magic potholes to goose them forward—all while using her mental connection to Katu to maneuver as best she could on the narrow track to avoid the lashing yellow tentacles that arose on either side. The beast flailed at her but, as she'd hoped, not with serious purpose. The tentacles that did connect flinched away after a few well-aimed swipes of her sword. In addition—bless that ley rider's bold and foolish heart—another carriage tried the ramp, arcing overhead, only to be smacked down mercilessly, diverting the tentacle creature from Cha and Katu.

The din of the crowd roared in Cha's ears along with the hot-blooded pulse of victory coursing through both Katu and her. *Bandit! Bandit! Bandit!*

They hit the other side and skidded across the finish line. With a mental nudge to Katu, Cha added a spin and a flourish. Never hurt to play to the crowd. Cha sprang to her feet, standing up in the low-slung, gleaming black carriage, pumping one fist in the air and brandishing her sword in the other. Scarlet banners unfurled from the heights of the nosebleed sections of the stands, proclaiming another win for her, the reigning champion, Cha's image on them ten times life-size, showing her tall, lanky form, cocky smile, and dark curls bobbed in the cut she'd made famous. No one would call her beautiful, but she possessed style in spades and that made up for a lot.

Another victory and a tidy purse to go with it. It wasn't like the old days with Dy, running contraband under the noses of the fae, but it was something.

And, except for the faithful Katu, it was all she had. Most of the time, that was enough. Unfortunately, Cha wasn't great at settling for "enough"—if anyone even knew what that was.

~ 2 ~

A Bit of Hot Goss

"Yo, Bandit!" Soaking wet, Garaile shouted across the tournament arena and jogged toward her through the still-settling clouds of scintillating white pixie dust, harmless now that it was separated from the ley magic. "Hold up, Bandit. I have news."

Cha climbed out of the jag parked at the terminus of the ley line, making sure to jump onto non-magical ground—people tended to get careless on the slow-moving parking leys, paying a fast and ugly price—and patted Katu's steaming hood. Accepting a towel from one of the arena-workers, she pulled off her goggles and mopped her face and hair clean of lake water and yellow ichor.

The crowds still roared for her victory, calling out her handle and sometimes her name, the die-hard fans even shouting *Katu!* while waving giant gloves with jaguar claws. They dispersed from the arena slowly, reluctant to leave the excitement of the race for their shops in town or the outlying farms that made up the six human principalities of Torocca.

The win felt great—especially as today's steeplechase had

been particularly challenging with that last trickster of a hazard—but the prize money felt even better. The purse would nearly double her dwindling hoard. Even as the reigning champion of quasi-legal racing, she didn't earn anywhere close to what she and Dy had once raked in on their smuggling runs. It wasn't like she had expensive habits, either. But the big races like this one only happened every so often, and the fae—and their human business flunkies—raised prices and taxes a lot more frequently. Each coin stretched thinner every day.

Cha didn't blame Dy for retiring and going legit with a steady job, what with the wife and kids to support, but the tournament gig left a lot to be desired—in income, the excitement of real danger, and having a purpose besides titillating the crowds. Maybe if Cha had ever found anyone she liked enough to settle down with, she'd be okay with the rest of it. She might as well wish to meet a fae prince and be crowned a faerie queen, however.

"Good news or bad?" she asked Garaile as he skidded up. "And nice showing out there. You would've won by taking the ramp if that tentacle hadn't snagged you."

"Hurt like a manticore sting, too." Garaile grinned ruefully, kicking his boot at the shoulder of the ley line and sending up a puff of sparkling motes. "Kind of you to say, but I know I ate it on that one. How'd you know not to take the ramp?"

Cha tapped her temple. "The wisdom of experience."

"Comes with age, I guess," he allowed, oblivious to Cha's huff of indignation. It didn't help that the prideful straightening of her spine made it twinge. She was only thirty, which was *not* getting old. "Kidding, Bandit," Garaile continued with a charming, dimpled smile. "It's a privilege just to be in the race with a legend like you. And Katu." He stepped back to admire the jaguar race-carriage. "He's got sexy lines, just like you."

Garaile was attractive, no lie, with his big shoulders and obvious hero worship. Still, while Cha might not be actually old, he couldn't be more than twenty, which was certainly too young for her. *Probably.* "Thanks." She kept the easy grin on her face. "News, you said?"

"Oh, yeah." Garaile's grin faded. "The bad kind. Monat got arrested."

"Damn." That was bad news indeed. Monat was savvy at her job, with a big-rig transport carriage that had eluded the authorities in any number of the human principalities, and even the occasional run to the first fae realm, Obsidian. "You got details?"

He pulled off his hat and cast a wary glance around them. With the final, climactic race of the tournament over, the other ley riders were dispersing, their race-carriages returning to animal form as the riders pulled them off the ley lines. Aware she should be setting a good example, Cha called Katu off the parking ley and onto neutral ground, mentally tapping the sequence that triggered the enchantment from being a carriage capable of traveling the ley line and carrying a rider and back to his natural, animal form.

Magic shimmered in a wave, the light-bending properties of the fae enchantment creating a prismatic effect. The carriage gave a last cooling purr, then shivered into the jaguar that was his original body. The metallic scales of the jag's shell clicked smoothly back into glossy black fur, the carriage compacting into feline form, legs extending and becoming big, soft paws that touched ground. The big cat settled happily onto his haunches at her side, Katu panting lightly from the race. He sawed a hoarse greeting and shoved his head under her hand for ear skritches.

The track manager gave Cha a salute of thanks for her effort. The ley lines in the arena were maintained by hired mages and expensive to keep active. The magic workers were already busily sealing the lines for the day. These weren't the locally and principality-maintained black ley lines governed by stable enchantments and regularly serviced by government mages employed by the human realms. No, to get the power and flexibility needed for high-velocity races and regularly tweaked obstacle courses, the arena owner paid out the nose for these ley lines, as well as for the Moonstone white pixie dust to keep them working at maximum speed.

Not to mention paying out the hefty bribes required to make sure the fae rulers turned a blind eye to the humans' entertainment escapades.

"I got details," Garaile promised in a low voice. "Got any ale?"

Cha jerked her head toward the changing rooms. "Walk with me." As reigning champion, she rated a private room. Catching the anticipatory gleam in Garaile's eyes, she shook her head to herself. These young bucks all seemed to think an invitation to her room meant they'd get to bang her. To be fair, sometimes it *did* mean that. Not today, though. *Probably.*

She palmed the lock spelled to respond only to her touch, gestured Garaile through the doorway, and pointed at the ratty couch. Private didn't mean posh. Katu strolled to his oversized pillow and flopped down, tongue lolling pinkly.

"Spill," Cha instructed Garaile, while she moved to the cooler and extracted a carafe of ambrosia. She poured a healthy draft into a bowl, the honeysuckle-sweet scent of it just a little too cloying, and set it before the cat. The enchanted carriage-beasts could live on regular food, like the animals they'd been born as, but to transform to and run as carriages, they needed the fae fuel to keep going. Humans called it ambrosia, because of the nectar smell and how much the animals loved it.

The fae, never fond of talking to humans, much less sharing secrets, wouldn't ever say where ambrosia came from. They simply sold the bottled liquid, along with other magical elements like pixie dust, for extortionate prices. Those imports had become key to human society. Once upon a time, the fae had existed only in stories. Then the Fae Wars had exploded, weakening the once-impassable boundaries between the fae realms and the world of humans. Those walls between separate realities had fractured, becoming porous. In some areas, they disintegrated entirely.

Humans were suddenly able to enter the fae realms—not a good idea today any more than it had been in the old fairy tales. Likewise, the fae invaded human lands, bringing with them arrogance, arcane magic, and monsters from myth. They easily conquered the pitifully vulnerable nearby principalities of Torocca.

As with all conquests, nothing had worked quite so effectively as introducing luxury goods to the newly oppressed population. The fae brought magic to the human world, enchanted conveniences that put an end to the misery of disease and starvation, and now no one could live without them. Which was good for Cha, because those needs—and the illegal methods for satisfying them—had kept her in coin. At least, until Dy went legit.

Garaile caught the iced bottle of ale she tossed to him with a grateful nod. "Monat was bringing a load of contraband pixie dust back here to Rockton," he said.

Damn and damn. Monat was an old friend. Dy would hate to hear this—so much so that maybe Cha wouldn't tell her. "Well, it won't be the first time Monat has had to talk her way out of a little jail time and a fine."

"Not this time. Apparently, she got the dust from a source on the *other* side of the border, and got picked up there." Garaile waggled his brows in titillated horror.

Cha winced. Lots of smugglers ran the risk of illegally transporting goods from the closest fae realm of Obsidian. It was no party, dealing with the fae hounds of the law. "Obsidian jail is no picnic," she conceded. "Still, Monat is a pro. She can handle it." At least, Cha hoped so.

"Not that side of the border. The *other* other side, you know?"

Cha waited for him to explain, but Garaile only nodded significantly and tipped back his ale.

"The other *other* side of the border…?"

"Yup." He counted on his fingers. "Not Obsidian, but the second one. Is that Citrine?"

Spare her Garaile's slow wit. Cha took a bracing swig from her own bottle. "Moonstone is the second fae realm," she told him patiently. "Are you *sure* Monat went to Moonstone?"

Humans took a chance crossing into the fae realms, full stop. Even the closest and lowest order fae realm, Obsidian, posed its dangers. Moonstone was that much worse. The way the six fae realms existed, you had to pass through the lower ones to reach the higher ones. They were kind of magically nested inside each other. Not that plenty of smugglers hadn't figured out how to bypass the import/export depot in Obsidian to trade directly with Moonstone, and the higher realms that worked through Moonstone agents, but it was a bad idea to actually *go* there.

Like the pixie dust they exported, the fae realms increased in power—and strangeness—the deeper in you went. The black pixie dust from Obsidian was the lowest test, which made Obsidian correspondingly the least dangerous of the fae realms, at least magically speaking. From there the dust ascended in power to Moonstone white, Citrine yellow, Amethyst purple, Cinnabar orange, and culminated in Ruby red. No humans had ever seen—to Cha's knowledge—the orange dust from Cinnabar or the legendary scarlet dust from Ruby. Probably because their faces melted off if they came within a league of that stuff.

Very few human magic workers could handle Amethyst purple dust or even Citrine yellow. Moonstone white dust was priceless for its potency and because more humans could deal with the stuff—like the mages working the racecourse—but Monat had taken a ridiculously dangerous chance, even for a haul of that.

"Getting to Moonstone and back is a fool's gambit," Cha

pointed out, just in case Garaile hadn't fully grasped it.

"You know that. I know that." Garaile shrugged. "Monat knows that. Or she sure does now."

"Did she make it back out of Moonstone?"

"Unclear. Word is, Monat is still in one of the fae realms—no one's sure which—in some fae jail. Maybe only Obsidian," he added, as if to make her feel better.

"Even if it's only Obsidian, they're more likely to send human smugglers home with a few added features as a lesson than let them off without punishment." And that was if they came home at all. *Dammit, Monat.*

Garaile grimaced, passing a hand over his forehead as if checking that he hadn't sprouted a pair of curling, brightly colored horns as had famously happened to a well-known smuggler caught out in Obsidian. Humans marked thus by the fae did not fare well, rarely surviving long. Mortal flesh couldn't endure that sort of modification.

Cha narrowed her eyes at Garaile. "Anything else?"

"You know as much as I do now," Garaile answered, holding up a hand as if denying personal responsibility. "Well, except one thing—some people think the law-hounds have found a way to listen to the underground path-channels."

Cha set down her ale abruptly, the *thunk* punctuating her dismay. "Is that verified?"

"Rumor, but a persistent one. Could be paranoia." Garaile shrugged, taking a thoughtful swig.

Could be. Nevertheless, she cursed. The human mage underground had established the clandestine path-channels so that regular folks could have conversations without going through the heavily monitored public networks. You never said anything on public path-comms that you didn't want the fae or human law to know and potentially arrest you for. The underground path-channels allowed anyone with the reasonably cheap—although also contraband—enchanted path-boxes to send and receive messages.

Despite the name, the path-boxes didn't depend on mental telepathy, instead working via a magical facsimile of that ability, which only the fae possessed. Also, the underground path-channels didn't work for private conversation, as anyone—anyone who knew the channel codes, that was— listening to the channel could hear the path-messages and potentially butt-in. Most people figured that was half the fun.

An unexpected side-benefit of the underground path-channels being open to anyone with the ability to chime in was that the various channels also allowed for a number of grassroots groups to organize judicious resistance to the iron-fisted control of fae nobles and their puppets, the human councils. That went beyond smuggling expensive magical goods. Some people were actually altruistic and cared about improving the world more than making their fortunes. Guess which camp Cha fell into.

If the law-hounds had figured out how to listen in… Well, a lot of people would suffer. Good people, not ones like Cha.

"Think that's how Monat got caught?"

"Going to Moonstone, anything could happen." The poor sods who returned mutated were the lucky ones. Only whispered rumors hinted at the dire fates of those prisoners never heard from again.

Garaile raised his bottle with a grim smile and Cha joined him in a solemn toast to Monat.

"Who was she running the dust for?" Cha asked.

"You don't know?" Garaile asked, squinting at her and apparently unsure if she was yanking his chain. Cute, nicely muscled, young enough he could probably go for hours, but really not that bright. Alas.

"How would I know?" Cha waved a hand at her surroundings. "I've gone legit. Mostly," she amended, since the tourney circuit wasn't *entirely* aboveboard. Still, it was as legit as she'd ever gotten.

Garaile snorted, shaking his head at her with a grin. "Oh, right. The day the Bandit turns law-lover is the day I stop riding the lines."

"Can't move anything without Dy's rig," Cha replied, swallowing back the old hurt and shaking her head. "You know who Monat was running for or not?"

"Yeah. Otto."

Of course it was. Cha seriously considered opening another bottle of ale, the first had gone down so easy. It just figured it was Otto. Always happy to profit off the smuggling of contraband magic ingredients so in demand by everyone from minor hedge-witches to the magic academies, then never around when the law came sniffing for the ley riders taking on all the risk. She was on the verge of asking Garaile if he wanted another ale—maybe he wasn't all *that* young and she didn't need sparkling conversation for a quick pressure-release— when someone rapped on the door.

It could be only one person and he *wouldn't dare.*

The door popped open and Otto stuck his head in, round face creased in what he no doubt thought was a charming grin. "Bandit!" he crowed. "Got a minute for an old friend?"

~ 3 ~

The Deal

"No," Cha answered, tempted to kick the door shut in Otto's face.

Naturally, he swanned into the room anyway, far too shiny in his sharp suit for the surroundings. Her perfectly nice, private changing room suddenly looked all kinds of shabby in comparison and Cha didn't care for it. "What part of 'no' don't you get?" she asked irritably.

"The part where you haven't heard my offer yet." Sweeping back his celadon tailcoat to reveal his substantial belly, Otto rocked on his heels, gleaming boots spattered with dirty white pixie dust from the arena. He eyed Garaile. "Number 54, right? You did okay out there."

Garaile beamed, actually blushing. "Oh, thanks, Mr. Otto, I—"

"Can you give me a bit of privacy with the Bandit here?" Otto winked broadly. "We got old times to talk about, doncha know."

Cha set her teeth against Otto's faux-folksy slang. Just one of the people, not a wannabe royal, fae-ass-kisser at all.

"Sure thing, Mr. Otto." Garaile stood, quaffed his remaining ale, and tossed the empty in the glass recycle. Putting on his hat again, he tipped it to Cha. "Later, Bandit."

"Thanks for the gossip," she replied.

Otto watched him go, then shut and locked the door behind him. "Little young for you, isn't he?"

"Did you or did you not see us fully dressed having a beer?" Cha snapped back. "We were just talking."

"Is that what you kids are calling it these days?" He grinned, went to her cooler and snagged a bottle of her ale for himself without offering her one. Just as well. Whatever he wanted, she was best staying sober for it. "You looked good in the race today, Bandit."

"I always look good."

He raised his bottle in a salute. "That you do." Leering, he raked her with his gaze. "Offer's open if you ever want to try a real man instead of your pretty boys."

"Why," she drawled, "do you know a real man I might be interested in?"

"Cute." He chuckled, unbothered. "The fans love you."

"Always have."

"Today's purse was… five-hundred silvers?"

He knew it was. "Something like that," she allowed with a shrug, as if she didn't much care.

He pointed the bottle at her. "What if I told you I could offer you a gig for one-hundred times that, for just twenty-four hours of your time."

Cha had to fight to keep her ears from visibly pricking up at that princely sum. Good thing they weren't pointed like a fae's. Folding her arms, leaning back against the massage table, she crossed her ankles and shook her head. "You can offer me a thousand times that and the answer is still no. I've gone legit." Though, a thousand times that would be, um, *a lot*. Math wasn't Cha's strong suit, but a lot of zeroes was always good when it came to money.

"No, you haven't. The day the Bandit goes legit is the day I give all my coin away and become a monk."

If only. "You're splitting hairs. Dy has definitely gone straight and I'm dead in the water without her. Same difference."

"Dy only went legit because that wife of hers keeps having babies."

Cha raised a brow. "So?"

"So, twenty-five thousand silvers will feed a lot of babies, for a very long time."

"It's not only a matter of feeding the babies." Cha had argued herself blue in the face with Dy over exactly this. When Dy was still speaking to her, that was. "Phinny wants a steady family life, her wife home every night, and a partnership she can count on. Not Dy running contraband while half the human principalities want to toss her in jail or hand her over to the fae for even worse punishment."

"Ironic," Otto snorted, draining the bottle, "since Phinny was Goldilocks's biggest fangirl, back in the day."

"Yeah, well, chasing the rainbow and sitting happily on the crock of gold are two different things."

"Phinny's not getting to play with her crock much with Dy out on the commercial lines six days a week on cargo runs."

Cha blinked at him, then gave in and grabbed another ale for herself. Since she clearly wasn't getting rid of Otto anytime soon, she graciously tossed him another. Company was company. "I'm losing track of the metaphors, here. What's your point?"

"We both know that you can talk Dy into it. The pair of you go way back, long before Phinny shook her bodacious ta-ta's at our blushing sorceress."

That much was true—at least the going way back part. Cha and Dy had met in school, two black sheep who quickly discovered a shared love of shenanigans. Like all humans capable of wielding or manipulating magic, they both had a bit of fae blood in their families. With Dy's sorcerous ability to alter or even create entirely new ley lines combined with Cha's extraordinary ley-riding skills, they'd begun a tidy business of smuggling minor contraband to the other students. They eventually escalated to acquiring more expensive magical supplies their instructors needed or coveted. What started as mischief turned into a lucrative career, one that provided excitement, made them decent coin, and garnered them enough enthusiastic groupies to get them both laid consistent-ly. That was all either of them had wanted for a good run of years.

Until Dy fell in love and got married. Something Cha still couldn't quite wrap her head around.

"I can't talk Dy into anything anymore," Cha said. "And that's if Phinny even lets me onto the property." Which she wouldn't. Not after the chicken incident, and that was nearly two years before, not long after their fifth kid was born.

Granted, Phinny had been dealing with some postpartum crankiness, but that had been the straw to shoot her clean over the edge into banning Cha from the property. You'd think Cha getting Dy arrested in Obsidian that time would have been the deal-breaker, but no: it had come down to the death of a single chicken. Though how was she supposed to have known Phinny had put out her prize hen to hunt the newly hatched bugs on a day Cha happened to stop by and Katu was feeling peckish?

"Ah." Otto nodded sagely. "You got old and soft. I should've realized."

"Screw you."

"Lazy, with the cushy tourney circuit."

"Hey, I work hard, asshole." She resisted the urge to suck in her stomach, which did feel a bit softer these days. Too much ale. Too little incentive to keep in shape.

"You work too hard for five hundred silvers when you could have a hundred thousand."

Cha looked at the bottle in her hand, wondering if she'd misheard the number via the wishful haze of strong ale. "Say again?" She might not be great at math, but she had a good memory for payouts and this one had just gone up substantially.

"You heard me. Fifty thousand for each of you, twenty four hours of your time. Boom. Done. Dangle *that* in front of Dy and she'll listen."

Maybe. Maybe not. And Cha would still have to get past Phinny. Still, that was a lot of coin. Knowing she'd likely regret it, she set aside her pride and good sense and succumbed to temptation. Wouldn't be the first time. "What's the job?"

Otto settled himself on the couch, not looking anywhere as good doing it as Garaile had. "You make a fast run across the border, pick up a package, bring it back here. Easy peasy lemon squeezy."

Not even remotely surprised, Cha stared Otto down. At least now she knew what had tempted Monat to take the risk. That amount of coin would last a very long time. For the rest of their lives in decent comfort, if budgeted well, even with inflation. "Over the border to Obsidian?" she asked, though she already knew that answer.

Looking at his nails, Otto sighed. "You know the rules, Bandit—deets are need to know and you need to know only after you sign the contract. Can't have my competitors getting the drop on me."

Cha blew out a snort of pure disgust. "You think I don't know that Monat got her ass arrested trying to bring a shipment of pixie dust over from Moonstone?"

Otto narrowed his eyes in surprised irritation. Bless Garaile and his gossip. "Monat got careless. And she didn't have you running distraction for the big rig. You and Dy are an unbeatable team."

"We *were*."

"And are. The Bandit and Goldilocks together again! An inspiration to the masses. Think of how excited the people will be. Plus you'll be providing a needed public service. Pixie dust prices just jumped again. Soon there won't be any ley lines to some of the outlying farm country."

"As if anyone in the countryside is using Moonstone dust."

"I don't expect you to understand the economics. The wealthy need white dust to run their businesses. They run out, the coin dries up, and the poor are the ones to take it in the teeth."

"Oh, right." No one believed in that trickle-down shit. "Like you care about anything but lining your pockets. What's your profit margin on this?"

"Enough that I can pay you a hundred thousand silvers." He lifted his brows significantly. "It's a prime deal, Bandit. You know it."

"If we get caught, we'll be rotting in some Moonstone nightmare prison with Monat, growing wings out of our asses or some such, and you won't be coming to bail us out. I know *that.*"

"The risk is why you get paid the big coin, dearie. At least you gals can have a nice chat behind bars, maybe a pillow fight in scanty lingerie. Wings are sexy."

"Wings are a myth. Sometimes I seriously worry about the depths of your depravity."

"So, you'll do it?"

Who was she kidding? The temptation was too much to resist. Even split, this would make them rich. And would give her a reason to try to sweet-talk Phinny into letting her come around again. A tasty bribe would help considerably. Cha put out a hand. "Half up front."

"Ten thousand up front—in gold coin for you to carry— another ten thousand when I see Dy's pretty face behind the controls of Big Betty, the rest when you deliver the package."

"I thought you were confident I could talk Dy into this."

Otto stood, dug a heavy coin purse out of his shoulder bag, and tossed it to her. "There's ten thousand in there. You run off with it, Bandit, I'll see the authorities get some interesting evidence on your more notorious escapades."

"Bastard." She shook her head in reluctant admiration as she opened the bag and took in the beautiful sight of the ten gold coins inside. He'd already had it counted out.

"Tell Dy to give Phinny a kiss for me," Otto added with a salute and a smirk.

~ 4 ~

Someone's in the Kitchen with Phinny

"**A**UNTIE BANDIT! AUNTIE Bandit!" Five kids came running at the sound of Katu's distinctive growl as Cha pulled into the drive at the picturesque rural cottage.

Phin Jr., the eldest and a kid with Dy's golden curls, was the first to reach the fence that protected the kids from contact with the static line. "You haven't been here in forever," he scolded.

"Yeah, where have you been?" Zazu demanded as she jumped onto the fence right behind her brother. A bright-eyed girl, she'd been named for Cha—poor thing—and, like Cha, never used her full name. Arantzazu and Arantxa were variants on the same impossible name, thus their much sassier nicknames of Zazu and Cha.

Behind them, the twins scampered up, covered in mud. Edur and Xavia sported Phinny's fiery red hair and similarly mischievous temperament. Edur hung back a bit, waiting for the barefoot toddler, Inigo, impatiently calling for him to hurry.

The ley line driveway came to an end and Katu halted

31

there with the cessation of magic. Because Dy could stabilize a ley line like nobody's business, which meant no concerns about wasting expensive magic, Cha left Katu in carriage form. That way he wouldn't be tempted to go after the chickens, like last time. Wincing at the memory of that foul—fowl?—incident, she grabbed the squirming, squawking bag from the passenger seat and climbed out the open top of the carriage. "I've been busy," she answered their questions with not quite a lie.

"Can I drive the jag, Auntie Bandit?" Phin Jr. called hopefully.

Cha squinted at him as she stowed her sword safely out of reach in the rear storage compartment and locked it. "How old are you now—six?"

"Seven!" he answered with the high dudgeon that only a kid many years away from driving age could muster.

"Gotta be thirteen before you can touch ley magic," she reminded him, shaking her head. Even that was an arbitrary age. What fae magic did to adult human nervous systems, it did even worse to developing ones. Kids that got sizzled never did grow up right. She should know—she'd started riding the lines way too young. Probably it had messed with her head, though it could be argued that she'd started out bad.

She handed the bag to Zazu who took it reverently. "Carry that for me? And," she said, returning her attention to the budding ley rider, "you'll need three more years after that to be licensed to ride the lines."

"But Auntie Bandit, the moms let me…"

Cha barked out a laugh. "I know that's not true, kid." Not

only was Dy too responsible of a sorceress to risk a kid's—any kid's, but particularly her kid's—brain development by letting them touch magic too early, but Phinny wouldn't like it. And what Phinny didn't like, didn't happen. She had bodacious ta-ta's and an even bigger will. "Edur and Xavvy, you know I love you, but no hugs until you wash off that mud."

"It's not mud," Xavia protested.

"Yeah," Edur chimed in. "It's actually—"

"I do *not* want to know," Cha interrupted.

"The moms wouldn't have to know about me riding the ley," Phin Jr. argued, tagging at her heels with the other kids as Cha picked up Inigo, who clutched at her neck babbling nonsense. He'd gotten so big since she last saw him. She carried him toward the cottage with pretty eaves and flourish-es worthy of a gingerbread house. Dy and Phinny had a nice spot here. Not fancy, but comfortable, with the spreading limbs of oak trees casting deep shade over the pond, rosy moss spun by tiny haltija fae wisping dreamily in the slight breeze. It was peaceful and homey, something Dy hadn't known she wanted until Phinny provided it.

"Your moms know *everything*," Cha told Phin Jr., smiling as sunnily as she could manage when Phinny burst out of the teal-painted doorway.

"That's right I do," Phinny declared, bodily blocking the doorway to the cottage, particularly effective with her very pregnant belly on assist. A big, wide-hipped, full-breasted woman with a mind as sharp as her tongue and a temper as hot as her fiery hair, Phinny seemed like a sweet-faced milkmaid until she opened her mouth. "And I know you are *not* allowed here, Arantxa Evermore!"

Cha managed to disguise a wince. "No need to break out punishing full names, Phinny. I just arrived and I haven't done anything."

"Being a bad influence already," Phinny replied with a sour expression for Junior.

"I told him no," Cha protested.

She sniffed, planting fists on curvaceous hips. "You need only *exist* to be a bad influence. Why are you here?"

"Visiting old friends?" Cha asked hopefully.

"No, you're not. Something's up. What?" Phinny wasn't magical herself, but she possessed a definitely uncanny ability to know what was going on with her family. But Cha hadn't even talked to Dy yet, so Phinny couldn't have picked up any vibrations, yet. Could she?

"It's been a while," Cha tried.

"It's been *a while* because you are banned from visiting," Phinny retorted. "Remember my prize egg-laying hen?"

"I left Katu in carriage form, didn't I? Besides, I brought you a present." She held out a hand and Zazu promptly handed over the bag. "Top breeder, they promised," Cha said, as Phinny took the bag and peered in suspiciously. "I never knew a chicken could be so expensive." She'd spent twenty-five silvers from her championship purse on the fluffy, irascible creature, but she considered it a business investment. "They're much cheaper already roasted."

The hen in the bag let out an indignant squawk that matched the expression on Phinny's face. "I don't care what you had to pay. This is basic amends," Phinny said, lifting the bag, "not worthy of a resumption of privileges."

"The news I bring is worthy," Cha assured her, not bothering to argue the merits of the fancy bird.

"What is it?" Phinny showed no signs of budging.

"I just need five minutes with Dy." As a diversionary tactic, Cha thrust Inigo at Phinny, slightly off-center, so the other woman moved to the side to reflexively catch her child in the arm not holding the irate hen. Cha took full advantage of the sliver of an opening between the door-dragon and the bright teal frame, angling her narrow body sideways and popping into the kitchen, feeling not unlike she'd skidded at high speed between a rhino-carriage and a scythe-tree. "It smells fantastic in here," she told Phinny with genuine enthusiasm, sniffing appreciatively as the other woman scowled and belatedly hastened after her. "Roast beast?"

"None for you!" Phinny snapped. "All you kids, outside. Xavvy and Edur, you wash off whatever that is at the well. Junior, take Inigo and do not, I repeat, *do not* touch that carriage. There's a fence around that ley for a reason." She handed him the toddler, then the thrashing chicken bag back to Zazu. "Give her the good roost."

The girl nodded enthusiastically, poking her face in the bag to coo at the chicken with a bravery that impressed Cha and worried her what kind of penalty she'd earn if her gift clawed out the eyes of one of the kids. "Here," Cha said, "there's one for each of you." She handed a bag of fancy spun-sugar fae candies to Junior, glancing at Phin as she did. "For after the littles are washed up."

Zazu, Edur, and Xavia banged out the screen door, happier

about the prospect of washing now, while Phin Jr. set Inigo on his bare feet, walking with him more slowly, fishing out one of the special—and expensive—treats for the delighted toddler.

Phinny whirled on Cha. "Spun-sugar, really?"

Cha smiled weakly. "I just wanted to—"

"I don't care. *You* will leave. You may *not* talk to Dymphna. She's asleep and—"

"Asleep?" Cha spun in surprise, glancing at the bright sun out the cheerful kitchen window as if she might have lost track of time. "It's late afternoon." Cha had timed her arrival for Dy's happy return home to a pretty cocktail and Phinny's home-cooked meal.

Phinny grimaced. "They've got her on the night runs," she admitted.

Cha gaped, not having to exaggerate for effect. She pointed at Phinny as if this was somehow her fault. "The whole point," Cha said slowly, punctuating her words, "of Dy taking this stupid *day job* was so she could be at home at night with you and the kids."

"I know that," Phinny ground out, then pressed a hand to her swollen belly. "Do you think I love this development? Well, I *don't*," she bit out before Cha could reply. "I hate it. I hate everything about it, but this is what we have. And it's still a hell of a lot better than me worrying about her being out on those runs with you, maybe getting arrested, thrown in jail, mutated by angry fae, or worse!"

"Neither of us ever got mutated," Cha protested. Though it had been close a few times.

"Luck!" Phinny nearly screeched.

"Skill," Cha corrected calmly. "A combination of smarts, experience, and talent. That's what Dy and I always had. That's why you fell in love with her."

Phinny stared at her wildly, then let out a little sob, pressing shaking fingers to her mouth. "Damn pregnancy. It's got me all over emotional."

Cha risked putting a hand on Phinny's shoulder. Once they'd been friends. Once they'd all been friends, thick as thieves, as the saying went—and which had been far too accurate, with Phinny serving as their fence, alibi, and lookout in the later years. Until Dy got arrested in Obsidian and nearly gained a few appendages, before they bribed their way into having the sentence reduced. "Maybe you're emotional because you're in a shit situation, hon."

Phinny nodded, face averted, not shrugging away from Cha's comfort, even leaning into her hand a little. "Dymphna is miserable. Oh, she won't say so, but I can tell. She's restless. The ley magic required for this job... It's not enough for her. She wasn't made for this life. She's too good of a sorceress and she's restless not being able to use all her talents. I'm ... afraid she's going to leave me."

"Never," Cha said with easy conviction. "Dy loves you and the kids more than her own life." More than the smuggling life, that was for sure, or she wouldn't have given it up—along with her best friend—for Phinny. Not that Cha was bitter. Or not much. She wanted Dy to be happy. She just hadn't realized Dy's marriage would spell the end of their friendship. It had happened so slowly...and then all at once.

"I only wanted her to be safe," Phinny whispered. Then

she lifted her head and gave Cha a flinty stare. "This is about a job, isn't it?"

Cha eyed her warily. "You told me I'm not allowed to propose any more jobs."

"Yes. So why are you here, wanting to do exactly that?"

"It's really good money, Phin. Big money. Once in a lifetime money."

Phinny gazed at her, clearly torn between hope and dread. She shook her head wearily. "Fine. Go ask her." She turned to survey the spotlessly clean kitchen. "Since you're here, you might as well stay for supper. I'll make some bread to go with it. I suppose you still love my rosemary twists."

It was a peace offering, one Cha hadn't even remotely expected, especially not this fast. Things must be even worse than Phinny had let on. "Nobody in all the realms makes 'em like you do, Phin. I've fair starved without them."

"You go on with your charming ways," Phinny protested, blushing. "I'm wise to your flattery, Arantxa Evermore."

Cha clapped her hand to her heart as if struck. "My full name, twice in one morning! If you speak it a third time, will I be exorcised from your home?"

"I only wish," Phinny retorted, but without venom. "Go wake her up. Say what you have to say. Then we'll talk." She gave Cha an impish smirk, the first real smile she'd produced so far. "Better you wake the fang-beast than me, for once. Consider it another penance."

~ 5 ~

Facing the Fang Beast

AS WAS TYPICAL of her, Dy had the blankets pulled up over her head, her petite body so perfectly cocooned that she resembled a chrysalis. The big difference was—and Cha knew this well from years of being Dy's roommate back at the magic academy—instead of a beautiful butterfly emerging from the covers, a newly-wakened Dy was a slavering monster of epic proportions. It had been a test of true love when Phinny first persuaded Dy to spend a full night in her bed.

Cha had tried to warn her, but did anyone listen to her? Clearly not, or the world would be a better place. Being a cautious soul—and experienced—Cha snagged a pillow and hurled it at the narrow lump in the bed, deftly hitting her mark despite the darkened interior of the room.

Dy burst from under the covers, golden curls snaking with life, a sparkling green fireball hurtling past Cha's head to smash into glitter, searing itself into the wall. Cha turned and observed the singed spot, whistling low. "Impressive."

For a moment Dy didn't reply, her pretty, snub nose screwed up, golden brows lowered in a black scowl. "Why are *you* here? I'm sleeping." She burrowed back under the covers like a worm going to earth.

"Oh, no you're not." Satisfied that her old friend was awake enough not to accidentally kill her if she didn't duck fast enough, Cha ventured close enough to the bed to jerk the covers away.

"Arantxa Evermore!" Dy shrieked, writhing as if the exposure to daylight would shrivel her to ash.

"Ah, it remembers me now," Cha returned cheerfully, ignoring yet another blunt-weapon use of her full name, drawing the heavy curtains back from the windows to allow the sunlight to pour in. "Time to wake up and smell the coin, sweetling."

"Does Phin know you're here?" Dy asked, wedging open one baleful, summer-sky blue eye. "Because she will absolutely cut me off from sex if she finds out you snuck in behind her back."

"Sex?" Cha repeated in disbelief. "She's so pregnant, she's about to burst like an overheated grape. Give the poor woman a break."

"I worry about your understanding of gestation."

"Not something I need to understand. Ever."

"Orgasms are very healthy in later pregnancy," Dy continued blithely. "Good for the circulation." Finally resembling something a bit more human, Dy raked back her snarled golden locks and grinned salaciously. "One of the great advantages of keeping your lover in-house, rather than having to constantly troll for a new one."

"I happen to enjoy the constant trolling," Cha replied with

dignity. "It's like target practice—helps to keep my hand in."

Dy rolled her eyes. "Like you need more practice."

"Thank you." Cha gave her a grin, then glanced pointedly at the burnt spot on the wall. "Looks like someone else could use some practice, though." Not quite a question, but Dy knew it for what it was.

"Don't start with me," Dy grumbled, moving to the side of the bed and scrubbing her hands over her face before assessing the daylight outside. "I don't have enough opportunity to express my magic," she admitted. "It's been building up on me. I didn't singe you, did I?"

"The day I can't duck one of your fireballs is the day I turn in my handle," Cha answered cheekily, and Dy snorted.

"Seriously," the sorceress said, standing up and stretching, her naked body petite and curvy, her breasts full and pink-tipped, waist narrow, and hips perfectly flared. With her ass-length golden curls, Dy looked like a storybook princess—a direct contrast to long, lanky, dark-eyed Cha. They'd made a good cruising team, appealing to opposite genders and preferences.

Blearily, Dy cast about for something to wear. Long familiar with her friend's habits, Cha handed Dy a pair of pants, holding a shirt at the ready. "To what do we owe the honor of a visit from you? Why *did* Phin let you in?" Dy's grudgingly waking brain caught up, her expression becoming alarmed. "Is something wrong with Phin? The kids!"

"No, no—Phin is fine and knows I'm here. I get to stay for dinner." Cha patted her flat belly—all right, slightly soft belly—in anticipation. "She's even making me rosemary twists."

"An evil spell," Dy decided, taking the comb Cha handed her and going to work on her wildly curling mass of hair. "You finally abandoned the last of whatever scruples you still possessed and purchased—most likely stole—a mind-wipe spell to make Phin forget how pissed she is at you."

"What a great idea—do they have those?" Cha asked, more to annoy Dy than anything else.

Dy threw the comb at her, which was—all things considered—a de-escalation from fireballs. Cha neatly caught it and motioned to Dy to turn around. "Let me get those snarls. I don't understand why you don't chop this mess off."

"I like it," Dy replied sullenly. "More important, Phin likes it. I meant to braid it before I fell asleep, but… I was tired."

"Hmm."

"Besides, we don't all look glamorously fabulous with a famous short bob."

Cha shrugged modestly. Just because "The Bandit" was a popular haircut didn't mean she'd planned it that way. She deftly worked the tangles from the bottom up with the comb, the simple task bringing back years of memories. "Phinny thinks you're miserable. She says they've got you on the night runs."

"Phin has developed a remarkably loose tongue all of a sudden," Dy commented acidly.

"There's a job," Cha began.

"I knew it!" Dy whirled, seized the comb, and shook it in Cha's face. "I promised Phin: no more smuggling. No more any of it."

"What if I told you that you could go out with me for a

night and a day—same as these runs you're doing—and come home with fifty thousand silvers?"

Dy goggled at her. "Are we smuggling the dead body of a freshly assassinated fae queen?"

"Nope."

"I see. We have to do the assassinating, too."

"No assassinating. Smuggling a package. Nothing new. You know this gig backward and forward."

"From where to where?" Dy asked with a narrowed gaze.

"Round trip gig. We pick up a package concealed in a few tons of pixie dust, bring it back to Rockton via the Gypsum route."

"Uh-huh. You say that like Gypsum doesn't have a dead-or-alive warrant out on you for that frozen ambrosia gig."

Cha waved that off. "Surely they've forgotten about that."

"Forget that you seduced the local lord's son and brought him back to Granite with you, causing the family to lose their hold on their ancestral lands?" Dy snorted in disbelief. "Not going to happen, Cha."

"First of all, it was not a seduction, as he met me more than halfway. Second, he *wanted* to leave. I was an excuse. An opportunity, not an objective."

"Good thing, since you dumped him."

Cha held up a finger. "The relationship parameters were clear from the beginning. It's not my fault he wanted more. And," she added, "he got more. Last I heard, he was in Princess Adalaja's entourage, knocking himself out trying to keep her *satisfied*. Having personally experienced how little staying power he had, I don't give him good odds."

Dy laughed, a hint of her former sparkle in it, though she quickly sobered. "I've missed you, Bandit."

If Cha had a heart, Dy's words would have squeezed it. She hadn't been sure Dy gave her much thought at all. "It's not the same without you, Goldilocks. You know that."

Dy nodded, then launched herself at Cha, seizing her in a fierce hug. Cha had to blink back a few tears. Nothing wrong with a bit of sentimentality at a moment like this. Probably it was the thought of all that coin that had her feeling emotional. She squeezed her diminutive partner with fervor. No, nothing had been the same without Dy. Their friendship was the only relationship in Cha's life that had ever mattered and it had hurt that Dy left her behind so easily. "Does this mean you want to hear about the gig?" she whispered in Dy's ear.

Laughing again, Dy pulled back and tapped Cha on the nose with a finger that tingled with a mildly painful spark of magic. "Bad kitty."

"That's Katu."

"You and Katakume, both. We can *discuss* the gig. *With* Phin."

"And with all the rosemary bread twists I can eat," Cha added happily. Maybe Otto was right. It seemed she *could* still talk Dy into anything.

Nice to know she hadn't lost her touch.

~ 6 ~

Goldilocks and the Six Kids

"ABSOLUTELY NOT." Dy propped her elbows on either side of her plate and clutched her head in her hands. "Go to Moonstone? No. There is no way in all the fae realms that we can pull this off."

"Done with that?" Cha asked, reaching for Dy's mostly empty plate.

"I can't eat any more. My stomach has soured at the prospect of my imminent death or mutation."

Cha snagged the plate and stacked it on top of hers, carrying it to the sink full of soapy water. Phinny was off ensuring the kids were all in bed—and safely out of earshot—so Cha had volunteered to do dishes. One could never lay the penance on thick enough. "If you're too used to a day job to take a little risk…"

Dy lifted her head and glared at Cha, mouth open in astonishment. "My realistic assessment of risk is all that kept us alive all those years."

"That's why I need you," Cha agreed cheerfully. "To avoid imminent death or mutation, as we've always so ably done."

"You two never took on a job like this one before," Phinny said flatly as she reentered the kitchen.

"What about Devil Run?" Cha gestured wildly, soap bubbles flying. "That was a fast turnaround. And dicey as the sixth hell with those little slime demons."

"That wasn't *this* fast, you didn't have to cross into freaking Moonstone, and slime demons are toddlers compared to the fae," Dy retorted. "If we'd gotten pulled over on Devil Run, they'd have slapped you on the wrist and then invited you to race in the next tourney."

"And you'd have bribed them with some ley magic," Phinny said fondly, running a hand over Dy's hair, then kissing her on top of her head. She sat with a relieved sigh. "Bless you for doing the dishes, Cha. I hate you one percent less now. But you can't do this gig. I'm invoking my veto."

"Give me your feet, sweetheart," Dy said, scooting back her chair and patting her lap. With a grateful smile, Phin kicked off her slippers and propped her feet on Dy's lap. "They're swollen," Dy commented.

"Every part of me is swollen," Phinny replied wryly. "I swear this one is a boy. They're always the worst."

"You know," Cha said conversationally, drying the last dish, "you two could always stop having kids any time you wanted."

"Don't start or I'll revoke that one percent," Phinny warned her.

"Phin wants an even dozen," Dy said with a smile in her voice. Putting the last dish away, Cha glanced over her shoulder to see the pair with eyes locked, goofy expressions on their faces. Love. It addled a person's brain, clearly.

"All the more reason to score this easy coin," Cha declared, snagging one more rosemary twist and swinging her leg around to straddle a chair backwards.

Phinny groaned. "Why did I let her in?"

Dy gave Cha a dry, warning look. "This coin is so very far from 'easy,' you'd be better off calling it impossible."

"Not impossible," Cha argued. "This is nothing we haven't done before. Just faster and in different territory."

"Calling Moonstone 'different' is an understatement, even for you," Phinny noted, head tipped back and face suffused with pleasure.

"Aside from the dangers we know about and the ones we can only guess at from rumor, they have ley lines we've never mapped, much less ridden," Dy pointed out relentlessly. "I hear the lines move around like they're alive with minds of their own. Something to do with the high energy of the white dust. Even away from the main ley lines and tourist areas in Obsidian it gets wonky. You know that."

"That's why we have you," Cha replied. "You can create, alter, or control any ley line on the fly and you know it. You've worked with Moonstone dust countless times."

"First, I don't know ley lines as they exist in any fae realm but Obsidian," Dy argued. "And pixie dust in its native environment moves differently. Even black dust inside Obsidian is whoa more powerful—it moves like lightning. Who can say what white dust would be like inside of the Moonstone realm?"

By the tone of Dy's voice, Cha knew Dy was intrigued.

This was the sort of professional challenge her sorceress partner never had been able to resist. Phin heard it, too, rolling her head to give Cha a resigned glare, her expression no longer at all pleased.

"Do we even know who our point of contact will be inside Moonstone?" Dy asked, frowning. "It won't be any operative we've worked with before."

"Otto promised details after he's assured you're in. He might be a money-grubbing ass, but he wants this shipment. His contact will be solid." *Even if they couldn't trust him past that...*

Dy only grunted in disgust. "Add in an unknown supplier. Plus, we'd have no local support." Dy ticked the points off on her fingers. "We don't know the populace; they don't know us. Worse, they *aren't* us, as most fae ignore humans at best and would rather swat us like gnats than deal with us. Obsidian is one thing, with all the human commerce and tourists, but we'd stand out like sore thumbs inside Moonstone, which means we'd be *lucky* if they only ignored us. We've got no idea where the ambrosia stations are for the carriage-beasts, or if there are any kind of pit stops for the humans. Can we even find human food in Moonstone?"

"We'll be in and out so fast, we won't need to eat. We take our own food and ambrosia. We won't even encounter any fae."

"You hope," Dy replied darkly. "What if we have an emergency?"

"That's where your sorcery comes in," Cha countered, then pretended to scrutinize Dy. "Unless you've gotten rusty, working the commercial grind for the powers that be and changing nappies."

"I know what you're doing and it won't work," Dy replied placidly, but Cha caught Phinny's quickly disguised wince as Dy dug her thumbs into a sore spot with more strength than necessary.

"Dealing with Moonstone ley lines will be tricky, I'm sure," Cha acknowledged with extra sympathy. "I don't blame you for being afraid to test your ability. Your aim was way off with that fireball, too," she added as a devious afterthought.

"It was *not* off." Dy tossed her hair back over one shoulder, glaring at Cha, her pretty blue eyes sparking. "I deliberately missed you, out of some misguided sense of nostalgia for someone who *used* to be a friend."

Cha snorted in derision, ignoring the pang that there might be truth buried in the sally. "You had no idea it was me. I could've been a fae law-hound coming to drag your petite ass off to jail for all you knew."

"I am not so rusty as all that," Dy snarled, leaving off her task to a whimper of protest from Phinny. "You think I don't recognize your stink by now?"

Cha spread her hands. "I'm just saying that, if you think you can't do it, just say so. I'll find someone else."

"Like you could find anyone better than me!"

"No way," Cha replied with perfect sincerity. "You're the best there is, Goldilocks, and all the world knows it."

"Do you two need a moment alone?" Phinny asked wearily and Dy shot her an apologetic glance.

"You know it's never been like that with Dy and me," Cha put in.

"I know." Phin tugged one of Dy's curls. "Cha is so not your type."

"And not only because she's incomprehensibly straight," Dy noted wryly.

"Hey," Cha protested, "I happen to like men."

"Like she said: incomprehensible," Phin replied, Dy chiming in on the last word—and they exchanged another of those soft-hearted looks.

Cha rolled her eyes. "Are we discussing my questionable sexual preferences or planning how we're going to become filthy rich?"

"We can do both," Dy answered sweetly. "And even though I am as proficient as ever—I defy you to find another sorceress who can do what I can with a ley line, in human or fae lands—having no idea how the lines lie once we cross the border is a major problem. Not stopping at all isn't an option. Even I need to get out and get a feel for the lay of the land once in a while. I'll especially need to in Moonstone, with white dust everywhere."

"That's why I'll be driving diversion for you," Cha pointed out calmly. "You need to stop, I'll distract any locals, law and otherwise, until you can move again."

"You won't know the ley lines either," Dy cautioned. "They won't feel the same to you. Riding them won't be like anything you've done before."

Cha shrugged that off. "Never met a ley line I couldn't ride." She could just imagine the speeds they'd get on pure Moonstone white, the native stuff, not the contaminated shit they exported for human use. Made her all tingly just to contemplate it. Better than sex. Okay, not really, but in the same general neighborhood. "Besides, if I get in trouble, I can call you for assist."

"True," Dy mused. "There's always the underground path-channels, at least for the part of the gig on this side of the Moonstone border. We know they work through Obsidian. Any human locals will be listening, so we could hit them up to find ambrosia sources and pit stops on the far side of the depot."

Cha cleared her throat. "About that…"

Phinny gave her a sharp glance and swore. "What are you not telling us? I just *knew* there was something more."

"There's a small possibility the law-hounds have found the codes to listen to the underground path-channels," Cha admitted, and braced herself.

$$\sim 7 \sim$$

A Daring Plan

PHINNY EXPLODED INTO motion—which, for a woman as heavily pregnant as she, was an impressive sight. "Manticores take you, Arantxa Evermore! How could you wait until *now* to mention that?"

"I wanted to present the information in a logical order," Cha began, "and—"

"And *you* are a scammer and always have been," Phinny declared pointing an accusing finger at Cha. "Your so-called logical order was all a subterfuge to sucker us into this hairbrained scheme, dazzling us with tales of piles of gold coin and riches, and now—" A sob burst out of her. "Oh, why did I let you over the threshold? I *knew* better!"

"Now, sweetheart," Dy said, rising and approaching her wife with wary concern, "try not to upset yourself. Think of the baby."

Phinny threw off Dy's reaching hands, batting them away like biting insects. "Don't you think-of-the-baby me, Dymphna Lockhart! Think about *me*, a widow, with six children—if I survive to birth *this* one—and no one to help me care for them.

We'll end up working the silver mines while you disappear into Moonstone forever."

"It won't happen," Dy promised her, "because I'm not going." She held up a hand at Cha's protest. "It's not worth it. Nothing you can say will make me want to go."

Cha sighed and drew her trump card. "Remember Monat?"

"She was at our wedding, so yes," Dy replied tersely. "Just spit it out."

Cha scraped her fingers through her short bob. She'd just known this would be the hardest part. She'd have told Dy anyway. It just kind of sucked to use the information as a lever. "Well, it so happens that she got arrested."

"*Arrested*," Phinny echoed, paling. "When? Where?"

There wasn't any getting around it. "Returning from a Moonstone gig. She's in jail somewhere between here and there, rumor has it."

Phinny's mouth worked, with no sound coming out. A blessing in the moment, but Phinny's wrath postponed was doom intensified exponentially.

"How did they get her?" Dy asked, the dread awareness already in her expression.

Cha winced, feeling vaguely guilty. Surely that was the uncomfortable emotion pricking her, unfamiliar though it might be. "You know as much as I do now."

Dy looked to Phinny. "We have to rescue Monat."

"No, we don't," Cha and Phinny said at the same time, pausing uncomfortably at the unprecedented occurrence of being on the same side of an argument. This had not been Cha's intention in mentioning Monat's disappearance. Maybe she hadn't thought it through—wouldn't be the first time—but Cha had thought more of a "do it in Monat's memory" kind of reaction.

"She would do it for us," Dy argued.

"No, she wouldn't," Phinny and Cha said together, once again.

Dy looked back and forth between them. "How can you two possibly agree on this? You never agree on anything."

"You're thinking with your heart, honey, not your head," Phinny said coaxingly. Cha let her field this one. That was the thing about Dy—and one of the reasons she needed Cha, and Phinny, too—she did have a soft heart. Too soft. If Dy could save all the world, she would. "It's one thing to go to Moonstone to earn money for the family, but staging a jailbreak to snag a prisoner from under the noses of the fae is not only wildly dangerous, it serves no one any good."

"It serves Monat," Dy replied stubbornly. "Since when do we abandon our friends, Phin?"

That was rich, coming from Dy, who'd essentially abandoned Cha in favor of marital harmony. Cha opened her mouth to say so, but Phinny gave her a beseeching look, clearly asking to Cha to back her up. Unaccustomed to having that particular shoe on the other foot, and finding that it pinched something awful, Cha searched her mind for an argument that could sway Dy. When she hit on it, she knew Phinny would never forgive her. Again. Still.

"Know who Monat was running goods for? Otto," she answered before they could ask. "Dy, he's desperate to have *you*—the infamous Goldilocks—on this job. You've got him in the palm of your hand on this one. Tell him you'll only do it if he'll find a way to bail out Monat. He's the one with the money and fae connections to pull it off. He just needs the right incentive."

Dy gazed at her, lips parted. Cha should've thought of this angle to begin with. Phinny braced her hands on the table, head bowed so her expression was hidden behind the fiery strands that had escaped her unruly knot of hair.

"Plus," Cha added, having saved this nugget for a desperate moment like this one, "he'll give us another ten percent down once he sees you behind the controls of Big Betty. That's ten gold coins you can give to Phinny right away on top of the ten in the bag I already gave you. You won't need to use your leave to do this gig. You can quit that commercial slog here and now."

"An even split would be five and five," Phinny said with a scowl, having always been the one to figure the finances. Part of why she'd made such an excellent fence before she went straight. "What about your cut?"

Cha waved that off. If, for some reason, they didn't make it back from this gig, she wanted Phin and the kids to have at least that much to keep them afloat. "I'll take my share from the final. And we split the pot three ways," she added on impulse. "Two thirds for you two, one third for me."

"That's not fair," Dy protested, though weakly.

"There's more of you," Cha replied, pointing out the obvious.

Phinny lifted her head and stared at Cha with a bitter chocolate gaze. "Is this a bribe, Cha?"

Reassured by the used of her nickname, Cha spread her hands. "Only in the best possible way. You can start spending this while we're gone. I just won a big tourney and—"

"You did?" Dy smiled. "Congratulations."

"Thanks." Rather than being pleased, Cha experienced a familiar surge of annoyance. Maybe it wasn't fair of her—after all, Dy was busy with a lot of stuff—but it hurt that her old friend clearly knew nothing about Cha's life. "Anyway, I've got the funds to buy more than a replacement chicken. I'll underwrite the supplies we need and cover any bribes along the way."

"Do you have gemstones?" Phinny asked, a challenging tilt to her chin, then shook her head at Cha's blank stare. "You've been out of the game too long, Cha-cha. They're not going to take human coin in Moonstone. The fae use jewels for currency. They only take coin in Obsidian because of the proximity to human lands, where they can use the stuff. Even then you'd be better with jewels for unusual circumstances."

Cha waved that off. "The fae act snooty about it, but they all take human coin if you offer enough."

Phinny shook her head. "Never what the coin's worth. You need gems."

"I'll get gems," Cha promised, wondering how in the seven hells she was going to afford *those*. But she couldn't take any of the advance now, after making such a big noble show of it and all. Teach her to be generous and thoughtful—it always came back to bite you in the ass. "Thank you for the sound advice, Phin. No one knows currency like you."

Phinny glared a moment longer, shook a finger at Cha,

then sighed and looked to Dy with resigned affection. "I don't like it, but I won't stop you from doing this."

"I promise to be careful," Dy said. "Thank you."

Cha discreetly contained her happy dance as Dy and Phin embraced. Finally, after what seemed like an unnaturally long hug, Phin released Dy. "Here's what we'll do," she said. "You two go to Otto and get that chunk of change. I'll light up my old network and get you all the maps I can of the ley lines in and out of the fae lands. Surely even the fae need to keep track."

"I wouldn't be sure of that," Dy commented darkly.

"Does this mean Fiery Wench is back from the dead?" Cha asked.

Phinny scowled at her, but there was a hint of mischief in it. "I'm changing it up. Fiery Wench needs to stay buried. Besides, she's not me anymore. Call me Mama Bear now."

Dy made a sound and went to her wife, giving her a long, lingering kiss. "Mama Bear, indeed, but you'll always be *my* fiery wench."

Cha studied the portraits of the kids on the wall, arranged in order of age, giving them privacy of a fashion, again.

Releasing her wife, Dy nodded crisply. "I'll contact the Academy of Mental Clarity and get the skinny on what they know about the law-hounds getting the codes for the under-ground path-channels. They can't have found all of the channels, or there'd be a lot more people getting picked up. We can develop a pattern to jump channels," Dy said to Cha. "Switch it up so they can't follow too closely."

Cha felt the anticipatory grin split her face. "And feed them false information on the ones we do know they're monitoring."

Dy stood. "Let's go get that first installment. I'll wake up Big Betty. And I'll need Warg, of course."

Cha goggled at her in sheer horror. "Warg is still alive?"

"Of course, he's still alive," Dy answered with considerable indignation. "It hasn't been that long and he's not that old."

Yes, he was. Cha met Phinny's gaze over Dy's head, and the redhead rolled her eyes, giving a little headshake of resigned disgust. The homely creature had to be even more ancient and full of slobber than ever.

"With the gold from Otto, you could take some coin to purchase a new lodestone," Cha suggested, a bit desperately. "Hell, I'll buy you one from my coin. Consider it an expense to do the gig."

"A *new* lodestone?" Dy was as aghast as if Cha had suggested gutting one of her children. "Warg has been with me for years. You know that, Cha. We're a package deal. I can't ground my ley-line magic without a lodestone and Warg is the best one I've ever worked with. If I don't have Warg, I risk having that ley magic crawl right back up my connection and fry my brains—and then where would you be? No ley worker is safe without a lodestone."

"I'm not saying go without," Cha protested. She'd never suggest such a thing. Not after that smuggling job when Warg chased after a gremlin, leaving Dy high and dry during an adjustment on a high-test white ley line—not incidentally their escape route. No longer grounded by the magically null lodestone, the white dust had surged in an uncontrolled backflow, knocking Dy unconscious. Stranded with Big Betty carrying a full load of contraband, no ley line, and the howls of the law-hounds closing in, Cha had been sure they were bound for a nasty mutation. Fortunately, Dy regained consciousness just as Warg returned and they all jumped onto the white ley line just before the hounds caught up to them. Without Dy's ability to close off the line behind them, their career would've been over then.

Dy absolutely needed a lodestone, especially with the high potency dust they'd be dealing with. Cha just wished she'd get rid of the stinking and tragically unreliable Warg.

"Then what *are* you saying?" Dy demanded with narrowed eyes.

"I'm saying…" Desperately, she tried to think of something to dig herself out of this rapidly deepening hole. "You deserve to level up," she declared, feeling inspired. "Warg is ancient, incontinent, and prone to chase gremlins."

"Oh, he's not that bad." Dy folded her arms and glared. "You can't possibly be suggesting I take on a mission of this magnitude with an untested, completely new-to-me lode-stone!"

"No." Cha sighed for the inevitability. "Get Warg and let's transform Big Betty. The sooner we get the next installment of Otto's gold, the happier I'll be."

~ 8 ~

Firing up Big Betty

B IG BETTY DOZED in the barn at the back of the property, an incongruous sight. The enormous elephant lazily plucked piles of fruit from a manger in her plus-sized stall while the much smaller horses and donkeys stamped nearby.

By the look of her, Big Betty hadn't been on the juice for some time. Animals that hadn't transformed to ride the ley lines in a while lost that glossy shimmer of magic, as the ambrosia that fueled them in carriage form gradually faded from their systems, and they reverted to resembling their more natural counterparts. Sometimes, the enchantment that gave them the ability to transform degraded entirely, rendering the creatures standard household pets forever more.

Cha squinted dubiously at Big Betty. "Haven't you been driving her?"

"When would I?" Dy demanded grumpily, though her scowl softened when Betty lifted her trunk in a welcome. She went to the great beast and patted the gray-whiskered cheek with affection. "The company has me driving *their* rigs— optimized for their proprietary ley lines."

"Then what's the point of having you at the controls?" Cha demanded. "Any baby ley rider can snooze in the cab of a transport and hit the switches at the junctions. You're wasted in that job."

"I know that," Dy ground out. "Not that I'm wasted—because of course any ley rider can follow the stabilized lines. But that's why I'm on the night runs now. There's been a lot of damage to the commercial ley lines. Vandalism on the proprietary paths the locals aren't supposed to use. They need me on the job because I can effect the repair on the fly and keep the delivery schedule and don't look at me like that! I'm good at my job."

"That's like saying the sun is good at drying piss on the pavement," Cha scoffed. "You're the most powerful, skilled, and inventive ley sorceress I've been privileged to know. Probably that exists anywhere outside the fae realms."

"That was someone I used to be maybe, a long time ago."

"Don't be ridiculous. You're still you—and you should be running that company, not working as some overqualified repair-mage."

"Well, now I'm doing neither, since I'm officially quitting."

"About time, too. You're way too special for the likes of them."

Dy paused, blinked at Cha. "Why are you the only person who ever believed in me?"

Cha snorted. "Phinny believes in you."

Shaking her head slowly, Dy caressed Betty's trunk, which curled lovingly around her tiny waist. "That's different. Besides, my mother never did."

"Your horrible mother doesn't believe in anything but herself. Bad example."

"And even Phinny was dazzled by the fame. You believed in me from the beginning and with unwavering intensity, even when I was no one."

"You were *never* no one." Cha tried to sound brusque, but the words came out a little rough. "You're my partner. I know what you can do, and you saved my ass more times than I can count."

"Likewise," Dy said on a sigh, then gave Cha a searching look, a vulnerability in it she hadn't shown in front of Phinny. "Do you really think we can do this?"

"If we can't, no one can."

"That's not a yes."

"Would you have believed me if I'd just said 'yes'?"

Dy barked out a laugh. "A valid point. You've never lied to me, have you, Cha? Despite all the rest."

"I've never lied to you and I never will."

The sorceress hesitated, then visibly came to a decision. "I want you to promise me something. It's important."

Uh oh. "All right," Cha replied evenly.

"Promise me you'll be responsible. Every minute of the way, and back again."

Cha nearly protested, but she caught the serious glint in Dy's pretty blue gaze. And it was true: responsibility had never been Cha's strong suit. "I'll be responsible, every minute of the way and back again."

"Promise."

With a groan, Cha lifted her eyes to the sky. "I *promise* I'll be responsible, every minute of the way and back again."

"Thank you," Dy said quietly.

"I believe we can do this," Cha told her, happy to have that done with. "So what if it's purple fae and ley lines that go bump in the night? We've never not made a delivery. We're not going to screw up now."

"We're out of practice."

"Rested," Cha corrected. "Ready to blaze."

Betty, as if understanding, lifted her trunk in a vigorous trumpet. From the far side of the cottage, Katu let out a purring yowl of agreement.

"The carriage-critters agree. Let's ride."

Dy held out a hand and they gripped forearms. "Bandit and Goldilocks, on the road again."

DY LED BETTY around to the ley-line driveway, the elephant lifting her ears and trunk in happy anticipation, a sprightly skip in her step. People argued about the ethics of enchanting the animals for use as carriages, but those who worked with the animals knew how much they loved the speed and excitement of riding the leys in more powerful, indestructible forms, maybe even more than the ley riders did. Only the fae knew how the actual enchanting worked, doing that bit of spell work in secret before selling the carriages to humans through various marketplaces. The bigger or faster the animal and carriage, the more expensive the price tag.

"Betty has missed our runs," Dy commented, echoing

Cha's thoughts.

"The carriage-critters aren't the sort to sit around any more than we are," Cha replied, running her hand over the Katu's wickedly curved fender. "They're raised to run and trained with the best, just like us. Once you get a taste, you can't get away from it."

"I can vouch for that." Dy guided Betty onto the ley line. The big elephant moved eagerly, caressing the currently inanimate jaguar with a thoughtful nuzzle of the flexible tip of her trunk, then stood stock still as the enchantment embedded in the ley line triggered the spell woven into Betty's physiology. The prismatic magic shimmered over Betty's gray and wrinkled hide as it became metallic, her body extending into a long, boxlike shape. Her head and shoulders clip-clapped into a shell, creating a cabin within. Feet tucked up, leaving the carriage bobbing some distance above ground before the motion settled out.

When the transformation was complete, all signs of Betty the elephant had vanished, replaced by the biggest transport rig on all the ley lines of all the human principalities. Maybe the fae realms too. Big Betty hummed quietly with power, ready to cruise the lines at full speed, empty or laden. Beside her, the jag picked up on the magic Dy had juiced into the ley-line spur, purring to similar life. The two carriages—Big Betty, huge and imposing, and the open-topped jag, low and sleek—shared a quintessential partnership. Like Cha and Dy, Katu and Betty had always been at their best working together.

"They look good together," Dy commented quietly.

Cha threw her an appreciative grin. "Yeah, they do."

Something gargled out a sound like a vomiting hound dog might make, and Warg ambled slowly up, belly dragging on the lavender-tipped grass and leaving a denuded trail behind. Basically a cross between a crocodile and a salamander—though in an unnatural shade of pink with violet, palm-sized spots—Warg had zero attractive qualities, but Dy squealed at the thing's arrival, crouching to embrace the irascible creature and kiss its slimy cheek. "There you are," she chided in a honeyed baby-talk she didn't use with her own kids. "Have you been swimming in the swampy end of the pond again, sweetums?"

Judging by the reek, the answer was a definitive yes, but Cha heroically said nothing. With a grunt, Dy lifted the stinking Warg into the cab of Big Betty, staggering slightly under its unwieldy, long-tailed weight as the creature nearly overflowed her arms. Once inside, Warg showed considerably more alacrity, sitting up almost like a person, tail curved under its lumpy rump and wrapped around in a circle. It propped clawed front paws on the dashboard as it gazed eagerly out the front window, tongue lolling between yellowed, serrated teeth.

"Look how happy Warg is to get on the line again," Dy exclaimed to Phinny as she joined them. Phin nodded, a sad smile gracing her strained face as she held out an overnight bag and food hamper. Dy went to kiss her wife and they embraced.

"You and Warg both look happy," Phin noted, then turned to Cha. "You take care of her or I'm coming after you."

"Of course, Phinny," Cha replied, a somber promise. "Always have. Always will."

"I know." Phinny nodded as if trying to convince herself. "That's the only reason I'm agreeing to this. Well, one of the reasons. Here." She reached into the voluminous pocket of her apron and withdrew a box made of polished, dark wood, fastened with a golden lock. She thrust it at Cha, who took it, bemused.

"The combination is Dy's birthday," Phinny said, pushing her fists into her now empty pockets.

Cha keyed in the numbers, opened the lid, and whistled. An array of gemstones glittered with perfect clarity, securely tucked in velvet nests. "Phinny…aren't you full of surprises?"

"For a rainy day," Phin replied, hunching her shoulders. "Or an angry fae, in case something from Dy's past caught up to her." She glared at Cha. "I figure you count as one of those somethings."

Cha let that go, as it was painfully accurate.

"You know the relative values?" Phin demanded. "I wrote out a key and put it in the bottom. There's no telling what any of them are worth in any of the fae realms but Obsidian, so that's what I noted for each. Still, the relative worth shouldn't change much. Start with the lowest and work up."

Cha didn't retort that even she knew that much. She might not be a financial whiz, but she knew how to bribe. "Thank you, Phinny," she said quietly. "I'll bring as many back to you as I can."

"Just bring home the one jewel that matters," Phin replied with dignity, quickly lost when Dy tackle-hugged her.

"We'll be back before you know it," Dy promised. "I'll have Otto's next advance couriered over, so start shopping!"

She whispered something in Phin's ear that had her blushing, so Cha turned away and climbed into the jag, all the home she'd ever needed.

Dy climbed behind the wheel of Big Betty, her sorcery palpably juicing the ley line that led out to the main drag. Cha loved to ride a line that Dy had magicked. Pure speed and the freedom of the road beckoned. As it should be.

"For coin, glory, and thrills!" Cha shouted to Dy, who grinned out the window at the sound of their old rallying cry.

"Let's haul ass!" she shouted in return, pumping her fist.

And they were off.

~ 9 ~

The Plan

"THERE'S MY GOLDEN-HAIRED princess of the ley lines!" Otto exclaimed with a fatuous smile creasing his shiny face, holding open his arms as if Dy would embrace him. "Give us a kiss."

"You can kiss my petite ass, Otto," Dy replied with barbed sweetness.

"I'd love to," he answered, grin turning lascivious. "Given up on the other team, have we?"

"Let's skip the sexual harassment and focus on important things like coin and deets," Cha suggested with silky menace, subtly interposing herself between Dy and Otto.

Not subtly enough, as Dy thumped her on the sword arm, making Cha aware she'd reflexively put her hand on the hilt.

"Don't slice up the boss till we get all the money," Dy said. "Besides, I can take care of myself." She flicked a finger and a tiny ball of sparkling white flew past Cha's head to put itself out on a yelping Otto's cheek. "Down, boy," Dy instructed with satisfaction, sliding Cha a smug glance. "See? Top of my game."

Hand clapped to his singed cheek, Otto gave her a wounded look. "Motherhood has changed you."

"Yeah—it's made me too tired to deal with stupid shit. I'm here, so extortion accomplished." Dy snapped her fingers and opened her palm. "Like Cha says: gold and deets."

"A true team." Unperturbed, Otto shrugged and went around his big, glossy desk. Outside the big windows of his fancy office, the human city of Rockton, capital of Granite, sprawled in varying degrees of relative splendor. Of course, nothing in the human principalities could compete with the elegance of the fae realms, both the sort humans had actually seen for themselves and the kind featured in the embroidered tales of bards and imaginative attempts at imitation. Still, the wealthy and nobles among the humans invested considerable coin in trying to *look* like they lived like the fae.

They built fanciful spires tiled in gleaming ceramics that counterfeited the palaces of the fae and ignored the rumble-tumble of wooden and sod shacks that encircled the city center like dead leaves shed from a living tree. Otto's office sat at the top of one such tower, where he pretended to be a legit businessman. Most of his expansive view centered on the racing stadium that stood not far away, a scintillating monument to illicit magical entertainment—and a pointed reminder of the true source of his wealth. Or, rather, one of those sources, all of them questionable.

Otto produced another of his ubiquitous velvet bags, the coin within clinking with softly musical promise. He set it on his side of the desk, well out of reach, as if they might snag the bag and run. Half-tempted to do exactly that, Cha reminded herself of the even greater wealth that awaited them if—no, *when*—they pulled off this job.

As long as they didn't die, get imprisoned, or mutated, that is. Not that she was worried.

"Please sit." Otto waved a hand at the visitors' chairs.

"We'll stand," Dy said.

"It can't take that long to tell us," Cha agreed. "What's the exact gig?"

"Your usual run over the border to Obsidian, plus a small extra step," Otto answered, shrugging as if it were nothing. "You'll hit the Obsidian depot for the camouflage shipment, then bypass to the other side, as you've done a thousand times."

"Hardly that many," Dy countered.

"And that's no mean feat," Cha added.

"Thus your exorbitant fee," Otto bit out meaningfully. "Once you have the cover shipment of Obsidian dust, you take the Obsidian Thirteen up to Moonstone, cross the border and follow the Moonstone Thirteen up to a location I'll give you. Meet my contact. Load the package. Come back here, deliver, and take your very generous payday."

"Let's see the location and contact info," Dy said.

Otto slid a document across the desk and Dy pounced on it like it was fae chocolate. Her steely gaze slid up to Otto and pinned him. "This is the same route and contact you gave Monat?"

Otto stepped back, nearly to the glass wall, and held up his hands like Dy had stung him with another tiny fireball. "Monat has nothing to do with this." He glared accusingly at Cha.

"What did you tell her?"

Cha decided to sit after all, sprawling sideways in a swank armchair and crossing her booted ankles. "Goldilocks and I have no secrets. You should know that. Neither do you, for that matter."

"You should also know," Dy said, sitting in the other armchair with considerably more grace, handing Cha the document, "that we're going nowhere until you agree to extradite Monat."

Otto goggled at her. At least seeing him caught so flat-footed mitigated Cha's irritation at Dy tipping their hand so early in the conversation. A wily negotiator, Dy was not. "I can't do that," Otto squeaked. "Nobody can help Monat now."

Dy stood. "Then we're leaving. Come on, Cha."

Well, Cha supposed, that was one way to negotiate. Otto sputtered out a protest before Cha had to abandon her comfy spot.

"You'd sacrifice a fortune for *Monat*?" Otto demanded.

"Some things are more important than money, right, Cha?"

Cha scanned the information on the document, in case Otto snatched it away. You never knew when this sort of inside knowledge would come in handy. They were to meet some fae operative going by the unlikely code name of Sugarplum at the Ice Lily Garden. One of her brows crawled up her forehead. Why couldn't it be a nice little squalid warehouse? Probably because the fae didn't have anything shabby.

"Hey!" she exclaimed as Dy swatted her on the head.

"*Right, Cha?*" Dy repeated meaningfully.

Cha transferred her rueful gaze to Otto. "You know how Dy is. She wouldn't agree to the gig unless rescuing Monat is baked in. You want your package in a hurry? Best just give in now."

Otto looked like he wanted to tear his hair out, though he gripped the edge of his desk instead. "You say that like I have any influence over the fae. The *Moonstone* fae!"

So, Garaile's gossip was good—Monat was in Moonstone jail. Cha waved the contact info sheet at him. "You got this much."

He sniffed, putting on a wounded face. "That's proprietary."

"Then proprietary yourself into extracting Monat," Cha suggested. Putting a hand to the side of her mouth as if to hide the words from Dy, she dropped her voice. "Don't make the scary sorceress angry."

"I don't have *time* to do that," Otto complained, nearly whining. "I'm not giving you a twenty-four-hour turnaround just for the fun of it. This was a rush job to begin with and now I'm way behind the clock. If I don't have a rig there by tomorrow at midnight, the offer expires."

"Why?" Cha asked and Otto released his chokehold on the desk to wave his hands frantically in the air.

"I don't know! You think I asked? They're fae. They call the shots."

"What's the package?" Dy asked.

Otto pointed at her. "That you do not need to know and, believe me, you're better off not knowing. My contact will know what to do. The cover shipment will obscure any magical signatures and I'm sure your sorcerous tricks can handle the rest."

Not ideal, but also not unusual for a smuggling gig like this. "Why do we have to get it back here so fast?" Cha asked the next logical question.

"You want to get caught by the hounds? Be my guest, but not with my product. Those are the terms and you're wasting time."

"No, you are," Dy retorted. "You clearly know where Monat is."

Deflated, Otto nodded. "But I can't get to her. I swear it. If that's your dealbreaker, then we have no deal."

He meant it. And no way Otto could find anyone else to get that shipment he so badly wanted in time. Cha assessed Dy, mutinously scowling. "Then give us Monat's location," she said, giving Dy a warning look when the sorceress rounded on her. "We'll handle the rest."

"You can't be late. Getting there or getting back," Otto warned, relaxing slightly. Pulling out a fancy quill, he scribbled something on a bit of parchment and held it out. Dy reached for it, but Cha was faster, springing up to grab the note and pocket it.

"We won't be late," Cha promised. "Trust me," she told Dy, who nodded reluctantly.

They settled into business, reviewing the route from Granite, through Gypsum, to the Obsidian border. That bit was easy, taking Ley Line Thirteen for most of it—commercial traffic all the way, a route they knew well—then into Obsidian.

The crossing should be straightforward. Dy's papers from Otto included a fake manifest for the big rig to show to the border guards. She'd be ostensibly picking up a cargo of black dust. Cha wouldn't need papers to cross into Obsidian as ley riders with racy carriages like hers went joyriding in the fun park that was the land of the Obsidian fae all the time.

From there it would get more difficult. Bypassing the Obsidian depot, the standard destination for the rigs legally transporting black dust, was always tricky. The law-hounds would be on the alert for those smugglers making contact on the fae side of the depot. That's when their special talents would come into play. Dy would move, adapt, or create ley lines for them to travel while Cha employed her considerable skills as a ley rider to keep them on track—and run interference for the rig.

Fortunately, that section of the Obsidian realm was a narrow band, and they should be able to shake any hounds when they crossed into Moonstone. After that, they'd have to be on their toes, play it by ear.

Then they'd have to reverse the journey, returning to human lands as fast as possible.

Getting Big Betty to the point of contact, loaded, and back to Rockton on schedule was top priority. As long as they kept the big rig intact and on time, the rest could be altered on the fly. Simple, really.

Of course, nothing was simple when it came to the fae.

~ 10 ~

Practice Makes Fun

"Goldilocks, this is Bandit. You read?" On the road at last, Cha let up on the glyph that activated the path-channel to send, ready to receive.

"You know it, Bandit," Dy's voice came back clear, Warg happily warbling in the background. The beast sounded like a hippopotamus with a severe stomach condition. "I'm on the Thirteen. Got a smooth black line and making time. Just passed the Lightning-Struck Oak Tree Milestone. Where you at?"

Cha took in the scenery. Thick-leaved trees lined the corridor cut by the major ley line. They were still in human lands, well outside of Rockton, but solidly still in Granite Principality, so the landscape hadn't yet morphed into sporting some of the more extreme weirdnesses that came from proximity to the fae realms. That would crop up in Gypsum, closer to the border with and into Obsidian. Angels only knew what the landscape would be in Moonstone.

The other traffic on the line looked pretty typical, so Cha flowed along at a reasonable speed, not yet taking advantage of

Dy's ability to tweak the ley line and thrust the jag into hyper-speed. The time for that would come. Best to save her partner's sorcerous juice for the crunches that would inevitably arrive, though it wouldn't be a bad idea for them to practice a bit.

Comparing the landscape markers to the glowing map globe Phinny had scrounged up and couriered to them, Cha made her best guess as to her position relative to Big Betty.

"I'm about seven leagues ahead of you, Goldilocks. Moving free and clear. No sign of any hounds. How are you on the clock?" They'd used some of Cha's funds to acquire magically synced timepieces.

"Running three hours and twenty-two minutes ahead of schedule. Looking good."

"Yes, you are, Goldilocks." It wasn't a huge amount of buffer time on a super-tight schedule—one incident could wipe most of that out in a hurry—but better to be in the plus column than the negative. "Bandit out." Cha clicked off, but the box immediately bounced live again.

"Hey Bandit! This is Grogmeister. Come on?"

"Well, well, well, Grogmeister," Cha replied. "Long time no chat, huh?"

"That's 'cause you went to the dark side and Goldilocks strapped on a ball and chain. You two really on the gig again?"

"Now don't be spreading tales," Cha cautioned. "Lots of ears on the trees, and I'm not talking the kind the witches put in their cauldrons."

Grogmeister snorted, the sound coming rough through the box. "We know all about ears out here away from big stone city, Bandit. Speaking of, you might try switching to the marcasite channel. You can talk a bit louder there, know it?"

"Ah, good tip, Grogmeister. Will take that on advisement."

"You need any little thing, you just shout, Bandit. You got time for a pit stop, you know where to find me. Got a deal on ambrosia, too."

"The last 'deal' you made me cost nearly a week's pay."

"It's a sad, sad day when the Bandit talks in terms of a paycheck."

"Don't I know it."

"No matter. You got friends out here still. You and Goldilocks, both."

"Good to know. Bandit out." As she clicked off again, Cha reflected that it was indeed good to know that. Dy had rightfully and logically pointed out that they'd have no local support once they crossed into Moonstone. However, they hadn't taken into account the longstanding support of the countryside they'd moved through all these years.

'Support' might be a strong word for the ragtag alliance of the various oppressed communities of the human principalities, but there was a conviviality in the boat of misery they all found themselves in. Though no one had much, what little they did have, they shared. That included information. It wouldn't be the same in the fae realms, but it could come in useful on this side.

The path-box lit up. "Bandit, this is Goldilocks. Come back."

"Bandit here, but word to the wise is that marcasite is the new gold."

"Gotcha." Dy clicked off and Cha switched the box to the new channel, silver-white light reflecting the color of iron pyrite. The underground path-channels had nothing to do with their alchemical symbol nicknames. They were just intuitive and convenient code for the colors the box took on when set to a particular wavelength.

"Goldilocks on marcasite. Anyone listening?"

"Bandit here. Go ahead."

"I've got a hound giving me the hairy eyeball. Human law. There's nothing to color me on the wrong side at this point, but I've had to slow down, and any fuss could lose us time. Besides…"

"Besides, this is good opportunity to warm up the old ties of partnership. I was just thinking we could stand a bit of practice. On my way to be the bogey. Give me a little goose?"

"On your signal, Bandit."

Cha spun Katu around, finding the reverse flow of the ley line to carry her in the opposite direction, back toward where Dy and Big Betty cruised down the commercial traffic groove of the Thirteen. She stayed at the speed of the rest of the line for the moment. She wanted to call attention to herself, but not so much so early in the game that she got herself flagged or, worse, ticketed. They'd budgeted for fines and bribes, of course—that was a function of doing business—but no sense racking up too much too early in the game. More than a few amateur smugglers had found their profits significantly eroded by bribes, and the fines when the bribes didn't work.

So, tempting as it was to weave through oncoming traffic, Katu seething to test his mettle in a real-life scenario again instead of on a carefully plotted racecourse, Cha jumped to the ley sideline, the jag juddering at the drop in speed and growling a little with impatience. Cha patted the dash comfortingly. "Just for a bit, baby cat. You'll get to stretch your claws eventually."

The traffic on the ley sideline plodded along at speeds more suited to the draft-carriages the bulk of people could afford to own or hire. Cha threaded her way through, just to get a feel for the line. With the exception of the commercial lines, every ley was different, created with varying amounts and compositions of pixie dust, even within the basic black category, and infused with the idiosyncratic enchantment of the magic worker who created it. Cha wasn't a sorceress by any stretch, but—like most of the top ley riders—she had just enough magic to give her an intuitive feel for the lines. They spoke to her in harmonies of color and texture. That sense allowed her to find the sweet spots in any line, the smoothest and speediest currents, and to avoid the inevitable bog holes.

She'd been on this ley sideline before, but it had been years ago, so she took the opportunity to assess. They'd be coming this way on the return trip, unless something went terribly wrong, so any opportunity to grok the currents of the main avenues was effort well spent, particularly the ley sidelines as they'd need those for evasive tactics.

Once she reassured herself she had a fix on the line, she pinged Dy. "Heads up, Goldilocks. Bandit's ready for a lighter shade of zoom."

"Lightening up, Bandit. In three, two, go!"

The ley line beneath the jag bunched with a burst of gray

as Dy's magic boosted the pixie dust one energetic level up. The ley line surged to a higher key, and Katu shot forward with a delighted growl. Cha whooped with sheer accelerating joy and fought for her new footing. Riding a boosted ley line in the wild was nothing like the manicured variety on the racetrack. Katu bobbled and slid sideways as Cha shot him around a slow-moving wildebeest carriage. The driver cursed her roundly, which she deserved, so she didn't respond in kind.

Close one. Too close. Dy had goosed the line far too much. No doubt all that bottled up energy she hadn't been using lately.

Done was done, though, and Cha shot up the ley sideline in nothing flat, flashing past Big Betty over on the main line and nimbly catching the attention of the rural law-hound pacing the big rig like a bloodhound on a deer.

Sure enough, as Cha flaunted the speed limit, the law-hound, a sleek and expensive-looking greyhound, shot to the ley shoulder, barely staying within safety margins as the rider braked, then found a side loop to carry them off the main and onto the side. Spinning a U, the law-hound coursed up behind Cha's jag.

She grinned to herself, slowing Katu by steering out of their personal current of gray, back into full black, the jaguar bridling in his impatience at being reduced to the stickier flow. Cha allowed the law-hound to close on her bumper, the scintillating fae-made lights flashing crimson, shrieking like banshees, demanding that she surrender to the law and pull off the ley line.

"Not today, asshole," Cha muttered under her breath, and

she released Katu's leash, slipping back into the line of Dy's juiced white current. A round of hoots echoing from the marcasite channel on the path-box demonstrated that she had an audience, so she added a bit of flair to the maneuver as Katu leapt ahead like an arrow from a high-tension crossbow.

Cha yodeled with delight, thrilled at the very real speed, leaving the law-hound choking in the silver-gray dust swirling in the wake of her accelerated passage. The cloud unfortunately billowed over the folks on the ley sideline, too. *Oops.*

Keeping an eagle eye on the slower traffic she wove around and through, Cha risked tapping the path-box back to the gold channel. "Bandit here, for anyone with ears on. I'm stirring up a bit of pixie dust on the side loop of the Thirteen. Sorry for the mess."

She tapped off, listening to the replies coming in, the side-chatter like a group of old friends at the neighborhood tavern. None of them angry—or, at least, not so much that Cha standing a round for the house wouldn't sweeten their tempers. Tucking her chin and smiling, she and Katu led the law-hound on a merry chase. Practice was always a good thing. Fun, too.

~ II ~

Picking up Prince Charming

I T WAS ALMOST too easy shaking the law-hound, and Cha said as much to Dy, back on the marcasite channel.

"Don't get cocky, Bandit," Dy warned, and Warg added bark-growl of agreement. "That was a local hound, a human with shitty skills looking to blow off the tedium. It'll get uglier from here."

"I can handle ugly," Cha replied. "Look at Warg."

"Ha ha."

"How much time did I buy you?"

"Three hours and forty-four minutes ahead of the clock," Dy admitted, her tone grudging. "Soon as you flew past, the whole ley kicked up speed to max on the black."

"And Fastcart here thanks you both!" another voice chimed in. "We're putting out the word that the juice is on the Thirteen. Anything you need, Goldilocks, we got you."

"Aw, thanks, Fastcart."

"Keep an eye on my girl, Fastcart," Cha said. "I'm looping back via the rural leys. Map shows I ought to come up behind you in an hour, maybe less, Goldi. Well before BX-time."

They'd agreed not to discuss their crossing the border into Obsidian, much less the next realm, not even among apparent friends on the path-channels. Too much exposure. Just because they weren't yet in fae lands didn't mean they wouldn't attract the interest of fae ears.

"Copy that, Bandit," Fastcart replied. "Watch your tail."

"It's a fine tail, so I can promise that...Well, well, well— what have we here?"

The rural ley, a dull black that moved so slowly under the feathering trees that it was practically molasses, had given Katu a breather. In a nice bonus, the pretty scenery had just gotten a whole lot prettier. A man stood on the side of the ley, waving her down. He was well back from the thick flow of the seething dust of the line, wearing an absurdly formal outfit for these parts. He frankly looked like he'd escaped from a royal ball. Cha didn't think it was a costume, either, but the real thing.

In fact, a small but glittering crown was affixed to his rather elaborately styled indigo hair. A violet silk cloak lined with eye-popping chartreuse streamed down his back, while the layers of the expensive suit beneath clung to a lithe, attractively masculine figure. Cha usually liked her men beefier, but something about this one appealed to her immensely. That was, besides the fact that he was available and in apparent need of rescue—both qualities she preferred in her men. The telltale sparkle in her pussy confirmed it. She liked this one.

"Bandit," Dy said, possibly not for the first time. "Come back. Did we lose you? What do you see, dammitall?"

"Candy," Cha replied, easing Katu to the edge of the sedate

flow and petting him into patience as he unwillingly came to a stop.

"No!" Dy shouted through the path-box. "No candy while we're on this job, Bandit! You said you'd be responsible."

"I'm not being irresponsible. We're ahead of schedule," Cha pointed out, very reasonably, she thought. The handsome, harried looking man was jogging up the dirt shoulder, waving to her as if she wasn't already taking in the enticing, lean flow of him. Nothing like a little juiced-up chase and smoking a law-hound to give her a sweet-tooth. "I'm just being helpful. You're always telling me I need to try to be a better person."

"Don't you do this to me, Bandit!" Dy shouted. "Not again. You *promised* that—"

"That I'd be behind you in an hour," Cha interrupted, rolling her eyes. "Probably less. You know I can catch up. Bandit out."

She tapped off transmission on the path-box just as the man reached them. "Hello sailor," she purred, quite certain Katu echoed it.

The man frowned, looking down at himself. "I'm a prince, not a sailor."

Oh yeah, and she was the queen of the fae. She sighed to herself. Did the pretty ones *all* have to be cursed with a lack of wit? "Even better. Where you headed?"

"Anywhere but here." He looked back up the ley line nervously. "As fast as possible."

"Happens to be where I'm going and I'm always fast." She added a salacious grin, but he seemed oblivious to flirtation as well as wit because he frowned.

"You can only go as fast the ley line flows," he pointed out.

Shows what he knew. "Hop in, Prince Charming."

"Bandit." Dy's voice lit up the path-box. "Come on, curse you."

"Who's Bandit?" the prince asked, eyeing the box dubiously as he leapt over the carriage rim with seductive grace and slid into the seat of the two-seater carriage, his cloak overflowing the side, causing him to fuss with it in frustration.

"No idea," Cha answered blithely, switching the channel to an obscure limestone. She wasn't going to be so cavalier as to turn it off entirely—she could always fast-tap to gold, or marcasite, in a pinch—but she didn't want any more interruptions to this introduction to the delicious princeling. "You settled?"

He determinedly punched down the voluminous cloak, which poofed up in his lap like a violet and chartreuse mushroom. "Can we please just *go*?"

He turned a beseeching look on her and Cha nearly choked on her breath at the surge of pussy-sparkle. His eyes were a shade of blue barely lighter than his hair, dominating a face so exquisite he could be fae. He must dye the hair to coordinate and what a stellar idea that had been. The human royals tended to get a bit absurd with their fashion excesses and endless mimicking of the colorful fae, but in this case she heartily approved.

"Now?" he added, his tone slightly sharper than his befuddled behavior had indicated. A hint of a predator showing fang beneath the fluffy camouflage. In truth, the imperious tone matched his tale of being a prince, but something was off here. Not only because princes had entourages, not relying on hitchhiking to get them about.

Cha frowned, wondering if Dy had been right to warn her about picking up strange candy. "Who are you, really?"

A chorus of high-pitched yowls echoed up from the intersecting ley about a league back and Prince Charming visibly blanched. "In case you don't recognize that sound, those are fell wolves chasing me. If they catch us, it won't be pretty."

Cha snorted. Fell wolves in human lands, especially this far out in the country? Not likely. "Tell me another tale," she invited.

"Go and I will. Or are you not capable of riding this ley?" he inquired with enough silky disdain that her hackles went up. Oh yeah, he was royalty of some kind all right.

She deliberately lifted her hands in the air. Not that she needed to touch Katu with her hands to direct him on the ley line, but Mr. High and Mighty didn't need to know that. Royals seldom knew how to do the day-to-day stuff of living. "We go nowhere until you tell me who you are."

"I'm roadkill, is who I am, if you don't move this thing along," he replied, all keen edge and zero befuddlement now.

She shrugged, kicking back in the sloped seat, putting her hands behind her neck and turning her face up to the gentle sunshine. "Not my problem," she noted mildly.

The overdressed fop practically seethed beside her. Were those magic prickles emanating from him? Cha had spent enough years around Dy to recognize the buzz of it. Interesting.

"I can make it your problem, *Bandit*," the man said quietly, raising a blue-tinted brow when she fastened him with a glare.

"I tell you I'm not him."

He shrugged, mimicking her earlier insouciance. "I beg to differ." With a flick of his finger, he popped the path-channel box back to the marcasite channel—not something a royal should know how to do, since they had staff for that kind of thing—and Dy's voice came ringing through immediately.

"Bandit! Come back. I swear, if you picked up some roadside piece of hitchhiking fluff while we're on a critical gig, I'll—" Cha cut off her partner, by changing off marcasite again.

"Roadside piece of fluff?" the man queried with that lifted brow, clearly striving for cool, but he was sweating.

"You have to admit you're quite floofy." Cha poked the billowing cloak. "And your implied threats don't work on me."

"How about aggressively stated threats? I can make life quite difficult for you, Bandit." The creatures howled louder, closing on them, and he barely restrained a wince.

"Not if you're reduced to flesh strips drying in the sun," Cha retorted cheerfully, although the howls did lift the hairs on the back of her neck. Surely they weren't really fell wolves, though.

"If you're a bandit, then you can be bought." He rummaged under his floral-embroidered vest, producing a platinum coin and proffering it.

Cha felt her own eyes bulge—not a pleasant sensation, but whoa, she'd never seen a real platinum coin, worth ten golds— and she reached for it. Quick as a wink, Prince Charming folded it out of sight, revealing only an empty palm. She huffed. "I resent the implication that I'm cheap goods for sale."

"Expensive goods," he corrected with a wicked smile that went right through her. The coin winked into sight between his nimble fingers and disappeared again. "A platinum coin should be enough to take you away from selling your…wares."

Cha nearly choked on the insulting implication, until she caught the calculating glint in his eyes. Maybe he wasn't so dumb. "Fine. I'll ride the line, do it fast enough to shake those slavering pups, and drop you where you like—as long as it's on my way—and I get the coin."

"For a platinum coin, I should think you'd take me wherever I want to go."

"Things to do. Places to be." The howls drew near enough to make even Cha a bit jumpy. If they really were fell wolves, they shouldn't attack anyone but their target, but you never knew…Still, unlike Dy, Cha was a champion negotiator and Prince Charming was sweating like an ice fae in the Summerlands. She tipped her head in the direction of the pursuing howls. "Whoever you are, someone wants you back pretty badly."

"Fine," he bit out. "Now does this thing go fast or not?"

Cha grinned. "Hold my ale."

$$\sim \textbf{12} \sim$$

Strip Tease

KATU LEAPT ONTO the main flow of the rural ley line, the bright sunlight temporarily dimming as the dull black pixie dust spun up into a cloud. Prince Charming let out a thin scream as the sudden acceleration flung him back in the seat—and the wind of their passage sent his voluminous cloak billowing into his face.

Maybe a better woman wouldn't have been amused, but as Cha's mother had always said, she was bad through and through and popped out that way. Deflating the pompous prince a breath or two wouldn't kill him. While he wrestled the cloak like it was a chartreuse slime demon sucking his life energy, Cha kept a keen mental eye on the ley line, wary of obstacles farming country tended to produce—livestock sometimes stupidly wandered into the black and got mired— and flipped the box back to the marcasite channel.

"Goldilocks, this is…" Cha flicked a sideways glance at the preoccupied prince. Ah well, no help for it. In for a silver, in for shiny platinum coin. "Bandit here. I need some juice on a rural ley. Dodging some fallen meat-eaters."

"*What?*" Dy practically screeched, echoed by Warg's disharmonious agreement. "Tell me you did not pick up a fugitive from…You did not say what I think you said. Especially not for a fancy piece of ass-candy."

"Such nice friends you have," the prince commented acidly, his expression set in lines of frustration as he bunched the pillowing, colorful silk in his fists.

"That friend is our ticket to speed, so shut it," Cha told him without rancor. "Goldi, hon—can we fight later?"

"Is this really that important?"

"It's been a while since we did the trick. We should practice anyway."

"Fine," Dy ground out. "Hide the dirty pics and open the door."

"Dirty pics?" the prince echoed incredulously.

"Hush." Cha punched the closest flailing limb.

"Ow," he complained, but said no more.

Good thing, as Cha needed the focus to clear her mind and open to Dy's.

She wasn't about to explain the trade secret that allowed Dy to link telepathically to Cha without mage support or a path-channel box and thus affect the ley line through Cha's connection to it. It wasn't the kind of thing taught at the mage academies, largely because humans weren't supposed to be able to do it. In truth, neither of them had ever heard of anyone besides fae capable of doing anything like it, and rumor had it that not even all of them could.

If she and Dy hadn't been bored and ignorant adolescents stuck at the academy over a holiday break together, since neither of their families wanted them home, they might never have sussed out the surprising ability themselves. That trick wasn't the only reason Cha had never found a partner to match Dy, but it was a big one. A big secret one.

Besides them, only Phinny knew the truth—because Dy had insisted on honesty in her marriage, whatever that had to do with anything—and Phinny would not only take it to her grave to protect Dy, she hadn't wanted to know too much about the details. Said she didn't need to think about what Dy saw in a filthy mind like Cha's.

Cha might've been offended, if it wasn't true. Thus, she did her best to clear the mental decks of any offensive dross before Dy looked in. Not that Dy would ever judge her.

Dy's magic flickered through Cha like the welcome touch of a favored lover, like a hug from her grandmother, long since dead. It wasn't erotic, as it truly hadn't ever been like that between her and Dy, no matter what the wilder tales claimed, but it did feel an awful lot like what people called love. Not that Cha would know, but if she loved anyone in the whole benighted world, it was Dy.

Well, Dy and Katu.

Cha opened the door to the ley line and Dy's magic flowed through her and into the line, kicking the pixie dust up to a very nice gray. Katu yowled his delight, ripping ahead with molten grace, and the prince shouted his incredulity. Cha grinned over at him. "Fast enough for you, princeling?"

"Remind me to kill you later," he bit out, finally freeing himself of the cloak. It went ballooning into the air, like an exotic flower set free to fly on the wind, spiraling away behind them. He set to work on the elaborately buttoned jacket that was the next layer, Cha watching with prurient interest.

"What are you doing?" she asked, one mental eye on the thankfully empty lane. The junction to the main road would be coming up quickly.

"Getting out of these ridiculous clothes," he answered in a tone of profound exasperation. Well, she supposed it *had* been a silly question. Almost as silly as his outfit, though she discreetly refrained from saying so. Who said she couldn't be diplomatic?

"Bandit," Dy said through the path-box, having withdrawn from Cha's mind as quickly as possible. "Time to explain who is currently disrobing in your carriage while you're going fast enough to kill yourself ten times over."

"I've never flipped on a ley and you know it," Cha retorted. "I know where I'm going—and what I'm *not* running into." Prince Charming had divested himself of the floral fitted coat and sent it flying, also, with a thin smile of grim satisfaction. "I wish you could see the sights though," she added.

"Pretty?" Dy asked, unbending a little. She might be totally into women, but Dy appreciated a good-looking boy for the aesthetic value. Dy had been the one to dub them "candy," because she—direct quote—wanted to gobble them up whole.

"Pretty as a princess in pink," Cha answered, earning a glower from her prince.

"And the part about who he is?"

"Undetermined. But I *am* determined to find out. Heh. Coming up on the junction. I'll be up on you in thirty at this speed, then you can take a gander."

"You don't need to burn that fast," Dy cautioned.

"Something tells me we need to put those meat-eaters well behind us."

"Now she thinks about it," Prince Charming muttered, sending his sparkling vest flying, leaving him wearing only a white shirt of such an exquisite cloth that the fine blue hairs on his chest glinted through. He removed the cuff links—amethysts, by the glint of them—carefully stowing those in a pants pocket, and rolled up his sleeves. Deep blue hair frosted his forearms, gleaming darkly against his paler skin and the very nice musculature. "Shouldn't you have your eyes on the road?" he asked pointedly.

Cha bared her teeth at him. What royal went to the trouble of dying body hair to match the head? Easier to wax it all off. Though it did make her wonder about the down-below… "Don't worry, I've got eyes in the back of my head, my juicy little blueberry."

"Don't call me that," he bit out, glaring daggers at her.

So prideful. Really, that attitude just tempted her to find out what lay under it. He removed the crown, grimacing as it caught in his hair and he had to untangle it. Cha's fingers itched to assist, but she kept her mouth shut, for once. Holding the crown in his hands, he turned it, seeming bemused. It was pretty—and obviously pricey—made of silver-white filigree that was probably platinum, and studded with deep violet-blue cabochon jewels that seemed to eat the light rather than reflect it.

"I can hold onto that for you," Cha offered in a friendly way, "since you're on the move and all. No luggage to stow it in."

He slid her a jaundiced and decidedly unfriendly look. "Thanks, but no."

"Just trying to be helpful."

"Your kind of help, I don't need," he sneered. "Just do what I hired you to do if you expect to earn the coin."

"I'd be careful about threatening to renege when I could dump you out on the line and have done."

He narrowed his eyes. "You wouldn't dare."

"Oh, you clearly don't know me at all." Cha looked again, but the crown seemed to have vanished. Sleight of hand, or actual magic? No time to puzzle it out. The junction flew toward them like a shooting star. "I'd hold on if I were you."

"You could only aspire to be me," he retorted. But he clamped a hand onto the jag's side.

That worked. "Brace yourself, Bridget," she told him.

"What?"

The prince sounded so aghast and confused—and so terribly offended to be in that position—that she nearly laughed. "Old joke. Means no time for foreplay," she explained. True, she'd never flipped her carriage on a ley line—besides which, Katu was far too balanced, strong, and experienced to lose his hold that way—but she'd also never taken a real world, not-banked racetrack junction at near full white either. This would be amazing.

Or a disaster.

Either way: an experience like no other.

~ 13 ~

Showing Off the New Candy

THEY HIT THE junction at explosive speed, the tide of white pixie dust slamming into the previously sedate black matter of the secondary line, exciting the slower pixie dust into higher states barely ahead of their passage. Katu fishtailed wildly, the ley-line feedback pouring up through Cha with orgasmic intensity, and she let out a long, happy shout of wild triumph. She had no attention to spare for Prince Charming, except to note that he remained safely inside the carriage, despite her threats.

Slower traffic scattered across the secondary line leading back to the Thirteen and Cha wove her way through it, making one lightning quick choice after another. When a heavy dray carriage unexpectedly—and stupidly—deflected directly into their path, Cha went on blind instinct, threading the needle through the narrow space between the lumbering carriage and the dead zone of the margin.

The differential between the high white beneath Katu and the fulminous drag of the black margin caught at them unevenly, sending them into a 360° spin. They skidded wildly, twirling like a top, and only long practice—and a heart of coldest ice—allowed Cha to steer them through it.

They came to a rest on the shoulder, facing backward, Prince Charming's eyes wide in feral terror. He looked like he might puke. "You almost killed us…" he whispered, gaze on the steep drop-off to the side.

"Not even close." With forked fingers, she pointed to her eyes and to the road. "The trick is to keep your gaze where you want to go; not where you don't."

He simply stared. "You can't convince me you have a philosophy behind this… this *behavior* of yours."

She shrugged cheerfully. "I'm a card-carrying member of the Sisters of Don't Give a Fuck. No celibacy required, in case you're concerned," she added.

"You… You're *insane*," he stammered again.

"You aren't the first to say so. I picked you up, didn't I?" Cha checked the traffic and goosed the jag into an opening. With reluctance, she gave up the white speed and tucked the ley dynamics down to pale black. That still had them passing the other carriages on the Thirteen with ease, though a number of them were drafting in her wake, she noted, taking advantage of the Bandit on a spree and juiced up with speed. Some cargos would be checked in for an early bonus today and Cha wished them well. Everyone deserved a gimme now and then. She glanced at her passenger. Definitely green, a shade that did not go well with the indigo.

"There's a cooler in the jump seat behind you," she told him. "An iced ale might help."

"At this point, I don't think drinking an entire vineyard

would make a difference," he snarled unhappily.

It shouldn't have been sexy, but so help her it was, and she laughed. "I'm not though," she said, feeling a bit of reassurance wouldn't go amiss.

"Not what?" He'd turned around in the seat, rummaging through the cooler anyway. Very nice ass. Since it was bobbing there beside her head, she allowed herself a long, leisurely look. *Mmm.* Lovely pussy-sparkle, more than she'd felt in quite some time.

"Insane," she answered, beaming angelically when he skewed around and glared at her. She tapped her temple. "I've been tested. Sane as they come, just a wee bit of irrationality when it comes to assessing risk." Well, and the criminal tendencies, including a disregard for authority and an icono-clastic drive to shatter rules just for the fun of it. She could hear the child psychologists as if it were yesterday. Good times.

"Just a wee," he muttered ungraciously, sucking down the ale. Then spewed it out. He examined the bottle with incredu-lity. "What in demon's spawn is this stuff?"

"Peasant fare, no doubt."

"Clearly." Apparently willing to lower his standards in this extreme circumstance, he drank again.

"And there she is," Cha declared with satisfaction.

"Who?"

"Big Betty." She tapped the marcasite channel live. "Heya Goldilocks, Bandit here sliding up on your delightful derriere. How'd I do?"

"Twenty-three minutes," came the grudging reply. "But I'm deducting five for every person you killed to do it."

"Then I'm golden because there were zero casualties." She might have emerged from the womb a criminal, but her disdain for rules didn't extend to taking lives, not if she could help it.

"Except for my stomach," the prince said sourly, "which seems to have flung itself into a pit, never to return."

Dy laughed, a sultry chuckle that Warg echoed in a far less appealing octave. "Been there. What's your name, pretty one?"

The man glared mutinously at the path-box, clamping his lips shut. Cha sighed, shaking her head. "He isn't saying," she answered Dy for him. "I'm calling him Prince Charming. Take a gander."

Deftly maneuvering Katu into the lane beside Big Betty, Cha positioned her pretty prince into Dy's line of sight. The sorceress didn't need to watch the road with her eyes any more than Cha did, but no sense taking chances. Dy leaned out the open window of Big Betty, a few long golden curls whipping out. "Yummy," she said through the path-box. "But what's he wearing?"

"Is that a *cargo transport*?" the prince asked, sounding as if he'd identified a rare species of demon spoor, after stepping in it.

Cha ignored him. "You should've seen him before he stripped down."

"Less clothes is definitely better," Dy agreed. "But you can't keep him."

"Aww, moooommmm..." Cha whined dramatically, doing a passable imitation of Phin Jr.

"The answer is no," Dy replied firmly.

"But—"

"*No.* Remember what happened the last time you tried to take a puppy on a trip. Giant Jo's Pit Stop is up ahead and you need juice after that burn anyway. Leave Prince Charming there. Put a sign around his neck if you have to. Surely someone will adopt him."

The prince tipped his head back and pinched the bridge of his nose between a thumb and forefinger. "What are the odds?" he mused aloud. "*Two* crazy women, in short succession."

"Really the odds enter a much more rational range when you consider we work together," Cha commented. "What?" she asked when he gave her an incredulous look. "I'm more than a pretty face."

"She's got a banging body, too," Dy commented. "Too bad she plays for the other team. Get that juice, Bandit, and ditch the puppy. I mean it. Be *responsible.*"

"Yeah, yeah, yeah. Will circle back when I'm fed and rid of the excess baggage."

"Hey!" the prince exclaimed.

"Got that. Be sure to circle up before the BX. Goldilocks out." Big Betty trumpeted as Katu sped up, leaving their partners behind in a cloud of sifting gray pixie dust.

"I resent being referred to as luggage. Or a sweet dessert. Or a juvenile dog," the prince informed her.

"Relax," Cha told him, giving him a last lustful and rueful look. Dy was right, curse her. Prince Charming was tempting, but she had no time to indulge. Nor could she afford any distractions. Chasing the sparkle with pretty men was her great weakness—and tended to interfere with the responsibility thing. "No harm meant. We just keep up the chatter for the ears."

"Ears?"

She pointed to the path-box. "Anyone can listen."

He stilled, face going hard in his concern, all vestige of foppish behavior gone. "*Anyone?*"

"Well, anyone who knows to hop on that particular channel." Which hopefully didn't include the fae law-hounds, or whoever held the leash on those fell wolves. She slid him a questioning look. "You do know how an underground path-box works, right?"

"Why would I?" His tone still held all the pompous arrogance she'd come to know and—well, not love, but lust after—but he looked genuinely concerned.

"You knew how to activate the channel."

"The magical mechanism is obvious." He waved that off.

"You really *are* a prince."

Now he gave her the side-eye. "Would I lie?"

"*Can* you?" she asked with alert interest. The fae couldn't lie. She tried to get a look at his ears, but his curling indigo locks covered them. Surely it wasn't possible, but…

His mouth twisted wryly. "Not saying. What's the BX your partner referred to?"

"Not saying." She simpered at him.

He set his teeth, sharp-edged jaw flexing as his eyes flashed. So sexy. Alas. "It could be important to me."

"It's definitely important to me." She tipped her head at the path-box. "Thus being careful."

"Ah," he breathed, eyeing the box. "Can anyone listen on that thing at any time?"

"Theoretically no, when it's off-channel, but it's made by human mages using a conglom of fae magic crafted to mimic telepathy, after a fashion, so there are no firm rules." She shrugged philosophically. "You know how it is, when magic's involved, all bets are off."

A sobering thought, if the fae guard had managed to infiltrate the path channels to the extent that they could passively listen in through the boxes at any time.

Something else occurred to her. "If you don't understand what we're doing with handles on the path-boxes, how did you know to leverage the knowledge that I'm the Bandit?"

He gave her a bland look. "I figured you being a 'bandit' was illegal. I'm not an idiot."

A bandit, not *the* bandit. She sighed for her own hubris.

"Handle is a code name then?" he asked, studying her intently. "What's your real name?"

She considered lying. Reconsidered, as—who was she kidding?—everyone knew who the Bandit was. "Cha." She held out a hand sideways, offering a friendly clasp. He didn't take her up on it. "And you?" she prompted.

"You can call me 'Your Highness.'"

"Ha ha."

"It's better for your long-term health if you don't know," he said, snootily as usual, but with a serious undercurrent. "What kind of a name is 'Cha' anyway? It sounds like a cough. Or a hairball."

"It's a nickname."

"What's your full name?"

She slid him an assessing glance. "Not telling."

"You're that much of a criminal?"

"It's that much of a mouthful."

"I can handle a mouthful."

Was it her imagination or did his coaxing tone—far nicer than he'd been to her thus far—carry a sensual buzz? He did have a very nice mouth. "Evermore," she confessed on a sigh. "Arantxa Evermore. The second is pretty normal. The first, however, is pronounced with a 'ch,' but spelled with an 'x.'"

"Ah, thus the seizing of the final syllable 'cha' for the nickname," he mused. "But Arantxa is such a beautiful name. Why bastardize it?"

She gave him an incredulous look. "It's spelled weird, no one can pronounce it, and it means thornbush."

"Sacred thornbush," he corrected, surprising her, then giving her a mischievous look with a hint of a smile. "Seems apt to me, oh thorny one."

She snorted, but couldn't help being secretly amused—and definitely intrigued. Too bad the timing sucked. "Look who's slinging stones, oh nameless one."

"How long till we reach this pit stop?" He shook his head in disgust. "I can't believe those words just came out of my mouth."

Cha chuckled, gauged the ley line and the landmarks. "'Bout ten minutes and you're rid of me."

"How about ten minutes of quid pro quo, answer for answer?" he suggested silkily.

"Sounds like fun. Me first: who and what are you running from?"

~ 14 ~

Quid Pro Quo

"T̲HAT'S TWO QUESTIONS," he retorted.

"One question mark," she pointed out placidly. "Besides, I doubt you could fully answer the question with only half the information there."

He grunted, which she assumed was him agreeing without being happy about it. "I thought you'd ask for my true name first."

"First rule of negotiating: never lead with the offer they expect." She pointed at the path-channel box. "Plus extenuating circumstances." Names held power and if this cagey princeling was in real trouble, as he appeared to be if actual fell wolves were on his ass, then he'd want to avoid any long-distance scrying that used his name to triangulate on his location. She flashed a grin. "This is why we have handles, Prince Charming."

"You gave your name."

"Because everyone already knows who I am. The price of fame." She added a sigh for dramatic effect. "Now, answer the question."

He tipped back his head to rest against the seat while he stared blindly at the sky. "I suppose it wouldn't do any good to answer that I'm running from fell wolves." He held up a hand to flick off her indignant rebuttal, his mouth quirking in an almost whimsical smile. "Never mind—I'll play fair, though the gambit was tempting. I'm running from my wedding."

Not at all what Cha had expected. She raised a brow. "Explains the outfit, I suppose."

"Nothing explains this outfit, believe me. At any rate, that is both the who and the what—my bride and my erstwhile wedding."

"Some bride who sics fell wolves on her beloved."

He huffed something that might have been a laugh. "I'm fairly certain it was her family, not her, who sicced the wolves on me. They don't really care what condition I'm in, so long as I'm alive enough to marry their daughter."

Cha turned that over in her head. The royals had all kinds of reasons to wed, and rarely did any of them have to do with affection between the bridal pair. Still, while the marital couple were often compelled by pressures they couldn't refuse— usually having to do with wealth and power, the sort gotten legally, but no more ethically than her methods, in Cha's opinion—seldom did they have to be dumped at the altar in a bloody heap. This only raised many more questions.

"Before you ask any of the questions obviously bubbling up in your pretty head," the prince said, "it's my turn to ask. What is BX code for?"

Cha bit back a sigh, wondering if she could convincingly lie about it. As a mostly full-blooded human, she was able to lie, and normally she was pretty good at it, but something told her the prince would see through most prevarications.

"I'll know if you lie," he cautioned her, proving her suspicion correct.

"Border crossing," she answered tersely.

"*Which* border?" he demanded in a sharp tone.

"Ah ah." She wagged a finger at him. "Tis my turn, Your Highness."

"Then ask."

"I'm constructing my question. Hush." To her surprise, he did remain quiet, his gaze on the side of her face as she idly drummed her fingers on the console. In truth, his name wouldn't do her much good. Not like she moved in those circles, so she'd be unlikely to glean anything useful from knowing it. She wasn't sure what information about him would turn out to be useful, given that they'd part ways forever in…less than five minutes. So, she opted to satisfy her curiosity. "What did you find out right before the wedding ceremony that was so terrible you opted to face fell wolves instead?"

He was quiet a long moment. "I'm interested that you assume I discovered something immediately before the ceremony."

"You were dressed up—in an outfit you obviously loathe—and thus clearly ready to do the thing that was asked of you. Seems logical that you wouldn't have gone that far if you already knew the thing that made you bolt. You don't strike me as the kind of guy who takes a while to make up his mind."

The prince regarded her thoughtfully. "You're not quite what I thought."

"Never am," Cha agreed cheerfully. "Though usually people begin with high expectations that quickly plummet into a miserable abyss of disappointment."

He actually snort-laughed. "I seem to be ahead of the game by starting low."

"Enough stalling. Answer the question."

"It's difficult for me to answer honestly as there is a geas involved, which is why I didn't discover the appalling truth about…well, my situation, until it was almost too late." He was quiet a moment, then shifted restlessly in his seat. "It's not my intent to dodge answering. I hope it will suffice to say that once I discovered… *something*—information her family not incidentally hoped to conceal from me until the blood-vows were made and unbreakable—I knew that I must sacrifice anything to escape."

Cha whistled. "*Anything?* That's not really a question," she added hastily. "I'm simply pointing out that a broad statement, or wish, like that is bound to get a fellow in trouble." She glanced at him and saw his jaw resolutely set in a hard line. "The *something* must have been serious."

"It was." He turned his head to look at her, blue eyes blazing. "Which is why I need to know—which border are you crossing and why?"

"That's two questions," she complained, mainly to give herself a moment to think. Though she'd yet to think up a convincing lie.

"One question mark and who's stalling now?"

Nothing for it. "Swear to secrecy."

"I so swear," he replied promptly.

She flicked a look at the path-box, making sure it was off.

"Gypsum to Obsidian."

He snorted indelicately. "Even I know that crossing into Obsidian isn't worth any secrecy. Tell me your ultimate destination or I'll assume you can't be trusted."

Ah, well—it had been worth a try. "Moonstone," she replied shortly, and mostly under her breath. "And I don't think I should have to warn you not to repeat that word aloud. We have a code name for a reason."

"No," he replied absently, gaze focused on the far distance, "you don't have to warn me. Finish answering the question."

"Why does anyone want to go there?" she replied philosophically. "To get the goods and bring them back."

"Then you *are* a thief."

"You think because you phrased that as a statement you're tricking me into thinking that's not a question."

"Your handle is a synonym for thief," he pointed out in an irritatingly reasonable tone.

"Yes, well, yours is 'Prince Charming' and we know *that* doesn't reflect reality."

"You chose that, not I."

"What would you choose then?"

He slid Cha a quick, canny look. "Is that your next question?"

"Withdrawn."

He chuckled. "As I thought."

"It's a moot point anyway," Cha declared, steering the jag to the slower margins and ratcheting down the drive, releasing the last dregs of the higher state white pixie dust, alas. "We're here."

~ 15 ~

Giant Jo's Pit Stop

THE PRINCE LIFTED his long nose and gave Giant Jo's ambrosia station and eatery a scathing assessment down the elegant length of it. "I'll give you *two* platinum coins if you'll carry me away from this... place. What did you call it? Ah yes: a pit."

"Pit *stop*. And it's not that bad." Bringing the jag to a halt on the slow-black lot surrounding the place, Cha cast an affectionate eye over the rambling establishment. Transports of all types and sizes, commercial and private, idled on the ley shoulder, while those converted back to animal form stood in stalls that delivered carefully metered draws of ambrosia, or stood docilely leashed in lines with their riders, waiting their turn. Yeah, it made for a churned-up pixie-muddied mess—especially as the animals tended to dump excretions once out of carriage form—and the area stank to the highest states, echoing with the hoots, cries, and howls of an exotic zoo.

Ley riders weren't always the most genteel of folk, either. Fae blood brought certain abilities, not refined manners. They were all still only human, and the kind that preferred running ley lines to any kind of polite, family life. Even Dy had her bad girl days before Phinny domesticated her. The riders who weren't fighting to control their restless beasts were shouting challenges at each other, one duo actively brawling. Prince Charming looked frankly appalled, and Cha clapped him on the shoulder. "Take heart. Just think how no self-respecting royal would imagine looking for you here."

He gave her such a sour look that she gentled her hand into a pat. "You know not to step on the ley line, right? Even this slow, it can—"

"I'm not an idiot," he snapped, levering himself up and leaping nimbly to the null margin.

"Pohtaytoh, pohtahtoh," Cha muttered to herself, resisting the temptation to show off her own athletic ease. All she needed was to catch her toe on a spur and dump her ass right on the ley where she'd told Prince Charming not to go. Slowblack or not, that would cloud her brains right at a time she needed them most.

In fact, Dy was probably right—as usual—and the last thing Cha needed to be thinking about on this epic and critical gig was man-candy, even if he was the finest piece she'd encountered in a long while. Maybe ever. The sooner she could divest herself of the alluring prince, the straighter she'd be thinking.

Mindful of the time—although Cha could easily catch up with Big Betty, dawdling led to the wrong mindset, and you never knew when you'd hit a setback—Cha efficiently triggered Katu's transformation back into animal form, ready with the leash and collar mandated by law in public venues.

And enforced by Giant Jo herself, if anyone dared cause a dustup by losing control of their animal.

"That's rather unsettling," the prince noted, an odd look on his face as he watched. Maybe he'd never seen the process before.

Katu was panting lightly, but looked in good form, placidly receiving the collar and eagerly padding toward the carnivore line. Cha wasn't the only one who remembered this place. She jerked her chin at the bar and grill. "Why don't you head inside and grab us a table? Order me a beast-burger, parsnip fries, and a bayberry malt."

"Peasant food."

She gestured at her rangy, decidedly unroyal self. "I am what I eat. Hopefully it won't taint your noble blood too much. Get yourself whatever you want." She eyed his lanky form. "You look like you could use a decent meal."

He drew himself up in a huff. "I don't take orders from you, Bandit."

"Fine, do what you like, but if you want to eat, you'll need something other than those flashy coins. Stuff like that doesn't turn up in the humble realms of actual humans."

He had the grace to wince. "They were for the ceremony. I didn't have time to grab anything else." As he said it, he also looked vaguely bemused. Cha suspected the prince wouldn't have known where to find commonly used coin even if he'd had more leisure before fleeing the altar.

"I'm not judging." That is, she wasn't anymore. Still—what kind of wedding ceremony required the delivery of platinum coins? She probably didn't want to know. Cha inched up in the line as a fine-looking lion finished its drink and its rider paid, swearing at the total. Prices had indeed gone up. "Point is, I'll cover lunch, since you're paying me so handsomely, but I'm on a ticking clock here so it would be good of you to bump up the timeline for me by going in and ordering."

He wanted to argue, she could absolutely read that in him, but he didn't. To his credit, he didn't flounce, either. Instead, he prowled off toward the bar and grill, the milling ley riders giving him a wide berth, their wariness making him look much like an unleashed carnivore in the herbivore line.

When it came his turn, Katu drank thirstily, but with elegant economy. A few ley riders complimented the animal, several more looking on with envy. Yeah, jaguars were pricey beasts, and Cha wouldn't have been able to afford Katu if she'd done everything on the up and up. Hey, when they stacked the deck against you, it paid to learn to have a few cards up your sleeve—and have the moral flexibility that allow for some judicious cheating. She stroked Katu's flat head affectionately and the cat purred, ready for a rest.

After Katu filled up and she'd converted him back to carriage form—also regulation—and parked him in the shade on the slow-black for a nice nap, Cha made her way inside, greeted by the cheerful sound of a fiddle playing a bouncing reel. One day she should get one of those magic music-playing boxes to listen to on road trips.

Giant Jo presided behind the grill, giving Cha a big grin and a fist-pump of solidarity. Rumored to have the blood of giant fae in her ancestry, Giant Jo towered over everyone and made magic with food. Cha reminded herself to grab Jo some of the effervescent blackberries from Obsidian that the mighty woman loved to put in her special pies. If she had time, that was.

Cha found the prince slumped in a booth, a pair of bayberry malts on the table. From the vibrant magenta stain on the tip of his striped paper straw, he'd at least sampled his. From the sullen look on his fine-boned face, he didn't love his first encounter with Giant Jo's cuisine. What would it take to make this broody bit of man-candy really smile? Too bad she wouldn't get to find out.

She slid into the seat opposite him, sucked down a fast and icy sweet berry-fest, then pinched the bridge of her nose at the instant ache. "Gah—brain freeze."

"Who *are* you?" he asked, sounding genuinely bewildered.

"Soon to be a cherished, if fleeting, memory."

He snorted. "Not in the least cherished, though I'll take fleeting. I can't wait to put this entire *incident* behind me." Glancing off to the side, his full lips set broodingly, eyes hooded, he looked briefly vulnerable and so troubled that Cha nearly reached out to pet him.

She opened her mouth to say…she didn't know what. Comfort wasn't her strong suit, and he wasn't the sort to want it, especially not from a peasant. Still—

"Cha, my beauty!" A man slid into the seat beside her, looped an arm around her waist, and drew her into a deep kiss. *Mmm.* She recognized that particular flavor.

Reluctantly withdrawing from the kiss—Tourqe had always been exceptionally skilled with his mouth and Cha allowed herself a dreamy internal sigh—she patted the cheek of the handsome blond ley rider. "It's been too long."

"*Much* too long," Tourqe agreed with a sensual smile, hands slipping familiarly over her hips. "Got a few hours? I can get us a room." He glanced at the prince. "Three could be fun. Remember that inn in Sandpoint? We could—"

"I'd rather be eaten and shat out by fell wolves," the prince spat.

Cha sighed for real, not at all dreamily. "Tourqe, this is Prince Charming, and we're on the clock sadly." Just then the waitress plunked down two identical plates. The prince had clearly taken the shortcut of requesting two of Cha's order. The server threw the prince such a fulminating glare that Cha could just imagine how he'd bungled that interaction. Cha gave her a nod of thanks and smile that promised a hefty tip, then wriggled out of Tourqe's stimulating grasp. "Gotta eat and fly, alas. Maybe next time?"

Tourqe kissed her cheek, giving her ear lobe a delightful little nip and tug, causing her ambient pussy-sparkle stirred up by the prince to glitter that much more, then withdrew with a warm smile. "I'm holding you to that, beauty." He tipped an invisible hat at the prince. "You're a lucky man."

Cha dug into her burger—delicious with tongue-searing fat, sharp cheddar, and Jo's special spicy red sauce—chewed the massive mouthful and, feeling the weight of Prince Charming's stare, met his accusing blue eyes. "What?"

"Who was that?"

She shrugged. "A friend."

"A *friend*." He made it sound like a banana slug.

"Yes, Your Highness. A sex-friend. It's something us peasants indulge in, to fill our miserably empty, poverty-stricken lives."

He picked at a parsnip fry, dunking it in a bowl of Jo's sauce, after observing her do the same, then made a face. "I can't imagine how cheap sex with strangers can possibly compensate for subsisting on *this*." He thrust the plate aside.

"First of all, this is the food of the gods. Second, sex with me is never cheap. Third, Tourqe isn't a stranger, demonstrably. And fourth," she added with a grin as she scooped his fries onto her pile and doused them with sauce, "sex, cheap or otherwise, has a marvelous way of making strangers into friends. I'd demonstrate, but…tick tock."

A reluctant smile tugged at his mouth before he squelched it. "My loss, I'm sure."

"Indeed," she replied in a lofty tone, giving him a conspiratorial wink, then signaling for the check and a go-box. "I assume you've called your servants or staff or whatever to come pick you up, however that works."

He sobered, not exactly nodding, but not refuting either. The royals had all sorts of proprietary tricks for pretty much everything, which was why they didn't need hacks like the underground path-channels.

"Well, good luck then."

"I have wealth, rank, and privilege," he replied gravely. "I don't need luck."

"Yeah, well, you've also got a vengeful bride and fell wolves on your enticing tail, so a bit of luck might not go amiss."

He hesitated, holding her gaze and seeming to be about to

ask a question. "Point taken," he said, which Cha was sure wasn't what he'd been turning over saying.

She slid out of the booth and shouldered her stuff. "Good luck to you then. It's been fun. Weird and occasionally provoking, but fun."

"I'm not sure I would call it fun."

She shrugged. "To each their own." Tossing off a salute, she strode out, firmly not allowing herself to look back. Never mind all the cautionary tales about the devastating shit that happened to heroes who looked back—and Cha was absolutely the hero of her own story—she just wasn't about the past. Walking away clean was always the best. So, though she imagined her wayward prince looking a bit slumped and lost in his finery, an exotic bird soiling his feathers in the grubby booth of Giant Jo's, she didn't look for herself.

He'd be fine.

She climbed into the jag, giving Katu an affectionate pet, then waved a jaunty acknowledgement to the ley riders calling out good fortune to her, several of them tuning up their own carriages with the clear intention of drafting her down the ley. That was fine. Some of them might even have legit business in Obsidian, so having a bit of traffic around them would only add to their cover.

She was about to tap the path-box to check in with Dy when ear-splitting howls rent the air, turning the already jostling scene into utter chaos. Herbivores stampeded in pure panic, dragging their luckless handlers behind them. Carnivores set up an unholy cacophony of challenge or solidarity— who could tell—and even the normally disciplined Katu trembled with an atavistic surge of challenge. Good thing Katu was in carriage form already, or Cha would've been hard-pressed to control him. Drawing her sword, Cha shifted in her seat to confirm what she was sorely afraid to see.

Fell wolves. A full dozen or more of them.

Well, fuck her sideways.

She'd glimpsed a few before, inside Obsidian, and seen horribly realistic paintings, but nothing like this. A deep, dull red with eyes such a bright yellow they burned like stars even in the daylight, the huge, shaggy creatures loped toward Giant Jo's at a ground-eating pace. At the same time, every other creature fled in the opposite direction, quickly leaving the grill a small island surrounded by a seething sea of malice. A living weapon aimed at one target: her erstwhile Prince Charming.

"Good thing we ditched him already, huh, baby cat?" Cha murmured, resolutely turning her back. "Or that would be us."

Not her problem. She had the shiny coin in her pocket and her responsibility—such as it had been—was done. Backing Katu out of the ley, she jockeyed for position among the other fleeing patrons, cursing the sudden traffic jam.

A shriek of righteous rage pierced the howling of the fell wolves. Despite her resolve, Cha looked. And bit out a curse that would melt bones if she had the sorcery behind it. Giant Jo herself had waded into the wolves, swinging her axe and bellowing for them to leave her place alone. This would not end well.

But, this was still not Cha's problem. Spying a narrow opening between a badly angled armored rhino-carriage and a family donkey-sedan, Cha goosed Katu forward. A commotion behind them had her looking a third time—and, just like with the doomed heroes in the tales, that backward look did her in.

Prince Charming had emerged from the grill and had come to Giant Jo's aid, indigo fireballs flying from his palms as he drove the fell wolves away from the giant woman. Oh sure, *now* he had to play the hero. And with real magic.

With a sigh, Cha told Katu to stay put, but be ready to peel out at top speed. Drawing her sword, Cha leapt out of the carriage and onto the grassy median, running back to the fray.

Dy was going to kill her.

~ 16 ~

Battle of the Fell Wolves

CHA HAD OBVIOUSLY never fought a fell wolf before, largely because she wasn't an idiot. Also, the beasts were sent after targets much higher than her pay grade. If there had been any doubt that these had been targeted at Prince Charming, it disappeared now. Though Giant Jo continued to hold the threshold to her place against the wolves, as soon as the prince appeared, they ignored her—and everyone else—and turned on him.

The sole advantage of this singular focus was that Cha could attack them from the back. The enormous disadvantage was that being on the other side of the wolves from Prince Charming put her in the path of the fireballs he was flinging about like a toddler playing flower girl at a wedding, the sort that misses the concept entirely.

Case in point: a violet-blue fireball hurtled right at her, grazing her left shoulder only because she dropped and flattened barely in time, scoring her flesh instead of boring through her face.

"Watch out!" Prince Charming shouted, sounding irate

rather than concerned.

Cha set her teeth and jumped to her feet, just as a fell wolf nearly backed over her as it reared to avoid a similar fireball. "Not. Helpful. Advice," she ground out as she laid into the shaggy red wolf, which stunk decidedly of sulfur. Why did people always shout at you to watch out for a thing *after* it had nearly brained you?

Hacking away at the wolf—which seemed not to notice her any more than it would a biting fly—Cha felt more like she was attacking a living pile of scarlet firewood with her sword. She rather envied Giant Jo's axe, a far more appropriate weapon in this instance. Prince Charming had his own, much bigger problems, grimly battling two wolves advancing steadily on him, while another circled behind. Cha's wolf seemed to gradually realize that she was a problem, turning on her and slashing with fangs that dripped red goo that she'd bet her now stinging and numb left arm was nasty fae poison.

Sure enough, a few flying droplets of the red ichor hit her sword hand as she lunged at the beast and it burned into her skin with acidic sizzling she could hear and smell. But Cha was no amateur to drop her sword at the first pinprick of pain. Instead she used the pain, pouring it into fury. Screaming in rage, she lunged at the fell wolf, driving it back with a flurry of sword-strokes, slicing across its muzzle and stabbing at its unnatural beady yellow eyes. The wolf scrabbled back, trying to evade Cha's blazing attack. It hit up against something that stopped its retreat, and with a cry of triumph, she stabbed into one eye.

With a yip, the wolf vanished in a puff of red smoke. Choking, stinking red smoke. Cha flapped her free hand—the one attached to the arm aching from Prince Charming's errant fireball—in a futile effort to clear the air. Her other hand burned like fire from the fifth hell, her grip slick on the hilt, and she decided she'd rather not look at it. Half the trick of courage was turning a blind eye to shit you knew would send you gibbering with fear. Time enough to gibber later when your life wasn't on the line.

Oh, wait—not *her* life but this deceiving piece of man-candy's. Speaking of, she could hear him through the smoke, yelling in a garbled way that indicated nothing good. Bravely, Cha waded into the murk, sword at the ready. Giant Jo was out there somewhere, still hollering about this shit being bad for business, and Cha really didn't want to run afoul of the big and angry woman's axe. A multi-limbed shape resolved itself through a thinning area of the cloud, giving Cha a sinking fear that something even worse had manifested—until she saw that it was actually two fell wolves, each with a mouthful of her Prince Charming, the struggling royal between them as they dragged him off.

"Now would be a great time for one of those fireballs of yours, Your Highness!" she shouted at him helpfully as she sized up the situation.

He snarled something back at her that she interpreted as being disagreement with her suggestion, along with an insulting speculation on the legitimacy of her birth and ancestral bloodline. All unfortunately true. It wasn't as if the humans who got themselves seduced by fae were fine upstanding citizens.

"Snob," she muttered. "I should let them carry you off to that demon-bride you no doubt richly deserve."

Still, the opportunity to wise up—oh, and stick to the very important smuggling job she was supposed to be paying attention to and had promised to be responsible about—had come and gone. Time was ticking away, and she was committed now, so best get this fight over with and either die or survive. On the bright side, if she got herself killed, she wouldn't have to face Dy and Phinny's wrath.

She stalked after the wriggling three-part creature that was the prince and his captors, leaving the stray members of the fell wolf horde to Giant Jo and her efficient axe, having to hurry as the beasts picked up their pace. She didn't know if they planned to carry him all the way back to his interrupted wedding, but she didn't want to find out either. She definitely didn't want to have to retrieve Katu and chase after her wayward prince in the entirely wrong direction, with maybe only rural leys available or none at all.

If she could just get a good angle on those yellow eyes, maybe these wolves would poof, too. Deciding to take out the lead beast first, she skipped ahead, intent on finding the business-end of the huge creature. Something crashed in the background and the prince gargled in a newly alarmed way. Cha frowned, opening her mouth to tell him she was saving him as fast as possible—when she collided with *something*.

Rocking back on her heels and regaining her balance only through long practice and natural agility, she brought her sword to bear and... goggled. A towering red demon stood before her, glaring down as if she were a little kid who'd thoughtlessly plowed into an adult at a faire. "Oops," she said, with a weak smile.

The demon growled, a sound that echoed through several dimensions, including magical, and an image popped into Cha's head of her being torn into very tiny pieces and scattered to the four winds. Great. Telepathic threats, as if the verbalized variety didn't annoy her enough.

Prince Charming made another garbled sound, which morphed into muffled shouting, resolving into: "Run! Save yourself, Cha!"

Sure. *Now* he had to be a nice guy and not an insufferably broody snob she could happily abandon to the wolves and demons. Not that she'd have done that anyway. *Probably.*

Summoning all her strength and considerable repressed rage, which she'd saved up from her miserable childhood for moments such as this, Cha gripped her sword with two hands and swung it at the demon's knees, hoping for a lucky strike at whatever served to hold its legs together and keep it upright.

She bounced off with a jarring impact as if she'd hit an iron post. Fuck if that didn't hurt her already throbbing hands. The right hand, the one already slick with ichor that burned like acid and probably a fair amount of her own blood, nearly slipped off the hilt, and she thanked her lucky stars she'd had a two-handed grip. The demon turned its back on her, jogging away, stomping a line of ambrosia pumps as it did. The wolves scampered at its heels, carrying her prince between them like a favorite shared chew-toy. Apparently the lot of them considered her duly chastened. They certainly moved too fast for her to run after them. Well, fuck it all.

The smoke had cleared and Giant Jo strode up, looking weary and irate in equal measures, her axe dripping with steaming ichor. "What in the seven hells, Bandit?" she demanded. "Look at my place! What kind of trouble did you drag in here? It's going to cost me a year of income to fix it up again. Even longer because I'll have to shut down, which means no income until I at least get the ambrosia tanks up and running again." She dropped her axe to the ground, despondent as the fire of the fight went out of her. "This is it. I'm done for. I'll have to close."

Though it hurt Cha's acquisitive heart, she dug out Prince Charming's platinum coin. And flipped it to Giant Jo. Easy come, easy go. "Don't close," Cha said. "We need you."

Giant Jo caught the coin reflexively, then stared at it much as Cha had. "Where did you get this?"

"Him." Cha pointed her sword after the gang of monsters. "He hired me to play bodyguard," she added, improvising, "which means I have to go after him."

"You can't give me this."

"I'll get another when I catch up to him." She hoped her confidence would put that out in the universe. Turning toward Katu, she started into a run, finding she could only limp, her thigh burning like fire. When had that happened?

"The coin is worth more than the repairs," Giant Jo called after her.

"You can give me free ambrosia for life."

"You wish," Giant Jo grumbled. "Here, I have something for you instead."

"Jo, I gotta fly if I'm going to catch them."

"You'll be glad to have it. Just hold your cats a moment."

Cha shifted from foot to foot impatiently. She didn't think they'd hurt the prince—they clearly wanted him alive enough to prop up at the altar—but with every moment that passed, she ran the risk of not being able to find him. Also, with every moment that passed, Dy would be drawing nearer to the crossing into Obsidian. The sorceress was probably turning the marcasite channel cobalt with cursing at Cha to respond and give a location update.

She'd started edging toward Katu, grateful that the impromptu beast battle had at least cleared the traffic jam, when Giant Jo came back out of the nearly collapsed diner. "Take this." She thrust a package at Cha.

"What is it?" Cha took the fabric-wrapped bundle dubiously, bemused at its lightness for its size.

"Useful for fighting iron-demons." Giant Jo cracked a grin and tossed the platinum coin in the air. "Now we're even." She raised her immaculately groomed brows. "Aren't you in a hurry?"

Biting out a curse, Cha tucked the unwieldy bundle under her good arm—which was the one with the bad hand, whereas the bad arm had a good hand—and dashed for Katu. Well, she hobbled, with most of her weight on the good leg. She'd kind of been hoping for a healing spell from Jo, but no such luck. She tossed the package into the jump seat beside the cooler—remembering belatedly and with considerable annoyance that she'd left her to-go box inside the now ruined diner. Depositing her sword in the passenger seat, she vaulted into the driver's seat, landing clumsily with a pained *oompf*.

Katu purred with excitement, clearly straining for action, having missed out on the last bit of battling. They spun out in a cloud of dull black, easing onto the rural ley leading to Giant Jo's, Cha casting her senses for a back-ley shortcut. That wolf/demon team had struck out overland at a ground-eating pace. She wasn't going to find them on a public ley line. Bad news was—okay, there was a shitload of bad news, but this stood out at the moment—the back ley was going to be slow as mud.

She really needed Dy's assistance, if she was still close enough. This was going to suck.

Mentally girding her loins, she tapped the marcasite channel and said, "Heya, Goldilocks. Bandit here. Um… Hi. How are you?"

~ 17 ~

Rescuing Prince Charming

"WHAT HAPPENED?" Dy shot back immediately. "And don't try to shine it up."

Cha hadn't really tried all that hard to dissemble. Not only was it next to impossible to lie to a sorceress, but also Dy had been her friend for way too long. She knew every nuance of Cha's voice, for better or worse.

"Ah, we had a bit of a dustup at Giant Jo's. In fact, any eavesdroppers should know the ambrosia pumps are down for a bit, but she could use cleanup help."

Cha had to have imagined Dy's audible sigh, as the box likely wouldn't have picked it up. "I'm an hour from BX. Are you telling me you're not going to make it?"

"I'll make it." *Maybe. Eh, probably not.* "If I don't though, you've done this crossing a thousand times. You don't need me until the next bit."

"Uh huh." Dy sounded supremely unthrilled and Warg made an unhappy sound reminiscent of a cat fighting a hairball. "Is this about the puppy?"

No sense prevaricating. "Yeah."

"Dammit, Bandit!" Dy exploded, spittle practically flying out of the path-box. "I told you—"

"The meat-eaters caught up to him," Cha interrupted. "I have to help."

The pause that ensued could have been weighed on a scale.

"Who are you and what have you done with the Bandit?" Dy finally said, dripping honeyed sarcasm.

"Ha ha. I'm not being altruistic." Was she? Inspiration struck. "I can't say anything, but I think he'll be helpful."

"Scratch your own itches," Dy shot back. "Mine are handled."

"Not that," Cha retorted irritably. "For the other thing."

Her skepticism leaked through the path-channel. Maybe those things transmitted more than voices. She sighed. "Honey—we can pull the plug. We don't have to do this."

The implication was clear: Dy thought Cha had lost her nerve. "I don't want to pull the plug," she ground out. "I can't explain, but I have to do this one little thing. Then I'll catch up."

"Can't explain on the channel or to yourself?" Dy asked softly.

"Yes." There, let her chew on that. "I'll catch up faster if you'll help me."

That sigh came through quite audibly. "Are you sure this is worth it? We don't have unlimited resources."

Yeah—her magic, their time, Dy's tolerance for Cha's foibles. "I'm only sure I can't turn my back." Though, she could. What was it to her if Prince Charming met his fate with his horrible bride? An hour ago she hadn't known he existed.

She owed him nothing. Even he would say so. "I have a feeling," she added, knowing she was playing her ace with Dy, and also it was true.

"All right then," Dy said, resigned. She never questioned Cha's hunches. Her "feelings" had gotten them out of too many tight scrapes. "Juice?"

"And a back ley assist."

"You don't want much."

"I'll owe you."

"Yes, you do. Put the porn away."

Cha cleared her mind of everything but love and gratitude for her bestie, the familiar feel of Dy's magic flooding into her for the second time in less than an hour. She let Dy feel through her ley-rider senses, finding the road. It was a lot to ask at this stage of their journey—for probably a wrong-headed reason—but Dy really shone in these conditions.

The ley-sorcery reached through Cha like spidery fingers, finding the rural ley line and subtly altering it. She keyed into Cha's mental image of the prince, along with the two fell wolves and the demon, a feeling of startled horror coming into Cha that wasn't her own.

"Some shit you stirred up," Dy commented aloud on the path-channel, an uncanny echo of her mental reaction in Cha's head.

Katu leapt along with Dy's juicing and on-the-fly creation of the ley-line, sending them shooting past farmhouses, fields, and lots of rocky land not useful for much. Very quickly, the towering red demon loomed in the distance. Bless Dy and her freaking amazing skills.

"Lay me a flat and get gone, Goldi," Cha said to the path-box, mentally reinforcing it.

Dy threw a ley-circle around the demon, thoughtfully layering extra white into the center line, with grays fading to inert black on the edges to the gutters. That oughta do it. She blew Cha a mental kiss as she withdrew, saying aloud. "Be there at BX or Mama Bear will eat you alive—and not in the good way."

Eying the iron demon, Cha didn't reply. Sensing Dy's magic, it had turned, scowling ferociously as Katu flew toward it, riding the new white at blazing speed. Reaching into the jump seat, Cha grabbed Giant Jo's package, biting out a curse as her hand stung with hellfire at the contact, and hoping whatever the thing was would turn out to be useful. Unwrapping the oddly shaped bundle—good thing she didn't need her hands to drive—she kept her eyes on the demon and her attention on holding Katu to the spiraling ley line as they circled the group.

So, it took her a moment to realize what Giant Jo had given her: a magic wand, one as long as Cha's arm.

And not a super cool, join-me-on-the-dark side magic wand, but one very much like the kind Zazu played with, glittering pink with a sparkle-covered star on the end. Cha groaned internally. No one could ever see the Bandit using this thing. It would totally ruin her cred.

It also looked beyond silly compared to the towering, heat-radiating iron demon. It tossed its head, black, curved horns gleaming against the gentle blue sky—a monster that shouldn't be in human lands. Though Cha's first impulse was to leap out and use her sword against the thing, she'd tried that once already to no avail. She didn't have much of a plan, and she was no genius, but she made a general point of not repeating her mistakes.

Except with men—and this episode potentially counted in that category—but other factors came into play in those cases. Some mistakes were *worth* repeating.

The fell wolves, still carrying their colorful burden, now lying limp in their grip, paused in confusion at the ley-line barrier to their progress. Magical creatures could withstand the concentrated pixie dust better than humans, but it still hurt or borked them up, depending on the species and which fae realm—or sorcerous creator—they came from. The wolves might have crossed the black leys, but that fresh white gave them pause.

With her quarry neatly trapped and a magic wand at her command, Cha elected to remain in Katu, racing circles at dizzying speeds as the iron demon spun ever faster trying to keep track of her, the annoying gnat buzzing around it. With no idea how to actually use a real magic wand—hopefully it *was* real and not an actual toy—Cha briefly wished Dy hadn't withdrawn already. But she was a big girl who could solve her own problems. This was like another steeplechase obstacle. Just weirder.

Waving the wand in the air, which left a trail of candy-pink sparkles in its wake, an encouraging sign for it being actually magic, Cha whipped the glittering, star-shaped end at the iron demon and yelled, "Begone!"

It roared and swiped at her, Katu fishtailing as Cha goosed him out of the way at the last possible moment. All right then, maybe the rule of three would work. If not, she didn't know what she'd do. Winding up the wand again—no idea if that made a difference, but—she again whipped the end at the demon and yelled, "Begone!"

(She'd briefly considered something more elegant like "I banish thee!" but figured she'd be better off repeating the initial command verbatim, in case the rule of three did kick in.)

The demon roared again, sounding pained, and clutched its horned head. Encouraged, Cha wound up the wand, pink sparkles filling the air and becoming glitter as they settled on Katu's upholstery, and yelled a third time as she pointed the wand at the demon, "Begone!"

For a moment, nothing happened. Then reality shivered, jolting sideways, and the demon collapsed in on itself, folding up like an origami, red-paper version of itself. The fell wolves turned to smoke, sucked in behind the iron demon as it grew smaller, becoming a tiny hole in the human world. With a pop, the last of the wolf-smoke vanished into the void, the hole closed, and the lot of them had vanished.

Leaving a crumpled pile of prince behind.

~ 18 ~

Rogue Fae

Pulling Katu to a halt and tossing the wand aside, Cha vaulted out of the jag and raced to the prince. She doubted he was dead, but if he was only close to death, what would she do?

It would be wrong to just leave him there, she figured. Even a cheerfully amoral creature like herself knew that much. But she also had a job to do and could hardly cart a mostly-dead/dying guy around. What had happened to the staff he'd supposedly summoned anyway?

Approaching him tentatively—even dead snakes can bite— she nudged him with the toe of her boot. Gently. She wasn't that callous.

He opened fulminous blue eyes to glare at her balefully. "What the fuck are you doing here?" he demanded.

So much for undying gratitude. "You're welcome," she retorted.

"I did *not* thank you," he said pointedly.

Rolling her eyes, she surveyed his lanky form. "Can you walk to Katu or do I need to throw you over my shoulder?

You're skinny enough that I could do it, though your masculine pride might suffer."

He huffed at that, pushing himself up from the decidedly soggy grass. His fine white shirt had absorbed the moisture, along with other best-left-unnamed fluids, and it clung to his lean chest in a way that shouldn't have been enticing under the circumstances. "I'm not skinny; I'm wiry."

She snorted. "Pohtaytoh, pohtahtoh."

"What does that mean?"

"Look, I'd love to chat semantics with you. I'd also enjoy peeling you out of your remaining clothes and giving you a sponge bath. But I have time for neither. Two choices, princeling: stay here or go with me."

"I could also go my own way," he pointed out, pushing to his feet without his previous agile grace, grimacing so much as he did so that she took pity and offered him a hand up.

"Grip my wrist," she advised. To her surprise, he did, a lovely buzz coming from the contact with his skin.

"You could," she agreed, happy she didn't sound breathless, "but from my point of view, that's the same as you staying here." She grinned. "I'll remember you always, just like this, outstanding in at least one field."

He didn't come back with a witty quip as she expected. Instead, now upright, he turned over her hand, still holding her wrist. "What happened to you?"

She tried to tug away, but he held on. Reluctantly, she followed his gaze, wincing at the state of her hand, which looked as if she'd dipped it in boiling oil for a while, then chopped at it haphazardly with one of Phinny's kitchen knives.

No wonder the fucker hurt. "I got ick all over it, from yon wolfies."

Frowning, he feathered fingertips over the abraded skin, as red as the monsters had been. Not how she'd imagined him caressing her. Her life sucked unimaginably. "Ichor, you mean," he corrected.

"No. I mean *ick*. That stuff was disgusting." She successfully jerked her hand from his grip, turned her back on him, and stalked away. Hobbled, curse it. Throwing up her good hand in the air, which only made that bad arm throb painfully, she called over her shoulder. "Stay or go, pretty boy. It's all the same to me, but I'm behind schedule from rescuing your fine ass and I have time to make up."

Unsurprisingly, as she landed in the driver's seat of Katu, this time holding back the groan of pain, the prince leapt into the passenger seat from the other side.

"Ow," he griped, fishing under that fine ass and withdrawing both her sword and the magic wand she'd carelessly tossed aside.

"Oops." She spurred Katu into the middle of the white and spun him in a one-eighty, not above smirking when Prince Charming yipped and grabbed the side. They shot back the way they'd come, taking full advantage of the juice Dy had left them. A glance in the rear-view assured Cha that Dy had set the enchantment to roll up behind them. No sense mucking up the countryside with corrosive pixie dust that wasn't supposed to be there. "Time to make up," she reminded him.

"Were we fighting?" he asked, giving a quirk of a smile when she slid him a droll look.

"Funny guy. I'll take that. Not that. *That.*" She pointed at the sword when he tried to hand her the pink magic wand. "The other thing you can toss in the back."

He held onto the wand, however, laying it across his lap as she snatched her trusty sword from him and slid it into the sheath at the side of the center console, then flapped her hand at the renewed sting.

"You should do something about that hand," he observed. "And the arm. And the leg. You look like shit."

"Yeah?" She gave him a jaundiced side-eye. "You look considerably worse for wear yourself, Prince Charming."

The path-box sparkled to life. "Status update, Bandit," Dy said.

"Peachy keen with cargo intact," she replied. "I am…" She checked the clock. Well, shit. "A bit over an hour to BX."

"How *much* over an hour?" Dy demanded.

"Almost an hour more than that," she admitted, and the prince made a sound of disgust, shaking his head. "Hey, I rescued you. You could show a little appreciation."

"Told you so," Dy said. "I left some high white for you. Try to make up the time, please."

"Have I ever let you down?"

"Consistently," Dy snapped and the box went dark.

"You two have a beautiful friendship," Prince Charming observed.

"I know." Cha allowed a beatific smile.

He bit out a sigh. "Give me your hand."

"Aww, I'm touched, but we just met. And you're already engaged."

"Are you always an asshole?"

"Yes, but I'm your asshole now, darling." She could've been wrong—it had happened once or twice before—but she thought he smothered a laugh. Reaching over he snagged her bad hand. "Hey! Watch the grabby grabby."

"You liked it well enough with that Tourqe idiot."

"Well, what he *does* think with, he uses very well and—ouch!"

"Don't be a baby."

"I'm not, I…oh, now that's nice." Her hand had abruptly stopped hurting, the cessation of agony almost orgasmic. She tipped her head back, closed her eyes, and sighed at the sheer relief.

"Shouldn't you be keeping your eyes on the road?" he asked.

"I am, metaphorically speaking." As promised, Dy had left a thin line of white down the network of rural leys, guiding Cha back to the Thirteen via a series of shortcuts. Mostly she just had to keep a mental feeler out for anything dumb enough to wander onto the white to get fried there. She could leave the rest to Katu. Cracking one eye open, she risked a glance at her maimed hand, pleasantly surprised to see it looking almost normal again. "What did you do?"

He shrugged, acting nonchalant, and released her hand. "A spot of therapy." He reached across her, gave her an arch look when she jumped, then laid careful fingers over her scorched shoulder. "You need to learn not to stand in the way," he murmured.

"Yeah, totally my fault."

"Good of you to admit it." As the pain in her shoulder lessened, he dropped his hand to her bum leg, healing the thigh wound, which turned out to be a fell-wolf bite she didn't remember getting. "All better," he told her, more than a little smugly.

"Th—I appreciate it," she said, amending her thanks at the last moment, recalling how insistent he'd been that he hadn't thanked her. If he was full or even mostly fae, then thank-yous were verboten.

"Least I could do given the rescue effort."

She flexed the hand, beyond relieved to have it back in working order, but unwilling to say so. Also: they really needed to talk about who in the seven hells he really was, but she was afraid to find out. She'd hate to have to leave him by the side of the road, after all the trouble she'd gone to. "I was hoping for another platinum coin," she told him instead.

"Isn't one enough?"

"I, ah, kind of lost the other one."

"You. Lost. A platinum coin. Is that what happened to your hand—the coin burned a hole through it?"

"Pretty much." And that was all she was going to say on the subject. "On-ramp coming up."

This entrance to the Thirteen went more smoothly—though it could hardly have been worse than the last one—as Dy had led her to a decently threaded ley meant to enter the main line at speed. They inevitably slowed, however, as they lost the high-test white and dropped down to a smattering of dark gray. Katu hit a nice cruising speed and Cha settled in for some serious catching up with Big Betty.

"Why did you come after me?" Prince Charming asked after a while.

"Told ya—I was hoping for another platinum."

"You could have endeavored not to lose the first one."

"Yeah. That goes on the list of precious things I've carelessly lost, along with my virginity, youthful optimism, and moral compass."

He made a snorting sound and she grinned over at him. It wasn't an actual laugh, but close. "You don't strike me as the sort to mourn her virginity."

"Not in and of itself—and certainly not the ensuing hijinks—but I didn't care for the manner of losing, thus the 'careless' qualification. But enough about me. We really need to discuss the fact that you're a sorcerer and probably a rogue fae."

~ 19 ~

A Spot of Sparkle

THAT SHUT HIM up for a full minute. And yeah, that had been a little over-the-top dramatic, calling him a rogue fae, especially since that was only a thing in stories. At least, Cha was pretty sure of that. She'd never heard of anyone meeting a real rogue fae, nor did she have any idea why they'd go rogue in the first place, since being full fae put you at the top of any heap anyone could pile up. Still, she'd gone with that instead of saying "you probably have enough fae blood to qualify for citizenship in one of the realms," as that didn't sound nearly so good.

"Rogue fae, seriously?" he demanded, looking down his long nose, currently wrinkled in regal disgust. "Have I tripped and fallen into some sort of serial melodrama?"

Yeah, okay, she deserved that one. "Aren't you just a little ray of pitch black," she grumbled anyway. "You know what I mean, what with the sparkly blue magicking."

"Should you be saying those things aloud?" he shot back, pointing a long finger at the path-box. He had a point. Discretion had never been her strong suit.

Rather than admit her error, she went on the offense. "You're ducking the question. And withholding pertinent information."

Another long silence ensued that would've been fraught, if Cha had the personal depth to experience fraught-ness. As it was, she hummed one of the tunes that had been playing back at Giant Jo's, once again considering that she should buy one of those magic music boxes to listen to on road trips like this. Maybe with her earnings from this job. Of course, with the earnings from this job, she and Katu wouldn't need to go on long ventures anymore.

"Is that why you came back for me?" the prince finally asked. "Because you figured I had something to contribute?" He waved a hand suggestively in the air, blue sparking from his fingertips in the vague shape of a fireball.

"That and your pretty face."

"If you want information, you have to give information," he chided. "Only true answers."

That was his problem if he thought that wasn't the truth. She shrugged. "I had a feeling."

"Clairvoyance?"

"Nah. Just human intuition. A hunch, nothing magical about it."

"You have fae blood if you're a ley rider."

She slid him a look. "I see what you're doing here, back to discussing me. Of course I have to have fae blood to be a ley rider, though I'm a bit surprised you know that."

"I'm not an idiot."

"No, but you are oddly ignorant of certain realities of peasant life."

"Can you be out of contact with your partner for a short time?"

Taken aback by the sudden change of topic, she raised her brows at him. "I assume you could reverse whatever you're planning to do at a moment's notice?"

"Yes."

"More precisely, the moment I give you notice?"

"Yes." He sounded impatient to have to repeat himself.

"I don't know…" It sounded like a bad idea.

"You can trust me."

Cha barked out a laugh. "Oh, no, my princely purple hitchhiker. I can see myself doing all kinds of questionable and filthy things with you, but trust is whole 'nother kettle of blueberries."

"You would bed someone you don't trust?"

The question gave her pause. In truth, answering something like that felt more intimate than a naked tumble in that theoretical bed. "When did I offer the—unquestionably enticing, once-in-a-lifetime, even for a royal—opportunity to 'bed' me, as you so quaintly put it?"

"You've been flirting with me."

She waved that off. "I flirt with everyone. Well," she amended, "everyone that gives me the pussy sparkle."

He made a choking sound. "Excuse me?"

"You know, chemistry. That indefinable spark. The genital awakening of interest when you encounter someone who rings your special bell." She waved at her crotch, just in case he missed her meaning.

"You seem to be defining it just fine," he replied in a

strained voice. "I've never heard it put that way."

"I don't know what you guys call it. Dick itch?"

"I'm pretty sure that's something different. So, you're telling me you'd have sex with someone who gives you this… sparkle, without having built trust with them?"

It amused her no end that he avoided using the word. "Uh, yeah. That's called having a healthy libido. Good sex doesn't require an intimate relationship."

"Healthy is not the word that springs to mind regarding your intimate relationships."

She slid him an incredulous look. "You've known me for five minutes, boy-o, and I—if I may be so blunt—am not the one running from a vengeful bride who did something so awful to you that you fled with only the fancy clothes on your back."

"And five platinum coins," he countered sourly.

The wealth of a small principality, yeah. She had no argument for that. "Whatever," she replied. Not her wittiest comeback, but she was still a little off kilter from the accusations about her approach to sex. Who was he to judge her? Dy and Phin got to give her shit about her disinclination to form lasting relationships—and there were reasons for that—not some random guy she'd just met. Talk about a sparkle-douser.

"I could do what I have in mind without your permission," he pointed out when she said nothing more.

"Now we're at threats? So much for the trust-building exercise."

He sighed in pure exasperation. "You're impossible."

She couldn't help an impertinent grin, indulging herself by

patting his lean thigh. *Ooh, yummy.* There, that was more like herself. She wouldn't let him get her down. "Now you're starting to know the real me."

He peeled her hand off his thigh, as if in distaste. Fine then. "You want answers," he pointed out. "So do I." He waved the wand around, grimacing when it poofed a burst of pink glitter that wafted over his face.

Cha probably should've controlled herself, but she snickered. "You look cute with pink glitter in your hair."

Holding her gaze, an irritated lick of blue flame in his indigo eyes, he tapped the wand against the path-box. A circle of crystal, mostly clear with a blue tint, enveloped the box. Even a mostly mundane like Cha could tell that meant it wouldn't send or receive. She frowned, deeply uneasy. "Hey."

"Trust me."

"No way."

"Only for a moment."

"A moment is all it takes."

"So cynical."

"You have yet to plumb the depths of my cynicism." With a sigh, she figured it for a done deal. "Spill already."

"First tell me how you happen to have a Moonruby wand."

"Moonruby? Never heard of that."

"And you call *me* ignorant. The wand is pink."

"I noticed."

"Thus a blend of magic from the Moonstone and Ruby realms."

"Whoa." Ruby was the highest-test magic, and the most mysterious of the fae realms. She looked at the wand with renewed respect. "No wonder it worked on the iron demon so well. I didn't know you could mix magic between realms."

Prince Not-So-Charming actually rolled his eyes at her. "I suspect what you don't know about sorcery could fill buckets."

"True enough," she agreed cheerfully. "Too bad I'm fresh out of buckets. Now give me my Moonruby wand." She reached for it and he snatched it away, tsking at her like some elderly schoolteacher.

"This is a powerful magic artifact," he told her in important tones. "Not to be waved about willy-nilly."

"I used that nilly to save your willy," she reminded him.

"I'm well aware," he replied gravely. "That kind of service means something to the...me."

"To the you?" She laughed, guiding Katu around a slow-moving hippo carriage piled high with crates, then turned in her seat to face him more fully. The pink glitter in his indigo hair should have made him look ridiculous, but somehow it came across as more delicious frosting on rich, chocolate (if chocolate was blue) cake. Damn if she didn't want to lick him up. "And what are the you, pray tell?"

"I can't tell you," he answered, then laid a finger over her lips as she snarled a protest. "*Can't*," he said with significance. "Geas, remember? Two things: yes, I have magic, and no, I'm not what you called me. Also, be very careful of what you do call me, Arantxa, in public or in private."

Serious pussy sparkle there. The word "private" had never sounded so sexy. Cha even quivered a little at the way her broody prince purred her full name, making it sound sensual and wonderful for the first time in her life. Maybe because he wasn't yelling at her, like most people were when they used her thorny moniker. Also, she could have imagined it—pussy sparkle could do that, leading a woman to all kinds of bad decisions and questionable fantasies—but it seemed like his finger lingered on her lip, tugging the bottom lip down ever so slightly as he withdrew.

"So, what *should* I call you?" Okay, her voice came out breathy, but hey—if he didn't want her turned on, he shouldn't be looking so edible and touching her in sexy ways, right?

"Your Highness," he answered with a quirk of a teasing smile. "I kind of liked that."

"You would. I'll just call you Prince, for short."

"I'll take Prince Charming as the 'handle,' but it's a bit much between us. Call me Azul, in private." He smiled, a hint of real charm in it.

"Azul," she said, trying it out. Pretty. Would sound mighty fine being shouted in the throes of passion, but... "Sounds a little demonic."

"I worry about your education."

"Hey, I might have been a scholarship student at Miss Mulry's Academy for the Magically Gifted, but the education was top notch. Tell me this," she continued, before he could retort. "If you can do magic, why couldn't you keep those fell wolves from carrying you off?"

"Ruby magic," he replied with distaste. "Higher than mine," he clarified with a raised brow. "Surely you have some sense of the echelons of magic use."

"Hey, I'm a simple ley rider. I just know that the higher the color, the faster I can go."

"I suspect you're far from a simple ley rider, Arantxa Evermore," he commented cryptically.

She noticed glossy black trees that lined the road now, along with the decidedly darker cast to the landscape. They'd crossed the invisible border into Gypsum and were getting close to the Obsidian border. Time and Katu had flown fast. "Sharing time is over. I gotta make contact with Dy."

He nodded—maybe she also imagined some regret in it—and tapped a finger on the globe he'd made over the box. Immediately Dy's voice came through.

"Bandit, what the hell now! I've got heat and not the good kind. Come back."

"What does that mean?" Azul asked.

"That means to strap in and hang tight."

"Is there a way to strap in?" He looked around, as if some kind of harness might suddenly appear.

"Nah. Figure of speech. Just don't fall out." She grinned as he groaned. "I need to catch up to her quick and what falls out, stays out."

"Stark, raving mad," he muttered, but he didn't sound nearly so annoyed as he used to. In fact…Was that a hint of a dimple from a suppressed smile?

What did you know? Prince Charming was starting to have fun.

~ **20** ~

In a Jam

Time to get serious—and talk Dy down from her current tree. "Goldilocks, this is Bandit. What's your status?"

No reply. *Well, shit.* Dy had just been on there. Had things gone that bad that fast? "Goldilocks, repeat, this is Bandit. Come back."

Still no reply.

"That's bad, right?" Azul asked. "I swear I didn't mess up the mechanism."

"No, she was just there." She switched back to the gold channel. "Heya riders. Bandit here. Anyone got eyes on Big Betty?"

"Upchuck here, Bandit. I'm drafting Big Betty on the Thirteen a couple of leagues from the big black line. She looks mighty fine to me."

Huh. What then? Cha thanked Upchuck absentmindedly, then thumbed back to marcasite. "Goldilocks, drop a clue. Pretty please, with sugar on top."

"Do I want to know why he's called 'Upchuck'?" Azul asked in a pained voice during the long pause that ensued.

"He earned the handle fair and square," Cha answered, frowning at the silent path-box, then glanced at Azul. "No, you probably don't want to know."

The box crackled and Cha's heart jumped in relief at the sound of Dy's voice. "I'm here. I'm just not speaking to you."

"Aw, honey. Don't be like that. I am responsibly right behind you and will hold your hand for BX. What kind of heat have you got?"

"If you were off eating candy, Bandit, I swear I'll sic Mama Bear on you and you'll be toothless."

"I swear I wasn't, was I, Charming?" She threw him an expectant look, pointing at the box.

He cleared his throat. "If that means what I think it means, then no. I remain unconsumed and intend to stay that way," he added with offended dignity.

"I was deaf for other reasons. Good ones," Cha said. "I'll explain face to face."

She wove through the slower traffic, ignoring the slight sting of Azul's dismissal. She didn't expect every man to want her. Sometimes the sparkle was sadly one-sided. Besides he was too fancy for the likes of her. And there was the fact that he had more fae blood than a person running around in human lands should have. Though the things she'd heard about fae lovers…Well, just say that there's a reason so many humans succumbed to fae seduction despite all the very good reasons not to. Like losing all memory of yourself and disappearing forever into the fae lands, dancing yourself to death or losing your humanity altogether. Or worse. She needed to keep those consequences firmly in mind. Even though the prince wasn't actually fae.

She was pretty sure. Just to verify, she sneaked a glance at his ears. No points protruding through his curling, deep blue hair. There was an iridescence to the color though, dark as a deep ocean with glints of indigo magic. It looked like the color emanated from the inside, the curls almost coiling of their own accord… Nah. It was just a really good dye job. Still, the color served to highlight his pale skin, his profile as delicately etched as a sculpture, made sensually alive by that full pouting mouth. She could imagine all sorts of things that mouth could—

"What?" he demanded, turning abruptly so that he caught and held her eyes, his as intense and full of secrets as that magically deep ocean she'd fancied.

"Just making sure you hadn't fallen out," she returned lightly as she wrenched her gaze away. Definitely *not* blushing, because she wasn't some inexperienced schoolgirl with a crush on the wealthy, unobtainable and noble, pretty boy. No, she was the Bandit. Hardcore and hard assed, with her pick of willing lovers. On a life-changing smuggling run fraught with danger. Now *that* was the kind of fraught-ness she thrived on.

"Arantxa," Azul began, a troublingly serious note in his voice.

To her relief, she caught the familiar buzz of Big Betty on the ley line ahead. That had been quick. "Aha!" she exclaimed, pretending she hadn't heard him, and hitting the path-box. "Good news, Goldi, I'm just about caught up." Dy didn't reply. Still pissed then.

Cha poured on the speed, weaving around the considerable convoy drafting Big Betty, all of them going awfully slow for that. A number of them sent up greetings as she passed.

"Do you know all of these… people?" the prince asked.

"What can I say? I'm a popular gal."

"Apparently," he noted drily.

She ignored the subtext he loaded into that observation. Traffic was slowing to a halt, a logjam of rumbling carriages filling the black width of the Thirteen. "What is *going on?*" she muttered.

"The traffic has stopped moving," Azul said helpfully.

"Thanks ever so, but I did observe that for myself," she returned acidly.

"You asked." The thin smile he produced positively reeked of false innocence.

She flipped back to the gold channel, as Katu purred to a halt, mentally unsheathing impatient claws. "Bandit here. On the Thirteen near the big black line—what's the hold up?"

Several voices chimed in with the unhelpful information that traffic had stopped moving. Azul gave her a smug smile. "We don't have time for this," she muttered, glancing at the timekeeper. It was one thing for her to fall behind, but Big Betty had to be on schedule if they were to make their payday.

Cha stood in the driver's seat, shading her eyes in an attempt to see ahead. Big Betty's bulk obscured a great deal, but it was obvious traffic was stopped ahead of her. No doubt this was what had Dy so riled.

"Sit tight," she told Azul. "I'll be right back."

"You'll what? But what if—"

"Katu knows what to do if traffic starts moving." She left him eyeing Katu's dash with decided suspicion, leapt to the safe margin, and made her way on foot past the stopped carriages, waving absently as ley riders called out to her. Reaching the passenger side of Big Betty, she hopped up and climbed in. Warg tried to lick her face with his big, decidedly slimy tongue, and she ducked with the agility of long practice. "Ugh, no," she told him.

Dy gave her a long, cool look. "Well, look what the cat dragged in." She tapped the timer, showing them now less than two hours ahead of schedule. "We're losing our margin."

"Like that's my fault?"

"I don't know," Dy answered, sounding just like when she caught one of the kids screwing up and was just waiting for them to fess up. "Is it?"

Cha leashed her temper. Dy had a right to be annoyed with her. Jerking her head outside, she said, "Step into my office." She hopped out again and walked over to a tree with leaves a normal green on one side and all black facing the Obsidian side. Dy followed a moment later, folding her arms and tapping a foot expectantly.

"I'm sorry I was radio silent," Cha said. "Prince Charming agreed to answer my questions if no one could overhear. He put a whammy on the path-box so it wouldn't send or receive."

Her eyes widening, Dy canted her head as if trying to hear better. "He's a sorcerer?"

"Apparently, and with a big dollop of fae blood, too." She wanted to tell Dy more, but thought better of it. If it so happened to be the case that her hitchhiker *was* full fae, however impossible that might be, then Dy would not take that news well. She would call a halt to Cha's association with

Prince Charming, probably enforcing her edict with sorcery.

It did occur to Cha that keeping her suspicions secret and going against what she knew would be her best friend's better judgment might not be the wisest course, but she felt oddly protective of Azul. Probably all of this pointed to bad decisions on Cha's part, but—hey—she'd never been known for her good ones, especially where pretty boys were concerned.

Dy pursed her lips in a soundless whistle at the news of fae blood. "Are you sure it was a good idea to go back for this guy?" Dy looked Cha over, radiating maternal concern. "Especially as you apparently suffered a fair amount of damage in the process—are you all right?"

"I'm fine." Cha waved that off. "He healed me," she added with a lift of her brows.

Dy didn't like that at all. She stared bleakly ahead at the stopped traffic. "Cha, sweetheart, this sounds like another of your—"

"Did you know that fae-realm magic could be blended?" Cha interrupted. "Giant Jo gave me a magic wand—it's pink— and Prince Charming says it's a combination of Moonstone and Ruby magic."

"I've read some treatises theorizing that was possible, but..." Dy shook her head. "That's beside the point. How did Giant Jo happen to have something like that?"

"Dunno. I didn't really have time to ask a lot of questions. There was an iron demon and—"

"What?" Dy broke in, aghast.

"I tell you, I've been through a lot," Cha said mournfully, not above milking it for sympathy.

Dy wasn't moved—or fooled in the least. "This is all going south already and we haven't even crossed into Obsidian. I don't like the omens on this."

Okay, this wasn't going the direction Cha wanted. "They're good omens," she insisted. "Giant Jo gave me a powerful magic artifact and I defeated an iron demon and a bevy of fell wolves!" She had no idea how many counted as a bevy, so that seemed like a reasonable vague number to pick.

"Cha, have you looked around you?" Dy shot an impatient finger ahead. "The border to Obsidian is closed. We're dead in the water before we've even begun."

"A small obstacle, easily overcome."

"What if someone knows what we're trying to pull off? They could have been listening in on the path channels, like you heard was possible."

"This situation is exactly why we have bribes," Cha pointed out. "Do you want to go back to Phin and the kids and tell them we have to give the coin back? That we gave up before we even crossed into Obsidian, a realm we've been in and out of hundreds of times? That people take their *kids* to for holidays and to play fairy?" When Dy's brow wrinkled into uncertainty, Cha pressed on ruthlessly. "Will you look into Phin Jr's face and tell him you hit a little traffic jam and bailed? Tell Zazu you got scared? Leave the twins to eat mud the rest of their lives?"

"You might be fancy free, but that family you're trying to use as leverage against me are people who love and depend on me." Dy retorted and Cha winced, knowing she'd pressed it too far. And she'd been doing so well, too. Dy raked her blonde curls back from her forehead, glaring at the traffic. "I will be missed if I don't return," she added so pointedly that it was clear they both knew no one but the crowds would notice if the Bandit disappeared, and they'd quickly forget her for the next racer.

What was this, pile on Cha for being an asshole day? "There are people who'd miss me," she said, sounding a little too defensive.

Dy glanced at her distractedly, then seemed to realize what she'd said. "Oh, honey, I'm sorry. I didn't mean that how it sounded. It's just been so long since I've done this and every league this job puts between me, Phin, and the babies is gutting me. Maybe I *am* too rusty, not cut out for the bandit life anymore."

This was even worse than Cha had feared. "Out of practice, maybe, but never rusty. This is a bump and it's natural for you to miss your family."

Dy gazed at Cha, her lovely blue eyes watery. "I do miss them. And I'm lonely. I thought this would be about you and me again—not you cutting contact and canoodling with some guy you picked up."

Ouch. And fair. "I'll ditch him now," she promised recklessly. "You matter far more to me than anyone else. I don't care how useful Prince Charming might be in the fae realms ahead," she added, not above reminding Dy of that salient bit of information, just in case.

Dy laughed, shaking her head, but at least no longer so upset. "You never change."

"Is that a good thing?" Cha asked hopefully.

"Promise me this," Dy said seriously, instead of answering. "Promise me you won't let this Prince Charming distract you. That you'll put me and this job first."

"I so swear." Cha seized Dy's hand, turned their joined hands to the side, and spit into the space between their palms, clutching tight so Dy couldn't immediately pull away.

Dy shrieked and extracted her hand with a small buzz of magic. "I can't believe you did that!"

"Think of it as Warg slime," Cha replied with an easy grin, "only cleaner."

"I hate you," Dy grumbled.

"Back at 'cha, babe. Get ready to fly. Those border fae won't know what hit them."

~ 21 ~

The Box O'Bribes

RETURNING TO THE idling Katu, Cha vaulted into the jump seat and rummaged in the rear compartment to dig out Phinny's box o'bribes, before sliding over and into the driver's seat again.

"Miss me?" she purred to Azul, who gave her a bored stare.

"I was enjoying the peace and quiet."

"Glad you savored it, as rest time is over." She pinged the gold channel. "Bandit here, hailing one and all of you poor suckers currently with thumbs up their asses stuck on the Thirteen by the big black line. I need a parting of the sea, stat, so I can unplug this toilet."

Azul slid her an incredulous look. "Do you say these things to deliberately disgust me?"

"Nope. I do it to disgust everyone," she answered cheerfully as the path-box chorused with cheers, rude comments on her metaphor, and—best of all—enthusiastic embellishments on the imagery. Given that Obsidian fae were involved, the conversation rocketed downhill rapidly. But the carriages also made way for her, parting to create a clear lane that Katu sailed

156

through, thrumming with pride. It was kind of like winning a race, albeit a bit sideways. Cha patted his dash. "Good kitty."

It took a bit of jockeying to get through the densely stalled traffic as they reached the border. It was defined by a wall, a black one, of course, towering to the sky and running as far as the eye could see in either direction. The silhouettes of black gargoyles perched at regular intervals at the top, ready to drop on anyone so foolish as to attempt to run the border. This wasn't the only crossing into Obsidian, but they all looked essentially the same.

The Thirteen ley line forked a short distance before the wall, the inbound leys leading to a series of gated arches. In keeping with theme—the actual fae tended even more towards dramatic architecture than their human imitators—the gates had been made to look like a spiked portcullis that lowered from above, as in a gothic tale. The gates were all down, filling the archways with overwrought iron twisting and twining like menacing black vines with bristling thorns and roses. Obsidian fae guards, equally spiky and gothic, stood sentry at the gates, while the border agents sat in their glass cubicles, reading books or having conversations with their colleagues, apparently at leisure—and totally ignoring the demanding questions from the carriages idling at the front of the lines.

On the outbound side, the gates stood open, allowing traffic to flow freely from Obsidian into the human realm. "Anyone can come out, but no one can get in," Cha intoned.

"I'm sure that's backwards," Azul said, eyeing the Obsidian fae.

Cha gestured to the two sides of traffic. "How is it backwards? You can see for yourself."

"What I can see is that the gates are down and we're going nowhere."

"Watch and learn, my darling blue devil." She angled Katu around a train of donkey carriages, whose driver rounded on her angrily. He'd been parked in front of a placid and towering Obsidian fae guard, who stared stonily past him, unmoved, possibly not even noticing the ranting, red-faced human as he implacably blocked the way.

"Look here," the angry ley rider shouted, "I'm—oh, hey Bandit. You're on the road again? Katu's looking in fine form, as are you." His gaze lingered appreciatively on her and Cha nearly pointed it out to Azul.

"Thank you, darling." She fluttered her lashes at the ley rider, whose name—real or assumed—she couldn't recall for the life of her. Had she slept with him? Maybe. He looked like her type. "Let me give this a try."

"Happy to yield to you," he said with a wink. "As you likely recall."

He revved his donkey carriages, optimistically readying them to move.

"Is there anyone you haven't bedded?" Azul hissed.

She tapped her chin thoughtfully. "Let me think… Hmm. Oh wait, you." She gave him a dazzling smile. *"So far."*

"You wish," he muttered.

Not dignifying that jibe with a response, she smiled up at the stony Obsidian fae blocking the way to the glass cubicle ahead. "Beautiful day," she observed. Nothing. Not even a twitch. "Mind if I pass, handsome?"

He flicked her a glance. "The border is closed."

She pointed to the outbound traffic. "Doesn't look closed to me."

"But it is closed to you."

Cha did a double-take. Mr. Stoic Obsidian Fae chose a bit of witty wordplay instead of ignoring her? Okay, yeah, it wasn't all *that* witty, but compared to his imitation of a wall, it was a step up. She pushed out her lower lip in a sultry pout, leaning an arm along the side of the carriage and arching her back to display her cleavage a bit better. Her bosom already looked pretty fabulous in the tight-fitting red leather jacket with the zipper conveniently at half-mast. (Conveniently and with foresight, because she'd lowered it when she got out of the carriage.) With her other hand, she raked back her short bob, hitting some dried ick leftover from the fell wolf battle and hoping it didn't show to disadvantage. "What would it take to…ease the opening?" she purred, letting her gaze slide over him, making the double-entendre obvious.

It wasn't hard to look interested. The tall fae had a nicely chiseled physique, along with big feet and long fingers that boded well for other parts of his anatomy. His dark eyes lingered on her with return interest, lingering on her breasts, but it was the glitter of the gem she'd palmed and held resting on the hand near him that truly caught his attention. He trailed a clawed finger down her bare forearm to her palm, the gem disappearing. "All I can do is get you to the border agent," he cautioned.

"That's plenty. You're my hero."

He actually cracked a smile. "Look me up on your way back through."

"I'll do that." She idled Katu forward as the guard stepped aside, the slow black was very slow here. Even if you wanted to try to run the border, you'd be going so stupid slow someone on foot could catch you.

"You're my hero," Azul said in a high voice no doubt meant to be hers. He added a snort. "I can't believe you'd trade sex to cross the border."

"I traded the promise of sex," she corrected. "Huge difference. Also a little sparkly jewel I figured he'd like."

"You did?" Aha, she'd surprised the arrogant prince. "I didn't notice."

"You weren't supposed to."

"The agent looks female," he observed. "What will you do now?"

"Who says I can't charm a female? Dy loves me. Most of the time," she amended, thinking how she'd carelessly hurt Dy's feelings by cutting off communication. You'd think she'd know better, having experienced how much it hurt when Dy's main focus went to Phinny.

"I'm sure it's a challenge for her."

"Never said I'm not an asshole. Now hush. Listen and learn." She pulled up to the booth. The Obsidian fae woman inside had her back to the lane, her long, white hair glimmering like magical moonlight. She leaned her elbows on the rim of the open window on the other side, deep in conversation with the agent across the way.

Without turning around, she said over her shoulder. "Border is closed."

"Damn bosses," Cha returned agreeably. "Never thinking

about the impact on the little people. Bet that pisses you off, huh?

Now the fae looked at her. "Doesn't matter to me. It all pays the same."

Cha nodded, making a face of annoyed agreement. "Not much, though, right? Shit wages, I'll bet." She tipped her head at the slot for identification papers, where a pretty jewel now sat. "People like us, we have to stick together, share the wealth."

The Obsidian fae woman glanced around, then snatched up the jewel with an avaricious smile, not nearly so smooth as the guard had been. "I can't let you through. Orders from above."

"Sure, sure. Makes it hard on all of you, though."

She frowned. "How's that?"

Cha jerked a thumb behind her. "Look at that jam. It's backing up for leagues. When they finally open up, you're going to be here way past quitting time, dealing with the backlog while the higher-ups are home enjoying the evening meal."

"I hadn't thought of that." She looked out over the long queue of growling carriages. "They can all go home themselves."

"How?" Cha held up her palms in helpless resignation. "There's no ambrosia station here. Everyone's waited for the cheaper one just on the other side. The carriages will run out of juice and revert to animal form, then you'll have real chaos on your hands." She shook her head. "I feel for you. I really do."

The Obsidian fae studied Cha. "Do you propose a solution?"

"Open the border," Cha answered promptly. "You and all your colleagues. Let us through and out of your gorgeous hair. It's really something, by the way—do you do something special to grow it so long and keep it so shiny?"

She put a hand to her hair, her claws long and polished with a moonstone color the same hue as her dramatic locks, starting to answer before she narrowed her eyes and dropped the hand. "If we let you through, we'll all be fired."

Cha had figured that. "I'm on a tight deadline and my own bosses are real jerks about it. However, they *are* invested in me and my partner delivering this shipment. How about a pretty for each of you to open the border? Then you quit and take a little sabbatical." She opened the case, flashing her considerable supply of gems.

The fae woman's gaze turned calculating. "Let me call the others over and we'll talk numbers."

$$\sim 22 \sim$$

Wings

"I CAN'T BELIEVE that worked," Azul commented, as Katu shot out of the border gates, the cat softly roaring his delight to be cruising in the lead.

"Why not?" After reassuring herself that no obstacles lay ahead, she surveyed the contents of Phin's bribery chest. They'd taken a hit, though not as bad as it could have been. Fortunately—thanks to Giant Jo's—Katu didn't need to be topped off with ambrosia yet. Better to make up the time now. She opened the gold channel. "Bandit on the far side of the big black line," she announced. "All clear to proceed. Our boxed-up friends made it possible, so if you have the means to be generous, it would be a nice thank you."

A chorus of cheers and thanks jumbled from the path-box for a bit and Cha pumped her fists in the air, as if to a shouting stadium audience.

"I suppose you see yourself as some sort of folk hero," Azul commented sourly.

"Nah. I'm as selfish as they come, but I do love the rush of the win." She grinned at him, which he didn't return, naturally.

"The reason I can't believe that worked is that all of those agents, possibly the guards, too, will now be out of a job. Just to do you a favor."

"For a financial windfall," she corrected. "Those gems will give them a buffer, time not living hand to mouth, to find better jobs."

"How could you possibly know they want that?"

"All people are essentially the same," she explained. "Fae or human, we all have the same motivations—we need coin or jewels or your preferred item of exchange to obtain the stuff we really want. The people who have most of the stuff expect the people with less of it to grub along, taking whatever shit they're doled out. And the workers do take it, because if they're in a crap job already—and believe me, border agent is bottom rung—that's the best they can get. So they grit it out, waiting for the moment they can leave for the day and go live the part of their life they actually enjoy."

He was quiet a moment. "I never thought of it that way."

"My darling sulky blueberry, that's because you're a prince. I bet you've never worked a tedious, low-wage job your entire life." She cocked a brow at him. "Or any job at all?"

"I have a job," he answered stiffly.

"I don't think marrying psychotic bitches with a kennel full of fell wolves counts as an actual job."

"Perhaps not, but it *is* a considerable amount of work," he countered.

"Did you just make a joke?" She laughed for him, since he didn't. "Answer me this—if you can," she amended, remembering the geas. "What did they have on you, to make you go through with this marriage?"

"What makes you think this undefined 'they' had 'something on me,' which I perceive is some sort of hu—" He abruptly looked off to the side. "—peasant colloquialism for extortion?"

"Did you almost say 'human' and substituted 'peasant' at the last second?"

He stabbed a finger at the path-box. Yeah, yeah. He still hadn't told her the truth when he'd had it encased in a cone of silence. Too bad the mystery only made him more interesting. She'd bet one of those gems she'd just used to bribe their way across the Obsidian border that the blue hair went all the way down to his nethers. *Mmm.*

"Here's what I think: you weren't marrying this chick for love," she answered his original question.

"As I'm not a superstitious idiot, correct," he replied drily.

"You regard love as a superstition?"

"Don't you?" he countered with a note of surprise. "The infamous Bandit, who's bedded every available male on the Thirteen and beyond, surely doesn't believe in anything so sentimental as romance."

She considered disputing that remark, but why bother? "Dy and Phin—Dy's wife—are in love. Have been almost from the beginning and no signs of it flagging. So, yeah, I guess I do believe in romantic love, in the staying power of a love like theirs, anyway."

He didn't comment. Since it was unlikely he was restraining himself out of courtesy, or some sensitivity regarding not wanting to stomp on her opinion, she figured he was thinking it over. "Why do you want to know what forced me into that marriage?" he finally asked.

She had to think back, having lost track of the conversation. "I had a point, I'm sure I did, about everyone being the same, having to do stuff we don't want to in order to survive. But also, I'm interested. We're kind of friends now."

"Your definition of friendship differs from mine."

"Check. Not friends. So, don't tell me. But we've got a drive ahead of us. Want to pick a different topic? Or you could sing me a song."

His head jerked around, as if in shock. "I'm not going to *sing*, now!"

Jeez, you'd think she'd asked him to disembowel himself. "Fine, fine," she said placatingly and lapsed into silence rather than provoke him further.

The Obsidian landscape rolled past, growing decidedly more fae with every league. Despite the implications of a word like "border," the demarcation between human and fae lands wasn't—to coin a phrase—black and white. With the failure of the natural barriers between the magical and non-magical realms, the landscapes had begun to overlap, rather than jutting precisely up against one-another. The phenomenon created a kind of bleed, where fae stuff filtered into the nearby human lands and where the non-magical world diluted the magic of the fae realm it abutted.

This mostly happened between Obsidian and neighboring Gypsum, though Cha had heard of other places in the world where magical realms had drifted up against the human ones. She didn't know what it was like in those places, but Obsidian was more or less like a human realm with a bit of a funky spin. And, contrary to what some stories assumed, not everything there was black. The black pixie dust did have a tendency to infiltrate many aspects of the realm, but mostly concentrated in certain places and objects.

Thus, the trunks of the surrounding forest were a gleaming black, but the canopy was green, if a deeper tone than in human lands and with occasional sweeps of black leaves. Same for the other foliage. Some of the flowers that bloomed in the meadows and the fruit hanging from the trees shone a disconcerting glossy black, but otherwise it was more or less human-normal. The road signs and ambrosia stations were a bit on the twisted side, but mostly familiar. It helped that she'd been there so many times. Moonstone would be much stranger.

"Family," Azul said, breaking into her thoughts. When she raised a brow at him, he shrugged, looking uncomfortable. "Family obligations are why I agreed to wed…her. I might not have to be employed for a living, but a life such as mine doesn't come without its pressures. There are some ways in which I must do as I'm told."

He sounded so bitter, in a most familiar way. She knew that particular flavor. "So, walk away from your family."

"Excuse me?" He sounded so astonished and offended that she nearly laughed.

"Cut ties. Lots of people do it," she told him, not quite able to interpret the complex rush of emotions across his face. If she had to put a name to it, she'd call him tormented. "If your family is shit to you, then you owe them nothing, let alone your loyal obedience. Cut 'em off. Go your own way."

"It's not that simple."

"It never is," she agreed. She knew that better than most. "But sometimes it's necessary."

They were quiet for a bit, this time more companionably. Cha suspected Azul was deep in thought. "That guard," he said finally, "the Obsidian fae guard at the border, if he had requested actual sex in exchange, would you—"

"Let me stop you right there, Your Highness, before you piss me off. I like sex; I make no pretense otherwise. I'd be interested in finding out if what they say about fae lovers is true—just mentioning that to you, putting it out there—but I indulge on my terms, for my own pleasure. *Not* as a commodity. Does that answer the invasive question that's none of your business?"

"Yes." He might have sounded a bit chastened, but then he asked, oh so casually, "What do they say about fae lovers?"

"Have you lived in a cave your entire life?"

"No, a palace," he returned immediately, expression so perfectly deadpan that Cha couldn't tell if he was yanking her chain or not. "We don't get a lot of gossip there," he added.

"Sounds stultifying. Nasty family. No gossip. What do you do all day—lie about on velvet settees and send servants running to bring you things you don't need?"

His perfect mouth twitched, annoyance or amusement—it was a toss-up. "Something like that. Come on, spill. I'm curious and we have a long drive."

"I can see you're learning from me," she replied without rancor.

"You've created a monster, indeed. What do they say?"

"Persistent little devil on this topic, aren't you?"

"I have an interest," he replied, almost primly.

It would be nice if that interest was related to her, but he sure hadn't taken her up on the fairly blatant offer. Not that she had time, but…A girl could dream. "Well, you've heard the old tales—that to be seduced by the fae is to lose all sense of yourself. Their lovemaking is utterly sensual, enveloping every sense so that you think of nothing else but the moment."

"And that's appealing?"

She slid him a look, but he seemed to be asking in earnest. "There's a reason human beings fall into doing stuff like drugs and alcohol. Yeah, not thinking and losing yourself entirely to the pleasure of the moment has a definite appeal. What wouldn't we give sometimes to have only pleasure and forget our cares?" Her words fell between them with a little too much weight, so she bared her teeth in a salacious grin and added, "And then there's the special features like claws, wings, tails, extra appendages, and who knows what all."

He barked out something like a laugh. "Those things are sexy?"

"Seven hells, yeah!" He looked so adorably perplexed that she had to keep going, just to see if she could make him squirm. "Sharp claws, grazing your skin, because a little pain makes the pleasure even more exquisite. Tails, because it's an extra appendage, and if it's prehensile, just imagine the orifices it could stimulate when everything else is occupied."

"And wings?" He asked the question with a slight burr to his voice, his blue blue eyes on her, glimmering with interest.

"Wings…" She shrugged cheerfully. "Just flat sexy. I can't tell you why. Incontrovertible fact."

"Interesting to know." He'd gone back to neutral, gazing out at the road ahead.

"Maybe because he'd, like, wrap you up in them, just the two of you in this sensual cocoon of naked fun."

"I thought you said you'd couldn't tell me why."

Yeah, it was perverse of her to enjoy the burr of irritation in his voice. Even more so that she was encouraged by it. "Maybe it's the feathers," she mused. "They're the perfect combination of soft and prickly, flexible and rigid, ideal for playing games of erotic torment."

"They might not be feathered wings, you know," he bit out. "Some fae have leathery wings."

"Ooh." She produced a shiver, making her bosom jiggle, quite effective as she hadn't returned her jacket zipper to its usual position yet. "Even better. So gothic."

"That Obsidian fae guard that caught your eye didn't have wings," he pointed out. If Azul hadn't been so clear about his lack of interest in her, she'd have called him jealous.

"I've heard they can hide them," she confided, giving him a wink. "Glamour, magic, whatever. They only come out at *special* times."

"I suspect that what you've 'heard' is a load of dramatic fiction liberally embroidered with titillating nonsense."

Definitely jealous. "A girl can dream. What about you— ever bedded a fae?"

~ 23 ~

A Jaunt Through the Countryside

AZUL'S HEAD WHIPPED around so fast that Cha thought for a second that something bad had happened. "Why would you ask that?" he demanded, eyes blazing. With the wind of their passage tossing his dark blue curls, he looked wilder, that sharp edge of danger peeking out from under the broodiness that she suspected more and more was a mask for his true self.

His true *fae* self, hidden by glamour, perhaps. That crown had gone somewhere. What else might he have hidden away from human eyes? She widened her eyes in innocence. "Just making conversation…but now I'm curious. You have, haven't you? And lived to tell the tale. What was he or she like—claws? A tail! Don't tell me they had leathery wings because I'll—"

"You'll suffer not knowing, is what you'll do," he interrupted firmly. "I'm not discussing this."

Allowing a few beats of silence, Cha surveyed the traffic. A few carriages had caught up with them, though most stayed behind, drafting her or Big Betty, who loomed solidly in the rear-view mirror. A cheetah carriage had blazed past them early on, followed by a few thoroughbred horses, showing off, windows blacked, and not bothering to offer thanks. Probably with noble or even fae riders. The rest of them were playing it safe and abiding by the speed set by the sweet Obsidian-black ley line, which was plenty fast for most purposes.

This side of the border, the embedded pixie dust shone with such purity the black seemed to glow. The fae naturally kept the best stuff for themselves, exporting diluted or even contaminated dust to the human lands. Thus, inside Obsidian, the ley line zipped along like black lightning, fast, smooth, and without glitches. It was exciting enough to go to the unwary human's head, which was why the fae law-hounds patrolled this section of the Black Thirteen—the name for the Obsidian side of the main road—with exceptional fervor.

She and Dy had figured this timing into their plan, knowing they couldn't afford to be pulled over, ticketed, and outrageously fined. (The incentives for the Obsidian fae law-hounds to levy sky-high fines were so egregious that bribes didn't work most of the time.) And it was critical to circumvent the Obsidian depot at night, under cover of full dark. Besides which, Moonstone—according to rumor—was obnoxiously bright to human eyes in daylight. Better to get in and out during the dark phase. This was all part of the plan.

Still, both Cha and Katu simmered with impatience, even at the increased speed. Neither of them did well with being law-abiding. It was so dull. Especially since Azul hadn't caved to the pressure of silence and was apparently not only not discussing whether he'd dipped his wick in fae juice—he totally had or his answer would've been an easy and emphatic 'no'— but had subsided into not talking, full stop.

Cha could almost wish for something to happen, but that was always a bad—

The marcasite channel blared so suddenly they both jumped. "Bandit, I've got a tail."

"And a fine one, too," Cha replied. "Can you describe?"

"Could be a hound in hiding. Not clear, but I've got a tingle and it's stuck like a burr. I'm concerned."

"But we're being angels. What did you do to draw attention?"

"I didn't, thank you for being a bitch. I'm wondering about that unusual border closure."

"Hmm. Yeah. Okay, keep on keeping on. I'll investigate and circle back for the depot."

Cha signed off and switched to the gold channel. "Hola Black Thirteen riders. Bandit here. Anyone spot a bit of a burr on Betty's tail?"

No response. Well, a few "nopes," but those counted the same. Most of their fellow transports, strictly legal or otherwise, could spot a law-hound drunk and with their eyes closed. Dy, being a sorceress, had an edge on knowing what most people didn't. Still, it was downright odd that no one else had copped to scrutiny.

"Huh," she said aloud after the box went silent. Dy was right about the coincidence—picking up a clandestine tail when they'd done nothing to attract attention and the border being closed for no discernible reason added up to nothing good. The possibility that the fae had been tipped off about their jaunt concerned her deeply. Surely this couldn't be a set-up. Who would benefit?

"Problem?" Azul asked, a line between his brows.

"Won't know till we know," she replied with forced cheer. "This is when it gets interesting."

"It hasn't been interesting so far?"

"*More* interesting," she qualified, sliding him a sly smile as she slowed Katu. "This is when I do my real job."

"I was wondering if you had a purpose besides looking hot in a race-carriage and flirting with everything on two legs."

"Aww, you think I'm hot!"

He rolled his eyes. "I can't believe that was your takeaway."

"I excel at takeaways that flatter my vanity," she replied absently, moving Katu to the slower outside lanes and trying to make it look natural. Several more carriages passed them, some hooting and honking. Big Betty sped past, Dy making an obscene gesture with the hand dangling out the window, and Cha chuckled. "Back at 'cha, babe."

"You two have a decidedly odd friendship."

"The stuff dreams are made of," she agreed. "What about you—any Azul besties out there?"

"No," he replied shortly. "My life is not one that lends itself to the acquisition of 'besties.'"

"How sad," she said, meaning it. She slid Katu into a gap, looking for the tail. Dy hadn't described the carriage, just in case they were listening in, but it could only be one of several. They knew the rhino transport lumbering steadily along, as she was a regular on the cargo runs between the Obsidian depot and Rockton. Kinda nice to see her still on the job after all this time. The carriage train of bison carrying loaded crates couldn't be the culprit—not nearly fast enough. That left the stork single-rider carriage, the zebra sedan, or the lemur.

"What happened to your staff anyway?" she asked, settling Katu back so she could observe the behavior of her three most-likelies from behind.

"What?" Azul sounded evasive, rather than surprised by the question.

She tsked at him. "Don't take me for a fool. Your people, the ones you called to come fetch you at Giant Jo's. The ones who didn't show and left your ass hanging in the wind for hellboy and his pet wolves to grab."

"Ah, those people."

She waited. He said nothing more.

"They fucked you, didn't they? And don't say 'excuse me' in that poncy tone. You know the what-what here."

Azul sighed, eyeing the carriages drafting Big Betty. "It's the zebra."

Oh now, that was interesting, even if he was avoiding the question. "How do you know?"

He flicked her a glittering blue glance. "I can see it. Or rather through it. There's a glamour on it."

"See? I knew you'd be useful." She clicked to marcasite. "Keep a finger on my pulse, Goldi, I'm going for a spin."

"I've got you," Dy replied, and Warg burbled as she drew on him to ground her ley magic. Dy was ready to give Cha whatever she needed to draw off the zebra. "A word to the wise—all this pure black might be a bit much in the wild. If you lose me, that's why."

"Understood. I'm a big girl." Back on the gold, Cha said,

"Steer clear, jockeys. The Bandit is stretching her legs."

"Is that wise to announce your intentions?" Azul asked, obviously a quick learner, bracing himself for the move to come.

"Being wise isn't part of my job description," she answered, revving Katu, and finding the slim line of white Dy had begun to subtly weave into the black. She ignored Azul's snort of derision and grinned at him. "Being bait is."

Sensing they'd fully centered on the white, Cha pulled up parallel to the zebra. Goosing Katu, she let out a defiant whoop, pumping her fist in the air. They leapt forward, Azul's screech sounding enough like a joy rider's to be convincing.

For a moment she thought the hound-in-hiding wasn't going to take the juicy bait she offered. It stayed stubbornly stuck to Big Betty. So, Cha darted across several lanes, causing a ruckus, though most of the other drivers had paid attention to her warning, and were alert for her antics. Still, the dullards not monitoring their channels helped with the show. They howled and skidded, Katu fishtailing as he crossed several ley speeds in succession, which made for a nice show. Dy had also slowed Big Betty to a sedate, sub-par pace.

Finally, the zebra bobbled, then shot out from behind Betty in a direct intercept for Cha.

That was more like it. With the predator now on their tail, Cha synced with Katu, concentrating on that delicious white streak. They shot ahead, Katu growling in triumph at finally getting to stretch his legs.

"They're gaining," Azul said. "Shall I dissuade them?"

"No," Cha barked. "We want them close enough to smell

our farts. Don't worry, sunshine—I won't let them catch us."

She poured on the speed, zooming up the Black Thirteen, the zebra right behind. No lights from them, but a magically enhanced voice boomed out for them to pull over immediately.

"They want you to pull over," Azul said, as if she might not have heard.

"Too bad I'm deaf in this ear," Cha commented, flicking an eye at the rear view. They were awfully close, the occupants of the closed sedan obscured by the window shading and probably whatever glamour kept them concealed. "You're royalty—do you do everything you're told?"

"I wouldn't know. You're the first person to give me orders."

"Except your family."

"Well, they—" He broke off. Sighed. "That's different."

"I can just imagine. I don't suppose your powers extend to moving or creating ley lines?"

"Not at all. Is that a problem? You should have asked that sooner, if—"

"Not a problem, boy-o. Just would've been convenient. Goldilocks is on the job. Any moment now," she added. The zebra carriage, still barking out increasingly loud instructions to obey, was close enough that if she slowed in the slightest, they'd plow into the back of Katu. "Come on, Dy," she muttered under her breath. "Anytime now."

"You could call her."

"Too distracting. She's working her sorcery to—Aha!"

The new ley line appeared off to the side, so abruptly that

it required a tighter than sixty degree turn to make it. Fortunately, Katu was light and responsive—and accustomed to sensing Dy's magic. They wrenched hard onto the ley, a bright, dazzling white. Bless Dy and all that bottled-up sorcery. Shooting off the Black Thirteen, they plunged across what looked to be a field of volcanic rock. Matte black, frozen in swirling flows, with occasional twisted bits of plant life struggling toward the sky, the bleak landscape looked like what most people imagined when they thought of the land of the Obsidian fae. When they weren't imagining a magical party land where they could play fae and pretend nothing was going to mutate them.

"Shit." Cha took several quick glances at the rear view, splitting her concentration between that and guiding Katu over the unfamiliar, twisting landscape via a brand-new, high-velocity white ley line that wasn't supposed to be there. "I think we lost them."

Azul, giving every impression of a man afraid for his life and clinging to his last thread of hope, gritted out, "Isn't that a desirable outcome?"

"No! We *want* them to follow us, to draw them off Big Betty."

"Then perhaps you shouldn't make it so bloody difficult for them."

"We don't want them to catch us either."

"A conundrum, to be sure."

"Yeah, a fine line to ride," she replied, ignoring the sarcasm. "So is this ley line. Fine, I mean. Not ideal, but Dy has been out of practice and she made this one with little warning.

I just hope that she didn't—*oof.*" The wind *whoomped* out of her lungs as they juddered to a slow down so abrupt it felt like hitting a wall, even though they were still moving.

Azul had already braced a hand on Katu's dash, so he wasn't thrown as hard as Cha, but he looked severely pained anyway. Or maybe that was just his normal, pampered-prince-forced-to-suffer-ignominious-peasant-life pained expression. "What now?"

"Dy did," Cha answered, maneuvering Katu around on the ley line they'd just been spat onto. It was high-quality slick black, like one would expect of a line on this side of the border, and fast enough by most measures, but after being temporarily spoiled by that lovely white, well… this felt like molasses. She also wasn't sure exactly where they were headed now. Squinting at the map, she flicked it with a finger, seeing if it showed their new trajectory. The globe spun wildly for a moment then, with an internal blizzard of magical black snow, then returned to exactly the same as it had been before, not showing their current location. *Uh oh.*

"Did what?" Azul asked with exaggerated patience.

Cha spared him a glance. "What? Oh—Dy. When she made us the escape line, she bridged it to an existing line—not unusual, and definitely easier for her, but a problem right now because I don't know this area and this fae back ley could be going anywhere and not fast. The map also seems to be on the fizzle—probably all the black pixie dust interfering—which means I don't know how to get back to the Black Thirteen."

"Can't we just turn around?"

"Might have to because I don't know where we're heading

and wherever that is could be really bad for us and—*Shit!*"

"Now what?" He sounded almost despairing.

"We didn't lose the tail. There they are and closing fast."

"I thought that was a good thing…"

"Yes and no. We drew them off Big Betty: Good. Can't turn around on an unknown rural ley in Obsidian: not so great."

"Then why are you smiling?"

She realized it was true—she was grinning ear to ear. "Cuz this will be fun!"

He groaned and thumped his head back against the seat. "I'm starting to hate it when you say that."

~ 24 ~

Suddenly: a Canyon

CHA'S GRIN SOLIDIFIED into a determined grimace. She'd drawn plenty of law hounds off Big Betty's tail over the years—exploiting the back leys to do it—but not on the wrong side of the Obsidian border. Guiding Katu on an unfamiliar ley line in foreign territory with an unmarked carriage carrying aggressive Obsidian fae trying to crawl up her ass, she fully and suddenly comprehended the extreme audacity of this gig they were attempting.

On the human side of the border, Cha had a feel for the rural leys. A true inborn instinct. Even the ones far from where she'd grown up had a familiar pattern to them, dictated in part by how people used them and how the human mageineers designed them. You could count on certain consistent elements—like that they wouldn't go through someone's house or barnyard or grain silo, for example. Or that no one would build a road through a frozen lava flow so inhospitable and saturated with background magic that the ley line kept vanishing into the surrounding rock, even to her keen senses for such things. Or, even more prosaically human, that the road went from here to there with some purpose.

She was beginning to worry that this one did not. Even worse, up ahead the ley line forked, one side going nowhere visible and the other going to the exact same nowhere.

"Which way?" she asked, tapping the map, which spun in an unhelpful and dizzying blur of black snowflakes. Snarling in frustration, she raised her voice. "Left or right?"

"You're asking me?" Azul replied, clearly startled.

"Only you and me here, buddy. Pick one."

"But I don't know what—"

"Pick!" she barked, the junction roaring up on them with daunting speed.

"Right!" he shouted back, grunting as she swung hard to the left, flinging him against the side panel. "Why did you even ask me to pick if you were going to do the opposite," he demanded, not posing it as a question.

She lifted a shoulder and let it fall. "Intuition. Sometimes I don't know what I should do until I hear the answer that sounds wrong."

"You are the most contrary person I've ever met."

"Thank you."

"It wasn't a compliment."

"Says you." They coursed over the twisting landscape of unrelenting black, going ever farther from the Black Thirteen and closer to absolutely nowhere at all. "Why is this ley line even here?" she muttered to herself.

"Do you want an answer?" Azul inquired with just a tinge of haughtiness. "Or am I to leave that to one of your other personalities?"

"Cute. You get more charming all the time, my pretty princeling. If you know the answer, that would be convenient, and—before you get snarky with me—by that I mean, yes, please."

"Mining." He pointed ahead and she squinted.

"I don't see anything but more of this lava field."

"Obsidian field," he corrected, then sighed at her puzzled frown. "What *did* they teach at that academy of yours? Obsidian is volcanic glass. The Obsidian fae mine it. Up ahead, obviously, is a mining refinery."

She shook her head. "I still don't see it."

He pointed again. "Right there. Towering on the horizon?"

"I see nothing but frozen black lava going... Oh. Those glassy castle-looking things?" If she squinted hard, and kind of looked from the corner of her eye, she could make out the fanciful spires made of such a finely transparent material they nearly blended into the sky deepening in color with oncoming twilight. Only the fae could make something like a refinery look like the spun-sugar candy treats she'd taken the kids. "I've never seen a mining facility that pretty though."

Azul snorted. "That's because you're hopelessly human."

"Aha!" She stabbed a sideways finger at him. "And you aren't?"

"I never said so. Nobles that consort with fae develop a different—watch out!"

"Whoops!" The ley line plummeted downhill precipitously. She corrected as Katu skidded on a too-tight curve, dangling their collective rear midair for a moment before she helped him dig claws into a meatier section of the ley. The line made a full circle before switching back the other direction as they dropped into the sudden canyon. Which shouldn't be a thing. Suddenly, there was a canyon! With all that black on black and increasingly dense magic, she hadn't seen or felt the defile.

"I hate this place," she observed, concentrating on the wildly curving ley line that descended in daunting angles down the side of the sudden canyon.

"At last, we agree on something," Azul gritted out. "Please don't drive us into the abyss. I'm too young to die."

"How young is that?"

"Not saying."

"Can you?"

"What—die? Yes! Why these questions?"

He was still being evasive. Not quite answering. She filed that away as they nearly spun off another curve so tight it wouldn't be legal in a human realm. "Just ticking boxes on my immortal fae test."

"Even the fae can die from irreparable physical damage," he gritted out. "Like being flung into an abyss because someone was chatting."

"I'm just making conversation. Did you need to be doing something else right now?"

"Obviously I'm nothing but a helpless bit of baggage here—"

"Attractive baggage, though," she put in.

He continued, talking over her, "But *you* need to concentrate on keeping us alive."

"Always top of my mind." Fortunately, the fae carriage chasing them had backed off, allowing her to slow Katu, making the tight curves somewhat less lethal. Then a bad thought occurred to her. Maybe it wasn't concern for their lives or carriage that had their pursuers confident enough to take their time. "So, if this is a mine—does that make this a quarry pit, not a sudden canyon?"

"I don't know what a 'sudden canyon' is, nor am I a mining expert, but I'd guess that yes, this is the extraction pit."

"Any knowledge on whether there will be a road back out?"

"Do I look like I have encyclopedic knowledge of the Obsidian Realm? Use your map device there."

"An astute observer would note it's spinning like a top and giving me nothing. Also, while I find the way you get even more arrogant and disdainful in times of crisis perversely charming, the reason I ask is that if this ley line terminates at the bottom, as one would expect for some sort of quarry, then we're trapped."

"Oh. That would be bad, wouldn't it?"

"As the sages put it, yes." She tapped the marcasite channel. "Goldilocks, you read me?"

Nope, the silence replied.

Cha switched to gold. "Bandit here. Anyone out there?"

Silence silence silence.

Just as she'd feared. "All this sodding pixie-dust infested glass is screwing up the magic," she noted. "We're on our own. Any brilliant ideas?"

"You should have gone right at the fork," he said in a helpful tone, actually smiling when she threw him a sour glare. "I can see why you like this sarcasm thing. Like a pressure-valve release."

"As if you weren't already the King of Sarcasm."

"Prince of Sarcasm," he corrected.

"Yes, well, Your Highness, all the sarcasm in the world won't help us when we hit bottom and we're quarry who are tragically trapped in, well, a quarry. Give me my magic wand." Despite everything, it was kind of fun to say that. She held out an imperious hand and he laid the wand in it.

"What do you plan to do with that?" he inquired politely.

"Magic." She tried to sound important and mysterious as she uttered the word, but who was she kidding? She had no fucking clue. "Maybe I can vanish the Obsidian fae carriage like I did the iron demon."

"Good luck with that." He said it the way people did when they didn't wish you good luck at all but figured it was a lost cause telling you that you were fucked in the head if you thought your plan would work out.

"Why?" She remembered as the bottom of the canyon rushed toward them, more of that lovely spun-sugar equipment at the bottom, swarming with ant-like Obsidian fae miners, growing larger with every switchback. Hey, she was busy and could be forgiven for forgetting a few newly learned facts. "Oh, because the wand is Moonstone and Ruby magic, and these are Obsidian fae."

"Give the woman a cookie."

"But wait, don't Moonstone and Ruby both trump Obsidian? So it should work."

"It might, if you knew what you were doing, which you don't."

She flipped the wand in her hand, thrusting it at him handle first. "Then you do it, Sorcerer Azul."

At least he took the wand, but he looked a little lost. The Obsidian fae miners had grown to bunny size, and had noticed the carriage chase down their road, several pointing, horned heads swiveling to watch. "What do you want me to do?" he asked, almost plaintively.

"I really don't care," she answered, trying not to snap at him. "Anything that gets us turned around and headed back to the Black Thirteen with skin intact, preferably with no more law hounds, well, hounding us."

"The ley line continues up the other side," he said, pointing helpfully at what she'd already noted.

"Yeah, and what are the odds it terminates in the glass castle of refining?"

"Pretty high," he admitted.

"Turning around it is." The bottom neared, the Obsidian fae the size of hip-high elflings now. "When I hit bottom—hopefully only literally and not figuratively this time—I'm going to spin Katu to face our pursuers. That will be your moment."

"My moment."

"To do your thang." She clapped him on his lean thigh, squeezing fast and removing her hand quickly before he could do it for her. "Dazzle me, my helpless and attractive bit of baggage."

By the time they hit bottom—literally and not figuratively, though the metaphorical variety might not be far behind—the Obsidian fae miners had grown to normal size. Half-again as tall as even Cha, who was no slouch in the height department, they were all charging towards Katu, brandishing various implements of volcanic-glass destruction.

As Cha had hoped, the ley line opened into a flat, wide area chock full of nicely charged pixie dust. The fae had none of the issues humans did with walking around on the stuff, and having it embedded in the very ground of the quarry likely helped the miners move stuff around. A number of enchanted vehicles of various kinds indeed scurried about, carrying loads of glistening black rock to bins or along the ley line that wound up the hill on the other side of the canyon.

Though the area teemed with equipment of all types, Cha knew her stuff and had just enough space to throw Katu into the promised one-eighty spin. As soon as he gained traction on the ley, he leapt forward with a predatory growl, heading straight for the unmarked carriage pursuing them.

Azul yipped, then shouted, "What are you doing?"

"Putting them off balance. Think fast."

They zoomed toward the still-descending law-hound carriage, accelerating despite the slope. Gotta love that pure dust for prime velocity. The fae carriage came around that last, hairpin switchback, and spotted Katu racing for them. A cloud of black pixie dust billowed up as they braked, and Cha cackled in glee, imagining their panicked expressions. "Eat me, you fae fuckers!" she yelled, goosing Katu faster.

Azul was making a high keening noise and—for a split second—she second-guessed giving him the wand. But he got ahold of himself, stood and aimed the wand at them, singing something in an astonishingly beautiful tenor voice, in a language she'd never heard. Pink glitter bloomed in the air around them, swirled menacingly in a way pink glitter never should, gathered itself, and arrowed at the oncoming carriage.

For a moment, nothing seemed to happen and Cha braced for a head-on collision. No way would she play the chicken and dive off the side. Only a courageous end for her. Then the glitter glommed onto the fae carriage, obscuring it in pink, then contracting. It narrowed to a pinpoint, then exploded into candy-pink vapor. It immediately cleared again, revealing a terrified zebra and two stunned Obsidian fae in the middle of the ley.

Well shit.

She didn't care about running over the fae, but the zebra was an innocent. It stood there frozen, legs splayed, muzzle down, staring with wide, shining black eyes at its onrushing demise. The fae had no such issues, scrambling over the side of the cliff and abandoning their poor, terrified beast, which only fueled her hate.

"Hang on," she told Azul, who groaned, sliding back into his seat.

"I'm beginning to hate that phrase, too."

She didn't answer, full concentration on Katu—and on hoping the zebra didn't panic and try dashing the wrong way. "Come on, baby cat," she murmured, and told him to leap.

Azul screamed thinly as Katu left the ley line, arcing to the steep cliff side rising above them. They collided with a rock outcropping—sending black glass shards flying—bounced off, and landed on the far edge of the ley line. Too far on that edge. They teetered for an endless moment, half the jag hanging over the drop, Azul clawing at the upholstery as if it could save him, before Katu found his footing, clawing at the ley line and heaving them solidly back to the meat of it.

They sped up the hill, Katu as happy as any of them to escape the sudden canyon of mining doom. In the rear view, the zebra shook its head, then trotted over to the side to grab a mouthful of scraggly foliage, as if nothing at all had occurred.

Very carefully, Azul tucked the magic wand into one of Katu's side pockets, letting out a long breath, saying nothing at all. Finally, as they made it to the top without further incident, coursing back toward the Thirteen, he took another breath, and said, almost philosophically, "I should have taken my chances with the fell wolves."

Saved by the Ambrosia Station

THEY MADE IT back to the Black Thirteen in good time. Dy had left in place the high white ley line she'd sorcelled up, thank the stars. Cha hadn't liked contemplating what they'd do if the rural ley petered out, or went in a different direction. With the map globe still on the fritz, she hadn't wanted to trust that the mine's ley line would take them to the Black Thirteen, instead of to, oh, a slaughterhouse for human cattle.

Azul would be fine in that case, but Cha had no desire to end up as a steak. Not that such things truly existed, but she'd seen enough dramas on the topic to want to avoid that particular fear.

But, all turned out fine and they made it intact. As it was, they were more than an hour behind Big Betty when they hit the junction and spun onto the Black Thirteen, traffic much more sparse as daylight faded and the bottleneck from the backed-up border had thinned out.

Like magic—ha!—the marcasite channel lit up at that moment. "Goldilocks here. Nearing the depot. Bandit, you close?"

Cha debated lying about it. On the one hand, knowing

they were so far behind her for the run around the depot would only send Dy into a frenzy of anxiety, which was never good for a sorceress who needed to keep a cool, clear head. On the other, Dy had that creepy, eyes-in-the-back-of-her-head maternal antennae for lies. She'd be angry at Cha for lying, and then anxious anyway when she dug the truth out. Cha sighed for her shitty luck so far.

"Bandit here. Good news is we stomped on that parasite that wanted in. Bad news is it took a while."

An ominous pause. "What's a while?"

"I'm back where I started. Sorry, babe."

An even longer, more ominous pause. "I hate you."

Azul tapped into the path-box. "Same, Goldilocks. Same."

At least Dy chuckled. "Prince Charming, do you swear on whatever you hold sacred that this delay was unavoidable and in service of the job?"

Cha groaned internally. Dy either had forgotten or didn't believe Cha's hints about Azul maybe having more fae blood than he should. The fae didn't take vows lightly. Odds were high he'd refuse to answer and, while that would be instruc-tive, that wouldn't help anything. "I already told you the truth," she inserted.

"I want it from a neutral third party."

"Hey," Cha protested. "Don't you trust your best friend?"

"No."

Azul gave her a sly half smile, indicating he was tempted to mess with her. Cha glared back, baring her teeth, promising painful vengeance. He shook his head in sorrow, pursing his lips in disapproval. That shouldn't have made her want to suck that lower lip into her mouth and bite it, but it did. What could she say? She was clearly a creature of her baser urges. They should all know that about her by now.

"I so swear," Azul said into the path-box. "We'll catch up in all haste."

"All right then," Dy said. "I'm back up to 36 minutes ahead of schedule. I'm going to juice up both Betty and me, let you get a bit closer for the depot. Don't fuck this up for me, Bandit. Goldilocks out."

"For *us*," Cha said to the silent path-box, then slid a glance at Azul. "This job is for both of us. And the kids."

"You have children?"

She barked out a laugh. "Me? Nooooo. Can you imagine me, responsible for keeping small humans alive?"

"Now that you mention it, absolutely not," he drawled, a hint of amusement in his voice. When she glanced at him, she caught a dimple in his cheek winking into existence like an evening star, though he still didn't crack an actual smile.

Declining to take the bait, she tapped the map globe. It swirled promisingly, then gave up a shower of sparks and went black. Not sparkly Obsidian-magic black, but dull, dead, giving-up-the-ghost black. "Great," she muttered. "I don't suppose you can fix that, Mr. Magic."

He gave the device a disdainful, narrowed look. "No. Who made that thing?"

"Some human mage. You know how it is for us, forever cobbling shit together out of fae scraps. Or *do* you know that?" she asked, pouncing.

It didn't work. He gave her a bland look. "As a royal, you

mean? No doubt our shit is higher quality."

"And it doesn't stink either, I'm sure," she shot back. "Are you ever going to tell me who you are?"

He leaned closer confidingly, even setting an elegant hand on her thigh. An unnatural heat flooded from that slight contact, rich indigo magic warming her blood and going straight to her groin. He caressed her thigh, slowly shaping the curve, going from knee to midway, teasing higher. The erotic punch surprised her, far more potent than such a relatively chaste touch should be. Was this how fae seduction felt? No wonder humans fell all over themselves to die for it.

"Oh, Arantxa," he murmured, bringing his lovely lips close to her ear, nearly brushing the sensitive shell of it, his breath warm and sweet, like berries in the sun. She leaned into him, inviting more, and he paused, mouth so close to kissing her. "Let me tell you," he whispered into her ear, "absolutely nothing at all."

She jerked an elbow at him, hoping to hit him painfully square in that enticing chest, but he evaded her, laughing. A real laugh and—like his lovely tenor singing voice—it sounded like bells on a holiday morning, clear and musical, pealing with the promise of something pure and real and not tainted with misery. "You're a right bastard," she told him, having to force the angry tone, as his laughing seemed to pull on her own, eroding her resolve to not smile.

Sobering, he touched a fingertip to his nose and pointed at her. Aha. A breadcrumb of information. A bastard, of human and fae blood, that much was certain, but weren't they all? No, he meant something much more relevant—that he was mostly fae? Perhaps gotten on the wrong side of the blanket. And who was this family that he'd alluded to? The fae tended to dump their partbloods into the human realm, but something about Azul made her think he'd grown up on the fae side of the fence.

She itched to ask the questions, but knew he wouldn't answer. Or couldn't, if she believed the geas thing, which she wasn't sure she did.

"Why did you want the map?" he asked, as if the interlude had never happened. "Isn't the depot right on the Black Thirteen?"

"It is." She contemplated the somewhat surprising fact that he knew that, then decided it was pretty obvious. Where else would one put a depot for transitioning goods traveling up and down the primary import/export route for the region? "I'm looking for an ambrosia station. Katu needs to fill up. Beats me why the fae can't use road signs like normal people."

"The fae have other ways of knowing."

"No doubt."

"I'd have thought you'd have planned for this eventuality."

"Some things you can't plan for. I know where the stations used to be, but it's been a couple of years and those things tend to move, except in the touristy areas, which I prefer to avoid. We could potentially get by, but I want to make sure we have plenty of juice to reach the depot and make the next BX."

"Do you know what you're getting into, over there?" he asked carefully. She almost thought he sounded concerned.

"I told you, we planned this. We're not amateurs."

"Where you're going is not hospitable to humans."

She raised her gaze to the seven heavens and their uncaring angels. "In the pithy words of my niece, Zazu: duh."

"You can't be caught there in the daylight," he persisted.

She waved her hand at the descending night. "Note the planning. Miraculously, it's night."

"There are other dangers."

"Why do you care all of a sudden?" she demanded, slanting him a glance.

He drew himself up stiffly. "I've realized how hapless you are. You don't even know where the ambrosia stations are in this realm."

"I know some of them. I just didn't expect to need a station this soon. Katu burned a lot of energy shaking that tail."

"Was it worth it?"

"Probably, but remains to be seen. The law-hounds—if that's who they were—shouldn't have picked up on us that fast. We were being good kitties. Nothing we did should've drawn attention."

"Besides bribing the border guards and agents to let you through."

She waved that off. "Yeah, but that's standard business, more or less." She glanced at him. "I mean, I've bribed my way over the border before."

"Color me unsurprised," he said drily.

"Exactly. The point there, also, is that if I'd triggered the fae law, they'd have been on my ass, not Big Betty's, see? And there's no reason the border should've been closed to begin with. They only do that if someone is running something they shouldn't."

"Which you are."

She stabbed a finger at the path-box, giving him the same arch look he'd given her. "No, we are not. Big Betty is running empty until we get to the depot. Then we're bringing back a perfectly legal shipment."

Letting his head fall back against the seat, he sighed. He sure looked edible like that, with his throat arched, the fluid lines of his collarbones framed by the winged, lacy collar of his white shirt. Cha allowed herself to savor the pussy sparkle he evoked. Even if she couldn't do anything about it, she could enjoy the sights.

"You lead a complicated life," he observed.

"Says the mysterious guy running from fell wolves, an iron demon, and a vengeful, potentially psychotic bride."

"Incorrect." He held up a finger. "A vengeful *fiancée*. An important distinction," he insisted when she snorted, "or I would be married and not hurtling on this wild ride through Obsidian with you."

"I guess it is your wedding night, huh? Not how you imagined spending it, I'll bet."

"No. Nor whom I imagined spending it with."

She very nearly apologized, but hauled the words back and jammed them down her throat. Sure, she wasn't some noble with sparkly fresh fae blood running through her veins. But she wasn't ashamed of who she was. Seven hells, she was the Bandit! Thousands cheered her name and emulated her style. And that was her authentic self. She wasn't some noble wannabe pretending to be something everyone figured was better than being human in stinking, mortal flesh. Fae weren't any better, just because they had magic. They wore meat suits, too, even if they did have a fancier variety that smelled like flowers or pastries and that lasted centuries longer. As Azul had pointed out, the fae could still be killed—it just took more work.

"What's she like?" Cha asked. "Besides psychotic." Yeah. She'd noticed that he'd left that part out of the descriptor.

He gave her a distracted, maybe confused look.

"The vengeful fiancée," Cha clarified. "We can call her VF, if you prefer. If you can talk about that part."

"Lenorae," he said, sounding faintly surprised. "It seems I can talk about at least her. And I wouldn't call her psychotic. At least, she never seemed so to me, or I wouldn't have agreed to marry her."

"You had a choice?"

"I had…a series of options and so, yes, chose her. I doubt she's behind sending the fell wolves after me. That would be her family and Lenorae might be as much a victim of their scheming as anyone."

Cha wasn't feeling charitable. Dy would be, but she had that soft heart while Cha's was hard as stone—and she didn't want to feel sorry for the woman. "So," she prompted, "what is this Lenorae like then?"

"She is…strikingly beautiful, naturally."

"Naturally," Cha echoed, restraining the urge to roll her eyes. If this Lenorae hadn't started out pretty, her family would've thrown money and magic at the problem until she emerged from their fabricated cocoon as the butterfly they figured they deserved—and could leverage to win them a mostly fae prince. That part almost might make her feel sorry for Lenorae, except for the hating her on principle. Cha would like to say she wasn't the jealous type—and typically she wasn't, generally happy to share the love—but what made this chick so special that Azul chose her out of a lineup when he clearly disdained all Cha had to offer? Yeah, she definitely hated this Lenorae.

"She's elegant, of course," Azul went on in a musing tone. "Perfect manners. Intelligent, very well educated. Witty, excellent conversationalist. Impeccable breeding. And she is…sweet. She has a gentle quality. Accommodating and graceful."

Let's just box her up and put on the shelf with a label saying "Perfect Woman," Cha thought viciously. But she managed to keep the snarky words from erupting from her big mouth. "She sounds like a yummy, candy-coated delight," she said instead, fully aware she wasn't being much less snarky—but then *she* was no perfect goddess—and wondering anew what happened to make Azul run from Miss Ideal Woman.

"Yes," Azul agreed absently, deep in thought. Or in delicious memories of his perfect fiancée. "I certainly thought so or, as I said, I'd never have chosen her, regardless of how my family—ah, there, I can't say more."

"Well, I'm sorry for your broken heart," Cha said, putting all her will into sounding sincere.

Azul glanced at her. "My broken—ah, no. No such thing, but…" He gave her a longer look. "You can't be jealous."

"No, I can't," she replied firmly. "Shows me for trying to be sympathetic."

"Arantxa," he began, "I—"

"Aha! An ambrosia station right over there."

Saved by the ambrosia station, in more ways than one.

~ 26 ~

True Lust's Kiss

Fortuitously, Cha spotted a roadside ambrosia station and pulled in, the place mostly deserted except for a couple of haulers. Evening had progressed enough that the tourists and joyriders had cleared out, leaving only the pros on the lines. She didn't recognize either of the male cargo jockeys, but she waved back companionably as Katu rolled onto the slow black and came to a halt.

Azul eyed them as he hauled himself out of the carriage. "More of your men in every port?"

"You can't be jealous," she taunted, throwing his words back at him and feeling ever so much better about herself.

"No," he answered on a sigh. "I can't."

Was it her imagination that he'd deliberately echoed her words, also, and that they carried a similar weight of regret?

Yes, Bandit, she told herself. *It is your imagination, so get a grip. You haven't mooned after an unattainable guy since Miss Mulry's and you're never going back to that pitiful state.* "Clear?" She rather snapped out the question, deciding not to tell Azul the truth, that she'd never seen either of those guys before in her life. Petty of her, but a girl had her pride.

He reached into the passenger seat and snagged the magic wand. "Now I am."

"Everything folds up in Katu when he changes," she explained. "You can leave that inside."

"You grabbed your sword," he pointed out.

"Force of habit—and you never know."

"Exactly," he replied, this time pitching his voice higher, clearly in imitation of her.

"You're not funny," she told him, triggering Katu to shift back to animal form. The carriage shimmered, clicking and condensing, until the black jaguar leapt onto the black grass, stretching and panting. She was glad she'd made the decision to stop. Katu looked parched and a little worn. She'd like to give him a rest, but that wasn't going to happen. "Come on, baby cat," she crooned, stroking a hand over his solid, glossy black head. "Let's get you fed."

Unlike Giant Jo's, this place had no restaurant, nor did it have—as she supposed was standard for the "we hate helpful signs of all kinds" fae—any posted rules. So, she left Katu off leash and guided him to the closest ambrosia station.

"Is that safe?" Azul asked, jutting his chin at Katu.

"Being off leash? Sure. Katu and I have been together since he was a kitten." She scratched behind his ears and he pushed his whiskers along her hand in affection. "He's my one true love." She waited for the scathing retort to that as she fumbled coins into the pump, swearing at the prices. But Azul said nothing.

As Katu eagerly drank, she stepped back and found Azul

leaning against a post with folded arms and crossed ankles, watching them intently. Her prince was always a broody one, but this felt different. "Something wrong?" she asked, not certain what that very serious expression meant.

His face cleared and he shrugged off whatever mood that had been. "I keep expecting fell wolves to emerge from the shadows. Or an iron demon. Or something even worse."

"There's worse?" she returned lightly.

"You don't want to know."

"Yeah, I probably don't. My motto in life is that I'm happier not knowing shit. Keep my eyes on my own work. Let the rest of the world take care of itself."

"Except for Dy and Katu."

"Even them. Katu is fine without me and Dy can take care of herself. She doesn't need me." Hadn't for years, which shouldn't sting. It was good that Dy had more people to look after her.

Uncomfortable with the conversation for no good reason, Cha checked the level in the trough. Katu still had a bit to go. She tapped a foot and crossed her arms, then felt like she was mirroring Azul, who still leaned against the post, observing her with that unnerving scrutiny, and uncrossed them again. She was restless to get going, that was the problem. Itching to get back on schedule. It had been ages since she'd been nervous around a boy and she sure wasn't relapsing to the bad old days.

"Can I ask you something, Arantxa?" Azul uncoiled from his lounging position and stepped closer to her. They hadn't spent really any time together when they'd both been standing up, and she realized now that he topped even her lanky height by half a head. For no good reason, her heart skipped several beats, then settled on a thudding, up-tempo rhythm that made her twitch inside her skin.

"I don't know why you're asking permission now—nothing seems to have held you back so far," she cracked, hoping to lighten the mood and lessen the tension. It didn't work.

"This is different. Personal. Important." He eased closer, that intent expression on his face stirring her blood to an even wilder temperature, a sultry hum in the air. "Intimate."

Well, shit. If he planned to ask what she thought—okay, *hoped*—he might, the timing stunk. She'd have to say no, since they had zero time for dallying, and she hated risking that he'd take the rejection badly. In Cha's experience, if you told a new guy 'no' once, even telling him 'later,' they got all butthurt and wrote you off. Sometimes, even the tried-and-true guys who should be reasonably sure you meant the 'later' in all sincerity still had hissy fits.

And none of this mattered, because there wouldn't be a later for Azul and her.

After she dropped him wherever he wanted to get to, they'd never see each other again. This could be her one chance to sample his sweet, deep blue delights and she had no choice but to bypass it. Being responsible sucked. She wanted to explain all of this to Azul, that she really wanted him, and not just as a temporary release, though that would be more than nice. But, wait, how *did* she want him then?

Well it didn't matter—see aforementioned imminent separation—and there wasn't any point in trying to explain any of this, especially since emotional competence wasn't her forte.

"So?" She drawled instead, emotionally incompetent jack-ass that she was. "Ask."

She'd meant to be all nonchalant, to soften the looming rejection she had to hand him, but apparently her body hadn't gotten the memo from her brain that they had to be responsible, because her voice came out breathy and her breasts rose and fell with excitement, very nearly brushing his spectacular chest that, in a fair world, she'd get to explore at leisure. But the world was very far from fair. She'd learned that young and shouldn't be forgetting it now.

He lifted a hand to feather fingertips along her cheekbone, surprising her with the gentleness of the sensual caress, delighting her that he was actually touching her, however chastely. Trailing his fingers along the sensitive skin on the underside of her jaw, he left sparking heat behind that burrowed into her system, frying it like pixie dust, but in a non-dead-soon way. Her heart thrummed like a hummingbird and the pussy sparkle leapt to life so hard she expected glitter to fly from her nethers.

"If I ask," he murmured, "do you promise to answer honestly?"

No amount of sensual allure could get her to agree to that. "Uh, no. Not until I hear the question."

Arrested, he stared at her, fingers still against her jaw, lifting her chin ever so slightly. "Seriously?"

"Hey, you just said you wanted honesty."

"Most women would just promise and then decide."

"Don't you mean most people?"

He canted his head, considering, then shook it. "I haven't had a lot of experience with broad swathes of…people."

Again, something in the way he said "people" made her think "humans." Instead of demanding to know just how fae he was, she asked, like a jealous bitch, "Just Lenorae?"

"And others of her…ilk."

Ilk. Interesting. "It's probably fair to say that I'm not like most people."

"No, you're not." His fingers tightened on her jaw and he searched her face. "Which I find oddly compelling."

Hoo boy. The pussy sparkle leapt like fireworks.

"All right then," he continued, still holding her jaw, hooded eyes drifting to her mouth. "I'm wondering, Arantxa, once this is done, would you consider…" He trailed off, his enticing lips hovering temptingly near. The scent of caramelized sugar and a hint of blueberry wafted around her in seductive tendrils. Not the sharp sweet of new blueberries, but the slow, lingering flavor of sun-warmed juices.

"Yes," she answered, not needing to hear the question. Her body closed the distance between them without her making a conscious decision, her lips seeking his with sensual hunger, pressing into him with aching need that blazed from smoldering coals to an inferno in the space of a thought. She threaded her hands behind his neck and into that deliciously silky hair, levering herself onto tiptoes to perfect the angle of the kiss. Even as she gloried in the taste of him—sizzling sugar browned hot enough to burn—she realized her mistake.

He'd stiffened in shock, not returning the kiss. How humiliating. She released him, words crowding to her tingling lips to form some kind of apology.

But—hallelujah!—he pulled her back via tightening fingers on her jaw. His other hand settled on her lower back, just above the curve of her ass, pulling her to him. He returned the kiss, as if answering a question she had asked, deepening it, opening his lips to hers and sweeping his tongue within as if tasting her, making a deep melodious sound like a growl.

He kissed her like a starving man, the hand on her hip vising into her flesh, sizzling into her bones, pressing her against his groin where he proved to be truly into her with impressive size and enthusiasm. Meanwhile, his lips on hers worked magic, richly, deeply stirring, slipping against hers with musical dexterity, a kiss like no other.

He felt slightly cool, as if he'd come inside from a winter storm, but the magic in him burned with sparking heat, the dual input frying her senses. She wanted that coolly sheathed heat all along her skin, inside of her, to writhe in wringing pleasure under him as he took her over and over again. Somewhere in the background, her newly minted responsible self shouted and banged its fists against the door of the closet her far more powerful, lustful self had shoved it into.

Katu sawed loudly, announcing that he was done with his meal, and head-butted her leg hard enough to make her stagger sideways, breaking the contact with Azul. Fantastic timing.

Actually, she realized, as she blinked away the sensual fog, seriously questioning all of her life choices—including a load of regret for both kissing Prince Charming and stopping kissing him in equal measures, which didn't help her mental clarity at all—it *had* been fantastic timing. Locating that mental closet where her responsible self sulked sullenly in the back of her mind, she unlocked the door and shoved her lustful self inside instead. A bit late and a lot painful, especially as her responsible self lit into an immediate tirade about Cha's many failings, while her lustful self wailed in frustrated disappointment.

"Both of you, shut up," she muttered under her breath. She couldn't win for losing.

"Arantxa?" Making her name into a question, Azul reached for her again and she forced herself to step back instead of climbing him like a tree. His face fell, briefly mirroring her own disappointment, then settled into rigid, brooding lines of his haughty expression that looked ever so slightly mean and turned her on even more. Dammitall.

"Katu's done," she said, pointing at the jaguar, in case Azul had forgotten the cat's name or something. "I hate to say no— only a temporary no," she hastily added, not that it would make any difference. "If that was the question," she added, belatedly and abashedly. Heat flooded her face, and not from desire, as he slowly shook his head from side to side.

"It… wasn't," he said, sounding like a man having the truth dragged out of him. "It didn't occur to me that you would—"

"Yes, well," she broke in, unable to bear it. "That's me. Impulsive. Man in every port, you know." She regretted that quip, too, as his expression shuttered.

"I know it doesn't mean anything to you," he offered, seeming like he was searching for the right words. "It's just that—"

"But it did," she insisted. "Because that was great. Really

great!" She searched her arousal-limp brain for a new, different, and better word. "Excellent!" So much for that effort. "I would absolutely be on board to keep going, but we're so lean on time that we should—"

"No, no. I understand." Azul interrupted her babbling and put even more distance between him and the crazy person. "Just as well."

Uh oh. "Just as well" was always a bad sign, though she could hardly blame him for thinking so, with her certifiable gushing. "We could pick up again later," she invited, hopefully enough that *that* sounded like a question.

He shoved his hands into his trouser pockets, looking off into some distance as they trotted back to the slow black. His white shirt had parted more—no doubt from her ravaging hands—and the lights of the ambrosia station made his skin gleam like pale blue moonlight. "No, it would be a bad idea. I had been thinking, but… no."

Cha restrained herself from suggesting a myriad of filthy things *she* had been thinking that perhaps had also been on his mind. "It's not a bad idea. It's a great idea," she insisted, really wishing the word "great" would stop coming out of her mouth. "It's just bad timing."

"It is bad timing—and I'm taking Katu's interruption as a sign," he replied grimly.

"It was a coincidence."

"There are no coincidences. Omens are important."

"You sorcerers and your omens," she grumbled.

"Only a non-sorcerer would dismiss the importance of such a precisely timed omen."

She couldn't think up an argument to that other than "nuh uh," which—aside from being pointless and juvenile—wouldn't be accurate, as it was true. Cha was always on the side of luck and coincidences, while Dy was forever chiding her for ignoring very real portents and omens. They'd been arguing about it since their school days and hadn't come to an agreement yet. Therefore, for once in her life, Cha seized the opportunity to keep her mouth shut and not dig herself in deeper.

She still had time and opportunity to make "later" happen. At least now she knew Azul wanted her as much as she wanted him. If Cha knew nothing else, she knew how to rig the game to win. She wasn't a champion for nothing, especially when the prize was so very enticing.

She could still win this one. She just had to find the path no one else had.

~ 27 ~

Prince Charming Has Left the Building

Reaching the slow black, Cha gave Katu a last round of chin skritches and kissed him on the head, murmuring to him what a good kitty he was, then sent him back into carriage form.

"Speaking of being a sorcerer," she said to Azul, as they both slid into their seats and he carefully re-holstered the magic wand, in neat tandem with her stowing her sword, "back at Giant Jo's, you didn't need the wand. You hurled those sparkly blueberry fireballs on your own, without any assistance. Or singing."

"And look how well that turned out," he replied grimly. "If not for your rescue, I'd even now be married to Lenorae and—" He waved a hand in place of words when his voice abruptly choked off.

"Why don't you have a lodestone?" it occurred to her to ask.

"I don't need one."

Very clipped answer from the broody prince. She could only hope he wrestled the same sexual frustration plaguing her. They glided with maddening slowness back to the Black Thirteen.

"Dy has one," she said conversationally. No big deal. Just chatting. No way was she going to sit in silence and think about that kiss while he ignored her. "A lodestone, that is. His name is Warg. Nothing attractive about the creature, but she's attached to him. And, obviously, as a *human* sorceress, she needs him to work magic without frying her brains." She let that dangle meaningfully.

He gave her a long, cool look. "What are you implying?"

"I'm just saying."

"Seven hells," he bit out.

"You can trust me," she insisted, watching the oncoming traffic, thinking his curse was for the proof she'd thrown in his lap that he was far more fae than he'd made himself out to be. That was the only explanation for his being able to work native magic without a lodestone. She eyed a substantial caravan of big rhino rigs, waiting for them to lumber past before she released Katu to climb the ramp, and told herself she wasn't being a hypocrite by using those words with him when she'd given that little speech on trust being earned.

"Not that," he spat. *"That!"*

She followed his pointing finger in the other direction and goggled. The landscape just beyond the ambrosia station seemed to be crawling toward them. "What is—"

"Demons," he answered before she even finished. "Ginger imps. And, call me paranoid, I believe they're headed for me. Go."

They would have to be on slow black when the ginger

imps attacked. Famous last words coming back to bite her in the ass. Despite the rhino blockade, she pushed Katu forward as fast as the side ley would take them, which was still slower than they could walk. Once she hit the fast black, she could dodge and weave around the caravan, though there'd be some hurt feelings. Better than dead-them though.

"Faster," Azul demanded, a hint of real fear in his voice.

"I *can't* go faster on the slow black," she said through her teeth. "Got to get to the on ramp."

"I could run faster than this," he said with even greater urgency.

"Yeah, but could you run faster than *them*?" She jerked her head at the onrushing imps, gaining with unnatural speed.

"You have a point."

"So do you," she conceded, eyeing the chittering mass of toothy demons in the rear view and using her expert eye to gauge the time to the faster black and their getaway. "We're not going to make it. Use the wand."

"Won't work," he gritted out, hands on the dash as if he could push Katu faster. "Ginger imps are Cinnabar magic."

She didn't ask how he knew—though in the rear view she supposed she could make out a distinctive burnt-orange glow to the creatures. Katu snarled, unhappy, clawing up the slow black, the fast black glowing so tantalizingly close, much too far to help them. "I thought Ruby trumps Cinnabar."

"Not when it's mitigated by Moonstone," he replied tersely, straining in his seat.

Cha had a brief moment of wrestling herself, though it didn't take much, even if her lustful self had somehow escaped her prison and had edged up beside her responsible self again, whispering naughty suggestions in her ear. They agreed on at least this one decision, uncharacteristically self-sacrificing though it may be. "I won't blame you if you want to run," she said, restraining a sigh, hoping he'd nobly refuse to leave her.

No such luck. He levered out of the seat, vibrating in cobalt agitation to run. Then paused.

"Come with me." He held out a hand to her. "I can get us both away."

She didn't ask the how on that, either. She believed him. She longed to take that hand.

She shook her head. "I can't leave Katu."

He nodded, unsurprised. "I'll draw them off, you should be fine."

"Wait—how will you get to your own BX?"

"I can find a way from here. Do I have to tell you to keep this safe?" He handed her the wand.

"I handled myself before you came along. I can handle things from here."

"Just, be careful, over there," he said, jerking his head in the direction of Moonstone.

"My middle name. Good luck resolving your marital woes."

Hesitating a long extra second, his blue gaze bored into hers. "Goodbye Arantxa."

And he was gone.

IT WASN'T THE lingering, romantic—or at least frustrated-lust-filled—farewell that Cha might've envisioned in her more idealistic moments. But it was probably for the best. Sharp and quick, like pulling the dagger out of your back.

Besides, they'd had no time for anything more.

Prince Charming had left her as if the demon spawn of the seven hells were on his heels—which, in this case, was almost literally true. True to his promise, the horde of ginger imps diverted, running in a smoldering red-orange river after him. Unfortunately, a few of the less bright imps leapt onto Katu anyway. They were mostly big mouths on spindly, claw-tipped limbs, and they chomped down with rows of serrated teeth on the first soft surface they could find.

Katu yowled in pain and protest, the carriage shimmering unsteadily as he instinctively tried to shift into his native form to fight back.

"Hold steady, baby cat," Cha urged, trying to sound soothing. The enchantment should hold Katu in carriage form, but sometimes the animal instinct overrode even fae magic. The last thing she needed was for them to take a spill on the verge of fast black. "I'm here for you," she added, as she pushed to her feet in the driver's seat. She didn't need a magic wand; she had her trusty sword. As it should be: Katu and her, a forever loyal pair. She wouldn't forget her priorities again.

She impaled a growling, munching, now squealing imp. The sword went right through it and the imp reached for her with weirdly long limbs, burnt-orange claws flexing as it shrieked and flailed on the sword. With distaste, Cha used a booted foot to slide it to the end, then whipped the sword like a slingshot to hurl the creature onto the fast black, where a ponderous rhino promptly ran it over, mashing it into the sifting pixie dust. Too bad that wouldn't be enough to fry the nasty imp, but it should work to slow it down. Hopefully long enough for Katu to be far away before it extracted itself.

She dealt the same treatment to the other three imps, counting her blessings that they hadn't been smart enough to turn on her *en masse*. She'd had enough of being chewed on for the next little while. By the time she'd dispatched her lot, Katu—calm again and focused on the task—had crawled up to the Black Thirteen, idling in wait for her go ahead. She slid back into her seat, and jabbed the gold channel into life. "Bandit here. Who's riding the rhino train by the ambrosia station on the Black Thirteen?" She hoped that would be enough detail. How many rhino trains in receiving distance could there be?

"Ho there, Bandit, this is Wailing Jenny. That you hurling toothy comets at us?"

"Apologies for that. I'll make it up to you. Can you give me a gap to get on and get going?"

"I'm holding you to that make-up gift. I like Amethyst wine." Cha rolled her eyes at that hint. A pricey apology. "Here's your window of opportunity," Wailing Jenny added, and the nose-to-tail rhino rigs parted, just wide enough for a sleek jag like Katu to slip through.

Cha barely had to prompt Katu to go—he leapt for the opening with fury and enthusiasm, more than happy to escape the place where those awful imps had dared to nip at him. He darted through the space Jenny had made for him and passed the laden beasts easily, pouring on as much speed as the Black Thirteen would allow. Checking the time, Cha verified that it would be tight, but she'd make it to the rendezvous with Dy and Big Betty at the depot, with a bit to spare. Then she'd have Dy's assist again, to power past the depot, over the border to meet their Moonstone contact, and out again to blaze back home with the prize.

All still according to plan, more or less. Minus a sexy fae prince or two.

It was only after a few minutes of cruising clear, the night wind ruffling her hair, Katu settling from his scare as he burned off the adrenaline in speed, that it hit Cha: Azul had taken off without giving her the platinum coin.

"Lost the boy *and* the coin," she muttered. "Doesn't it just figure."

THE LIGHT TRAFFIC had lightened even more, the Black Thirteen narrowing to a single lane, as they neared the depot. It was a big, sprawling complex, mostly horizontal, with none of the stereotypical fae spires and towers. That was because humans had helped to design the thing, optimizing the structure for the relay of Obsidian exports. It was a rare example of fae-human collaboration, practically a historical monument, and had an actual guided tour and gift shop.

The fae also imported goods from the higher fae realms and funneled those through the depot and into the human realms. A much smaller volume of human-realm stuff went through in the other direction to the fae that handled distribution from there. The fae-element of the design made the complex look like a glittering starfish, if a starfish had more than five arms and was encrusted in gems.

The design of the Black Thirteen, which terminated at the depot, played a role in slowing the transports, taking them from cruising speed to a more leisurely approach in the single lane, before splitting off into smaller, slow black ley lines that conveyed them to various arms of the starfish, according to the nature of their business.

On the far side of the complex, a smaller section handled the relay of the few human-realm imports the fae actually wanted, with a ley line leading from there to lines that splintered off to parts unknown in Obsidian. One fat ley shot straight for the distant, opalescent glow of Moonstone and beyond. That was the ley they wanted.

Someone had been clever in the depot's design, with all the cargo transfer handled inside the building, which meant no ley lines connected from the human-facing side to the Moonstone-facing side. A nicely passive obstacle to the law-abiding, but not insurmountable for the wily smugglers. Dy hadn't invented the trick of creating ley lines to bridge normally unbridgeable distances. Plenty of smugglers before them had found ways to manipulate the magic to circumvent that simple obstacle. No, Dy hadn't originated the workaround, but she was the queen at this game.

Cha and Dy had maintained path-box silence, as the law-hounds would be listening in on depot-related chatter if they could be. They didn't need to talk through this part through anyway, as they'd run the depot countless times. Cha spotted Big Betty at one of the pixie-dust export arms, getting loaded with their decoy shipment of black dust. Hopefully that part of the plan was going smoothly, anyway.

Cha motored off onto a side ley that led to a small village that served the depot tourists and traffic. And, not incidentally, hosted a robust smuggling trade for those small-time crooks who couldn't manipulate ley lines. A number of inns and larger hotels formed the outer ring, in varying degrees of faux-fae style. On the plainer end were the places that served the transport riders—functional, some nicer than others, but all geared toward the comfort of regular human people with no fae-wannabe aspirations.

For the tourists, bigger resorts sparkled with lights positioned around fanciful parklands and pools, their towers spiraling up in twists of rainbow color. Between the two, a picturesque village sat, with torchlit, cobblestone streets bordered by shops and restaurants glowing with fae lights. Cha sat in the slow-black parking lot—threaded through with human-safe walkways in iridescent white stone, so it looked uncomfortably like a vast spiderweb to her jaundiced eye—and waited for the minutes to tick by until the rendezvous with Dy and Big Betty.

With nothing else better to do, and determined not to moon over Azul and that bone-melting kiss, she concentrated on the people strolling through the village like it was her job to keep an eye on them. Many wore costumes, playing at being fae for the night, with pointed ears and transparent wings. Some even had kids with them, she noted, to her disgust, acting like they were frolicking in some amusement park and not in a literal fae realm where actual monsters lived that loved to snack on the small and vulnerable.

Not her problem. Served those parents right, really. Maybe if the children got munched, then the stupid would die out from that branch of the human race before it could go any further. Cha caught herself on that at best uncharitable, at medium bitter, and at worst truly monstrous thought and had to recognize her foul mood. Losing a shiny platinum coin and the shiniest pussy sparkle she'd experienced in a considerable amount of time would do that to a girl.

But soon she'd be rich beyond her wildest dreams. The prospect should have brightened her more than it did. They'd be on the move soon, and that would occupy her attention. No time for moping when she was riding for a fortune. Coin was better than pussy sparkle any day. Only a few more minutes and Big Betty would be pulling out and they'd be onto the next—

"Seven hells!" she swore. A little kid—decked out like one of the Amethyst fae, entirely in purple, with wings, horns, pointed ears, and a second pair of arms flapping beneath the wings—scampered away from the village and into the shadowed meadow beyond the parking and hotel area. Cha waited a moment longer, with an attitude too cynically edged to be called hopeful, for the kid's parents to wake up and give chase.

No such luck.

"Dy is so going to kill me," she observed, trying to recall how many deaths at Dy's furious hands that made on this gig alone. Even Cha probably didn't have that many lives left. Sword in hand, she vaulted from the jag, leaving Katu idling at a purr, and raced down the network of shimmering paths toward the fading purple blur.

Of course the pathways weren't a straight line shot. Set up to be stupidly fanciful and as twisted as fae hearts, they curved through pretty statuary of the cutesy versions of monsters, like fauns and mermaids, then split again to fan into smaller lines between each parking spot before coalescing again. Probably people on vacation enjoyed the meandering maze of pathways; for someone with a ticking clock who needed to get to a nummy tidbit of a human kid before whatever fae monster luring it got to swallow them, it sucked mightily.

Finally, Cha made it to the shadowed meadow, beyond relieved to be able to step onto solid ground instead of dancing around between brain-frying pixie dust islands. In the darkness, she couldn't make out the bouncing purple blob. She did, however, pick up the sound of a pretty, tinkling bell and Cha's already pounding heart skipped a few beats, feeling as if it dropped into her stomach.

"Fuck!" She picked up speed. Behind her, in the village, someone started shouting in alarm. "Glad you finally noticed," Cha hissed at the unknown parent.

The sound of the bell—so lovely and compelling, even to her, who knew better—grew louder. She put on a last burst of speed.

Which meant she nearly crashed head on into the Eloko.

~ 28 ~

Sweet Silver Bells

IT WASN'T TERRIBLY large, the Eloko being members of the gnome family, but no less terrifying for that. Covered in grass instead of hair, creatures of its ilk loved meadows like this. It held the little bell, still tinkling attractively in one clawed paw, and embraced the happily wriggling child in the other. The kid, fully under the spell of the bell, giggled merrily as the Eloko licked their face, pointed teeth ringing a circular jaw widening to swallow the kid's head as its eyes burned like coals latching onto dry kindling.

Just fantastic.

Cha didn't waste time telling the monster to drop the kid—it didn't understand words and wouldn't relinquish its meal even if it did—and that cursed bell was sounding better to her every second. In a few more moments, Cha would be snuggling up to be the next meal. Going for the most efficient shortcut, Cha used the momentum of her run, swung the sword at the Eloko, and chopped off the hand holding the bell.

It gave a last jangle and fell to the ground. The spell broken, Cha's head cleared. The kid, who might be naïve but wasn't an idiot, began screaming, and the Eloko shrieked in pain, spurting blood the color and consistency of mud. The latter didn't last long, as Cha carried through the counter swing to sever the Eloko's other arm while it was distracted by losing the first, separating it from the kid, who fell to the ground like the bell. Instead of jangling, however, the kid burst into tears and began crying for their parents.

The Eloko fastened glowing red eyes on Cha and waved the stumps of its arms, clearly not quite comprehending that it had lost its primary weapon, the bell useless in the grass. Torches and shouts heralded the approach of humans combing the meadow, calling the kid's name. The kid, bedraggled, covered in muck, screamed back. Cha slashed the sword at the Eloko, who cringed, then turned and ran. Just as well. It would be harmless without its bell. Possibly it would grow a new one? Cha didn't know and didn't much care. This was the Eloko's territory, after all, and it wasn't the creature's fault that stupid humans had dropped a tasty treat in its lap.

"Bartholomew!" A person—possibly the dad—arrived with torch in hand, decked out as an Obsidian fae, complete with bat wings and horns so tall and twisted that, if they were authentic instead of hollow fakes, they'd topple a real fae. "What did you do?" he demanded, thrusting the torch at Cha like *she* was the monster.

This was why she had a non-interference policy. The kid—Bartholomew, apparently—wailed louder and launched themselves at the man, crying "Daddy!"

Cha pointed her sword at the bell. "Eloko," she said by way of explanation.

"I don't even know what that means and I see only you here," the man spat, hampered by Bartholomew, who seemed intent on climbing the man's body.

"It's a fae monster," she said, wondering why she bothered. "You're in a fae realm, not an amusement park. You shouldn't let your kids wander."

"How dare you tell—"

"Don't touch that bell," she advised. "I've got an urgent appointment." Before the stupid human could aggravate her further, Cha took off running.

She was going to be so late.

"YOU ARE SO late!" Dy hissed as Cha and Katu pulled up beside Big Betty on the little used side ley that was their longtime rendezvous point. "I don't even want to hear your excuses."

"Good thing, cuz I don't have any," Cha replied. "Only a sincere apology."

Dy, who'd been pacing the adjacent walkway, arms folded and golden curls flying in a magical wind, whirled and paused, narrowing her eyes as she surveyed the empty passenger seat. "What happened to Prince Charming?"

"Easy come, easy go," Cha answered nonchalantly. "And no," she hastened to add when Dy's glare turned even more suspicious, "there was no coming. No hanky or panky. We were attacked by Cinnabar imps and he drew them off. Besides, the deal was that I'd get him across the Obsidian border and now he's on his own." Doing whatever he did when he wasn't running from vengeful fiancées.

Dy sniffed. "You don't smell like imp. That's Eloko blood."

"Really? Dammit." She surveyed herself, realized she still had the jacket unbuttoned so as to show off her cleavage, and corrected that. No one to entice now. Alas for that. "I thought I avoided the spew."

"Why were you fighting an Eloko?" Dy asked on a sigh.

"Long story and we're running late. We need to go."

Dy shook her head. "Running *too* late. We can't make the turnaround now."

"Sure we can. Moonstone is right there and our rendezvous not that far past the border." Cha checked the clock. "Only 45 minutes behind. We can make that up."

"And if we don't?" Dy demanded. "If we fail to make Otto's deadline, then we forfeit everything. Big Betty is loaded with crates of pure black dust. Why not run it back now—perfectly legal—and take what bank we can?"

This again? Cha wasn't sure why Dy kept wavering in her resolve, but clearly the last pep talk hadn't stuck. She raked a hand through her short hair and climbed out of Katu. "Let's say we do," she offered agreeably. "You really think Otto will give us any payment out of this decoy shipment? We could end up with no pay, out the gems I already spent on bribes, plus the other coin we've already spent, and you're minus a day-job to boot."

Dy blew a golden curl out of her eyes, glaring in mutiny. "Which is all your fault."

"You know what, Dymphna?" Cha countered, surprising herself with her sudden anger. "I've had enough of this. You could have said no. At any point when we discussed this, you could have turned me away—as I might point out you've done plenty of lately—and kept me cut out of your nice, cozy, happy life. I offered you something more. Doing something you *used* to love that would have the delicious side benefit of getting your family out of a financial jam.

"Fine if you want to bail on this gig and slink home with your tail between your legs. I'm glad you have someone to go home to. Believe me, I am so happy for you. But don't you dare blame this on me. I'm here. I'm ready to go and do this thing. You've asked me to make promises to you that I'll come through on. I did and I have. I've *never once* bailed on you. But Dy, you bailed on me. You turned your back on me and cut me out of your life like something disgusting you needed to scrape off your shoe."

Dy had paled, gaping at her, and Cha was surprised to find herself shaking with emotion. She had no idea where all that emotional vomit had come from. "Never mind," she bit out, waving it off as if to clear the bitter words from the air. "I've had enough of this shit. Let's just go home."

"Wait. Cha." Dy put a hand on her arm, holding her back. "I didn't know you felt that way."

"Oh yeah? How *did* you think I felt? Is that something you actually thought about?"

Dy shrugged helplessly, her hair no longer dancing with magic, but flattened with unhappiness. "I thought you were happy," she answered in a small voice. "You're the one leading the glamorous life, with the racing and your adoring fans and hordes of pretty men falling at your feet. You're not the one with the stupid corporate job, diapers to change, and snotty kids bickering at each other day in and day out."

"I thought you were happy, too," Cha said, more than a little chagrined.

"I am happy," Dy insisted. "That's just day to day shit. I have what I want and I thought you did, too."

"I didn't have you," Cha said quietly. "I just never thought there would come a day that we stopped being friends."

"I thought I was too boring for you," Dy admitted, tears swimming in her big blue eyes. "I didn't want to be the domestic stone around your neck."

"Oh honey." Cha pulled her into an embrace. "Never. You're my favorite person. And I love my snotty, bickering nieces and nephews. After the chicken incident and Phin was so mad... I thought you didn't want a bad influence around your kids."

"Phin worries," Dy agreed, "but even she didn't mean for you to stay away for so long. You're part of the family, Bandit."

"You know that you're the only family I've got." She braced herself, as heartfelt confessions really weren't her thing. "I guess I've been lonely."

"Oh, honey, I feel terrible." Dy sniffled against her. "I guess we should've talked. Why is that always the answer and also always what we don't do?"

"Yeah, well, water under the bridge, Goldilocks." Cha stepped back and tugged one of Dy's spiraling curls as she said it. "We have a decision to make right now. Go forward or go back? I believe we can still make the turnaround, but not if we keep burning our time. We'll soon hit the point of no return."

"And we're out of time to rescue Monat," Dy said on a sigh.

"Not necessarily." Cha considered, wondered if she'd kick herself for this later. She should wake up and smell the Eloko blood, most likely. Heroics were for suckers. But Dy was more important than the rest. "Our gig relies on you getting Big Betty back with the shipment," she pointed out. "Otto will pay you whether I'm there or not. Once we meet the contact in Moonstone, you can hightail it back to Rockton. I can see you clear over the border, then circle back to grab Monat."

Dy hesitated, clearly torn. "You would do that?"

"Just said so, didn't I? But it means you would be on your own. If we go now, you should be able to travel back at legal speeds, but you'd have zero margin for mistakes or hang ups."

"I can handle that part, but…." Dy put a hand on Cha's arm. Squeezed lightly, her magic effervescent and calmingly familiar as the hug had been. "I don't want you to risk yourself."

"You know I'm too selfish to do that," Cha cracked.

"Right." Dy dropped her hand and planted fists on her hips, all annoyed mama now. "What I do know is you'd only have fought an Eloko if some kid needed rescuing."

Cha snorted. "Seriously? Better to clear the gene pool of the idiots, I say."

Dy gave her a knowing look. "You call me a softy, but I know you, Arantxa Evermore."

Cha clapped a hand to her heart. "Not the full name! Please, I cry uncle." It made Dy laugh, but that heart Cha wished wasn't quite so soft panged at the sound of her name, Azul's voice speaking it in that caressing way echoing through her mind, her lips burning with the memory of that kiss. Any minute now, he'd leave her thoughts and quit haunting her. He was like that Eloko, a fae creature with an alluring magic trick. *Son of a Bitch.* Had Azul used enchantment on her? Seduced by the fae was such a tired old tale, but she clearly wouldn't be the first of her family line to fall for that silver bell of adventure sex.

"We go," Dy said, breaking into her thoughts that jangled like the silver bell hitting the ground, and—fortunately—bringing her back to the moment. "If you can get to Monat, great," Dy continued, "but only at no risk to yourself."

"Yippee!" Her cheer sounded hollow even to herself. Spinning on her heel, Cha headed for the purring Katu. "Let's ride." She pumped a fist in the air, trying to be her old self again, not quite sure where she'd left it.

"Cha," Dy called after her, not yet moving. "I'm sorry about Prince Charming, whatever happened there." The sorceress always did read her too well.

"Not a thing," Cha replied with forced cheer. "In every sense." She hopped into Katu and pulled out, waiting for Dy to lay them a line through the dark to the ley to Moonstone.

And told herself she didn't miss the broody prince. Not one bit. No way could you miss someone you'd known for all of five hours.

"Easy come, easy go," she chanted under her breath, willing herself to believe it. Maybe repetition would work to break the spell. Soon she'd have forgotten all about him, except as a colorful footnote on the greatest haul of their lives.

~ 29 ~

Through the Veil of Stone

WARG WARBLED FROM Big Betty's open windows as Dy anchored her ley magic to him, her sorcery dense in the air like the smell of ozone before a lightning strike. Though the sorceress had done this part any number of times, it still required finesse, creating a whole ley line where one not only hadn't been before, but wasn't supposed to be. The fae authorities weren't fools. Far from it. They knew smugglers used temporary ley lines to circumvent the depot and its customs agents, and they'd enchanted the ground all around to prevent the creation of new ley lines.

That was one of the many reasons Dy was the best—she could outpower that enchantment. But it required a sizeable portion of her magic plus unbroken concentration to focus on keeping it all circumscribed so as not to trip any magic-sensitive alarms and alert the fae. To get the job done, Dy and Cha needed fast, but they also needed discreet. Too much power tended to radiate increased magic along several dimensions not detectable to human senses.

Other magic-workers could create new ley lines, and obviously did, as Bandit and Goldilocks were far from the only smugglers out there—and likely quite a few teams had cropped up to take advantage of the lucrative business Cha and Dy had abandoned—but Cha seriously doubted any had tried to connect to the Moonstone Throughway. Instead, they'd done what Cha and Dy had always done before—created short hops of ley lines to meet up with their fae counterparts off in the backwoods beyond the faux fae village and other rural areas around the depot. The area was littered with clandestine meeting points, some shrouded in permanent enchantments to hide them from all but the key players. Dy and Cha had one of those on the far side of the depot, a snug little hidey-hole that would hopefully still be there for them to use on the return trip, if necessary.

For this gig, though, they needed something different. The ley line Dy spun out from her core of magic was created by her from beginning to end. She wasn't moving a nearby line or modifying one of the many natural ley lines most landscapes boasted. The Obsidian fae had chosen this plain for the depot deliberately, because it was mostly void of natural magic and any ley lines that had built up over time in the eternal struggle of life to prevail had been ruthlessly destroyed. That told you a lot about the fae, right there.

Also, unlike most middle-tier smugglers, Dy would create a ley line much longer than the typical short spur, this one curving well around the busier areas of the depot before connecting to the major fae artery where humans really weren't supposed to be.

It was painstaking work and Cha kept alert for any signs of

interruption that could fatally break Dy's concentration and leave her too depleted to begin again. With her own ley-rider magic, Cha sensed the line running out through the dark, narrow and precise. It was almost like that falsely fragile looking ley line from the racecourse, though even more tenuous-seeming on the surface. But Dy's work was gold. She hadn't cratered a ley line yet. Tonight would not be the first time. It looked barely there from above, to hide it from notice, but it would be solid beneath.

Dy's illusion magic settled over them like the shroud they needed, and Cha sent Katu purring along Dy's newly created line. Confident in the road ahead, they took the lead—as point, scout, decoy, and canary in the coal mine—showing Big Betty the way. Ironic that Dy could create and move ley lines at will, but her ability to follow and ride them lagged well behind Cha's. Yet another reason they made a great team.

They coursed along in the pitch dark, no distinctive ley-line glow to light their way, only Cha's ley-rider expertise keeping them from stumbling off the fine, nearly invisible line. Big Betty a lumbering shadow behind them, mostly distinguishable as a blacker silhouette against the star-laden sky, Katu cruised forward, following Dy's magic with the familiarity of lovers holding hands.

Bad analogy. For the umpteenth time, Cha scrubbed thoughts of Azul from her mind and focused on the notably dangerous task at hand. The only division of her attention she allowed herself was keeping an ear out for sounds of alarm from the depot.

But it was quiet. Not *too* quiet—perfect quiet. Almost serene as they glided soundlessly, lightlessly through the night. Up ahead, the Moonstone Throughway glowed with opalescent brilliance, thanks to the high-quality moonstone pixie dust used to construct and stabilize the big ley line. Though Cha narrowed her eyes to scan along the shimmering length of it, she didn't see any traffic. They'd chosen this timing to hit the thoroughfare when hopefully few, if any vehicles would be on it. Dy could disguise them to some extent, but her illusions could only stand up to so much scrutiny, especially by the magical fae, well experienced in constructing and penetrating glamours of all types.

It made her wonder how much of Azul's appearance had been fae glamour. Very few humans could see through a well-constructed glamour, and Cha wasn't one of them. Neither was Dy for that matter, as her talents, exceptional as they were, lay in a different area. Her illusions came from bastardized human magic, whereas fae glamour was—something else entirely. So, Azul, with his cryptic hints and hiding behind this supposed geas that kept him from telling her much of anything at all, could have been—

"Dammitall," she bit out—albeit quietly and under her breath. "*Not* thinking about him, remember?"

Fortunately, for her peace of mind if nothing else, Dy's ley line pulsed gently into the Moonstone just ahead. This part would be a bit tricky. To keep their improvised route unnoticeable, Dy had kept it very low test, gathering black pixie dust from landscape, which meant it was low quality, unrefined, and full of inclusions. That helped the ley line blend in better, and it was what she had to work with, but that meant they'd been going dead slow. Not as slow as slow black, but far below the velocity of that pure, high-test Moonstone white ahead.

Though Cha had, of course, ridden white-infused pixie dust ley lines many times before, she and Katu had never experienced a pure, fae-constructed white line. She suspected it would feel like being launched to the moon and she thrilled to the new challenge. As long as they could navigate that big bump from dirty Obsidian background dust to high-test Moonstone white, they'd be rocketing along and gliding toward the border.

The junction hit hard—even harder than she expected—nearly jolting Katu off the lines entirely. He growled, fighting for purchase, as the Moonstone dust threatened to spin them off into a trajectory of doom. Cha had little time to hope Dy had observed their difficulty and would be able to hold Big Betty through the substantial punch, as she reached through Katu and wrestled the Moonstone magic, helping him adapt to the sheer power of the thoroughfare.

Then the flow of the Moonstone had them in its grip, and Katu surfed it, his excitement palpable, and Cha held on, the pair of them screaming through the night, faster than they'd ever gone.

Once she felt certain Katu had it under control, Cha risked a glance back at Big Betty. The elephant carriage followed close behind, looking unruffled by the speed or the rough transition. In the cab, Warg, swollen with the magic he was grounding, nearly glowed in a most unlovely way, his violet polka dots larger than usual and radiating into a spectrum she couldn't entirely see. He'd pressed his snout up against the clear windscreen, slobber falling from his long tongue in enthusiastic drops. Dy was frazzled, her corkscrew curls nearly white in the reflected light, and standing out like a halo all around her head. She looked like a tormented angel, which really wasn't far off the mark. More than once some wit had described Cha as the devilish accomplice to Dy's angelic loveliness. Fair enough, but that didn't account for Dy's demonic streak.

Reassured that Big Betty had the Moonstone speed handled and that Dy remained strong and steady in the seat—critical for her being able to maintain the illusion cloaking them—Cha watched for any traffic or other obstacles and bent her attention to the upcoming border.

To all accounts, and naturally there weren't many of those, the Obsidian/Moonstone border wasn't guarded and blockaded like the ones from Obsidian to the human realms. It kind of bent Cha's brain to try to understand how the physics worked—blame magic there—but Moonstone nestled entirely within Obsidian, like a pit inside an avocado, only it managed to have as much land or more. Outside the avocado lay the human realms, like an ugly rind, she supposed. Inside Moonstone lay Citrine, entirely encapsulated, also without being any smaller. And so on, with each realm up to Ruby, nestled in the center like a compressed jewel no human could comprehend.

Moonstone held considerable mystery, but humans *had* been there. Mostly envoys of nobles being entertained by high fae, lesser cousins left as ambassadors to emerge years later with no memory of their time behind the Moonstone veil.

Otherwise, the humans entering and returning from Moonstone fell into two groups: the legitimate business entrepreneurs and the smugglers.

Neither of which traveled this particular trade road. It was a gamble to run the border this way—the sort of calculated risk Bandit and Goldilocks had built their fame on, and the sort Otto had hired them for—and Cha only hoped they'd planned it correctly. This border wasn't guarded or blockaded because it didn't need to be. The natural veil that separated the fae realms from one another took care of that.

And it loomed now on the horizon, drawing closer with daunting speed, as if a massive predator raced toward them, even though Cha knew in her head that they were the ones moving. It glowed white, curving away like a sphere, blocking all sight of anything on the other side.

Going into that apparently solid wall looked so much like recklessly barreling into certain death that Cha could barely override the fear in her animal self and still maintain calm confidence in Katu. The jaguar had to sense her trepidation, but he rushed forward without hesitation, trusting her utterly. Cha closed her eyes, since they only fed her instinctive panic about looming disaster. She didn't need sight to follow the ley line streaming clear and fast through the wall, and she certainly didn't need to be any more afraid.

Telling Katu all was well, hoping she wasn't lying to him and getting all four of them killed—five, if you counted Warg—Cha led them straight into the big white wall protecting Moonstone.

~ 30 ~

Death and Beauty

I T HURT.

It hurt beyond what Cha could have mentally prepared for, even if she'd taken those fairytale warnings seriously. It hurt on a level beyond nerve endings and tissue damage. She felt as if she'd been turned inside out and then reassembled as something *else*. No wonder humans who spent time on the other side of the veil lost track of years or more. Her body seemed to have been forcibly disconnected from anything like the logical progression of time.

In a distant part of herself still capable of thought, for some reason she thought of Katu going from natural form to carriage and back again. He never showed any sign of pain from the process. None of the animals did. And yet some nagging observer in the back of her mind connected the two, as if she'd just been similarly transformed by her passage through that veil dividing realms.

She was so shaken by the non-experience, which had taken forever and no time at all, that she only checked on Katu, and then on Big Betty much, much later. In doing so, she realized she still had her eyes closed and that she actually needed this thing called vision to look in her rear view. After a moment, she figured out how to open her eyelids—which at least were still a part of her—and then forgot what she'd meant to do with looking because she was entirely dazzled. It became brilliantly clear why humans who visited here seemed to be able to only describe it as beautiful and terrible in one.

Where Obsidian looked more or less like the human realms, but progressively twisted sideways with increasingly potent magic, Moonstone was truly *other*. It was no more entirely white than Obsidian was entirely black, but white pixie dust infused everything with opalescent radiation. It glowed with ambient white dust, nearly as bright as a human-realm day, and she could only imagine what sunrise would bring. The sight put Cha in mind of a rare snowfall in her childhood, one that had followed on the more usual freezing rains.

She'd gone to bed in her narrow cot, shivering under the threadbare quilt, listening to the sound of rain pounding on the wooden roof and pinging through the cracks to drip merrily into the worn pots her mother had set out. Sometime in the night, the sound had stopped, and she'd awakened to an altered world. She'd looked out between the wintertime boards mostly covering her tiny attic window to see every-thing changed into shrouded white.

Even familiar objects looked new and strange. The usually muddy hog pen was gone beneath a pristine surface of snow. The hen house barely a swell in the frozen sea. The barn, always lopsided, leaned ever further toward its weak side, somehow looking graceful and serene in its impending, slow motion collapse. It was all so pretty, Cha could almost forget about the cows and horses about to be crushed in the listing barn, or the hogs and chickens nowhere in sight.

Everything looked so beautiful that it seemed impossible for the snow to be dangerous. It could only be magical. The sun had come out to frostily shine on the landscape, making every crystalline bit sparkle like tiny rainbows. Cha had never witnessed anything so magical in her entire short life thus far and, for the first time, she felt something of that joy in being alive that the stories talked about.

Only when the barn did collapse, and the tree branches began falling with great booms like thunder and lightning combined, did her new sense of happiness also fail. In the long, cold, wet, and miserable days following, as her family and her neighbors dug out from the destruction, dealing with the deaths of livestock and people, she began to understand that something beautiful could also be deadly.

She'd forgotten all about that long ago time—until this moment. Moonstone was exactly that: shrouded in white to the point that only some things had familiar shapes, excruciatingly beautiful with rainbow refraction in every crystalline mote, and clearly lethal, possibly in ways she could never predict. Her frail mortal self cowered in terror.

Taking herself by the metaphorical scruff of the neck, she shook herself out of the astonished stupor. She was no longer a child, helpless in the face of forces of nature. Cha had come a long way since that dismal little farm—with a decent helping of luck but also through her fiercely determined will—and she wouldn't be cowed now. Fuck Fairyland and its pretty tricks.

As if the thoughts had helped clear her brain of a lovely, but freezing fog, she abruptly regained her focus. Katu cruised along the Moonstone Throughway, seeming unperturbed. Big Betty streamed along behind them, Warg hanging out the passenger window so that his floppy ears blew back in the wind of their passage, leaving a comet tail of shimmering rainbow sparkles. Dy was there, but Cha couldn't discern her friend's condition.

Wondering if the path-box magic would even work, Cha opted to try that first. Stopping would be more dangerous than being overheard. Keeping to the marcasite channel, she tapped it open with caution—kind of silly because, what was she afraid of?—that it would blow up in her face? Actually, yes. Everything felt so magically charged that it seemed not at all impossible for ordinary objects to suddenly explode. "Goldilocks, you there?"

Dy took so long to respond that Cha was working out the details of discerning the boundaries of the side leys—if there even were any—and finding a place in the glittering anti-landscape to pull over.

"I'm here," Dy said, sounding drunk. "Though... whoa. That hit hard."

"You on the level?" That didn't mean what most people thought, part of the code they'd worked out long ago when jealous schoolmates or teachers hung up on malicious compliance could listen in.

"I'm as level as can be," she answered, less slurred this time. "But hungry—both of us. Let's grab a snack at the first opportunity."

Uh oh, that wasn't a good sign. She meant that Big Betty was low on ambrosia, which was not according to plan. Big Betty should've had more than enough juice to get to their contact and back again, to fuel up in at least Obsidian, but preferably one of the stations near the border. Most ley riders figured their carriage's fuel supply through experience, knowing their animal well, and intuition that shaded more or less toward guesswork, depending on their native talents. But Dy's sorcery gave her better insight than most and she'd never have planned wrong, which meant that the crossing into Moonstone had drained Big Betty far more than expected.

Katu, though he seemed fine, could therefore be running low, too. All bets were off on this side of the usual reality.

Even more concerning, Dy saying she was hungry, too, meant she'd run low on magic. Hopefully they wouldn't need her to spin ley lines out of whole cloth—not until the return trip anyway—but they would continue to need her illusion cloak. "I don't know about that opportunity," Cha said. "We still dressed for company?"

"Barely decent but socially acceptable," Dy answered wryly. "SOL for a pick me up then?"

"Maybe." Cha peered around, barely picking out anything recognizable, let alone obviously an ambrosia station. It nearly made her nostalgic for Obsidian with their lack of signage, an annoyance that seemed like a fond memory now. Not to mention the ambrosia station there, and that kiss, with blue sparks fountaining around them and... She banished that thought with a snarl.

"What was that?"

"Katu growling. How far to the party?"

"You don't know?"

"My moral compass is more on the fritz than usual." Cha kicked herself for not mentioning her map going wonky to Dy back at the depot. Too much else on her mind, clearly, and of the wrong things entirely.

Dy's sigh came through like a gust of wind. "I make it no more than fifteen from here. I can take point."

"You know where to find me if you need to change up." Cha moved Katu as far to the side as seemed wise, relieved that at least Dy knew where they were going. Fifteen minutes wasn't too long, and matched up with Otto's specs. Though it didn't *look* like nighttime with all that brilliant white, the throughway remained deserted and the clock indicated it was still the wee hours. They needed to get back into Obsidian and past the depot before daybreak there, to use Dy's discreetly created bypass ley and rejoin traffic like the fine, upstanding, and perfectly legal cargo haulers they pretended to be.

Nighttime in Moonstone meant nighttime in Obsidian, so they were on track for that part of the plan. Among the many things Cha didn't understand about how the fae realm magic worked that made bigger places fit inside of smaller ones, was how they all had basically the same sun, moon, and stars. Regardless, given how bright Moonstone was at night, she gave thanks they'd escape before sunrise when it would surely become blinding.

Big Betty passed them, blowing up a cloud of radiant white pixie dust, and Cha held her breath. That was the downside of the open coupe design of the jag. It allowed her freedom to battle off various beasties, giving them an advantage over other ley riders, particularly in races, but in circumstances like this, she didn't want to be inhaling even liberated pixie dust.

Theoretically, once it departed from the ley line or whatever other magical source had grown it, the dust lost its potency—which was why it had to be mined, magically stabilized, and packaged for transport by the fae. Humans couldn't pop over the borders and fill their pockets. Still, given how charged this pure stuff felt, not to mention the way it had fucked with their magical devices, Cha didn't want to know how this shit would affect her body.

Come to think of it, maybe the fae didn't have to apply mutation-punishments to interlopers. They wouldn't have to put themselves out. They could just allow the ambient pixie dust have at their frail mortal flesh. Great. Now she'd be sprouting moonstone scales or opalescent horns from her forehead or fragile wings like Bartholomew had, only in shimmering white and not detachable at the end of the holiday.

Come to think of it, no wonder Azul had been cranky about the whole "wings are sexy" conversation, aside from her deliberate and accurate poking at his dignity. The idea of having permanent wings attached to herself wasn't even remotely sexy. What did the fae *do* with them during sex anyway? She seriously doubted you could lie down on them and you couldn't have both people on top. Maybe, you could do a standing up thing. Or a sitting up lap-straddle. She supposed doggie style could work, too, which would allow for—

Realizing she'd drifted dreamily into yet another lust-infused daydream about her new favorite unattainable rich, pretty boy—who, by the way was gone forever, never to be seen again, he was *that* unattainable—she shook her head to focus. Good thing, too, as apparently time had flown by and Big Betty was moving to a side ley and thus slowing. Cha squinted suspiciously at the timepiece, not at all convinced time was flowing as it should, sensual daydream or not.

Big Betty, going ponderously enough they could be on slow black, curved into what looked like a dazzling blizzard. Perhaps Dy's sorcery, even at low ebb, allowed her to see through the Moonstone-blindness in a way Cha couldn't. She dearly wanted to ask, but couldn't think of a decent code phrase and, besides, it wasn't all that important. Neither she nor Katu much liked being the horse with its nose in the tail of the one before, but they couldn't always be the lead.

She patted Katu's dash. "Soon we'll be on our way and fancy free again," she told him.

They'd get whatever package would be disguised inside the crates of decoy black Big Betty was carrying and get that delivery on the road in time for payday. And then Cha would go looking for Monat. There had to be some clues as to where she'd gone, if the rumors had made it back out of Moonstone all the way to the human world.

Though, at the moment, she had no idea how they'd possibly find Monat in this boundaryless place. Oh well, not like she had anything better to do.

~ 31 ~

Deception of the Sugarplum Fairy

AHEAD OF HER, Big Betty slowed to a halt, though the blizzard of prismatic white dust didn't abate in the least. It swirled and eddied like real snow falling from the sky would, and Cha experienced a jolt of dislocation, for a moment unsure of where she was.

"Get a grip," she instructed herself. No wonder all the tales of humans visiting the fae realms carried a common thread of people becoming confused to the point of forgetting themselves entirely. Because she'd never had (much) of a problem in Obsidian—except for that time she drank too much black stout in that little tavern and ended up dancing the soles off her boots—she'd underestimated the impact of Moonstone. Just as Azul had cautioned, the jerk.

She waited for Dy to exit Big Betty, knowing the sorceress would know where to step. Dy held the door for Warg to lumber out, holding her free hand high in a thumbs up. Well then. Cha climbed out, too, eyeing the shrouded footing uneasily. But it felt solid enough. And the soles of her boots hadn't fried into pixie dust oblivion, so things were looking reasonably optimistic. Just to be sure, though, she holstered the magic wand along with her sword, one on each hip. If Dy was bringing Warg, then the sorceress anticipated she might need magic. Tucking her thumbs loosely in her belt loops, ready for a quick draw of either weapon, Cha swaggered up to stand beside Dy.

Warg gave her a happy howl and a slobbering kiss on her hand, oblivious to her disgusted glare. "This is the Ice Lily Garden?" Cha demanded of no one in particular, gazing around at the somewhat industrial-looking flat area—as industrial-looking as the fae got, anyway—and seeing nothing resembling lilies or gardens, though she supposed the pervasive and scintillating white dust handled the "ice" part.

"According to my notes, yes," Dy answered tersely.

"Now what?" Cha asked, staring into the swirling white as if she saw anything but that.

"Shh," Dy answered very quietly. "Sugarplum is coming."

Cha strained her eyes, still seeing nothing. Dy was tense, her golden hair curling tightly as if in a mist, though the air felt quite dry.

A silhouette formed in the foggy swirl, a darker shape of white on white, impossibly tall, at least twice Cha's height. Multiple alabaster white antlers forking in an impressive array of lethally sharp tines, glistening like diamonds, added to the impression of looming height. A long, delicate muzzle dipped toward them, making a triangle topped by doe-like, liquid brown eyes, fringed with heavy lashes. The rest of the Moonstone fae was draped in a voluminous robe of dappled ivory, blending into the background pixie dust. It occurred to

Cha that this was its version of wearing a dark cloak in the shadows of a back alley for this clandestine transfer. She choked back an irreverent snicker.

"Have you lost your way, humans?" the Moonstone fae inquired in a fluting voice, so lovely Cha wanted to curl up at the creature's feet and purr. Another manifestation of the enchantment lure, like sirens in the ocean or a grass-gnome waggling a pretty bell. The Departments of Fae Studies at the various academies theorized that fae and humans had actually co-evolved, with the fae races developing niche predatory skills entirely to prey on humans. Otherwise these entrance-you-into-stupidity abilities wouldn't work only on humans. Cha didn't quite get why—Dy was the brainy one—but she could see the point.

"We're looking for the sugarplum factory," Dy answered, giving the code phrase Otto had provided.

The creature didn't exactly smile—its pointed face didn't seem to be constructed for that—but it dipped its statuesque head in the facsimile of a nod. "You are very nearly late," it said.

Its voice no longer held that musical note that fogged Cha's brain and she scowled at the creature. Not very polite to poke them with a metaphorical sword first before verifying their identity. "Very nearly late isn't 'are late,'" Cha pointed out caustically. The Moonstone fae didn't acknowledge her with even so much as a flicker of one of the pointed ears crowning its triangular head.

"Bring the transport inside," it told Dy. Lifting one, scarily long limb, it gestured with a multiply cloven hoof-hand—

enough segments to seem vaguely like fingers and disturbingly unlike them—that looked like it was made of pearl.

Cha had an increasingly bad feeling about this. "Inside where?" she demanded.

Dy cast her a cautionary glance. "I can see where."

"You can?" Sometimes Cha really hated having just enough magic to get herself into trouble and not enough to get herself out again. "I'll follow you then."

The Moonstone fae finally deigned to acknowledge her existence. "You will remain here, human. Or leave. We do not care, but you shall not enter."

Oh, so Cha was "human," but Dy got the princess treatment? *Nope.* "Where she goes, I go."

"Incorrect. You will remain here, human. Or leave. We do not care, but you shall not enter."

"Practiced those instructions, did you?" Cha muttered, and Dy frowned.

"It's fine, Bandit," she said. "They want us to get this cargo back as much as we do. There's no purpose in getting me inside for any other reason."

"Unless it's to fatten you up and roast you in the oven," Cha pointed out, glaring at the Moonstone fae, more than tempted to pull her sword. Or the magic wand. *Bet a little Ruby infusion could fry your ice lily white ass.*

Dy raised a golden brow at her, moonstone pixie dust sparkling in her curls, making her look more angelic than ever. "Now *you* are the one balking?" she hissed. "We made it all the way here, with you haranguing me the whole trip, and now you have cold feet?"

"It's all this snow," Cha retorted. She was shivering, though it wasn't actually chilly.

"It's pixie dust."

"I know that." It had been a stupid argument, start to finish. "Go on then. But keep your antennae uncurled. I'll be waiting right here," she declared in a louder voice, glaring at Sugarplum.

"I would never think otherwise," Dy told her with a smile that said everything. Yeah, despite the rough waters under the bridge, they'd never failed to have each other's backs. Like someone trying to shove a large water balloon through a narrow window, Dy wrestled a squirming Warg—trying to lick the pixie dust from her face—into the cab of Big Betty. Sugarplum disappeared into the sparkling mist and Big Betty sailed forward with silent grace, gradually fading away like a schooner in a fairytale being enveloped by a mystical fog.

Cha shivered harder at the image, hoping this foreboding wasn't a real omen, as she emphatically didn't believe in such things. "You've just inhaled too much pixie dust," she told herself. "Getting all paranoid and dreaming up crazy scenarios."

To make herself feel better, she drew her sword, the hilt comfortingly solid in her hand. She'd like to pace off the nervous energy, but without really knowing where she was stepping, that wasn't a great idea. She could stay where she was or sit in Katu, neither choice great for her nerves.

She also minded the clock, having nothing else to do. The time ticking by did nothing to make her feel any better about the situation. Getting the clandestine shipment from Sugarplum only marked the halfway point. They still had to get the stuff back to Otto by the deadline or they'd be out the final payment. The deposit would go a long way, but nothing like the payday they'd planned for. Once again she kicked herself for forgetting to get that platinum coin from Azul.

Wherever he was, she hoped he had made it all right. Unlikely the imps had gotten to him, but he'd seemed like he had some distance to travel and then there was that oddness with his people not showing up for him. Knowing what little she did—that his family had pressured him into the marriage with Lenorae and that there'd been some hidden component, something so terrible that he'd run rather than deal with it—it was entirely possible that his family had prevented his staff, or whatever, from coming to his aid.

Which meant he was on his own out there. Not her problem, but she still worried about him.

And she worried about Dy and Big Betty, carried off by Sugarplum. What if this whole escapade was some elaborate scheme? There'd been something off from the beginning, with attention from places that shouldn't have noticed them. And Monat getting caught in the first place... Was this how it had happened? Maybe the Moonstone fae were collecting human sorceresses for some nefarious purpose. Something even worse than a fae barbeque party or whatever they did for fun.

Nearly half an hour had elapsed. If Dy didn't reemerge, what then?

Staring at the opaque, swirling mist until her eyes prickled from the strain and her stomach lurched from the dizzying prismatic effect of the sparkling white dust that her brain continued to insist was snow, Cha considered her options. Which were basically no options, but it sounded better in her head than being utterly fucked, and not in a good way.

1. Turn around and go home. (Not really an option, but listed first so she could cross it off.)

2. Keep waiting. (This was the default option, but not one that could last forever.)

3. Go do something else entirely. (Also not really an option, but included for thoroughness.)

4. Charge straight forward, heedless of the consequences.

Who was she kidding? The choice was obvious.

At twenty-seven minutes since Big Betty had vanished into the malicious Moonstone mist of doom, and a lifetime of imagining the worst, Cha had settled on the only option she could live with and still be herself.

Sliding into the driver's seat of the idling Katu, she brandished both sword and magic wand, then signaled the jag to zoom straight into the mist after Dy. Into what, who knew, but she imagined a fae version of a loading dock, perhaps with a shimmering Moonstone door lowered and barred against entry. She'd never deliberately crashed Katu before, and wild doubt suddenly stabbed through her.

Was she crazy? Maybe *this* was how the fae eliminated humans with the idiotic bravery—or desperation—to invade their realms. The fae simply messed with the humans' heads until they put themselves out of their own misery. The poor sods staggering back into the human realms with mutations, additions, deletions, or simply not who they'd been when they went in, were the lucky ones.

All of this flashed through her mind in the time it took Katu to leap into the mist on slow white that was still faster than most fast blacks. Snowblind, and feeling more than a little crazed, Cha gave herself up to fate.

And braced for impact.

~ 32 ~

All Is Lost, Including Herself

ON THE UPSIDE, they didn't crash into anything solid enough to kill them. On the concerning side, several soft, grunting things went flying—to the side and over the top of the jag, close enough that Cha had to duck—and she could only hope none of them was Dy. Or Warg, she supposed, since Dy was fond of the appalling creature.

Katu skidded to a stop so abruptly that he skidded sideways, hitting a few more soft, grunting things with the side of the carriage. Cha took in the scene with one, sweeping assessment.

Sugarplum—or its mostly identical twin, hard to say—held Dy wrapped in several appendages, holding the sorceress still so she couldn't move enough to hurl a spell, one cloven-hoofed, weird finger-hand thing securely slapped over her mouth. Another Sugarplum-looking fae held Warg, quite a bit less securely, probably as it's not easy to hold onto the equivalent of a greased and pissed-off water balloon. Warg twisted and howled with ear-piercing shrieks, trying to bite its captor with no success, but liberally spraying the creature with

253

slobber, which—judging by the disgusted expression on the fae's otherwise serene face—was just as bad.

Big Betty, still in cargo transport form, trumpeted in quiet distress as swarms of pearly imps with cherubic faces and stubby wings carried crates stamped with the Obsidian logo out of her cargo compartment. Others lay in various grunting piles scattered about the big room, clearly the things Katu had hurled about during their dramatic entrance. Cha didn't know what species of fae they were. Some kind of Moonstone imp.

Black pixie dust swirled in the air from several broken crates, combining with the ever-present white dust to make a gray haze. For a second, Cha winced at the waste of all that expensive Obsidian dust, thinking she and Katu had broken the crates—then she saw one of the imps smash an intact crate with a sledgehammer three times its size.

Check: cherubic Moonstone imps are super strong.

They also didn't seem to care about the rest of their co-hort, singing an annoying song as they continued with their carrying and smashing of crates task, ignoring their injured fellows and Cha with equal blissful obliviousness.

Not so much the case with the Sugarplums around the room, who now converged on them, even as Dy made wide, blue eyes at Cha, attempting to convey some mute message. Cha had no idea of the specifics, but the general "we're fucked here" gist made it right through.

All of this took barely the time to blink and, before Katu had quite finished sliding to that sideways stop, Cha leapt to her feet, one foot on the center console and another on the dash, waving the sword and magic wand at the advancing

Sugarplums. "Don't do it," she warned in her finest menacing style.

Which did nothing to slow them. Charming.

Figuring her best bet lay with the wand, since flesh wounds didn't slow most fae much, with their super-quick healing, Cha tried to recall how she'd banished the iron demon and its puppy brigade. Moonstone and Ruby combined should work on Moonstone fae, right?

Hopefully this time wouldn't take three tries. Just in case, she tried building in a three on the first try, since magic liked threes so much. "Once, twice, thrice, I banish thee!" she shouted flinging pretty pink sparkles onto the nearest Sugarplum. Yeah, she didn't know why she used old-timey language either.

It flinched like a demon spattered with angel blood, emitting a faint scream like a melting snowflake, then vanished. The other Sugarplums halted in their tracks. Oblivious to the ruckus, the Moonstone imps continued carrying, singing, and smashing.

The Sugarplum holding Dy—their personal Sugarplum, perhaps—said, "What is the meaning of this rude and arrogant intrusion, human?"

Rude and arrogant? Cha had just poofed one of its friends. Gotta love a species that worries more about manners than, you know, life itself. Though maybe Cha had only banished the thing, not murdered it. She'd like to think that way because, though she'd do literally anything for Dy and she had a rep as a cynical badass bandit, but Cha really didn't like to kill anyone. She was an asshole, not a murderer. A girl had to have *some* standards.

"Release Dy and Warg," she commanded, pointing the wand—gently—at the Sugarplum holding Dy.

She'd expected some back and forth, but maybe the poofing had served as sufficient intimidation, because Dy's Sugarplum immediately released her and Warg's Sugarplum dropped him to the ground, wiping its hands off in the universal gesture of relieved disgust. Warg, unfazed by the fall, scrambled to Dy, who crouched to put her hands on him.

Within a breath, the white and black pixie dust whorled into a funnel, spinning with tornadic glee into Dy, who looked momentarily like a monstrous toad—with wildly spronging golden corkscrew curls—as her mouth expanded to inhale the dust. Cha barely had time to reach toward Dy, to do what, Cha didn't know, before Dy exhaled again, freezing all the Moonstone imps in mid-carry, sing, and smash. Even the Sugarplums froze in mid-sneer.

The ensuing silence was crushing. Cha checked to make sure she could move. Fortunately, the answer was yes. She didn't know how Dy had managed to exempt her from the cloud of frozen doom, but good for her.

"What in the seven hells happened?" Cha demanded, jumping down from the idling Katu.

"Probably whatever happened to Monat," Dy retorted, standing and lifting Warg in one easy movement. "We need to get out of here. I don't know how long my spell will last."

"Agreed, but…the shipment?"

Dy, having shoveled Warg into the cab of Big Betty, turned and shook her head. "I don't know. The Sugarplums kept asking where the astra was. Then," she continued when Cha opened her mouth, "when I also had no idea what they were talking about, started having the puttoes unload and search the supposedly decoy shipment."

"Puttoes is what you call the imps, huh?" Cha asked absently, collecting her wits when Dy glared, then clapped her friend on the arm and squeezed. "I feared the worst."

"This is pretty damn bad. Otto fucked us."

"Yeah, he did." Cha sheathed the sword, but not the wand, and climbed a few steps up the ramp to Big Betty's interior. Since they seemed sturdy and she was in a bad mood, she grabbed the puttoes in her way and chucked them off to the side, methodically clearing a path. "Hurts my mercenary heart to see all this dust spilled and wasted."

"Whatever the Sugarplums were talking about," Dy said, climbing in behind her, "they clearly expected to be receiving something, not giving us something to return to Otto."

"Which means Otto never expected us to return. He sacrificed us to a one-way delivery."

"No wonder he was willing to promise so much coin," Dy agreed. "He never intended to pay us the rest." In an uncharacteristic display, she punted a nearby putto off Big Betty's bay. "What?" she asked when Cha eyed her. "That song of theirs was getting on my nerves and they were carelessly hurting Betty." She stroked the inside of Big Betty's cargo bay and the elephant rumbled sadly, Katu sawing in sympathy.

"Want to kick some more of them?" Cha offered, and Dy's worried frown dissolved into a reluctant smile.

"Yes, but we should get out of here before enchantment frays too much. You arrived in the nick of time, Cha—thank you."

"Late, I would say."

"You didn't wait our standard thirty minutes, I notice."

"You know me," Cha replied with a grin. "Do you think Monat did complete Otto's delivery and ours was the second?"

She surveyed the unbroken crates. The spilled stuff was mostly worthless now, so no point in gathering it up, much as that, too, pained her mercenary heart. The value of the remaining cargo wouldn't come anywhere near Otto's promised payday. It wouldn't be worth even the platinum coin she'd carelessly squandered, but the remaining crated dust would fetch a tidy bit of coin. Enough to keep Dy off the corporate circuit for a while and the kids in new shoes, or whatever they went through so fast.

"This decoy shipment had to cost Otto," Dy observed. "Even if he was smuggling something to the Moonstone fae inside this stuff, how was he getting paid?"

"I don't know," Cha agreed. "It makes no sense, but I'll tell you what does make perfect sense: whatever the Moonstone fae wanted, it's still in here. Let's get this stuff back over the border to the human realms, find out what's in here that had everyone so excited, and get Phin to locate a buyer for the dust. We can salvage something from this ill-gotten gig."

"Steal it?" Dy asked thoughtfully.

"Yeah." She gestured at the putto-strewn loading bay. "I'll clear a path. You rev up Big Betty and Katu and I will blaze us back down the Moonstone Throughway."

Dy looked doubtful. "It'll be daylight soon."

"Go fast," Cha advised. "Light up those leys, sorceress."

"That'll burn ambrosia," Dy warned, "and remember that

Betty is low."

"I know a station right past the Moonstone border. We can make it." She hoped. But, really, what other choice did they have?

Dy jerked her chin in a nod. "Let's do it."

They quickly booted the remaining putto workers from Big Betty, having to peel a couple off the crates they'd grabbed, while the stubby-winged imps glared at them balefully. Once done, Dy closed Betty's gate and bumped fists with Cha. "We can do this."

"You betcha we can, Goldilocks," Cha replied, moving a broken crate from the path to the door leading outside, and trying not to inhale more dust than she had to.

"I'll lead the way," she said, hurrying around to the cab. "Try to keep up."

"Cute," Cha called after her. "Just get your adorable ass moving." She hustled, moving crates and puttoes as Dy reversed Big Betty out of there.

A bit of movement caught her eye. One of the Sugarplums twitched, its colorless eyes tracking them, pointy muzzle moving in soundless shouting that would soon be real shouting. Cha hurried even more, saying nothing to Dy, lest her partner hesitate in her escape. They could still make it. Her still-sore shoulder twinged as she wrested the final crate at an awkward angle, but she got it cleared.

"Go go go!" she yelled to Dy, who goosed Big Betty, reversing out of the docking bay in a whoosh of Moonstone dust.

Once she confirmed they were clear, Cha dashed for Katu. At that moment—probably as Dy's rapid departure attenuated the spell—the Sugarplums and puttoes all unfroze.

They all dashed straight for Cha.

She was still several lengths from Katu, with considerable obstacles in the way, but this wasn't her first fae rodeo. Cha drew her sword and lashed the wand at the nearest onrushing Sugarplum. The pink sparks shot weakly, then sputtered out with a whine. Just fantastic.

"Once, twice, thr—" She broke off with a grunt as a putto body-slammed her groin at the perfect angle to be breathtakingly painful. Hopefully it wasn't a pussy-sparkle-killing blow. That would just be the sour cherry on the shit sundae of her life. The thing sunk pointy teeth into her thigh, adding insult to the pussy injury as the bite didn't hurt nearly as much. All qualms about murder lost to the moment, she stabbed it with the sword. The putto weighed no more than a marshmallow, so she used the sword like a slingshot to fling it into the face of the closest Sugarplum.

"Thrice, I banish thee!" She finished the invocation and whipped the wand around. That didn't work at all. Not even a feeble squirt of pink glitter. Seriously worried her wand had gone impotent, she tried one more time from the beginning. "Once, twice—"

Her breath choked out as unnaturally strong, ivory arms encircled her from behind, pinning her arms to her sides and squeezing all the air from her lungs, cracking a few ribs in the process. The Sugarplum—possibly her personal Sugarplum—lifted her off her feet like she was a bit of thistledown.

"Fuck me," Cha muttered, which didn't work either, and passed out.

~ 33 ~

Fae Jail

CHA BLEARILY SWAM up from dreams of trying to eat sugary marshmallows and choking on them instead, opening her eyes to what could only be a fae jail cell. She'd always kind of figured this day would come. In fact, at one point in her admittedly troubled adolescence, her mother had predicted this very thing. No one would be surprised to hear she'd come to this. The Bandit meeting her comeuppance at last.

Still, she'd expected to find herself pacing an Obsidian-black jail cell, not one that looked like the inside of an egg. With the curved walls descending evenly to a shallow bowl at the bottom, there would be zero despondent pacing. She wasn't even sure she could lever herself up from being a puddle on the polished opalescent bowl of a floor. Also, it leeched some of the drama of her situation that the thing looked like it could be spun of sugar candy instead of bleak as dying coals.

Come to think of it, being despondent worked pretty well lying in a puddle, which seemed to be all her body wanted to do at the moment. Her ribs ached with a dull throb, regular acute stabs of agony grabbing every time she took a breath. The rest of her didn't feel much better. Had the Sugarplums held a dance party on her unconscious body? Sure felt like it.

Nevertheless, she ignored the seductive lure of lying in a dramatically wilted heap of her own failure and pushed to a sitting position, then to her feet, allowing herself to groan and wheeze all she liked, just so long as she got the job done. Sure, she had to brace one hand on the curved wall to keep herself vaguely vertical, especially with the curved floor unbalancing her, but it was a start.

The cell looked little different from a standing position, basically a sphere of semi-translucent white with subtle rainbow shimmers. No windows or apparent door. The lack of facilities to relieve herself concerned her greatly. Possibly the fae didn't realize that human bodies had those needs.

Or they planned to just let her die in here. Cheerful thought.

What had they done with Katu? In general the fae valued the carriage beasts, so hopefully the Moonstone monsters would care for him. He'd be missing her, though, and wondering why she'd abandoned him. The thought made her want to weep and she wasn't the weeping kind.

More optimistically, she hoped Dy had gotten away clean. Maybe she and Phin were even now fencing the stolen cargo of Obsidian black dust, along with whatever valuable object Otto had been sending to Moonstone, and planning their retirement. The thought made her happy enough to momentarily forget how much her current situation sucked. If she had to sacrifice herself to a lonely death in a fae jail, then that was the best possible reason to do it.

The glow didn't last long, and neither did her stamina. Besides, with pacing impossible and standing downright painful, the questionable virtue of being upright quickly faded. At least the curved wall allowed her to slide down in a glide that was, if not gentle, at least slightly less excruciating than a full drop. Experimenting, she found the ideal position, an angle that accommodated her long legs while not compressing her aching ribs too much.

Despite her bone-deep exhaustion, she couldn't sleep. She was in too much pain and had too much anxiety about her situation. But there was also nothing to do but think and worry. All of her bad choices and multitudes of regrets paraded through her mind, jeering at her, taunting her former and now shattered bravado.

And topping the list, the biggest regret of all: losing Azul. Why hadn't she at least shagged him super fast before nobly letting him go? Responsibility sucked—and if this was the reward for it, then she failed to understand the virtue of it.

Much as she didn't want to jinx herself by wishing for something to happen—no doubt anyone coming to fetch her would not be invested in making her situation better—she began to long for change. She also really needed to pee.

Cha was no mathematician or scientist, but she began calculating what would happen when she inevitably had to pee in her little egg. Much better than obsessing about certain tasty blue fae princes. Would she drown in it before her body ran out of the stuff? Maybe not if they never gave her any food or water. Still, soaking in a bath of her own urine was so far from a badass way to go that she deeply regretted that she hadn't gotten killed in the fight.

But then... why hadn't they killed her? Seemed like it would've been easier than wasting an egg on her.

The shell shivered around her, interrupting the morose thoughts. The top of the cell went transparent, then vanished entirely. Cha struggled to her feet, even more difficult this time, as she'd stiffened up during the long sit. A Sugarplum-type fae peered in at her. "Come out, human," it said, its fluting voice so alluring that she practically longed to do its bidding, and probably would have even if she wasn't desperate to escape her cell.

"How?" she asked, hoping her leaning against the wall looked saucy and cynical, rather than a desperately needed surface to prop herself against.

The Sugarplum simply reached in, fisted a hand in her jacket, and lifted her like a kitten by the scruff of her neck. Just delightful. Fortunately, it plopped her down before she gave into instinct and struggled like a frantic kitten with no claws. She managed to stay on her feet, just barely, and produced a sneer for her jailer. The man wouldn't keep her down, even if the man was some gender-indeterminate, Moonstone fae.

They seemed to be on a walkway that surfed along in a sea of shimmering white egg-shapes. How unsettling. Was Monat in here somewhere? Cha had no idea how she'd find out or begin searching, but she had promised Dy, and that could be something fruitful from this shit situation. So, this was actually semi-close to the original plan, with a few setbacks.

If you counted Cha being also trapped in fae jail and probably dead soon as a "setback."

"I'm free to go then," she suggested to the Sugarplum. Couldn't hurt to try.

The Sugarplum sneered mightily, doing a much better job than Cha had. "You now face interrogation and trial," it said. "I seriously doubt the verdict will include freedom."

"I have some lovely shinies you might care to look over," Cha said, wondering if she *did* still have them. The chest of Phinny's gems was in Katu still, wherever her baby cat had ended up.

The Sugarplum didn't even pause to consider that half-baked bribe. "Come with me."

"I need to pee first," Cha said, not budging.

Can a sneer deepen? If so, that's what happened. "Humans are disgusting."

"Yeah, basically sacks of shit and pee," Cha agreed amiably. "Good reason not to keep us around. I'll just be on my way then."

The Sugarplum—probably not her personal Sugarplum anymore, she was pretty sure, but it wasn't like they wore nametags—seized her again by the back of her jacket and perp-walked her along at a truly uncomfortable pace for her traumatized body. Happily enough, however, they ended at a toilet facility that seemed to be designed for humans. Once Cha got over the relief of being alone inside, relieving herself, she received the extra delight of finding a shower within and various grooming supplies.

Bathing and removing the various goops out of her hair absorbed all of her attention at first. Finally clean and dressed again, she felt considerably less miserable. Surveying herself in the mirror, she found she looked, if not her best, at least reasonably put together. Then she met her own dark, snapping gaze in the mirror and asked, "Is it at all weird that they have a facility designed for humans here? Yeah. That's what I thought, too."

Something caught her eye in the corner of the mirror, a bit of dark metal and, saliently, *not* any shade of white. Cha pried it out from behind the pearlescent glass, the steel ring falling into her palm. The smooth metal circle was tipped with grinning skulls. Monat's nose ring. Monat had been here. And she'd clearly removed the nose ring, screwing the skull head back on, before leaving it deliberately behind. Cha's spirits, already abysmal, cratered further.

Though she'd locked the door, the Sugarplum opened it. "Come, human."

"The name is Arantxa Evermore," she replied jauntily, pocketing the nose ring, "though everyone calls me Cha."

The Sugarplum simply reached in and dragged her out. She was getting more than a little tired of that. The restroom had been as windowless as the rest of the place. Even if they hadn't disappeared her sword and magic wand—worthless piece of crap *that* had turned out to be—she didn't really have much in the way of options for escape. Without Katu, she could hardly get anywhere in Moonstone, even if she could figure out which way to go. Hitchhiking along the Moonstone Through-way would be a real treat. She snorted at the image and the Sugarplum smacked the back of her head with an extra appendage. "No laughing," it said.

"Man, fairyland sucks," she whined, earning another smack. Oddly it made her feel better.

THE "TRIAL" PORTION that ensued was, of course, a travesty, though mostly harmless. Her expectations remained low to abysmal for any happy outcome for her and she couldn't follow most of it. The trial involved a lot of posturing by various lovely, prancing Moonstone fae who argued amongst themselves in such ethereal, fluting tones that they sounded like an angelic choir. Cha might have enjoyed the pretty music, if not for the part where the lyrics were no doubt all about her imminent execution.

Trapped in a booth like an egg with the top cut off, pain washing over her in waves, and strapped in so she couldn't even adjust to alleviate the stiffness setting in, and surrounded entirely by fae speaking in a language she didn't understand, Cha had never felt so miserably alone in her entire life.

I will be missed if I don't return, Dy had said, and it hit Cha with full, humiliating and agonizing force that she was going to die alone, and no one would know what had happened to her. And no one would miss her, not really. Dy would have Phinny and the kids. Azul would probably never give her another thought.

Depression set into Cha like a damp, winter chill, making her heavy and lethargic. She couldn't do anything to affect her fate and that ground down her spirits even more.

And that was before the interrogation and accompanying

torture began.

Abruptly done with their arguments, the Moonstone fae all turned to her, forming a loose circle of sneers. One produced the Moonruby wand and shook it in Cha's face, demanding to know where she got it.

"It just appeared one day," Cha replied with her best innocent expression.

The wand-wielding fae punched her in the face with the cloven hoof hand fisted around the wand. It hurt exactly as much as you'd think it would. Stars in her vision, blood in her mouth, Cha missed answering the next question, until a hoof-punch to her sternum sent streaks of pain straight to her flagging brain, waking her up a little. Unfortunately, that also kicked her thoughts into awareness that something might be seriously wrong with her inside, that she might already be dying.

Another fae demanded to know where the astra was, to which she responded, "I have no idea what you're talking about." That earned her even more punches to the face and her already battered ribs. Her breath became labored along with an extraordinarily sharp stabbing feeling in her chest that she worried might be a piece of fractured rib lodged in her lung. On top of having no food or water for an indiscernible amount of time, Cha began to feel seriously weak and light-headed.

Both of the answers she'd given had the benefit of being true, which allowed her to lie freely about everything else, at least as much as she could get the words out. Not that it saved her from the increasingly violent and damaging blows, but lying allowed her to protect Dy.

That was one of the few benefits to being human as opposed to fae: the ability to lie and do so outrageously. If the situation had been less dire and had Cha felt a tiny bit less like her mortal flesh was being stripped of in tiny pieces, she might have enjoyed the tales she spun for them. Because the fae were unable to lie, the concept of it pretty much baffled them. Just as they had contempt for humans in general, they seemed unable to comprehend that humans could do what they couldn't.

So, Cha lied. She lied colorfully and extensively—possibly delusionally, given her weakened state of mind—weaving a complex history behind her appearance in Moonstone that sounded improbable even to her own ears. She lied so extravagantly that she countered her own assertions several times, tripping over her stated timeline, and belying things she'd said only minutes earlier. These mistakes only further confused the fae interrogators who could only believe that the conflicting truths were somehow simultaneously valid.

Cha only stuck to the truth on those two key points so as to be sure not to reveal anything important. She didn't know how Giant Jo had come to possess the magic wand, but no way would she get the woman in trouble with the fae. And, regarding the astra, whatever it was, Cha retained the hope that Dy and Phin could profit from it, so she wasn't risking losing control of that information. Not that she really had any to begin with, but she kept hoping that the Moonstone fae might spill more details in their quest to get coherent information out of her.

Of course, information-gathering was unwarrantedly optimistic of her, as that was assuming she'd live to make use of that information. Or that her bruised and no doubt bleeding brain from all the blows to the head would retain any of it. Eventually, the fae began discussing her immediate execution in tones of resignation, as she clearly had nothing to offer about this astra they wanted. They discussed that part in her language, clearly hoping that would break her where nothing else had. Ha to that. Cha could die on her own without their help.

When they began seriously debating the least-effort way to kill her that would also efficiently dispose of her human corpse without polluting their pristine environment, Cha found the prospect of her imminent death less consoling. She considered that her approach of claiming total ignorance about astra had been a Bad Idea. That information was likely the only reason she'd lived this long.

Unfortunately, she couldn't figure out a way to walk that back. She was furiously concocting an alternate storyline that wouldn't contradict what she'd already said more than necessary, when they settled on dropping her in a pit of acid.

That experience would probably be just as bad as it sounded.

Worse, part of their argument for that method involved a discussion of a human who could only be Monat having been tossed in this same pool and disappearing with a satisfying lack of lingering human stench. If Cha hadn't already been weeping from the torture, she'd have broken down at the news of Monat's terrible and lonely death. A miserable fate Cha would share, and she hadn't even contrived to leave a clue behind. And back in Rockton, Garaile would share the gossip about Cha's disappearance, sharing a beer with someone else. And Dy and Phinny and the kids would have a little memorial by the pond for Cha, eventually, when they finally gave up hope, Zazu tossing petals onto the water in memory of her ill-fated auntie.

Even though sobbing hurt her lungs and ribs worse, Cha couldn't help it as two Sugarplums lifted her between them and carried her out of the courtroom, handing her over to a small herd of puttoes. The cute and nasty little creatures crowd-surfed her with those strong, bruising, and careless white doughy hands, through twisting corridors of breathtaking architecture. They seemed intent on hurting her as much as possible along the way, as if taking revenge for how she'd treated their fellows in the docking bay.

She refused to be entirely crushed by it all, however. Maybe no one would ever know it, but she'd be damned if she'd go to her death sobbing like a toddler deprived of a toy. From the depths of her will, she summoned the energy to curse the brutal puttoes in an unrelenting streak that at least made her feel better. She'd at least be able to tell herself that she'd gone down fighting to the very end.

They brought her into a circular hall with a high, beautifully arched open dome revealing a dazzlingly bright white sky beyond. Beneath, an unpleasantly piss-green pool vented noxious steam that burned Cha's lungs and made her eyes water. Not how she imagined going.

As they chanted to the count of three, giggling all the

while, and tossed her in, she punched both hands into the air, middle fingers high.

Fuck them if they couldn't take a joke.

~ 34 ~

Damsel in De-Stress

"HOLD," CALLED OUT a smooth voice.

As if obeying the command despite gravity and all those related laws of physics, Cha's body froze in midair, suspended over the acid pit. Nice that she still had both middle fingers upraised in her final act of defiance. Not so great that she was arched in a grotesque twist with arms and legs splayed.

"Prince Azulejah," a Sugarplum said, sounding both surprised and deferential. "Your Highness. We are honored by your visit."

"Are you?" The bored and haughty tone was excruciatingly familiar, but Cha didn't trust her hearing. It couldn't possibly be Azul, here and now—and somehow halting her imminent execution by slowly dissolving in agony. But then the blue glitter in the air did look like his. And, despite the proximity of the stomach-turning, eye-watering acid bath that produced steam that burned her skin even from a distance, the pussy sparkle leaping to life felt like his, too. She really wanted to be able to turn her head to see, but that freezing enchantment currently saving her life wouldn't allow it.

"But of course, Your Highness Prince Azulejah," a Sugarplum babbled like a frantic birdling. "You elevate our humble dwelling by your very presence. How may we be of service to such an august personage such as yourself?"

Cha longed to roll her eyes at the obsequious words. Apparently she couldn't do that either, though they watered freely enough. Probably that was good since she could also still breathe, which was important for her continued not dying.

"You can return my human to me," he answered, managing to sound both certain of their capitulation and as if he couldn't care less whether they complied.

"Your Highness's human?" The Sugarplum's anxiety came through clearly. "But, forgive me Prince Azulejah, this human is a criminal, found guilty of breaking multiple laws of the Moonstone Realm and—"

"Do my laws not supersede yours?" he returned with such chill condescension that even Cha shivered, though he was ostensibly rescuing her.

The concept finally penetrated her clearly overtaxed brain: Azul was somehow, however improbably, here and was actually saving her life. So much relief and joy wrung through her that she briefly lost track of the conversation, but next she knew, she was floating through the air and deposited in an ungainly heap at Azul's feet as the enchantment released her on safe ground. To be honest, she wasn't even embarrassed and had to restrain the impulse to kiss his shiny boots.

That impulse died a quick death as he nudged her with a toe of one shiny boot, none too gently, gazing down at her with an arrogant expression, one brow disdainfully arched.

"Do get up, human," he said, prodding her again. "Such a pitiful lack of decorum."

Cha was delighted to discover she retained enough contrariness to glare at him. He might have saved her life, but she didn't have to take anyone's shit. Especially not someone so clearly fae.

For his current appearance removed all doubt, if she'd really still had any.

Azul looked even taller—though that could be her perspective, piled at his feet as she was—and radiantly beautiful in fabulous garb in shades of blue. His curly, indigo hair waved back from his moon-pale face in perfect ringlets, pierced by high, delicately curved, and elegantly pointed ears. He wore a crown again, though not the gaudy one he'd had when she picked him up a day before and forever ago. This was a simple diadem of some unearthly glowing metal set with an amethyst of remarkable clarity.

And then there were the wings.

They lay mostly folded against his back, not feathered but composed of a thin membrane of such a deep violet they looked almost black. Like a bat would have, claw-tipped thumbs crowned the points of the wings where they towered above his head, framing him with regal lethality. Also like a bat, the lower part of his wings were tipped with clawed fingers that flexed restlessly, the only indication of restiveness in his otherwise statuesque poise.

He glanced down at her when she didn't immediately obey, blue gaze coolly distant. "I gave you an order, pet."

Deciding that particular moment wasn't ideal for demonstrating that she was no one's "pet," let alone some fae prince's, Cha took the hint and pushed to her feet. Unfortunately, her body had apparently had enough of, well, everything and dizziness swamped her as she staggered up. Azul clamped a hand to her upper arm, dragging her to her feet with a hiss of impatience. The grip also steadied her with welcome strength, so she didn't try to yank away, simply letting him hold her upright, hanging her head in what she hoped looked like submissive obedience.

"This is your human pet, Your Highness?" a Sugarplum inquired in a fluting voice, sounding doubtful and fawning at once.

"Yes." Azul gave her a little shake. "A disobedient one. I shall remove her and deal appropriately."

"Ah, Your Highness, if I may…" a different Sugarplum began, and paused respectfully. How messed up had her life become that she could tell Sugarplums apart by voice alone? Answer: seriously messed up.

"What will you know?" Azul replied, an edge of warning in his tone. He didn't scare Cha—she'd seen him fighting a chartreuse, life-eating, silk cloak after all—but even she wouldn't want to cross him in that moment.

"I beg your pardon and indulgence, Your Highness," the Sugarplum answered, "but there is the matter of an, ah, astra."

If possible, Azul cooled further beside her, emitting a wintry chill. "Excuse me?"

"It was being smuggled into Moonstone by this *human*," the Sugarplum replied stiffly, hastily adding, "Your Highness.

And my superiors have concerns, as you might imagine, Your Highness."

"I fail to see what that has to do with me," Azul replied with such icy disdain that Cha felt a little afraid. "Surely you're not implying that my realm has anything to do with an astra smuggled into Moonstone?"

"No, Your Highness! Not at all. But we have reason to believe this human may have knowledge of the astra."

"You have a curious way of extracting knowledge, unless you expected bits of information to bubble up from the human's dissolved neural tissue."

"Well, we did attempt interrogation and torture, Your Highness, but..." The one Sugarplum trailed off as it seemed to realize it was admitting to harming the Prince's property. Several others chimed in, disavowing knowledge and protesting various other things.

Nearly smirking at the Sugarplums' back-pedaling, Cha was glad to have her head hanging.

"Enough," Azul declared, his single command sufficient to shut them all up instantly. "I am uninterested in your problems. Now, return my Scepter of Nialis to me and I shall leave you to your... activities." The final sneer said everything about his opinion of their pursuits.

The Sugarplums squabbled quietly about the location of this scepter, which must be Cha's magic wand. "My sword, too," she muttered to Azul.

"I'll get you a better one," he muttered back.

"I liked that one."

"Hush."

Fine, it wasn't that great of a sword, but… "And Katu." She wouldn't save herself by sacrificing her cat. "Non-negotiable."

"Handled," he answered shortly. A putto ran up, presenting the wand to Azul with a deep bow and Cha risked glancing around the room. All the assembled fae appeared chastened, some bowing deeply, some fully prostrate on the floor. A better person wouldn't have enjoyed the sycophantic display, but Cha had never been above pettiness.

"I shall leave you," Azul informed them as he tucked the wand away. He spread his wings.

Cha gaped, despite herself and despite her resolve to remain totally cynical and unimpressed. With a span three times his height, Azul's wings shone with eye-blinding beauty. Unfurled, they went nearly transparent, the light shining through them a glorious, pure violet.

Azul pulled her hard against him and Cha reflexively struggled, startled out of her momentary trance.

"Hold on," he told her, and she had a moment to realize what he planned and wrapped her arms around his lean torso, enveloped in the haunting scent of ripe blueberries. "Close your eyes and press your face against my chest. The sun in Moonstone is too bright for mortal eyes."

Well, if he *insisted*. She turned her face into his silk-clad chest, closing her eyes tightly, and inhaled, savoring the moment. Who could blame her?

He flexed, his body gathering and wings whooshing. Her feet left the ground, her breath whistling out in a panicked wheeze. Azul nuzzled her hair. "I've got you, Arantxa. I won't let you fall. You can trust me to keep you safe."

For the first time in what felt like days, she let go of the horrible dread and tension, trusting him despite herself.

Though she told herself she had no reason for it, she believed him.

~ 35 ~

The Prince

"KEEP YOUR EYES closed," Azul advised, sounding infinitely more gentle than he had only moments before.

"I don't want to see how far I am away from the ground anyway," she replied.

His chuckle reverberated musically through the chest under her tightly pressed cheek, the muscles there flexing with his wingbeats in a most alluring fashion. She'd like to see him without a shirt doing this. Okay, fine, she'd like to see him totally naked doing just about anything.

"I can't believe you lied to me about the wings," she said with a fair amount of petulance.

"I didn't lie," he replied. "As you've no doubt astutely surmised by now, I cannot lie."

"Because you're fae."

"Because I'm fae."

"And not any kind of part blood fae, either. You're the high octane, pure, all the way deal."

He laughed again, full-throated, with all the velvet of his

beautiful tenor singing voice. "I wouldn't put it that way, but yes."

"What in the seven hells were you doing in the human realms marrying a mortal woman then?" she demanded, forgetting and opening her eyes to glare at him. With a yip of pain, she closed them again instantly, stars dancing burning points against her retinas.

"Told you," he said on a sigh. "A moment longer and we'll be inside. You can ask all the questions you like. But I warn you, the geas I spoke of is still in effect."

"Who could put a geas on a prince of Amethyst?"

"Another question I cannot answer."

The light blazing against her eyelids dimmed, a blessed shrouding dimness falling around them. And—praise be to the seven heavens—her feet touched solid ground.

"We're there, but it's still too bright for you. Keep your eyes closed a moment longer. Can you stand?"

"Been doing it all my life, save a few months there at the beginning." Unfortunately, when she tried to put weight on them, her legs buckled.

With a soft curse, Azul swept her up in his arms and carried her into a deeper dimness that made her sigh in relieved delight. It definitely wasn't because some hitherto unknown sappy, romantic place deep inside thrilled to him carrying her. "Must you always be stubborn?"

"You ask that like you don't know me at all." She risked squinting her eyes open, relieved to find herself in a place of normal human brightness. Correction: a palace. Azul currently carried her through a spectacular hall lined with what appeared to be pure amethyst. Ahead of them, purple light blazed with headache-inducing intensity, but as they progressed, golden shades descended over the arched windows, reducing the hall to a comforting lavender glow.

"Just how powerful are you?" she asked, trying not to stare too much. If he'd been enticing before, he fully entranced her now. She'd be worried, but it wasn't as if she could run away. Dying in his arms would be a far better fate than the acid pit from the fifth hell, so she wasn't going to overthink it. A skill she'd refined over the years.

"It depends," he answered with a quick glance at her and away.

"Prevarication isn't lying?"

"You ask that like you don't know me," he retorted. "When you're unable to lie, dancing around the fuzzy gray borders of the truth is all you have." He carried her into a grand bedchamber and laid her on a bed the size of a small lake.

"Why, Azul," she cooed, fluttering her lashes, "if you wanted to seduce me you could just say so."

He cocked a brow at her, his wings half-mantled for balance as he crouched, pulling off one of her boots, then the other. "Oh yes, because half-dead humans are irresistible."

She flopped back, acknowledging the truth of that. In truth, she felt more than half-dead. Was three-quarters dead a thing? She was somewhere between three-quarters dead and mostly dead, she decided. And she was seriously punch drunk, which didn't bode well for her brains. She should try to rally. "What is this place?"

"My pied-à-terre in Moonstone." He rose to fetch something.

"Aren't those supposed to be small—a pied-à-terre?"

"This place *is* small, comparatively, and it's my home in Moonstone, a sovereign piece of land where I have sole authority. Sit up."

"Sit up. Stand up. Throw up." Her head seriously swam, threatening that very thing as she tried to lever up.

"Just the first," he replied, amusement threading his voice. He sat on the bed and slipped an arm under her, lifting her to lean against him. "Drink this."

She eyed the eerily glowing goblet in his hand, the purple liquid within sizzling as if boiling, giving off a heady fragrance like violet honeysuckle. "You're bossy all of a sudden, Your Royal Highness, king of your sovereign realm."

"Prince," he corrected. "And yes, that includes you at the moment, stubborn one, so drink lest I be forced to pour it down your throat." His arm tightened around her as she tried—okay, feebly—to pull away. "You'll feel better, Arantxa," he said in a quieter, coaxing tone. "I promise."

"Well, since you can't lie," she grumbled, feeling a little foolish for resisting, but also like a weenie for capitulating. But she wasn't going to have him feed it to her like she was a sick kid. She took the goblet and sipped, the liquid gloriously delicious and refreshing. She gave it another long look. "Is this...ambrosia?"

"A form of it. Purer than what you feed the enchanted animals. It won't turn you into a carriage," he teased, humor lighting his deep blue eyes.

"Speaking of," she said, refusing to be charmed, "where is Katu?"

"Let's make a deal. I'll talk as long as you're drinking that." He dipped his chin at the goblet while holding her gaze.

"I've always been told to never make a bargain with the fae."

He smiled, brushing some hair out of her eyes. "Too late for that, my sweet Arantxa. Your first mistake was saving my life." He raised his brows at her surprise. "Implicit bargain. Drink if you want answers."

She sipped, telling herself it was because she already felt better from that bit and not because he was ordering—or extorting—her into it.

"Katu is here," he said as soon as she lifted the goblet to her lips. "He is well-fed and resting. When I felt your distress and came looking for you, I found him first and brought him here. Keep drinking. Yes, I sensed your trouble and sought you."

"Wait—so you can read my mind?"

"No."

"I've heard that some fae can—"

He laid a finger over her lips, closing them. "Some fae, yes. Not me. Besides, listening to people's thoughts is an exercise in chaos and cacophony. I don't wish it on anyone."

Hmm. Then how did he know that? She wanted to ask, but fae couldn't lie, so... "If you can't read my mind, then why could you feel my..." She refused to call it distress, but she also didn't want to whine.

"Not thoughts," he filled in, saving her from the word search. His fine lips twisted in a rueful smile. "Just very strong feelings of being in trouble, of your life being in danger. The life debt gives me no choice."

"I had no idea."

"It's not something the fae publicize," he replied drily. "Imagine if that were commonly known, the sordid elements of humanity who would seek to take advantage of that."

"You think I'll be hurt that you just called me sordid, but I'm at peace with myself."

He met her gaze levelly. "I did not mean you, as you are possibly the most trustworthy human I've ever met."

Awww. Her heart did a disconcerting flippy-floppy thing.

"Why aren't you drinking?" he asked, eyes glittering, expression stern, and her pussy sparkle leapt to join the impromptu heart-dance.

"You just saved my life," she pointed out, very quickly between swallows. "Doesn't that balance us out?"

"That doesn't cancel the connection between us, only deepens it," he replied somberly. "To answer your other questions, I'm very powerful when on my own sovereign land, less so when I'm not. Even less so the farther I am from it."

"You're a prince of Amethyst," she said, showing him the empty goblet.

With a satisfied nod, he took it from her and set it aside. "*The* Prince of Amethyst," he clarified.

She should have known, but that was extraordinary enough information that she forgave herself for assuming otherwise.

"I was in your human realm to get married," he said drily, "to Lenorae, as you already know."

"And who the hell is she that *the* Prince of Amethyst was marrying her?"

"That I cannot answer, but you asked earlier who can put a geas on a prince of Amethyst and I can only suggest you remember what little you ever learned about the order of power of the fae realms."

"*The* Prince of Amethyst," she corrected, just to poke at him. "Only Cinnabar and Ruby are higher than Amethyst."

He smiled slightly, tapping her nose. It could have been any gesture of random affection, but she knew it was a yes to her assumption. For such a casual touch, it also lit her up inside. Okay, lit her up even more. "Do I have to call you 'Your Highness'?" she asked, wrinkling her nose to banish the tingle.

"Why start now?" he returned drily. "If you began according me the respect of my rank, I might not know who you are."

"Excellent point. We wouldn't want that."

"How do you feel now?" he asked.

"Much better. In fact..." Oh, seven hells, what was she thinking, lolling around and having heavy-lidded, pussy-sparkling thoughts about the Prince of Amethyst? "Dy! Where is she? Did she make it back?"

Azul shook his head, the ambient lavender haze deepening the blue of his curls as they bounced. "I don't know. It's you I sense, not her."

"I have to go find her." She tried to scoot off the bed, but he restrained her. Gently, but with that implacable fae strength. "Let me go, Azul," she growled. "You might be King of all you survey here, but you're not the boss of me."

"Prince," he corrected, then had the audacity to smile at her glare. "It matters. My father, the actual King of Amethyst, would take it very much amiss were he to learn that I allowed anyone to apply his title to me."

The King of Amethyst was Azul's father. No wonder the Moonstone fae had been so agog. This just got more and more surreal. Azul's smile deepened at her obvious consternation. "While I have you temporarily speechless, let me explain two things. The first is that it is daylight outside and your human eyes can't take the brilliance of the light. You'd go blind in minutes and be no help to Dymphna at all."

"I don't need to see to ride the ley lines," she insisted stubbornly. "I don't have a lot of magic, but what I do have works without sight."

"And everything else you need to see?" he asked, holding her gaze, and she had to drop hers in acknowledgment. "Second," he continued, "though you're clearly feeling much better, you're still injured and need to be healed. I can take care of that and we can leave at nightfall. Non-negotiable," he added with a lift of his brows, making it clear he'd learned that little phrase from her.

Though she hated to give up without a fight, he'd made excellent points. Then what he'd said struck her. "We—you're coming with me?"

"Well, I need to get back to Granite and I thought I'd see if you're willing to be my ride." He grinned. "I can pay."

~ 36 ~

A Nice Afternoon

H E SMILED HOPEFULLY at her, looking nothing like the guy who'd moped nonstop on the way there.

"I thought you hated my driving," she said.

"Only the terrifying parts."

"You're immortal."

"And yet, not impervious to pain or fear of losing body parts."

"Ha ha. Yeah, of course you can ride along. I'd be glad of the company." Maybe a little *too* glad, but she was only human, as the fae loved to mention on a constant basis. "Should I ask why you're going back when you were so het up to get back into the fae realms?"

"I needed to get back to Moonstone, specifically to this place." He waved a long-fingered hand at the palace.

"To regain your power."

"Yes." He held her gaze. "Now I go back and finish what Lenorae's family started."

She really wanted to ask more, but figured both that he likely still couldn't say much and that she probably didn't want to know. The last thing she wanted to hear about was the perfect Lenorae who somehow got herself affianced to *the* Prince of Amethyst. Knowing that Azul's father was king at least explained the family pressure to wed as they decreed. Though the information changed her assessment of who Lenorae and her family were. They had to be Cinnabar or Ruby fae, or affiliated with those realms, to have put the geas on Azul. She tried one more question. "Why was the wedding in a human realm?"

He considered, seeming to be trying out different answers to see what would come out of his mouth intact. "It was a politically tricky situation," he finally said, then shrugged to indicate the vast array of things he couldn't say.

Yeah. She figured. "All right then. No more questions. How long till nightfall?"

He glanced at the sky beyond the lavishly gilded ceiling. "About six hours."

"That long? I thought I was stuck in that Moonstone jail a lot longer than that. They picked me up right before dawn."

"You were jailed for several days. That's in part why you were so weak."

"Several…" She couldn't finish, rubbing a hand over her face. Anything could've happened to Dy in that time. "This is really bad."

"Not as bad as you dying there and not getting back at all," he replied gently, no longer restraining her, but rubbing her back lightly. It felt really good. Too good. "And remember that time in the fae realms moves differently than in the human realms. I wondered before if you factored that into your calculations for returning with your cargo on time."

"No," she admitted. "No one seems to have worked out the math on it."

"There is no math—at least, not of the kind humans use. The oscillations of time and space that set the fae realms apart from the human ones aren't based on the same laws of physics. It changes all the time, depending on various factors that don't follow a pattern."

"Oh, that explains everything," she commented sourly. "Otto said the timing would work and he was invested— literally—in us bringing back his cargo on time. What is the astra anyway?"

"You don't know?" he asked cagily, his expression shuttered, and Cha was put in mind of how he'd reacted to the Moonstone fae speaking about the thing.

"I said I didn't know what it was, didn't I?"

"Yes, but *you* are capable of lying, Arantxa darling."

"Hey, I haven't lied to you." Much. She tried to think of any outstanding lies she'd committed with him.

"Uh huh." He chucked her on the chin. "Let's finish the healing. Why don't you bathe first, then you can have a nap until it's time to go."

"Hey, not all of us naturally smell like berries."

"No, you don't smell like berries." He leaned in, inhaled deeply, and hummed. "You smell like Arantxa Evermore, the most interesting and enticing woman I've ever met."

She drew back to squint at him. "What is this about?"

"I'd think a woman who's had as many lovers as you would recognize a seduction. Are my techniques so lacking?"

Okay, that she really hadn't expected. She had to work to keep her jaw from falling open. "You want to seduce me?" she nearly squeaked.

He frowned. "You had made your intentions clear. Have you changed your mind?"

"What about the whole bad omen, bad timing thing?"

"It *was* bad timing," he answered with implacable logic, "as the subsequent attack by Cinnabar imps unequivocally proved."

Well, he had a point there. "And the timing is good now?"

"We have hours to kill," he answered on a purr.

Who was she kidding? She was totally up for this. One upside of stewing in your regrets in a fae jail cell is you emerged with your priorities rearranged and crystal clear.

"I have not changed my mind." She grinned. "You might recall that I really wanted to find out about the wing thing."

He leaned in, brushed her ear with his lips, then bit gently—sending lightning straight to her groin. Apparently at least that part of her hadn't suffered lasting damage and still felt great and ready to party. "I do vividly recall," he murmured into her ear. "And I fully intend to wrap you up in my wings, just the two of us in a sensual cocoon of naked fun."

Her pussy sparkle rocketed right up to Ruby level. "I think I should take that bath."

"Let me help you," he practically purred. Sweeping her up into his arms, he stood at the same time with effortless strength.

"I'm pretty sure I can walk now," she said, a little embarrassed.

"You don't like me carrying you?"

She nearly gave a flip answer, to deflect the intensity of the moment, then remembered the whole honesty thing. With a sigh, she admitted, "I like it too much."

Though she'd rather expected him to tease her, he instead gave her a long, fulminating look. "I know what you mean."

She decided not to question that as he carried her into a bathing chamber as elaborate as the bedroom had been. He set her on her feet next to a sunken pool of amethyst-dark water. "Why is everything purple?" she asked. "Like, is it a branding requirement, that you must uphold the realm theme in everything around you?"

He regarded her with some amusement. "It's the magic. Our realm generates a vibration of magic that you perceive as shades of purple. It doesn't look that way to us."

"Oh." Well now she felt like a stupid human, like a dog capable of seeing only a few colors compared to her more sophisticated superiors. *Human pet.* She narrowed her gaze at Azul, who watched her intently. "It's a wonder you can put up with us at all."

A slow smile spread over his face, his wings expanding in an eye-catching way. She supposed he had to have big rooms just to flex them, and she absolutely supported him flexing those wings as much as possible. "You have your appealing qualities," he replied, nimbly unbuttoning her jacket.

"Uh, you're undressing me?" she asked, since she hadn't been exhibiting her denseness enough already.

"Demonstrably," he answered smoothly. "I've been wanting to do this almost since we met."

"Why are you being so nice to me now?"

He paused on the jacket, raising his cobalt-blue gaze to hers, then settled his hands on her hips. "This might be all we have, Arantxa. You have to know that, right?"

Well, she did, but that hadn't been something she'd wanted to contemplate too closely. "You won't be my first one-night stand," she answered glibly, "and I doubt you'll be the last," she added, just to make herself feel better.

"Then we understand one another. My situation is …complicated. After this one-afternoon stand," he said with a sly smile, "we might never have another opportunity."

"Will you still marry Lenorae," she asked with intense curiosity and an annoying stab of jealousy, "after all that happened?"

"That remains to be seen. There are …things to sort out. But the reasons I agreed to the marriage in the first place remain. I am not the master of my own fate, in this regard. The most I can do is seize this time with you. I would like it to be 'nice.'" His smile turned almost shy. "If that's all right with you."

"I can do nice," she said, feeling a bit silly about the insistent way she said it. "I mean, I like nice. I can be nice."

"Don't strain yourself. I find I'm perversely attracted to your mean streak."

"I don't have a—" His lips cut off her words, hot and silky, fanning the excitement racing through her body like high-test pixie dust on a perfectly inclined race course. Oh yeah. This worked. He busied himself with her jacket, sliding it off her shoulders and letting it fall. Rather than immediately proceeding further with the undressing, he smoothed his hands over her shirt, tracing the curves with what seemed like reverence.

"Mean and sweet," he whispered against her mouth. "The perfect combination."

Oh wow, she hadn't expected to feel like this. She wasn't a woman who indulged in the softer emotions. Sex was sex and they were better keeping it that way. Levering him away from her, she smiled into his concerned frown. "My turn," she informed him. "I want to see these wings without a shirt in the way."

"You're kinky for wings," he accused, but amusement quirked his lips and lightened the frown.

"Put it down to one of my human failings. How does it come off?"

"I'll do it." He stepped back a bit more, clearly enjoying giving her a good view, judging by his smug expression, wound long fingers into his shirt and pulled, ripping it clean off.

~ 37 ~

Wings and Things

CHA HAD OFTEN said that she wasn't easily impressed. Certainly not by a hot male body, as she'd seen—and caressed—any number of fine specimens in her day. But Azul as he posed for her, shirtless, wearing only tight, dark pants that rode low on his slim hips, those deep violet wings framing his lean body and that gorgeous chest muscled from flying ... Well, he made her mouth go dry.

"I wish I had a painting of this moment," she said artlessly, fresh out of chill, and unable to think of anything saucier to commemorate the moment. Then she compounded the misstep by adding breathlessly, "You're so beautiful."

"I'm glad you approve," he said gravely, going right past the opportunity to rightfully mock her.

"Can I see from behind?" she asked, and he turned, smiling only a little, giving her the equally spectacular rear view.

With so much of their admittedly brief acquaintance spent seated, Cha hadn't really had the opportunity to check out his ass—and boy how she savored the moment now. Small and tight, like a pair of apples she'd like to sink her teeth into. And his back… Oh, angels would weep black tears to have wings like this. The transparent lavender of the thinner membranes deepened to violet near the bones, and almost black where the wings joined his shoulders. The skin there was equally dark, emphasizing the shadows between the ridged muscles before radiating out in lighter shades until paling into the barely-blue moonsilver of the rest of him. Gothic, wicked, and unbearably alluring.

"May I touch?" she asked, her voice whiskey-hoarse, and he glanced over his shoulder, cocking one lean hip, and giving her that smile she couldn't resist.

"Yes, but be aware—they're very sensitive."

"Like, arousing sensitive?"

He held her gaze and nodded slowly. She approached carefully as he seemed wary of her now, and she recalled their conversation about trust, which seemed so long ago. She ran light fingers over his shoulders, his skin twitching like a horse besieged by flies. "You can trust me," she told him, meaning it.

"I know," he answered quietly. "But can you trust me?"

Instead of answering, she smoothed the caress, soothing him as he took in a shuddering breath, hanging his head and bracing one hand against a pillar. She trailed her fingers over the skin of his back, which felt like the finest sueded leather, then softly, barely touching, transferred to the thickest bones protruding from his back. The thin membrane covering them felt barely there, sueded like his skin, but so delicate. He shivered, grating out her name, "Arantxa…"

"Too much?" she asked innocently, lightly scraping fingertips farther along.

Abruptly, he furled his wings and spun, seizing her. "When I want you this much, yes."

Holding her with that easy strength, he pressed her back against the pillar he'd been propped against, his lower wing-fingers catching her ankles to wrap them around his waist so that he snugged up hard and tight against her pussy. Cha was already so tightly wound, she nearly came right then. "This is only the first round, right?" she asked on a strangled gasp.

"The first of many," he agreed, fastening his mouth to her neck and sucking hard, making her convulse.

"Then screw nice for now," she suggested with some desperation.

"I might have to save nice for the third round," he agreed, growling as she nipped his shoulder. "Maybe the fourth."

She nearly melted. "I can wait for nice, but we're wearing too many clothes still."

Lifting his head, he kissed her hard, then gave her a feral smile. "Easily handled." His wings unfurled and closed around her, the thumb and finger claws shredding her clothes with lethal speed and only just grazing her skin, the sensation exquisitely erotic.

"Seven hells," she panted, going absolutely liquid, held up mostly by his hands on her. "Those are the only clothes I have."

"Getting you new clothes seemed much easier than waiting another moment," he informed her tersely. "I also took the liberty of ridding you of the blood and the 'ick,' I believe you called it, which had been coating you rather extensively."

"Much faster than a bath," she agreed, then gasped and

wriggled as one wingtip claw trailed down her spine and into the cleft of her ass. She realized he'd also disposed of his pants when his naked body pressed against her, his cock long and hard against the slickness of her most intimate tissues. "Yes?" he asked, body straining with tension. "I know its fast and human women can take longer to—"

"Yes," she nearly shouted, grinding against him. "Shut up and fuck me, Azul."

"Oh, Arantxa darling," he said in a dangerous voice, "I do believe I shall." Brushing his lips along the shell of her ear, he whispered, "Brace yourself, Bridget."

Holding her with one hand and a wing cupped around her for support, he positioned himself and slid smoothly inside her. They both stilled, their gazes locking. The sensation for Cha was like nothing before, shimmeringly perfect, completing her in a way she'd have scoffed at had anyone suggested it to her. "Now I know why humans go for fae sex regardless of the dangers."

"Am I a danger to you, Arantxa?" he asked on a purr, flexing his hips to move into and within her, sending furious sparks of passion shuddering through her. "You have to know I'd never harm you."

"That's not what concerns me," she answered, her thoughts scattering to the four winds. His wings closed around her, shrouding them in that violet haze of erotic steam, her edges dissolving with pleasure as he rocked inside her, flexing his hips with inhuman and sinuous grace. She clung to him, aware that *this* was the danger. She wanted to hold on and never let him go, to keep and hold him forever. Who had she become? Another bedazzled human woman seduced by a beautiful fae man.

Azul didn't reply, seeming as lost in her as she was in him, his lips pressed to her temple, his breath coming in rough pants, hot and sweet, his body flexing all along hers. Maybe she only thought she'd said it aloud, which was for the best. Apparently she'd turned into putty in his hands, at least sexually, but that didn't mean she'd stopped being the Bandit. She wouldn't lose herself to this man, no matter how perfect. Her resolve firmed, she shored up the walls around her heart and gave herself over to the spectacular pleasure he brought her.

A LONG TIME later, they lolled bonelessly in the deeply hued water, post-third round, which had occurred in the massive tub. The second round had been a real banger on the jewel of an amethyst floor and Cha's knees might never be the same. Still, she'd do it again in a heartbeat. As soon as she could move again.

The water fizzled with effervescence against her sensitized skin, smelling faintly of grapes and also like violets. In her stunned, completely enervated state, she didn't care that the two things smelled nothing alike. Every fingertip of her throbbed from Azul's thorough assault of her senses and she could barely lift her head. She might die from his attentions, but she'd die a happy, if sadly mortal, woman.

"I apologize," Azul said on a quiet sigh.

She indeed couldn't lift her head, but she could roll it to look at him. "Going to have to renege on the promised fourth round?"

He pursed his lips impatiently. "As if you could take another round. In my… zeal, I neglected to pay attention to your fragile mortal condition."

"Hey, buddy, I'll see your 'zeal' and raise you. No man has worn me out yet."

"I'm not a man," he pointed out.

"If you're fishing for compliments, I'll give you that one. You, my most succulent of blueberries, are far better than any mortal man." She didn't mind admitting it, especially feeling as if he'd wrung every cell of her body dry and replaced the fluid with the finest bubbling wine. Not to mention the wings. It had never occurred to her that the wing fingers—and don't forget those wicked thumbs at the other end—would demonstrate such dexterity, nor that the wings themselves would be so flexible. Having those oh-so-soft wings sliding along every bit of her skin and basically three sets of 'hands' stimulating her, along with his most excellent cock doing the work of angels had been the pinnacle of an already pretty stupendous life of sexual adventuring. "And now I know what you do with the wings during sex."

"Everything I *can* do with them," he agreed warmly, holding out a hand to her and managing to make her blush, before he sobered, interlacing their fingers. "No, I meant that I should have healed you first. I was being selfish and could have waited until you were—"

"I couldn't wait," she interrupted. "Did not want to. I will concede, however, that a bit of healing wouldn't be amiss before this theoretical round four." She gave him a considering side-eye. "If you're capable that is."

With a growl of mock-anger, he used their joined hands to tug her to him, and she went eagerly, more than ready to be overcome again. But he gathered her close and stood, stepping out of the bath, wings spread for balance. Water sheeted off of them, helped along with his magic, a warm-honeysuckle breeze swirling around them so that, by the time they reached the bed again, even her hair had dried.

"Handy," she commented. "Too bad you can't use all that magic in the human realms."

"Whether I can depends on a number of conditions," he replied, laying her on the bed with infinite care, stretching her out, then running hands along her body, one wing also dipping to caress her side as he sat beside her. "You are all over bruises, Arantxa."

"Fortunately all these blues and purples are your favorite colors." She made a joke of it, but she did look pretty terrible, with plenty of greenish browns in the patterns radiating over her body. She didn't remember getting most of them. "I'm surprised I don't feel worse."

"These are all peripheral remnants," he replied absently, taking one foot in his hands with a barely-there touch, his wing cupping beneath her knee to support her leg. "The elixir I gave you initially took care of the internal healing at least."

"I should have bathed in *that*," she joked.

He raised a brow. "You did."

Huh. "Then why—*ahhh*," her breath sighed out of her as

his lips pressed to her swollen ankle. The relief from that minor pain felt like cool water on a hot day.

He smiled against her skin, tracing the strained ligaments with his clever tongue. "There's internal. There's surface. Now I'm getting the in-between."

"My in-between is enjoying this very much," she admitted, melting into the bed. Maybe her knees *would* be the same again, a cheerful thought if she ever got another chance at that particular flavor.

"From this end, too," he told her in a voice as soft and sueded as his wings. "The turn of your ankle here, is so lovely. And the arch of your foot." He pressed a kiss to the spot, sending warm tumbrels of sensation up through her. "Such long toes, and the second toe is the longest."

"That's supposed to be a sign of fae blood in a human. Or intelligence. You can take your pick which is more likely with me."

He chuckled, music in it, and drew that toe into his mouth, suckling lightly before releasing it. "Charming," he comment-ed before giving each of her toes the same loving treatment, then moving up her calf.

This was new to her, being ministered to, being cared for. Yes, he was using his magic to heal her with blessed generosi-ty, but it felt like more than that. Not that she would un-barrier her heart—that was a non-starter—but she could relax into this feeling of...being adored. Inside her head, she could admit to that, though she'd deny it at the top of her lungs if anyone else suggested it. For the moment, bathed in amethyst light and Azul's unwavering attention, she could enjoy. Was this how trust felt?

Whatever it was, the delicious feeling made her wonder what else she'd been missing in life. Well, she would go on missing it, because this was only for now.

Azul continued his intimate inventory of her body, describing how enticing he found every aspect of her mortal flesh, in detail, caressing, kissing, licking, healing, and nipping as he went. He reminded her of Zazu reading for herself for the first time and insisting on reading the book aloud to every adult of her limited acquaintance, over and over, pointing out the words as she did, and frequently pausing to recap the story so far.

Except that Azul's enthusiastic exploration and discussion was, fortunately and of course, actually sexy and fully engrossing. Unfortunately, Azul's study of her body was also exceedingly more frustrating. The man who hadn't been able to wait to be inside her a short time ago had transformed into one with an excruciating amount of patience. Several times, she attempted to seize him and end the healing/teasing, but he resisted her easily, using his wings to pin her in place like velvet-covered ropes of woven steel.

"I'm not stopping until you're entirely healed," he informed her with that arrogance that perversely appealed to her. "Also, this is my first and likely last opportunity to properly worship your body. I'll not allow you to rush me through it."

Cha squirmed in futile rebellion, simultaneously wrung out to the point of wilting and fulminating with need. She didn't like to think about this being the end of their time together, so she didn't pursue that angle. There was nothing to argue there anyway. "Surely I have nothing you haven't properly worshipped before," she said to the ceiling, shuddering with the erotic intensity of his ministrations, trying to think of ways to hurry him up.

"I've never been with a human woman before," he replied, slowly licking the underside of her breast.

She ignored the completely unreasonable ping of delight at hearing that. *Yes, yes—you're totally special, Cha. Temporarily. Get over it.* "Are we so different?"

He lifted his head and slithered up her body, rubbing his naked self against her like a cat, then kissing her deeply. Lifting his head, he held her gaze. "Yes. And you, Arantxa, are unlike anyone else. Stop fighting me and let me have this."

"I'm not fighting you," she said, oddly chastened and also touched by his words. And fragile, deep inside, rawly vulnerable in a way she never was. "I *can't* fight you," she pointed out, managing to add some asperity to her voice, demonstrating by struggling against the wings holding her. His thumb claws curled in response, scraping gently, erotically against the surprisingly sensitive skin at the pulse points of her wrists, making her convulse and hiss out her breath.

"I mean in here," he murmured, placing a kiss on her forehead and shifting to plant a more lavish one between her breasts, over her thudding heart. "And here. Can't you trust me, just a little?" he asked almost wistfully.

"I'm here aren't I?" she returned. "In your evil fae lair letting you have your way with me."

"Evil, hmm?" He mused over that, humming in that lovely

tenor and brushing light kisses over her breasts. He seemed particularly fascinated by them, loving to play with her nipples, along with her belly button, likely because he didn't have either. "I'm not evil."

She wrapped fingers around his thumb claws, drawing the pads of them along the lethally curved edge, and shimmied against the wing membranes draped lavishly over her skin. "Gothic," she whispered. "My violet prince, pretty as a devil."

"You haven't seen many actual devils if you think that," he said with a slight smile, "but I'll take the compliment as intended, my beautiful, sacred, and thorny lover." He settled more deeply against her. "Spread your thighs for me, Arantxa," he urged quietly.

Though she kind of wanted to defy the order for form's sake, she also wasn't going to cut off her nose to spite her face, so she obeyed eagerly, wrapping her legs around him. He sheathed himself in her, slickly, seamlessly, both of them shuddering at the final click of that lock and key fitting together. As if that key unlocked something deep inside, she unraveled, coming apart in slow increments too gradual to be called climaxes, too intense to be anything else.

The sensation rolled through her, ongoing, shredding every last boundary, Azul's face poised above hers, indigo eyes sparking amethyst and locked on hers, body similarly riveted to hers, his wings spreading huge and high, violet night shrouding them from the world. As he crested, they opened to full expanse, radiating magic that poured into and through her, infusing her with wellbeing she'd never before experienced.

He released and relaxed, burying his face in the side of her throat, wings folding to embrace her, along with the arms he wrapped around her. Safe and protected, entangled in every way, even the dangerous ways, she fell into blissful rest.

~ 38 ~

On the Road Again

AZUL WOKE HER some time later, by raining kisses on her face. "Feeling better?" he asked on a laugh when she swatted at him.

"I don't feel like a beautiful butterfly emerging from that cocoon," she informed him groggily, sitting up and stretching. Her body felt amazingly good, however. "I'm the caterpillar that got stepped on by the big bad fae."

He actually rolled his eyes at her before striding naked into the bathing chamber. The sight of his adorably tight ass framed by the deep purple points of his partially mantled bat wings did a considerable amount to wake her up.

"What was that?" she called, following him, but not quite hearing what he'd muttered in response.

"I said you're more like Katu in animal form, lacerating me with your claws," he answered, glancing at her in amusement as he went to an open corner of the room with a lacework floor.

"You're the one with the claws," she replied, but absently, quickly forgetting the thought as purple rain commenced showering over him. Amethyst water drenched him as he stood, his head tipped back to allow it to sheet over his body, his wings stretching and angling to be evenly rinsed. She wanted nothing more than to lick every drop of moisture away.

He cocked a brow at her and curled a wing in a come-hither gesture. "Care to join me for round five?"

"Do we have time?" she asked, knowing the answer. Even she could tell dusk had gathered outside the shaded windows. As she asked, the shades lifted themselves, baring windows that revealed a landscape illuminated by pearly twilight. "No," she answered for him, being her most responsible self. The choice wasn't even difficult—worry for Dy chewed at her and her lustful self sprawled in satiated somnolence, like a drunk after a five day feast.

"I'll let you shower alone," Azul agreed ruefully, "as I don't trust myself to keep my hands off of you." The water stopped and he shook himself, wings rustling musically. As he passed her, he paused and framed her face in his hands, wings arching in an echo of the embrace. He kissed her softly, even affection-ately, then searched her eyes. "It's been an honor and a true pleasure, Arantxa," he said solemnly. "I'll never forget this interlude. Or you."

"Yeah, well," she extracted herself lest she give into the craving to hold onto him, "you can't, right? That life debt and permanent connection and all."

"Not what I meant," he said quietly.

"How do I turn on the water?" she asked, ready to be done with the uncomfortable conversation. "Oh!" she exclaimed as the water sheeted down the moment she stepped onto the lacework flooring. "Thank—" she started to tell him, turning back to smile.

But he had already left.

AZUL DELIVERED ON the clothes, though they were—why didn't she see it coming?—all deep shades of that dark purple that looked black in most lights. Form-fitting to the point of hugging every line and crevice of her body, the pants, shirt and jacket clung to her skin with a sensual warmth that reminded her far too much of the feel of Azul's skin. Cha also couldn't tell what they were made of. Nothing that existed in the human realms, that was for sure.

"What is this?" she demanded, plucking at the decidedly low neckline. "Fairy skin?"

"Disgusting concept," he chided her, batting her hands away and adjusting the neckline, hands casually brushing her breasts as he did. "Leave it now. You look incredible." He circled her. "Coming and going."

"Yes, well, I still need a sword," she reminded him. She'd fetched Monat's nose ring from the shreds of her former clothing and pocketed it.

"I haven't forgotten," Azul replied lightly. Suddenly, a sword lay across his outstretched palms, glowing with golden light, a distinctly orange-red quality to the metal.

She peered at it, hesitant to touch. "Is that…"

"Cinnabar magic," he confirmed, deftly spinning the blade

to offer her the hilt. "A bit of assistance for you, just in case. Since you seem to be in dire need of assistance in keeping *your* skin intact."

She eyed him. "That sounds quite a bit above my pay grade. Just a plain mortal, remember?"

"I wouldn't give you something that could cause you harm," he replied with strained patience.

Apparently trusting him at least that much, she wrapped her hand around the hilt. It felt good, solid, exquisitely balanced, and maybe a little weirdly alive, but she could live with that. Most important, it didn't immediately fry her nervous system and send her into paroxysms of death. She didn't really think Azul would do that to her, especially having gone to so much trouble to heal her, but old cynicisms die hard. "Cinnabar magic just in case I need to level up over someone from, say, Amethyst?"

He regarded her gravely. "We're not out of Moonstone yet. And who knows when you might decide to hare off in Obsidian and save some child with foolish parents from an Eloko."

"Some child…Hey, how do you know about the Eloko?"

Feathering fingers over her cheek, he smiled. "I kept track of you. You big softie."

"Watch it with the insults, Your Highness." She danced back, pointing the tip of the sword at him. It was an outrageously good weapon, like holding sunlight—fast, bright, weightless, and powerful. "Besides, I'm a big sharpie now."

"And may you save many mortals with it," he replied solemnly. "But do be careful. That is a powerful weapon you have currently pointed at my heart."

She rather thought he didn't mean only the sword, but she couldn't allow herself to fall into the implications of what he might mean. Carefully, she sheathed it, feeling as if she also put her heart away. "We should go."

With a courtly gesture, he waved for her to proceed. "After you, thorny one."

KATU WAS BEYOND delighted to see her, the jaguar in animal form came galloping over the grass and leapt fully onto her, knocking Cha onto her back with big soft paws on her shoulders, pinning her down while he licked her face with his raspy tongue. "Aw, baby cat, sweet kitten," she said to him, scratching his whiskery muzzle and chin. "I missed you, too. Now stop, stop..." she began laughing helplessly as he continued to lick her.

Finally she levered the happy cat off of her, struggling to her feet to find an amused Azul watching her. "I would never have predicted you're a giggler," he remarked.

"I do not giggle," she replied with dignity.

"You giggled just now."

"That was laughter."

"Giggling."

"I'm happy to see my cat. Which way to the slow white?" She refused to be embarrassed, walking in the direction he indicated, a hand on Katu's head as he sawed quietly, nudging her thigh with affection. "He looks good," she offered, grateful that Azul had seen to the cat.

Azul dipped his head in acknowledgement, both that she couldn't thank him and in ironic understanding that she appreciated his care, for her and her own. They reached the slow white and Cha, giving Katu a last, long chin-skritch, triggered the enchantment to send him into carriage form. The transformation went fast and slick, barely any transition, and she whistled low, impressed. "Is that the Moonstone dust or the high-quality ambrosia you clearly fed him?"

Azul set a hand on her back, kissing her cheek. "A bit of both."

She checked out Katu's jump seat and boot, sighing when she noted everything that hadn't been attached was gone. Not that the cooler of food and ale mattered now, but it hurt her mercenary heart to lose all those gems of Phinny's. "Fucking Sugarplums," she muttered.

"Everything all right?" Azul asked.

"Just a bit of highway robbery," she answered on a sigh. "But I have my skin intact." Because she couldn't thank him, she gave him a kiss, lingering as she should not. "We should go."

"Shall we then?"

"Let us shall," she answered in a plummy voice.

"I do not sound like that," he told her, his wings vanishing.

"Awww... do you have to?" He looked plenty delicious without the wings, but...

"They're awkward for sitting in a carriage and for explaining to authorities, so yes, I have to."

"You're *the* Prince of Amethyst," she pointed out, sliding

into the driver's seat. Oh yeah. This felt good and right. The last bits of herself still out of place from her ordeal settled. *The Bandit is back.* "Which authorities could possibly bother you?"

He slid her a look. "Recall that there is discretion involved, Arantxa. Out there, I'm not even fully fae, or even mostly fae." As he spoke, his appearance shifted subtly, his ears rounding, his sharply elegant features softening, the iridescent blue of his hair and eyes dimming. He still looked like himself, but also much more like the frivolous human noble playing at being fae that she'd first thought him. The change was a bit disconcerting.

"I always thought glamour was supposed to make people prettier," she grumbled, sending Katu down what looked like a stately drive through a manicured park, "not the reverse." Though evening had fully fallen, the light remained bright enough to make her squint. She had to admit, if only to herself, that she could not have endured full daylight in Moonstone.

Azul picked up her hand, turned it over, and kissed her palm, sending a sensual susurrus through her body, arousing that which had been fully sated not long before, her lustful self shaking off the sleepy bloat and sitting up with renewed interest.

"I appreciate the compliment," he said, with a sly smile. "But 'glamour' in the original sense meant enchantment. It's only the humans finding the fae beautiful and enviable that gave the word the sense of making something more attractive."

"Well, losing the wings is definitely the wrong direction, but that could be my personal kink, as you say. So if glamour means enchantment, does that mean they are actually gone, not just invisible to human eyes?"

He considered, and she knew his expressions well enough to know that he was calculating how to explain within the constraints binding him. "Yes," he answered, grinning when she glared. "Invisible to *all* eyes, however," he corrected, "and touch, as you know." His smile turned intimate, reminding her of when she'd thrown herself at him and generating that answering pussy sparkle she no longer had time to indulge, no matter how alert and now yammering for satisfaction her lustful self might be now. Probably they'd never get to indulge again. And didn't that just figure. Fuck her life.

~ 39 ~

Sex, Lies, and Ley Lines

THEY LEFT THE walls of Azul's estate behind very high walls topped with what appeared to be razor-sharp chunks of amethyst, guarded by a faceted, gothic wrought-something gate that opened at their approach and faded invisibly into the walls behind them—and plunged into the whiteness of the Moonstone landscape.

Azul directed her through the rural leys and soon they hit the Moonstone Throughway. Cha eyed their erstwhile sanctuary dwindling in the distance in the rear view, vanishing to a dot, then quickly gone.

"Something wrong?" Azul asked, turned partway in the passenger seat to watch her.

Cha shook herself. Bad enough that she was having all these weird, softhearted feelings; no need to compound that with spinelessness. She produced something that felt close to her usual insouciant grin. "Just very ready to put Moonstone behind me. How long to the border, do you think?" Even at the blazing speeds on the fast white, she agitated to go faster. She also kept wanting to look over her shoulder for pursuing

Sugarplums and puttoes.

"Less than an hour, subjective time," he replied, patting her on the knee. He meant it to be soothing, she knew, but the gesture mostly served to annoy her by making it so clear that he saw through her bravado.

"*If* we don't hit trouble. Or traffic. Or troublesome traffic," she commented darkly.

"We won't."

"You're so confident?"

"I do have increased power still. Enough to do that much for you."

"For *us*," she corrected. But he only smiled blandly. Yeah, he could clearly handle anything that came at him here. "The fae realms just aren't for humans," she said on a sigh, feeling every cautionary tale about humans lost to the fae in the chilled marrow of her bones. Marrow that at least hadn't been sucked out of her cracked bones by Sugarplums.

"I tried to warn you."

"Yeah, well, you're in excellent company with all kinds of people of my acquaintance then, from my parents and siblings, to my teachers and professors, to my lifelong best friend who I can only hope is still alive."

"You have a family?" he asked, sounding more interested than she'd have predicted.

"Did," she answered on a shrug.

"Oh, I'm sorry."

"For what, that I had them or that I don't anymore?"

"Interesting question. I always thought humans liked their families and so were sorry to lose them."

"Don't the fae like their families?"

"I could be biased," he answered after a pause, gazing down the sparkling white ley line. "I don't like mine, for obvious reasons."

She absorbed that, wanting to ask more, knowing he likely couldn't say. Plus, he looked sad, so she didn't want him to dwell. Bad enough that he was headed into this fucked-up wedding scenario. He didn't need to ponder why his clearly awful royal family had sacrificed him to a situation so terrible he'd run from it. She understood Azul well enough now to know he wouldn't flee unless he had no other choice.

"I didn't *lose* my family," she told him, her attention on the flow of the ley line, internal gaze focused on the past, "not to mortality anyway, if that's what you're thinking. It's more that they lost me. I was a problem child," she continued, glancing over to find him raptly listening. "Always getting into trouble. They were happy to send me to Miss Mulry's and have done. Not just happy—relieved." That had stuck with her more than anything, the utter relief on her mother's face as she said goodbye and went back to the hired carriage that brought them there, Cha's younger siblings already arguing about who got Cha's room.

"How old were you?"

"Ten. That was the youngest you could board a kid. I was lucky Miss Mulry's took me on as my family was poor. Scholarship student, you know, on account of my extremely awesome ley-riding talents." She smirked at him, but he was frowning.

"How bad can a ten-year-old be?" he asked.

She rolled her eyes. "You know me."

"Yes, I do, and you're not a problem person."

"I'm incorrigible," she confided with a wink. He still didn't smile. "Oh, come on! I'm badass. I'm the Bandit. I didn't earn that rep by being all law-abiding. I didn't think you harbored illusions about me that way."

"I know not many people would have picked up a rude, stray prince on a rural back ley."

"You were understandably out of sorts, what with the fell wolves and all. Besides, I thought you were pretty. Never could resist a bit of candy, you know."

"Softhearted," he whispered, smiling now.

"See how you are with the insults?" she huffed. "Dy is the softie. Everyone knows it. She's going to be broken-hearted about Monat."

"Like you."

Sighing, Cha wrestled the unexpected surge of grief. She and Monat hadn't been close, but they'd been friends. She'd been too busy worrying about her own shitty fate before to give way to the very real sorrow over Monat. Even worse would be having to tell Dy. Cha couldn't think about it too much and keep herself together. Azul was watching her closely, maybe seeing the dank emotions that threatened to sap the ferocity she needed to keep going.

"I'm sorry for Monat's shitty fate," Cha said with deliberate lightness, shrugging it all off. "She was good people and didn't deserve that end, but I was mostly upset that I nearly ended up the same way. Anyhow," she continued when she saw he was about to insist she possessed some kind of sweet, gooey center, which she emphatically did not, "my mommy didn't want me, my daddy left early, wah wah. I don't know about fae, but that kind of tale is more common in human families than the opposite. Getting dumped at Miss Mulry's Academy for the Magically Gifted was the best thing that could've happened to me because that's where I met Dy. Speaking of..." She frowned at the path-box. "This thing stopped working when I crossed into Moonstone. Can you whammy it better, now that you're all full of Amethyst piss and vinegar again?"

"I contain neither piss nor vinegar," he replied in a snotty tone, passing lightly caressing fingers over her hand, telling her without words that he would let the topic go. Continuing the movement, he spun a web of violet magic that formed a net around the path-box. "If Dy is in range, she should answer. Use the amethyst channel."

"There is no amethyst channel."

"There is now," he replied, looking all smug and self-satisfied.

"You know, you could have been a lot more useful before," she grumbled.

His smile faded, leaving him broody again. Grief and anger, she realized, just like her own demons. "I'm aware," he said with biting regret.

See? She wasn't a good person at all. "Sorry," she muttered, and he waved off the apology. She tapped the path-box until it turned purple—an unearthly shade that didn't occur in nature, at least, not in the human realms. "Oh, that little display won't raise brows or anything," she told him.

"You should probably not use it in mixed company," he

suggested, unrepentant.

"Goldilocks, Bandit here. You out there?" The box shivered with waves of lavender and she threw Azul a look. He shrugged.

"Bandit!" Dy's voice came through with frenzied relief. "Where in the seven hells are you?"

Cha's lips actually wobbled with emotion at the welcome sound of Dy alive. "In the Big White, headed for the reverse BX. You?"

"I'm at the rendezvous and you're nearly three hours late. I was starting to worry!"

Three hours? Azul looked amused at her stunned reaction. "I told you time moved differently in the … 'big white.'"

"You don't have to put air quotes around it," Cha told him. "You are so uncool."

"Is that Prince Charming?" Dy asked, her voice rising to a screech. "Bandit, if you've been—"

"I haven't," she interrupted and Azul raised a brow at her, making a shocked face. Well, she *had* been, but … "It's a long story," she amended. "I'll tell you later. Can we still get through?"

"I hope so. We'll be hitting the work-around in daylight."

"We will?"

"Um, yeah."

Cha looked around at the Moonstone night, which still looked like day to her. So confusing. "Can't be helped, I suppose."

"Agreed. The alternative isn't one. Bandit, there's no room for *screwing around.* You have to—"

"I have to be there soonest. Will do," Cha interrupted and tapped off.

"It's fascinating to watch you lie," Azul commented. "It's a kind of human magic we can't match."

"First of all, I wasn't *lying*, exactly," she protested. "I didn't want to air the details on the path-box, so I talked around it."

"No, *I* would've talked around it. You said you weren't when you were. Magic."

"It's not magic," she retorted.

"Lying again." He laughed musically and with real delight. "No wonder I adore you, Arantxa."

Her mood surprisingly light, she gave him the middle finger, listening to the music of his laughter as she coaxed Katu into a bit more speed.

~ 40 ~

A Perfect World

CHA SIGHED WITH relief when they burst through the big Moonstone wall and into sunny Obsidian daylight. She shook her head, refocusing her eyes. "It truly isn't nighttime here. How does that even work?"

Azul shrugged. "I've tried to explain this to you already."

"Yeah, yeah—time moves differently, blah blah blah." Still, it sucked that it seemed to be well into the morning here in Obsidian, the golden light more like her normal world, the sound of birdsong more comforting than she'd have guessed. Never would she have predicted that the surreal, twisted landscape of Obsidian would feel familiar. Almost like coming home. A sign of trauma right there, when a fae realm seemed like home.

But then—she glanced over at Azul, who was fiddling thoughtfully with the Moonruby wand, caught her looking, and gave her a warm smile—when your boyfriend was fae, maybe that wasn't such a long shot. She caught herself, tripping on the thought. *Azul is decidedly not your boyfriend,* she told herself firmly. *You had a great interlude, but that's it. You're both moving on, so no matter how bone-melting he is in bed, he's still just a guy who was a lover, past tense emphasized.*

She was excused from wrestling herself further by their arrival at the designated rendezvous, basically a wide spot on a side ley, surrounded by trees. It looked empty, but that should be Dy shrouding them in illusion. Still, she wanted to proceed cautiously. "I don't see them," she confided to Azul quietly, "but—"

"But they're right there," he interrupted, pointing.

"How can you see through my illusion?" Dy demanded. Actually, it looked to Cha like a bush asked the question in Dy's voice, but it quickly morphed into the petite blonde. Big Betty shimmered into view behind her, giving a muted trumpet of greeting, while Warg spilled halfway and haphazardly out the window of the cab, warbling happily, a single line of drool spilling from his jaw to the ground.

Azul squared off with Dy, looking slightly taller to Cha's eye than he had a moment ago. "Your sorcery is very good," he told her in his usual nonchalant style, which meant he sounded arrogant as a...well, as a fae prince. "It is not, however, better than mine."

Dy's corkscrew curls practically unscrewed themselves as she puffed up in righteous fury, poking Azul in the chest. "Listen, you. I don't know who in the seven hells you are, but I do know you've been a nearly fatal distraction for my best friend and if you think you can just seduce her, ruin our gig, and stiff her the coin you owe, then—"

"Dymphna," Cha said, interrupting and interposing her body between them. Azul took the opportunity to surreptitiously palm her ass, so she elbowed him in the ribs, eliciting a satisfying grunt from him. "He saved my life."

Azul made a tsking sound and Dy's eyes widened into pale blue halos around suspicious black pits. "You shouldn't say that aloud, Cha."

"No, she shouldn't," Azul agreed. They exchanged a look of surprise, reminding Cha of her unexpected synchrony with Phinny.

Dy soon returned her furious scrutiny to Cha. "And this outfit? It positively reeks of Amethyst magic. Do I even want to know where these clothes came from and what happened to your old ones?"

Cha barely resisted looking at Azul. "It really is such a long story and I promise to tell you all of it when we are safe. Let me just say that I spent some time in Moonstone jail."

"What?" Dy's sweet face whitened to a mask of tight horror. "Oh Cha. No. Did you go after Monat then? What did you—"

"Monat is dead," she told Dy without preamble, figuring it was best to rip the bandage off. "I'm sorry, but she died in Moonstone. I found evidence."

"What evidence?" Dy asked in that even tone she used when she was fighting not to melt down, her big blue eyes swimming with tears that Cha viciously hoped Dy wouldn't shed. If Dy started crying, then she would, too, and that would wreak at least a first hell on her badass reputation.

Cha fished out the nose ring and laid it in Dy's palm. "I found this in the washroom for humans. You know she'd have only removed it for one reason."

"To leave a clue," Dy said, wrapping her fingers around the ring, her voice watery. "How did she die?"

"You don't want to know. No," Cha said firmly when Dy opened her mouth to argue. "I will not tell you, but it nearly happened to me. Would have if Az—" At his hiss of warning, she hastily corrected, "if Prince Charming here hadn't gotten me out."

Dy closed her mouth. Nodded to Azul. "Fine."

"Fine," he echoed grinning at her cheekily.

She turned back to Cha, visibly gathering her poise. "What happened at the Moonstone meet? You were right behind me and—"

"Do we have time?" Cha asked. "No, we don't," she said firmly when Dy looked mutinous. "I promise to tell you everything later. On the porch at your place, over ale and Phin's rosemary twists."

"Fine," Dy agreed, then added, not too grudgingly, to Azul. "You're invited, too."

The fae prince looked puzzled and taken aback. Cha had half expected him to refuse with his characteristic hauteur. She had to admit, she really couldn't picture the elegant man chilling his ass on Dy and Phin's rustic porch, the kids screaming and flinging mud and fish slime.

"I would like that," he said slowly, as if the words felt strange in his mouth. The truth, of course, as he couldn't say anything else, but flavored with the regret of knowing it would never happen. He met Cha's gaze over Dy's head and nodded minutely in mutual understanding.

She was the first to look away, clapping her hands together

briskly. "Let's get the parade moving. Were you able to juice up?" she asked Dy, tipping her head at Big Betty.

"Yes, but have you?"

Unable to repress a smile at how very well she and Katu had both been replenished, she nodded, catching the pleased glitter in Azul's eyes.

Dy made a sound of exasperation. "It's like being caught in a heat ray standing between you two. Were Phin and I this bad?"

Cha nearly answered yes, then realized Dy's implication. "Not the same thing at all," she answered crisply, wrenching her gaze from Azul's compelling one. "Ready to do the thing?"

"Ready," Dy said, looking between them with a quiet somberness Cha didn't care to explore. Dy fastened her gaze on Azul. "Since your sorcery is so much better than mine, Prince Charming, can you assist with hiding us if I falter?"

He bent in a sweeping bow that gave Cha an absurd wave of pleasure, including a surge of pussy sparkle that would never again be satisfied, curse it. "I would be honored, Goldilocks."

"For coin, glory, and thrills!" Cha pumped her fist in the air, wishing she felt it more.

"Let's haul ass and get home already," Dy agreed, with a similar air of deflated resolve.

It wasn't quite their old rallying cry, but it came close. Rest in peace, Monat.

"WHAT HAPPENS NOW?" Azul asked as they slid into their seats in Katu.

"Ideally, in a perfect world, Dy will easily establish her workaround ley, we'll hop on it, loop around the depot undetected, come out the other side and blend with the normal import/export traffic. Then we cross the border back into Gypsum with no trouble, hightail it to whatever fence Phinny will find for us, hand off the Obsidian dust and the astra inside, which you still haven't told me what it is..." She trailed off hopefully.

"It's better off in the human realms is what it is," he replied in clipped tone.

"So you're not going to tell me—or is this a geas thing?"

He gave her a long, serious look. "I don't actually know what the astra is. That's a generic term for something quite politically tricky within the fae realms and you are better off knowing less than more. Do you understand what I'm telling you?"

"Well, if that's your way of warning me off, it won't work. I'm going to have to find out what it is to sell it."

He smiled thinly, unhappily. "Just...go carefully, Arantxa. Don't mix with things beyond your ken."

"I'm a pro," she assured him breezily. "This is totally my ken."

"Keep my words in mind. Promise me you will."

"You know promises aren't binding to humans."

"They are to you. Promise me anyway."

"Fine, fine. I promise I'll bear in mind that this is all politically tricky and my ken isn't up to snuff for comprehending it all."

He smiled. "That works."

"Anyway," she continued, "once we identify the astra thing, we'll sell it, and it won't be our problem anymore. We'll take our big pile of coin and head to Dy and Phin's cottage for ale and rosemary twists. Peasant food," she added with a sly smile for him, "but delicious."

"No doubt." He set a hand on her thigh and caressed the inner curve. "I've discovered a recently developed taste for all things human and peasant."

"All?" she countered archly.

"A select few," he allowed, then pulled his hand away, alas. "You know I can't go."

To Dy and Phin's cottage for ale and rosemary twists. Yeah, she knew that. Dy had laid down the beginning of the work-around ley line, so Cha sent Katu down it. It prickled the back of her neck and between her shoulder blades to be doing this in broad daylight, but she trusted Dy—and Azul—to keep them hidden. The ley line felt good, maybe a little too good, not nearly as fragile as the one Dy had created on their way in. Likely the sorceress had abandoned using a thin line to keep attention away and was relying on her and Azul's ability to glamour to protect them.

The teamwork that included Azul gave her a warm, fuzzy feeling that she resented mightily. Probably she should enjoy the moment, but the looming future where all this would be gone gnawed at her. Might as well embrace the disappointment now and get used to it. Speaking of which… "I assume you want to be dropped off at Lenorae's family domicile of doom?"

He considered. "How close can you get me?"

"Well, as I don't know the *exact* location, I can't answer that with authority, but I can get back to the spot where I picked you up."

"I can guide you from there, unless you'd rather not get too close."

"Hey, door-to-door service is all part of what we provide here at Bandit Express." Besides, she really wanted a good look at Azul's future bride. How else would she torment herself at night imagining him with *her*, wrapping the bitch in his glorious wings and doing to her what…Yeah, self-destructive was Cha's middle name and she was at peace with that.

Unfortunately, she couldn't think of a way to resume semi-normal conversation after that exchange. Mostly the demand to know *why* he had to go back to that unsavory situation battered at the backs of her teeth. He couldn't answer and, even if he could, she wouldn't like what he had to say and it would change nothing, so she clamped her jaws down hard to keep any whining and clinging from escaping.

Azul sensed her mood. Or felt the same. Whatever, because he was quiet for a while, the silence stretching uncomfortably. "It's never a perfect world," he finally said.

At first Cha thought he meant their inevitable parting and his even more certain dismal unhappiness at Lenorae's hands. Was it so wrong to hope Azul would be miserable with his ideal bride? A better woman would be able to wish him happy, but Mrs. Evermore's little troublemaker had never been destined to be a better person. Cha viciously hoped Azul would pine away for her, forever regretting that he didn't stay with her and…and what? Live a cozy cottage life with her like Dy and Phin? Have half-fae/half-human babies and send the sulky, criminally minded critters off to Miss Mulry's? No no no. She shuddered at the image. No amount of rosemary twists could make her want that life.

"Not even a close to perfect world," she agreed. "It's all right. I know you have to go get married to *Lenorae*." She didn't quite spit the woman's name and was proud of herself.

He gave her a quizzical glance. "I meant your list of all that needs to go correctly in the next little while."

Oh. Well, fuck her life and her stupid heart blabbing out nonsense. "That's why they pay us the big bucks—this isn't a corporate cargo run. This is dangerous living and we're the best." The depot loomed nearby, not nearly as sparkly as at night, but still glittering like a bedazzled starfish in the morning light. "Besides, we nearly have the first bit done."

She really shouldn't have jinxed them like that because right then, Dy's sorcery flickered through the ley line, slowing them. "Bandit," she said on the amethyst channel. "We've got a problem."

"I've got a solution," Cha replied. "Give me a slingshot."

"Won't help. Take a gander."

Cha stood in the driver's seat and shaded her eyes. An Obsidian blockade sat across Dy's ley line, a row of winged Obsidian fae holding spears leveled right at them.

"Fuck me," she said, on a sigh. It really never was a perfect world.

~ **41** ~

Hitting the Mobstacle Course

"I DON'T SUPPOSE you could just use your magic to vanish them?" Cha asked Azul, waving a hand at the line of warriors.

"I actually *could*," he answered, "but there would be repercussions."

Well, things were looking up. "What kind of repercussions?"

"Unpleasant repercussions."

"More specific, please."

"War between Amethyst and Obsidian, with the other realms taking one side or the other."

That didn't sound so bad to her.

"Worse than the war that originally fractured the veil between the fae realms and the human ones," Azul added in a philosophical tone. "Likely with enough wild magic to completely destroy all mortal life." He smiled placidly when she gave him a sour look. "But I'd do it for you, darling. Allow me to sweep this minor obstacle from your path and let's not worry about the fate of the world. All that matters is our love."

"You're not funny," she told him with a scowl, covering up the stupid stutter of her heart at the mention of love, which wasn't possible, as they'd barely met and were as meant for each other as a fish and a bird. "How about a solution somewhere between us dying here or destroying creation in an effort to avoid death?"

"Your wish, my command," he replied easily, uncoiling with inhuman grace from the passenger seat and leaping nimbly from the carriage, deftly avoiding the ley line and strolling toward the line of Obsidian warriors as if out for a walk. Cha marveled that she'd ever thought him less than fully fae. Even with the glamour, he radiated a charismatic light all his own.

"Bandit," Dy said through the path-box, "what is he doing?"

"I don't know but let's hope it works." Cha eased Katu forward in Azul's wake, drawing the Cinnabar sword and keeping it ready, in case he needed back up.

Azul posed there, hipshot, looking unbearably sexy—Cha even imagined a shadow of violet wings in the air around him—waving his hands as he spun some story. Or perhaps sang a song? The Obsidian warriors sagged, their spears drooping, then one by one crumpled to the ground, apparently asleep. Azul dragged a couple of the big men off the ley line as if they weighed nothing, then gestured Cha forward. He leapt in as she pulled up.

"What did you do?" she asked right as Dy asked the same question via the path-box.

"Sang them a lullaby," he answered calmly. "It won't last

long now that I've stopped singing, so we should go."

"Don't have to tell me twice." Cha fired Katu ahead, Big Betty right behind. The depot sparkled with promise, bustling with business. "Not much farther to go. We should be in the clear."

For the second time, she jinxed herself with her big mouth. A flood of law-hounds poured out of the depot, headed their way on newly laid ley lines. "Fuck me," she commented.

"It's almost like you should stop saying stuff like that," Azul said.

"Amen, Prince Charming," Dy put in.

"Don't you two tag-team me," Cha bit out, understanding a bit more how Dy felt on the rare occasions Cha and Phinny agreed. "Dy, make yourself useful and put on the lightning."

"We can't outrun them," Dy protested.

"You don't have to. That's why you have me." She grinned at Azul. "Ready to make yourself useful?"

"I thought I already did."

"You did and you will. Don't glamour us until I say so. Hiding the dirty pics, Goldi."

Dy's sigh came through audibly, but she also swept into Cha's mind, potent and poised to act.

"Time to go cross-country, boy-o," Cha told Azul. "This is when it gets interesting."

He sighed dramatically. "Every time you say that I—seven hells!"

Katu pitched over a gully, nearly expelling the unprepared prince, Dy's impromptu ley line uncoiling bare arm's lengths ahead of them. It was fast, but rickety-fragile, being spun up so fast on unfriendly ground. Cha whooped, drawing attention as they emerged from Dy's protective illusion. "Can you pied-piper them?" she called over the wind of their passage.

"Can I what?"

"Don't you know any human tales?"

"Why would I?"

He had a point, but she growled in frustration. "Use your magic song thingy to get them to follow us instead of Big Betty."

"I think that's not a problem," he replied, craning his neck. "They're following us—and gaining fast. Why does this feel oddly familiar?"

"Just like old times," she agreed. An unexpected surge of nostalgia hit her that she and Azul already had old times together. "Only I doubt there's a convenient sudden canyon down to an Obsidian mine nearby."

"My heart breaks."

She laughed at his dry humor, knowing better what it was now. Also that gave her an idea. "Hey Goldilocks—you know Santa's Village?"

"You want a shortcut to it?"

"Please and thank you."

The ley line shifted, careening abruptly to the right, and she followed it, Katu bouncing over the magical equivalent of potholes in the hastily constructed ley line. The ground beneath, salted to prevent exactly this kind of thing, resisted Dy's sorcery in fits and starts, sending Katu flying into the air to jounce down again. "I hate your world," Azul gritted out.

"Technically this is your world, not mine," Cha replied,

though privately she agreed with the major level of suckage at the moment. It was too jolting to even be exciting.

"Obsidian is no more my world than yours," Azul said with a sneer she didn't need to see.

The tourist village rushed toward them, in all its fanciful gingerbreading and tinkling music, the narrow, rainbow-cobblestoned streets thronged with tourists. "This will be a treat," Cha noted.

Dy's ley line threaded them straight for the main street, the law-hounds doing their best to crawl up Katu's ass, shouting orders and sending up sparkly flares. Fortunately, the show alerted the people—human families and fae shopkeepers and performers alike—of their high-speed arrival. The music squealed up to a glass-shattering pitch of alarm, then cut off, replaced by the screams of scattering people. Katu shot past colorful stalls selling ribbons, horns, wings and assorted other souvenirs. "Need anything—new wings, maybe?" she asked Azul, sparing him a sly sideways grin.

"Cute," he answered huffily. "My own are much better."

"I'll say."

Behind them, the fae law-hounds slowed—not because they cared about not hitting the people, but because the ley line was breaking up—and one skidded sideways abruptly as one end of the carriage hit a null spot while the other had a hold of a bit of ley line still. The carriage careened into a stall full of false wings, sending up a cloud of rainbow glitter along with an Obsidian fae rider, then abruptly popped into lion form. The lion shook herself, roared her displeasure, and promptly took off chasing a screaming human.

"Oops," Cha said to the rear-view. Couldn't be helped though. Katu was mostly going on momentum at this point, Cha basically bouncing him from one point of ley magic to the next, like a rock skipping over a pond. She aimed for the shortest cut through to the parking ley, hoping they could make it. "Once we're past the crowd, drop the cloak," she told Azul.

"Got it."

"Here we go." Urging Katu into a last skip through the decaying ley line, Cha pushed him up and over a magic slide in the kiddie playland, taking advantage of the extra boost to send him flying through the air to land with a bang on the parking ley. Slow black is slow, but at least it was steady, unlike the patchy shit that was all that remained of Dy's impromptu ley line. With any luck, Dy had made it around the depot and even now cruised down the Black Thirteen to the border.

Navigating the molasses-slow parking ley, Cha kept one eye out for kids popping out from behind parked cars— something that happened with unnerving frequency—and popped on their private Amethyst channel. "Shook the tail in fantasyland," she reported. "You clear?"

"Free and clear, sailing down the noir one-three to the BX," Dy replied. "I've got some extra juice so I'm leaving some white behind. Quite the party here."

"Excellent. Catching up."

"Translation, please?" Azul inquired on a drawl.

"Dy is adding Moonstone white to the Black Thirteen ley line to speed things up. Other ley riders are jumping on the free speed boost. That's a good thing," she added with a glance at him. So pretty, with his hair disarrayed by the ruffling breeze, golden late morning light dancing over him. "If everyone is exceeding the standard ley speed, then it makes it harder for the law hounds to pick out any one violator."

"Then we're on the ideal side of the equation?"

"Not quite yet, but getting there."

As she tore her gaze away, Cha contemplated that "ideal" was the last word she'd use to describe how this had all played out. Translation: shitty situation normal for her.

~ 42 ~

All Fucked Up and Nowhere to Go

D Y'S WHITE GOT them across the border lickety-split. In no
time, it seemed, Cha was veering off to the side ley that
led to Lenorae's family manor, promising to meet Dy at the
fence Phinny had arranged.

"Remember that invitation, Prince Charming," Dy said via
the path-box. "You're welcome to visit any time, as long as you
don't mind children. Dirty ones, I should warn you."

"I'll remember that," Azul replied, a bemused half smile
ghosting over his lips.

"I would say the thing, but I know I can't say it," Dy added.
"Just know it means everything to me that you pulled Bandit
out."

"It does to me, too." Azul tapped the box off.

"We're coming up on where I picked you up," Cha noted,
trying to sound casual and not at all emotional about that
conversation, or the prospect of saying goodbye to Azul
forever. "Remember that you're directing me."

"It's just up here. Turn in that drive."

"Which drive? I don't see any—oh." The landscape beside

her, which had been the usual countryside standard farm, field, livestock, cottage, barn, field, etc., rotation, wriggled as if water had flowed across it, then morphed into tall gates made apparently of red roses, set into an opaque wall of a crimson so deep a hue it appeared black. Cha was no genius, but even she could catch a clue after a while. The pet human figuring out that she might not see magic like a fae did, but she could tell that this thing where a color looked kind of black and shimmery meant magic in spectrums beyond her mortal understanding. "Ruby magic, huh?" she commented, trying to sound nonchalant as the gates glided open with soundless grace.

Azul glanced at her in faint surprise, momentarily losing his pose of studied boredom. He was tense, she realized, assuming hauteur and practiced indolence as a mask to cover his anxiety. She marveled a moment that she knew this about him so clearly, then set it aside.

"As you say, darling," he answered with a dip of his nose that seemed longer than it had before, maybe only because he was looking down it so effectively.

"Are you sure you want to do this?" She had a bad feeling.

"What I *want* doesn't enter into the decision." Taking her hand, he kissed it, holding her gaze. "Remember that, Arantxa. If I could do as I wished, things would be very different. But I can't, and so they won't."

Katu sawed a mournful agreement, smoothly following a flowing ley line unlike any Cha had ever experienced. "What is this place?" she asked, mostly wondering aloud.

"Somewhere neither here nor there," Azul answered absently. "And here we are."

"In nowhere?"

"Precisely."

They glided to a halt on a circular drive, apparently isolated in a meadow of bloodred poppies. Cha opened her mouth to ask—and closed it as a palace shimmered into existence. It hurt her eyes to look at it and she shaded them, then had to avert her gaze. "I don't like this," she muttered, gripping Azul's hand as if she could hold onto him forever. Not that she wanted him forever. Did she? "Come with me. We'll figure something out."

He smiled sadly, cupped her cheek with his free hand, then pulled her to him, the scent of sun-warmed blueberries teasing the edges of her senses. "I cannot," he whispered. "You will indeed be a cherished memory, though far from fleeting."

Abruptly releasing her, he leapt from Katu and tossed her the Moonruby wand. "Be careful with that."

"The thing barely works."

"I believe you're mistaken, Arantxa darling." He grinned, then turned as if someone had called his name—though Cha had heard nothing. A woman stood on the steps of the palace, strawberry pale hair flowing nearly to the ground. She was breathtakingly lovely and Cha hated her on sight. Well, she would have, if she hadn't hated the woman on principle already. "Lenorae," Azul said, bowing formally.

"Your Highness," she replied, clasping delicate fingers together. "We have much to discuss."

"So it would seem," he said, inclining his head graciously.

Lenorae frowned at Cha. "Who is this?"

"No one," Azul answered smoothly. "My ride and nothing more." He flicked his fingers and he, Lenorae, and all of it disappeared, leaving Cha sitting in Katu on a slow black country lane, surrounded by nothing but farm. No poppies in sight.

"Well, goodbye, Prince Charming," Cha said, having planned to snarl the words in sheer offense at the abruptness of his departure, but her voice broke halfway through and—to her utter chagrin, she sobbed, tears suddenly pouring down her face.

No one. My ride and nothing more.

"Get a hold of yourself," she said out loud, fiercely through the tears. "Since when do you cry over a guy, Cha? Especially one you knew for four fucks. You knew he was candy from the beginning. Enjoy the sweet; move on when it's gone."

Except this hurt like he'd been more than that, like he'd been a meal. Like he could have been forever, and how absurd was that? Cha wasn't a forever kind of gal. Certainly not with a real fae prince. She was the lowly fish trapped in her little pond, gazing at the beautiful winged creatures and knowing they'd always be beyond her.

With a breaking heart, she swallowed the bitter reality of Azul's feelings for her, of what he'd said within her hearing, quite deliberately. He could have poofed her a moment before that, so he'd wanted her to hear, to know the finality of his words. She was no one to him. A ride and nothing more. That was the truth.

Because he couldn't lie.

~ 43 ~

Truth and Consequences

T HE RENDEZVOUS WITH the fence Phinny had arranged for them was satisfyingly shady. No fairy spires in sight, no glittering dust of any color, except for the back alley slow black Katu prowled along. Parking Katu, Cha slid out, approached the smaller, human-sized door next to the big one for cargo rigs and knocked. An eye-level window slid open and Cha offered the passcode Dy had sent.

She slipped through the barely opened door that turned out to be thicker than her body and greeted a cloaked and hunchbacked person of indeterminate gender who'd answered. "Heya, Bandit. Call me Igor," the person said, mostly shrouded in the filthy cloak, but showing enough of their pitted face for their wink at the ironic name to be obvious. "This way."

As she followed Igor, Cha took in the busy shop, which appeared to be engaged in filing off the identifying characteristics of any number of magical artifacts. It was dirty, painfully loud, and smelled of old food and unwashed humans. Everywhere she looked, something illegal occurred, and Cha breathed a sigh of relief. This was her element, where she belonged.

She'd been born a scruffy mortal, a problem child with a shitty moral compass and she didn't aim for higher company than that. She was no Lenorae.

In the next room, Big Betty idled. Dy, with Warg draped over her shoulder so he drooled gleefully on the floor, seemed to be in deep conversation with Phin and a third person. A crew of disreputable humans in protective gear carried out the crates of Obsidian dust.

"We're observing protocol," Igor said in a scratchy voice, scraping back the hood of their cloak. "No one wants an accidental mutation."

Cha eyed the sharp, piss-green ridge of spines protruding from Igor's backbone. "No, I wouldn't think so."

Igor jerked their head at the spines. "Not accidental, obviously, but mine to keep, whether I want to or not."

"I'm sorry," Cha said with all sincerity, knowing them to be empty words.

"Eh, don't waste good sympathy on me," Igor replied, shrugging philosophically, which sent the spines rippling musically. "At least I made it out alive. I heard that Monat didn't."

It was almost a question, so Cha confirmed it. "I wish I could say otherwise, but I'm sure of it—and I nearly met the same fate, so I feel you on being glad to be alive."

"And yet you made it out intact," Igor observed, so neutrally—and hoarsely—that Cha couldn't determine if they resented her for it. "Did you really go to Moonstone jail?"

The memory of that beautifully lethal, horrifying place hit

Cha hard and she shook the memory away, then nodded when Igor looked puzzled. "Yeah," she answered. "I was there." A real non-answer, but she found she really hated to say anything more, or even think about the place. Or about how Azul had rescued her. Or those last words of his. *No one.*

"What's Moonstone like?" Igor persisted.

Cha was already shaking her head. "I can't really describe it."

With a disgusted snort, Igor looked away. "That's what Goldilocks said."

Dy looked up then and waved Cha over, giving her a quick hug when Cha walked up, holding onto her shoulders and searching her face. "Everything go okay with Prince Charming?" Dy asked.

"Right as rain," Cha answered cheerfully, turning away from Dy's dubious frown, and holding out a hand to Phin. "Hi there Mama Bear."

Phin surprised her by yanking her into a fierce hug. "I know you sacrificed yourself to save her and I'm grateful to you for the rest of my life," she whispered in Cha's ear.

Cha nearly squirmed in discomfort. "Remember that when I tell you how I lost all of your bribery gems."

"What?" Phin screeched—right in Cha's ear. She jerked back, but Phinny held on. "Arantxa Evermore, how in the seven hells did you use up that *entire box* of gems?"

Dy flashed Cha a look of sympathy. Clearly there hadn't been time to tell the whole story. "I'll tell you over ale and a basket of rosemary twists," Cha told Phin, pinching her on the cheek.

The fence, who'd gone to check with the cargo supervisor, returned right then. "Lucky Ducky," he said by way of introduction, holding out a hand to Cha to shake. "An honor to meet and fence for you, Bandit." He dipped a chin at Dy. "The tale of you and Goldilocks getting to Moonstone and back is making the rounds. If you weren't famous before this, you would be now—and you'd have no trouble getting high-end gigs, even with Otto blacklisting you."

That was news. Dy rolled her eyes at Cha's questioning look. "Yeah, somehow Otto got wind of us heading back and has vanished, but not before putting out the word that *we* fucked *him*."

"The nerve," Cha commented.

Lucky Ducky cackled. "Best advertisement he could put out there. Everyone knows Otto got Monat done for and the fact that he ran rather than pay you or take you to task for supposedly screwing up his shipment speaks volumes. At any rate, you two will be able to pick and choose, because guess what was hidden in those crates you picked up in Obsidian?"

"Which crate?" Cha asked, privately betting it was one in the very back.

"All of them," Lucky answered.

"All?" Dy echoed. "But we saw dozens cracked open in Moonstone and the fae never found a thing."

"They didn't know what they were looking at. Come on, we'll show you." Lucky gestured for them to follow.

The four of them trooped over to where a group of workers clustered around an opened crate, and accepted ventilation masks from one very short gal who grinned manically. "I'm

Nerd Girl," she said, "scientist and sorceress. Lucky Ducky brought me in to analyze your cargo." She waved a hand at the crate on a draped table.

As opposed to the puttoes' wanton destruction back in Moonstone, this operation had been conducted with surgical precision, the lid delicately pried open and the seething, living pixie dust within exposed.

"What are we looking at?" Cha asked, perfectly willing to be the ignorant one of the bunch. "I see a bunch of Obsidian pixie dust, which we already knew was there."

"Is that *all* you see?" Nerd Girl drawled. She pointed at Dy. "Use your sorcery. What else is in there?"

"It's agnicurna," Dy said in tone of hushed awe. "All through the pixie dust. Now I understand."

"Well, I don't," Cha told her. "They said they were looking for astra, remember?"

Dy gave her an impatient look. "Did you really ditch the entire semester on the Fae Wars?"

"Pretty much," Cha admitted. "Can you learn my ignorant ass now?"

"Astra means weapon in the old language," Dy explained. "It's not specific. The Moonstone fae were worried about a weapon being smuggled in."

That's what Azul had said, Cha recalled. *I don't actually know what the astra is. That's a generic term for something quite politically tricky within the fae realms and you are better off knowing less than more.* "And this invisible agnicurna is the weapon?"

Dy nodded somberly. "But it's not invisible. Agnicurna translates as fire-powder. Black powder that can be used as an explosive. It's mixed all in with the Obsidian pixie dust—almost the same color—and the ambient magic of the dust obscures it unless you know what to look for."

"And looking with the correct lens," Nerd Girl agreed, tapping her temple. "Gotta have the right smarts."

"So," Cha said slowly, thinking hard, which kind of hurt her brain, "Otto was being paid to smuggle a human explosive into a fae realm. To what purpose?" *...something quite politically tricky within the fae realms and you are better off knowing less than more.*

"Nothing good for them," Nerd Girl answered solemnly.

"And what's bad for the fae is usually even worse for us," Phin noted glumly.

"Because of the wars between the various fae realms?" Cha asked. "But those don't involve us."

Everyone gave her sardonic looks ranging from gentle to incredulous. "You mean," Dy said with raised brows, "except for the ones that shattered the veils between worlds to begin with and allowed the fae and their magic into ours, making humans a conquered and oppressed people?"

Oh, yeah—there was that. Cha's brain continued to churn away, Azul's words, the ones he'd made her promise she'd keep in mind, going around and around. *Politically tricky.* What else had he said about that? That's right. *It was a politically tricky situation,* he'd said as a non-answer, when she'd asked why a fae wedding would take place in the human realms. And he'd told her to keep the Moonruby wand, to remember the order of the fae realms and their relative power. Was Azul somehow in the middle of this? Marrying someone affiliated with Ruby and allying Amethyst with them? Shaking the thoughts away, she focused on the now—and on the sinking feeling in the part of her that measured the value of coin and shipments.

"I'm guessing this agnicurna is worthless in our realm," she said, and they all nodded.

"Worse," Dy said, eyes somber above her mask, "the contamination makes the Obsidian dust worthless."

"And the box of gems is gone, too," Phinny said, rubbing her belly as if it pained her.

"At least we have the deposit gold and what it bought us," Dy replied, looping her arm around Phinny's considerable waist. "Though we owe Cha her share."

Lucky Ducky cleared his throat.

"After we pay you all, of course," Dy agreed. And they set to haggling.

~ **44** ~

Endgame

I T WAS A sober group that gathered on the porch of Phinny and Dy's charming cottage, despite the cold, aged ale and fresh rosemary twists. The shrieks of the kids splashing in the pond with Katu and Big Betty in their animal forms, the latter spraying everyone with water she sucked up into her trunk— including the adults sitting on the porch—helped to lighten the mood, but didn't lift them entirely out of the glums.

"I can't believe Otto fucked us," Cha commented.

"Language," Phinny said in mild reproof.

"They're a mile away and I know they've heard the word before."

"I can't believe Monat is *dead*," Dy said, elbowing Cha. "Priorities."

"Well, Monat would be dead, regardless, but we still could have gotten paid," Cha told her, earning a fierce glare from both women.

Cha shrugged and took a swig of her ale. It went down cold and just the right bittersweet to match her mood. Even the rosemary twists didn't give her much comfort. Something was tugging at her, a nagging worry, a particular purple dread that she strongly suspected had to do with Azul and this connection he'd spoken of. He'd known she was in trouble; would she sense the same? The big problem there was that *he* had had the power to save her whereas *she* couldn't even begin to find him. She even swallowed her considerable pride and drove Katu out to that rural ley, looking for the bloody rose gates or the field of poppies or even a something that looked like a nothing. She'd gone up that stupid slow rural ley several dozen times, hoping against hope that her princely hitchhiker might appear.

No joy.

If they did have some connection—and if it mattered—it existed only because of mutual life-saving. He'd said so himself. And he'd said, clearly and honestly, that she was no one to him. Nothing more than a ride. In every sense of the word, no doubt. Well, at least she'd sated the pussy sparkle for a while. And quite satisfactorily, too. She'd banged a full fae prince and lived to tell the tale. She could dine out on that for quite some time. Which, she might have to, as Otto's disappearance meant no races for a while and a girl needed to eat.

"Lucky Ducky sent another offer our way," Cha finally said.

"No," Phin and Dy said in unison.

Cha raised a brow at them. "It's all this side of the borders. Totally human to human job."

Phin sighed heavily. "Can we just—"

She broke off as Dy put a hand on her arm. "Someone is coming," Dy said, lifting her nose as if she could sniff out the unexpected arrival. "Plenty of magic, probably fae."

"Wonderful," Phin grumbled, pushing to her feet. "You kids—get to the barn and hide out in there. Because I said so!" she added to the chorus of protest.

That was a kind of magic, the unruly children immediately trooping off, Phin following behind to scoop up Inigo, casting a warning look over her shoulder at Dy that spoke volumes. Even Katu and Big Betty followed Phin obediently and Cha fervently hoped someone would keep an eye on the chickens with Katu around.

She and Dy strolled out to the parking ley, with studied nonchalance, and stood hip to hip, waiting. Dy's magic bristled in the air and Cha rested her hands comfortably near the Moonruby wand and the Cinnabar sword. Her heart, however, tripped along in a happy, hopeful beat that made her want to stomp it under her bootheel. The optimistic little fucker only brought her pain.

"Do you think it's him?" Dy asked quietly.

Cha snorted in deliberately vulgar fashion and cocked a hip. "Otto? No. I wouldn't be surprised if he's dead."

Dy slid her a knowing look. "I meant Prince Charming and you know it."

Cha knew it. Sometimes she hated how well Dy could predict her. "It's not him," she replied with certainty. That wasn't just her cynicism speaking, either. "Not his flavor of magic."

"So, you know the flavor of his magic that well, hmm? You know, you never did tell me exactly what—"

"Shh. They're here."

A carriage rolled up, not one enchanted from an animal, but something fully fae and looking like a giant soap bubble made (mostly) solid. It came to a halt and a woman stepped out, standing on the slow black ley like it was nothing, which it was to her. Her knee-length, strawberry-blonde hair shimmered with an unearthly glow. She looked between Cha and Dy, then rested her gaze on Cha. "You," she said. "Bridget."

"Hi Lenorae." Cha decided on the wand and drew it slightly. Only Azul could have told her that name, but that didn't mean he'd sent her.

"You know this…person?" Dy asked, the pause just perceptible. "Why is she calling you Bridget?"

"Long story. This is Prince Charming's bride that was," Cha answered in a cool, uncaring tone. "Or is it official ball and chain now?"

"I don't know what that means," Lenorae said, then tossed something silver at Cha.

Cha caught it reflexively, knowing what it was when it *thunked* into her palm. She showed it to Dy, who whistled. A platinum coin.

"I was told you'd know who sent this," Lenorae said, her voice lifting at the end in almost a question.

Cha nodded, feeling flat-footed and not at all sure what to make of this.

"You need to come with me," Lenorae said.

"Oh, honey," Dy drawled. "Bless your heart, but I don't think so. I suggest you drop the glamour before I strip it off for you."

Lenorae made a pretty O with her mouth, a lovely, innocent expression that faded immediately. The air around her flickered, magic fluttering in a cloud of crimson rose petals. And in the pretty woman's place stood a glowing red demon, with huge, outstretched wings, and Lenorae's eyes.

Cha suspected she knew what Azul had seen to make him flee the altar. Though, who knew? Maybe demons were his kink.

"Now will you come with me?" the demon asked in Lenorae's fluting tones.

Dy started to say no again and Cha stopped her. "I have to go."

That nagging connection that said Azul jumped up and down in affirmation.

Giving her a long fulminating stare, Dy seethed for a full minute, then threw up her hands. "Fine. I'll get Warg and fire up Big Betty."

Cha grabbed her into a hug. "Thanks, Goldilocks."

Dy returned the embrace. "Always, Bandit." Then she pulled back and rolled her eyes.

"Phin is going to kill us," they said as one.

This story continues in *Blades, Books, and the Bandit*

Coming May 2026

Writing as Jennifer K. Lambert

NEVER THE ROSES
Never the Roses
Among the Thorns

Titles by Jeffe Kennedy

FANTASY ROMANCES

THE FAST AND THE FAE
Love. Lies, and Ley Lines
Blades, Books, and the Bandit
Princes, Potions, and Pixie Dust

BONDS OF MAGIC
Dark Wizard
Bright Familiar
Grey Magic
Familiar Winter Magic
(Also available in Fire of the Frost)

RENEGADES OF MAGIC
Shadow Wizard
Rogue Familiar
Twisted Magic

WARRIORS OF MAGIC
Reluctant Wizard
Strange Familiar
Magic Reborn

HEIRS OF MAGIC
The Long Night of the Crystalline Moon
(also available in *Under a Winter Sky*)
The Golden Gryphon and the Bear Prince
The Sorceress Queen and the Pirate Rogue
The Dragon's Daughter and the Winter Mage
The Storm Princess and the Raven King
The Long Night of the Radiant Star

THE FORGOTTEN EMPIRES
The Orchid Throne
The Fiery Crown
The Promised Queen

THE TWELVE KINGDOMS
Negotiation
The Mark of the Tala
The Tears of the Rose
The Talon of the Hawk
Heart's Blood
The Crown of the Queen

THE UNCHARTED REALMS
The Pages of the Mind
The Edge of the Blade
The Snows of Windroven

The Shift of the Tide
The Arrows of the Heart
The Dragons of Summer
The Fate of the Tala
The Lost Princess Returns

THE CHRONICLES OF DASNARIA

Prisoner of the Crown
Exile of the Seas
Warrior of the World

SORCEROUS MOONS

Lonen's War
Oria's Gambit
The Tides of Bára
The Forests of Dru
Oria's Enchantment
Lonen's Reign

A COVENANT OF THORNS

Rogue's Pawn
Rogue's Possession
Rogue's Paradise

CONTEMPORARY ROMANCES

Shooting Star

MISSED CONNECTIONS

Last Dance
With a Prince
Since Last Christmas

CONTEMPORARY EROTIC ROMANCES

Exact Warm Unholy
The Devil's Doorbell

FACETS OF PASSION
Sapphire
Platinum
Ruby
Five Golden Rings

FALLING UNDER
Going Under
Under His Touch
Under Contract

EROTIC PARANORMAL

MASTER OF THE OPERA E-SERIAL
Master of the Opera, Act 1: Passionate Overture
Master of the Opera, Act 2: Ghost Aria
Master of the Opera, Act 3: Phantom Serenade
Master of the Opera, Act 4: Dark Interlude
Master of the Opera, Act 5: A Haunting Duet
Master of the Opera, Act 6: Crescendo
Master of the Opera

BLOOD CURRENCY
Blood Currency

BDSM FAIRYTALE ROMANCE

Petals and Thorns

Thank you for reading!

About Jeffe Kennedy

Jeffe Kennedy™ is an award-winning, USA Today bestselling author works include novels, nonfiction, poetry, and short fiction. She has won the prestigious RITA® Award from Romance Writers of America (RWA), been a finalist twice, received the Wyoming Arts Council Fellowship for Poetry, been a Ucross Foundation Fellow, and was awarded a Frank Nelson Doubleday Memorial Award. She has 68 published fiction titles and her work has been translated into seven languages. She is a Past-President of the Science Fiction and Fantasy Writers Association (SFWA).

She also writes as Jennifer K. Lambert™.

Kennedy's fantasy romance/romantic fantasy—or romantasy—career initially took off with the trilogy *The Twelve Kingdoms*, which hit the shelves starting in May 2014. Book 1, *The Mark of the Tala*, received a starred Library Journal review, was given the RT Editor's Pick for June, and was nominated for the RT Book of the Year while the sequel, *The Tears of the Rose* received a Top Pick Gold and was nominated for the RT Reviewers' Choice Best Fantasy Romance of 2014. The third book, *The Talon of the Hawk*, won the RT Reviewers' Choice Best Fantasy Romance of 2015. Two more books followed in this world, beginning the spin-off series *The Uncharted Realms*. Book one in that series, *The Pages of the Mind*, was nominated for the RT Reviewer's Choice Best Fantasy Romance of 2016 and won RWA's 2017 RITA Award. The second book, *The Edge of the Blade*, was a 2017 PRISM finalist, along with *The Pages of the Mind*. The final novel in the series, *The Fate of the Tala*, released in February 2020, along with a short novel epilogue, *The Lost Princess Returns*. A high fantasy trilogy, The Chronicles of Dasnaria, taking place in *The Twelve Kingdoms* world came out from Rebel Base books in 2018, and was translated into Czech. The novella, *The Dragons of Summer*, first appearing in the *Seasons of Sorcery* anthology, finaled for the 2019 RITA Award.

Other romantasy series by Kennedy include A Covenant of Thorns, originally published by Carina Press, *The Forgotten Empires* published by St. Martins Press, the indie series *Sorcerous Moons*, and the wildly popular dark fantasy romances in *The Bonds of Magic, Renegades of Magic,* and *Warriors of Magic* series. Her *Heirs of Magic* epic fantasy romance series includes *The Long Night of the Crystalline Moon, The Golden Gryphon and the Bear Prince, The Sorceress Queen and the Pirate Rogue, The Dragon's Daughter and the Winter Mage, The Storm Princess and the Raven King,* and *The Long Night of the Radiant Star*.

As Jennifer K. Lambert™, she's written *Never the Roses*, an instant USA Today bestseller, and *Among the Thorns*, forthcoming in July, 2026.

Jeffe Kennedy lives in Santa Fe, New Mexico, with her husband of over thirty years, his chocolate-lab assistance dog, two Maine coon cats who assist no one, and plentiful free-range lizards.

Jeffe can be found online at her website: JeffeKennedy.com, every Tuesday and Friday on her popular podcast, First Cup of Coffee with Jeffe Kennedy, and on most social media. She is represented by Sarah Younger of Nancy Yost Literary Agency.

jeffekennedy.com

facebook.com/Author.Jeffe.Kennedy

bsky.app/profile/jeffekennedy.bsky.social

goodreads.com/author/show/1014374.Jeffe_Kennedy

bookbub.com/profile/jeffe-kennedy

instagram.com/jeffekennedy2016

tiktok.com/@jeffe_kennedy

youtube.com/@JeffeKennedy

Sign up for her newsletter here.

jeffekennedy.com/sign-up-for-my-newsletter